Margaret Domvile

Life of Lamartine

Margaret Domvile

Life of Lamartine

ISBN/EAN: 9783337415501

Printed in Europe, USA, Canada, Australia, Japan

Cover: Foto ©Raphael Reischuk / pixelio.de

More available books at **www.hansebooks.com**

BY·

LADY MARGARET DOMVILE

LONDON

KEGAN PAUL, TRENCH & CO., 1, PATERNOSTER SQUARE

1888

LAMARTINE.

CHAPTER I.

1780–1811.

THE father of Alphonse de Lamartine was a cadet of an old Burgundian family; his mother the daughter of M. des Roys, an officer in the household of the Duke of Orleans. There had been in the circumstances of their marriage more of romance than is usual in France. Mademoiselle des Roys, while still a child, received a nomination entitling her to become a canoness in the richly endowed Chapter of Salle, and, having reached the age of fifteen, was shortly to take vows which, though not cutting her off from the world, would have bound her to a single life, when she met, at the house of his sister (herself a canoness of Salles), the Chevalier de Lamartine. A few weeks later the Chevalier obtained Mademoiselle des Roys' consent to ask her hand in marriage. The want of fortune and family prejudices were formidable obstacles, but the lovers remained constant, and, after three years of hope deferred, they were united just at the eve of the Revolution.

Their early married life was clouded with heavy trials.

B

M. de Lamartine was among the few devoted defenders of the Tuileries on the roth of August. Wounded, and a prisoner, he owed his life to the kindness of a municipal guard, who helped him to escape the terrible September massacres. For a time, he and his wife lived unmolested in a remote Burgundian village, but in 1794 the whole Lamartine family, including the aged grandfather and grandmother, were thrown into prison. Only the younger Madame de Lamartine, who had just given birth to a daughter, was allowed to remain, guarded by soldiers, in the family house at Mâcon. A little later, the Hôtel Lamartine being wanted as a barrack, she got leave to move into a pavilion at the end of the garden, formerly occupied by servants, which, by a happy chance, faced the Convent of the Ursulines where her husband was a prisoner. Lamartine's earliest recollections are of the dreary months spent in this abode, when the silence of the streets was only broken by the rough jolting of the tumbrils, carrying their load of victims to the scaffold, or by wild snatches of revolutionary songs, which he, poor little unconscious child, used to catch up and repeat, wondering at his mother's tear-dimmed eyes. Sometimes Madame de Lamartine had a momentary glance at her husband when, guarded by gaolers, he passed along the prison corridors; for this she used to stand for hours watching at the window, holding up her boy in her arms.

After eighteen months thus passed, came the welcome news of Robespierre's fall, and then the worst was felt to be over. The prisoners were allowed to creep away one by one, till at length the Hôtel de Lamartine received back all its inmates. There they lived on in fear and trembling, in poverty and seclusion, for the reign of Terror did not cease at once. It was not till nightfall that a few old friends, faithful to the habits of a lifetime, would venture through the streets with little paper lanterns in their hands, and, taking their seats at the card-tables, resume the game that only a Revolution could have interrupted.

These childish reminiscences seem melancholy enough, but there came at last a happy, ever to be remembered day, when a long file of bullock waggons came to the door and carried the whole family—parents, children, servants, and household goods—off to Milly, a little country house standing not far from the high road to Cluny. Here, in a quiet Burgundian valley, the Lamartines brought up their family of five daughters and one son. In two books, " Le Manuscrit de ma Mère " and the " Mémoires Inédits," which Lady Herbert's translations have made familiar to the English public, Lamartine has described, with much detail, the years passed in the lowly home, which did not differ, in outward appearance, from the houses of the neighbouring peasants save for the large courtyard and double flight of granite steps leading to the massive hall door of worm-eaten and blackened oak. Everywhere the Revolution had left its traces : the principal sitting-room had been used by the peasants as a *salle de danse* on Sundays, and their heavy wooden shoes had broken the encaustic tiles into minute fragments ; while the iron plate of the hearth, too useful to be sacrificed even on the altar of patriotism, had been turned inwards, so as to hide the obnoxious "fleur-de-lys " which showed that some former owner had been a Chevalier de St. Louis. But the village

mason quickly replaced the encaustic tiles with equally
serviceable bricks ; fires of vine-dressings burned as brightly
as ever in the spacious chimneys, and the joyous laughter
of the young mother and her happy little brood chased
away the ghosts and filled the room with sunshine, while
the vines blossomed and the fruit-trees bore as they used
to do in the years before '89. The furniture consisted only
of a few beds, chairs, and tables, so that before long every
one had found his or her place in the house, and the family
settled down to a life in which refinement and culture were
combined with incessant and laborious industry ; an
annuity of a hundred a year and the little property of
Milly being all they had to depend on. But with much
greater people than the Lamartines, money was scarce in
those days, and the want of it did not interfere with their
happiness. The whole household rose early, and after
prayers said at their mother's knee, the children breakfasted
on the vine-dresser's soup, and then trotted off to weed the
vines, or to watch their father's sheep grazing in the forest,
till the Angelus bell brought them back to the midday
meal of meat and *bouilli*, eaten with two-pronged forks out
of little red earthenware bowls ; and after dinner, their
mother, when her household tasks allowed, heard them say
their lessons.

In the long summer days friends used to come in relays,
sometimes from long distances—much in the pleasant, un-
ceremonious fashion described in Eugenie de Guérin's
journal. In winter, when the wind whistled at its will
through the corridors, the family gathered round the fire in
their mother's bedroom, the father reading by the flickering
light of a tallow candle, the mother playing such old-

fashioned airs as Rousseau's " Devin du Village " on the
clavecin, or talking to her elder children as she rocked the
youngest to sleep in the heavy wooden cradle. Some of
the most charming of Lamartine's writings, alike in prose
and in verse, are those in which, with a poet's delicate
perception of every detail, he recalls those early days.

The most delightful and exciting period of the year
was the gathering-in of the vintage. For weeks before, he
and his sisters used to watch, with the eager eyes of childhood, the cleansing and preparing of the wine-vats which
heralded its approach. Then came the keener delight of
being allowed to join the grape-cutters, who, selected among
the cleverest and handiest of the village girls, used with
deft fingers quickly to clear a whole plant, throwing the
white or purple clusters into bins, which the men then piled
on a huge waggon. When it was fully loaded, the bullocks,
at a word from their driver, lifting their massive heads
under the yoke, moved slowly away ; the children, regardless of stained pinafores, following the cart dripping with
crimson rain, gathered up the bunches that fell, to give as a
reward to the patient oxen, sometimes rushing away to
greet a fresh band of workers with cries of delight.

" The joy ran like the wine from hill to hill."

Then, intent on being useful, they set to counting the carts
as they came in, running in turn to bring their father
the reckoning—a matter of no small consequence, for the
produce of the farm was the only source of income on
which the family, in those days, could securely count.
But even on the sunny slopes of Burgundy the vintage is
not always gathered in with rejoicing ; more than one

entry in Madame de Lamartine's journal tells of anxiety and loss. In the spring of 1801 she notes the delicious smell of the vines in flower, adding, " If all these blossoms turn into grapes, we shall be rich this year." A few weeks later she writes, " A terrible hailstorm has come down in full force on the vines. It is all the worse because they were laden with grapes. My heart is indeed full when I think of the possible failure of the crop and of the suffering this would entail on our poor people as well as on ourselves." The final entry is, "God's will be done ! We have had another fearful storm, and the rain has entirely ruined the crops. I am sick at heart with fear and anxiety."

Another red-letter date in the sylvan calendar was the shelling of the walnuts, when friends and neighbours gathered round the great table in the kitchen, which was lit up for the occasion with rude, flickering lamps, called, not inappropriately, *creuse-yeux.* The men brought up from the cellars heavy sacks of walnuts, the contents of which soon covered the floor. Before each worker was then set a light hammer and a pile of nuts. When the latter were broken, the good ones were put aside for sale, and the rest sent to the oil-press.

On other winter evenings long hanks of silk or yarn were got ready for the travelling merchants who came at stated times to buy them. Though the presence of the house-mistress was doubtless a gentle restraint, there was plenty of mirth and chatter at these gatherings. When village gossip was exhausted, other more exciting topics took its place. The pedlars, who at the beginning of the Revolution had been busily employed disseminating political pamphlets in the remotest villages, now carried in their packs newspapers, giving thrilling accounts of French victories with vividly coloured illustrations of "Massena in Switzerland," or "Hoche in the Palatinate," driving the enemy before them, or the storming of the bridge of Arcola by a hero even more famous than Horatius. Not that the price to be paid for these glories was ever forgotten by the simple country folk; the conscription, which then carried with it the additional bitterness of being a new and hitherto undreamt of blood-tax, pressing far more heavily than the *corvées* it replaced, was loudly and deeply cursed. The first real sorrow Lamartine had to bear was when a comrade, a few years older than himself, was carried off, despite his unwillingness, by the pitiless recruiting sergeants, and never heard of again. Claude Chanet was, it is true, only a peasant; his father being M. de Lamartine's head vinedresser. But the boys were from early childhood companions in long rambles over hills and dales, and a friendship had sprung up between them, the remembrance of which laid the foundation of the strong sympathy for the peasant class which always distinguished Lamartine, and enabled him to give the world those vivid, faithful pictures of rural life which, though taken perhaps too frequently from its mournful side, yet indicate its lights as well as its shades, its joys and compensations as well as its sorrows and its burdens, and which form his best title to enduring fame. "Hier sind die tiefen Wurzeln seiner Kraft."

Another playfellow was the little Chevalier de Pierreclos, the heir of a somewhat eccentric family, who were the Lamartine's nearest neighbours. The old Comte de Pierreclos had never been popular, and in 1790, on the famous and hitherto unexplained day called "la journée du brigandage," when the peasantry throughout the whole of France rose simultaneously, destroyed an immense amount of property, and then returned quietly to their old ways, his Château of Bussières had been completely sacked, the family owing their lives to the fidelity of a handful of retainers. The Chevalier de Lamartine, hearing what had happened, came out from Mâcon with a party of young men, well mounted and armed to the teeth, and drove off the incendiaries, of whom a considerable number were slain in a skirmish near Cluny ; a service which the old count never forgot. Unfortunately, his memory was equally tenacious of injuries received. " Look," he used to say to the boys, " look at the traces of those brigands. Here is the mark of the hatchet of one ; here of the pickaxe of another ; a third has left his mark there. Never, in my time, shall the memorials of these outrages be effaced ! " The countess had died in prison, and the household was ruled by the count's only sister, who was a clever woman in her way, but who, like her brother, clung with eccentric persistency to the habits of her youth. She used to come into the drawing-room at eight in the morning, and settle herself in a curtained seat, whence she dealt cards to all comers—brothers, nieces, visitors, who had each to take a hand in succession. Resting for a little towards midday, she began again in the afternoon, and so passed the day until supper-time. Another inmate of the house was the Chevalier de Pierreclos, an old cavalry officer, who, having run through his fortune at an early age, seemed to have no function in life save to agree to everything proposed by his elder brother, to bring in flowers for his nieces, and

inexhaustible supplies of faggots for the great fireplaces;
"kindly and obliging, he lived the life of an animated
piece of furniture." Meanwhile, the sons and daughters of
the house grew up with as little care or training as the
saplings in the forest; the girls, handsome and *piquantes*,
were chiefly employed in worshiping their younger brother,
who already gave every promise of becoming, what he
eventually turned out, a brilliant and amiable scapegrace.

Very different were the discipline and training which
reigned in the well-ordered home at Milly, where incessant,
often laborious industry was combined with perfect refinement, and with a more than average amount of culture.
People are tempted to think there is something conven-
tional in the way so many Frenchmen have of beginning
their autobiographies with enthusiastic laudation of their
mothers. In Lamartine's case this filial worship was certainly as sincere as it was ardent. Perhaps the most
prominent trait in Madame de Lamartine's character was
a tender and exalted piety; an intensity of faith, the
recollection of which always remained to her children as
evidence, stronger than any argument, of the reality of the
unseen, spiritual world. But there was nothing narrow or
austere in her religion; if it made her severe with herself,
she was so lenient in her judgment of others that, living at
a time when party feeling, both political and religious, ran
very high, she had often to bear bitter reproaches on account
of the moderation of her sentiments and her toleration of
opposite opinions. There are two points mentioned by
Lamartine in his mother's teaching, which unquestionably
influenced his character—she never allowed him to laugh
at his own faults or even at his mistakes, but bade him

remember he was a being endued with reason, whose actions all had a certain importance ; and also—while most anxious to encourage and stimulate him to study—she carefully checked all tendency to rivalry by never letting him compare himself with another. Of the first rule the wisdom is doubtful ; it might have been better for Lamartine if, instead of always taking himself seriously as was his wont, he had sometimes been able to indulge in a laugh at his own expense. But to the second he may have owed the remarkable absence of envy or jealousy in his character, which explains the affection with which he was, all through life, regarded by his brother-authors.

In her girlhood, Madame de Lamartine had, both at the Palais Royal and at St. Cloud, glimpses of a very brilliant and intellectual society. After that period her life was passed in extreme seclusion, and within a narrow circle. But she was one of those people who, by reflecting on all they see, hear, and feel, draw more profit from a little experience than others do from a much wider range. It was from her Lamartine inherited the love of nature and of simple things, the delicate perception of detail, the warm, far-reaching sympathies which were not the least of his gifts. In what her son calls "her slightly Roman education," Madame de Lamartine had acquired the habit of allotting, at the end of each day, a certain interval to reflection and self-examination, the results of which she noted in a journal. And when the first troubled years of her married life were past, and she had settled quietly down at Milly, she resumed this habit, "in the hope," as she writes, "that by noting my daily thoughts and anxieties I may learn to know myself better, and so correct my faults. It will also, I hope, be of use in the children's education, to keep a record of the gradual development of their characters." Accordingly, every night, when the rest of the household were asleep, and the silence of her room unbroken save by the regular breathing of the sleeping children, the more wakeful among them used to see their mother seat herself before an antique bureau incrusted with ivory, and take out of a secret drawer a little grey book, such as were then used for keeping accounts. Often her pen would travel over the paper for a couple of hours without interruption, as she recorded the domestic annals of each day, sometimes of each hour.

One of the first entries is dated June, 1801, when the Lamartines had lately recovered possession of the sequestrated estate of St. Point. The château, situated amid beautiful scenery, just where the first spur of the Jura mountains rises up from the Burgundian *côteaux*, was a much larger and more imposing structure than Milly, but, as it was a good deal out of repair, the family only occupied it in the summer. Later, it was restored by Lamartine at considerable expense, and became the home with which his brightest and likewise his saddest memories are associated. In its churchyard he laid the ashes of those he most loved, and there he now rests himself.

"*St. Point, June*, 1801.—We came here for the first time yesterday. It had been somewhat difficult to provide for all our little people, and I was very tired. Towards evening I went to pray for a short time in the church which adjoins our garden. As I passed, I noticed that a grave was being dug; the funeral took place this morning. A young girl, daughter to the deceased, on hearing the first

spadeful of earth fall on her father's coffin, fainted away.
I fetched some smelling-salts, and then brought her into
the house, where I gave her a little wine and some biscuit,
which revived her. But what really gave her consolation
was, that I wept with her: then the children, seeing
my tears, began to cry also, and so this poor man was
mourned by people who did not even know his name.
The daughter said some things which moved me deeply.
There is nothing which touches these poor country folk so
much as to see their sorrows really understood by those
whom they think of as beings almost of a different nature
to their own. In the evening, we brought the poor girl
back to her home, where we found her two little brothers
watching for her. They ran out to ask if their father was
not coming too. I was glad my little girls should gain,
as it were by accident, some knowledge of the terrible
separation death brings, and which they will themselves
have one day to suffer. Life should not be masked to
children ; they should be allowed to see it as it really
is, such as God has made it, with its sorrows and its
joys.

"I have been to see an old maid of eighty, who was
left a little pension and a room at the top of the château.
The beadle's wife gives her all the attendance she needs ;
she has for her only companion a hen, which is as tame as
any pet bird can be. Her name is Mademoiselle Félicité,
her hair as white as the wool of her distaff, and beneath
her wrinkles can be traced the remains of great beauty.
My husband has consented to her remaining here as long
as she lives, even though it should put us to some incon-
venience ; old plants should not be uprooted. At her age

a room is her whole world. Places we have lived in long become as it were a part of ourselves.

"Yesterday we took a long walk with the children to the highest peak of the range of mountains which divide us from the valley of the Sâone. These hills, which rise and fall like clay moulded by the hand of Him 'who made the earth of matter without form,' are covered with pine and birch, mingled with broad patches of golden broom or with long slopes of purple heather and of grey sward, cropped close by countless flocks of sheep, which, seen from below, look no bigger than fowl. Little torrents, whose course can easily be traced by the deeper green of the willows which grow on their banks, or by the flakes of white foam they throw up, glittering like snow in the sun, rush down the mountain side. My husband walked with the keeper, while the children and I rode donkeys led by little boys— the old beadle, who owns the donkeys, acting as our guide. It took us three hours to reach the highest point, although, looking at it from my bedroom window, I had thought to climb it easily in half an hour. But distances on mountain ranges are as deceptive as the flight of time, only in the reverse sense. Mountains seem close at hand when they are really far away, whereas time which we think long is very short: sometimes it seems endless; then, as we are reckoning it, 'tis already gone! We spent the whole day walking about with the children, or seated on the grass, gazing at the glorious panorama spread out beneath us. On one side, the Mâconnais, with its little white villages, from whose belfries we could hear the Angelus ringing out at noon; on the other, 'La Bresse,' with its endless meadows, reminding me of pictures of the Dutch Polders which my eldest brother, who was Secretary of Embassy at the Hague, used to send us as children. And far away on the southern horizon soared Mont Blanc, at first dazzling in its whiteness, then changing to soft rose-colour, and at last to a deep, dark violet in the rays of the setting sun, like a piece of iron which becomes white or red as it passes through the fire of the blacksmith's forge. We dined on the grass, and then, mounting our donkeys, returned home by another path through the chestnut wood. The clattering of our donkeys' hoofs on the rocks, the voices of the children, the whistling of the blackbirds as they flew away, the crack of my husband's gun fired at the coveys of red-legged partridges, the chatter of the donkey boys and the beadle, made our little party so noisy that a stranger might have thought a troop of banditti had taken possession of the mountain. And so seemed to think some poor little shepherds guarding their goats and sheep at the edge of the wood, for they fled in terror and hid themselves in the heather. Presently we came on a fire lighted between two big stones in the middle of the path, and by the side of this rustic hearth was a pair of wooden shoes. Evidently the owner had been too frightened to stop and put them on. I proposed, to the delight of the children, that we should give the fugitives a pleasant surprise, putting into each *sabot* a half-franc piece and some sugar-plums the children had saved from dessert. As we went on, we talked of the fright of the poor little shepherds, and, when they had gathered courage to come back, how delighted they would be. They would be sure to tell their mothers, at night, that the 'good people' who are said to haunt the mountain had given them these treasures. And so it

proved. The children, finding their *sabots* full of money
and sugar-plums, gave all the credit to the fairies. But
their parents were not so easily taken in, and, with the tact
and refinement so often found among our peasantry, determined to show how much they appreciated our kindness
by giving us a surprise in return. The following morning,
when our servant opened the door, he found on the step
four little red baskets filled with walnuts, cream-cheeses,
and little pats of butter made into the shape of *sabots*, the
bearers of these little presents having run away, so as to
give us back mystery for mystery. We were all delighted
with the gratitude and delicacy of feeling shown by this
anonymous offering. Such acts of mutual kindness between
the poor and those whom they call 'the rich' are what I
most wish my children to see and to practise themselves."

When Lamartine was eleven years old the question of
his education began to be discussed. It was not easily
solved, for the Revolution had made a clean sweep of the
old public schools, and the few which had as yet taken their
place, being mostly private speculations, did not inspire
much confidence. At last the family council decided on
trying an establishment lately started at Lyons by a
Monsieur Papineau, and thither his mother, with a heart
as heavy as his own, brought him. "I came here yesterday," she writes, "to bring Alphonse to school. My heart
is bleeding. This morning I went to Mass in the house,
and could get but a glimpse of his beautiful blonde curls
among all those little heads. As I went out I felt as
Abraham must have done when he sent Hagar and Ishmael
out into the desert; neither the beautiful mountain of the
Sâone, nor Fourvières, nor the Ile Bach, floating in golden

light, gave me the least pleasure. I shall stay on for a week, and go as often as I can to see my poor Alphonse, who cannot accustom himself to his prison, and to get myself used, little by little, to this cruel separation."

The change from home to school, under any circumstances, would have been trying to a boy of so sensitive a nature, and, according to Lamartine's account, the Maison Caille was little better than a French edition of Dotheboys Hall. However, the longing to leave his dreary prison as soon as possible had the fortunate effect of pushing him on in his studies, and, though he started in the lowest class, his healthy country upbringing had strengthened both mind and body, and he soon rose to the highest. But the violence and brutality of the master, who was continually beating and threatening his pupils, became more and more intolerable ; and at last, in the third year of his school life, after a frightful scene, ending in a violent struggle, in which a boy was well-nigh murdered by the infuriated master, he resolved "to stay no longer in these shambles," and with him two other boys, also from Mâcon, laid a plan for escaping to their friends.

They managed, one half-holiday, to slip unperceived from the playground, and, having walked for two hours, considered themselves so secure that they turned into a *café* to dine. Hardly were they seated when the door opened and the master walked in. With a playfulness more awful than his wrath, he merely said, "Another *couvert*, garçon ; I am going to dine with these gentlemen ! " But when the meal was ended, a gendarme was summoned, and the culprits, thus publicly disgraced, were marched back to the Maison Caille. Here fresh humiliations and punishments awaited them. Lamartine, who persistently refused to ask pardon, was kept a whole month under lock and key, in a little room under the leads.

At last the holidays came, and his mother, when she heard all that had passed, took his part, and, instead of having to return to Lyons, he was sent to a Jesuit college recently opened at Bellay. He describes the change as if from *L'Inferno* to *Il Paradiso.* Indeed, the Fathers, in their long black coats, reciting the office as they paced the secluded alleys, reminded him of the shades in the Elysian Fields. The college, with its imposing masses of building looking down on the leafy valleys, its tennis courts and playgrounds and *salle d'armes ;* the courteous and kindly Fathers ; the comrades who did not ridicule him, even when with streaming eyes he sat watching his mother's carriage toiling up the steep road which led to Mâcon,—all offered the greatest possible contrast to the Maison Caille. The discipline was doubtless strict enough, but it was maintained by kindness rather than by punishment, and in this genial atmosphere Lamartine's character and talents quickly expanded ; he formed the rapturous friendships of boyhood, gained the confidence of his masters, and returned home each half-year laden with prizes, perhaps too easily won. Many of the Fathers were learned and accomplished men, but in the years of dispersion they had lost the habit of teaching, and, before there was time to build up anew, a fresh storm burst. Napoleon, though he tolerated the Jesuits for a while, never intended the order to revive. A quarrel broke out on their account between him and their patron, Cardinal Fesch. The college was dispersed, and Lamartine returned home, his education only

42

half completed. However, he had been spared the years
of mingled revolt and dreariness which make up the
school life of so many Frenchmen ; and his teachers, if they
did not send him forth a very finished scholar, at any rate
inspired him with an eager love of knowledge, and especially of literature, the one possession which he never lost.

On leaving college, and for many years afterwards,
Lamartine felt acutely the want of a profession. His
position was a peculiar one, and in order to explain it one
must go back a good many years. His grandfather, who
owned very large estates in Burgundy and Champagne,
and received beside, as his wife's dower, a considerable
property in Franche-Comté, had been, like most of his
contemporaries, prodigal and extravagant, passionately
fond of society, and entirely neglectful of his affairs. But
his eldest son, who began life as an officer in Louis XV.'s
Chevau-légers, was of a different temperament. He and
his brother, the Abbé de Lamartine, belonged to the group
of cultivated and philosophical young aristocrats who
ardently espoused the ideas of constitutional government,
the abolition of monopolies, and national representation ;
and, in their own opinion, contributed far more to the
triumph of the principles of '89 than either the middle class
or the people. " Ideas come from above, not from below,"
was their formula. At any rate, a group which included
such names as that of Mirabeau, the Lameths, Mounier,
Virieu, La Rochefaucauld, and Lafayette, represented
tolerably advanced opinions. M. de Lamartine, however,
was practical, even more than philosophical. Finding that
his father's management was leading to financial ruin, he
resigned his commission and the attractions of Paris to

devote himself for some years to reorganizing the family affairs, in which he thoroughly succeeded. The younger children had been provided for according to the custom of the time: the three daughters as canonesses of rich chapters; the second son was a beneficed abbé, the third a soldier, with the little estate of St. Point as his patrimony. Then came the famous *nuit des sacrifices*, in which all privileges, including the right of primogeniture, were voted away. But that any Parliamentary vote should leave their eldest and favourite son only a share of their estates, that his brothers and sisters would consent to rob him of his birthright, was an idea the old Count and Countess de Lamartine never could be brought to entertain. The Chevalier was equally faithful to old traditions, and when called on at his father's death to claim his share, absolutely refused, the habit of respecting his parents' wishes was to him a higher code than any written law. The other brothers and sisters did not, apparently, share his views, for long and painful discussions followed, ending, however, in an arrangement by which the Abbé de Lamartine received an estate near Dijon, the three sisters good incomes, while the bulk of the property remained in the possession of the eldest brother, who, thanks to the Chevalier's generous self-abnegation, was still the head of the family.

Although the months spent in Republican dungeons had modified his political views, the Comte de Lamartine showed his independence of character by refusing to offer the Imperial *régime* any homage but that of silent submission. When, in 1809, the emperor spent some days at Mâcon, he sent for M. de Lamartine, and after questioning him closely about various matters concerning the province, ended with his usual autocratic formula, "What do you wish to be?" "Nothing, sire," was the somewhat abrupt reply. Napoleon, who disliked no class of men so much as those who wanted nothing, turned angrily on his heel. The answer did honour to the Comte de Lamartine: but it was hard on his nephew, when he left college, conscious of talent, eager, ambitious, to find every road to employment or advancement barred by an iron will; for his uncle expected all the members of the family to regulate their conduct by his. At first the trial was not so keenly felt; the enjoyment of an amount of liberty, which, if not very great, had the charm of novelty, the amusements of provincial life, the high spirits of youth, sufficed, as his correspondence shows, to make his life pass pleasantly.

Hitherto, what has been told of Lamartine is taken from journals and memoirs edited by him shortly before his death, but with his return from college begins the two series of letters published by Madame Valentine de Lamartine in 1871–1876, which cover a period of nearly forty years. They do not pretend to any positive literary value, but the earliest ones are written in a crisp, natural style, which most people will prefer to the author's later manner, along with a good deal of fun and humour. The friends to whom the earlier letters are addressed are M. Aymon de Virieu and Guichard de Bienassis. The latter appears to have been an amiable, commonplace young man who, from his father having enriched himself by a plebeian marriage, belonged rather to the *bourgeois* than to the aristocratic section of Burgundian society and was tiresome from his false modesty, requiring continually to be assured of the undiminished affection and consideration of his friends,

Aymon de Virieu was a very different character. His father, the Marquis de Virieu, had been a Revolutionist in 1789, but died two years later fighting on the Royalist side at Lyons. Apparently, his son inherited from him a love of conflicting opinions, for he is described by Lamartine as "a mixture of Rabelais and Socrates," constantly turning even his own most cherished convictions into ridicule. This was intensely irritating to Lamartine, whose tendency it was to take everything rather too seriously. However, Virieu, when he saw he was really giving pain, gradually corrected himself, and developed into an amiable and friendly Socrates, without disciples, but also without the prison or the hemlock; for after a not very stormy youth and a short but creditable diplomatic career, he married, settled, and developed into a much respected country gentleman. The tie between him and Lamartine was no passing schoolboy fancy; during their whole lives they were dear and intimate friends.

The first few months following Lamartine's return home were, as we have said, of unalloyed enjoyment. He was delighted with the room his mother had fitted up for him, with ample bookshelves, and overlooking her favourite avenue of old walnut-trees. "My father," he goes on to say with amusing pomposity, "has bestowed on me the three gifts which in our modern days represent the toga which the Romans conferred on young men who had reached manhood—a watch, a gun, and a horse; as if to tell me that time, space, and liberty were henceforth mine." Through the pleasant summer months his days were divided between long excursions through the far-stretching woodlands, grooming and exercising his horse, a limited amount of

reading under his father's direction, and an unlimited
amount on his own account in the hitherto unexplored
realms of poetry and romance. Among his favourite
authors he enumerates Madame de Staël, Chateaubriand,
Madame Cottin, Richardson, Prévost, and translations from
Shakespeare, Tasso, Milton, Dante, and, above all, Ossian,
whom, with the enthusiasm of so many foreigners of that
generation, he thus apostrophizes : " Ossian, bard of the
vague and of the infinite, foam of lonely sea-shores, spirit
of the mist, voice of the wild north wind, cloudrack swath-
ing the mountain peaks of Scotia ; as great, as majestic as
the Dante of Florence, but more tender, more pathetic,
more human ! "

So passed the first eighteen months of Lamartine's
home life between Milly and St. Point, diversified by
occasional excursions and visits to friends and relatives.
But in 1810 his father purchased a *hôtel* in Mâcon, and
thither the family moved thenceforth every winter. In a
volume of youthful reminiscences, published under the
name of " Confidences," Lamartine describes Mâcon in the
early days of the century in very flattering terms, calling it
" the Weimar of France, the Gallic Florence, a centre of
good taste and good breeding, in which art, literature, and
science throve and flourished ; an alluvial deposit of the
old *régime* which had collected, as if fortuitously, on the
banks of the Sâone." Before the Revolution, it had been
a rich episcopal see ; the last bishop, a *grand seigneur* of
the most accomplished type, outshining by his magnificent
hospitality the richest nobles of the province. Next to the
bishop, the most important personage was the Comte de
Montrevel, who never went to Paris, and spent his revenue

of 400,000 livres in Mâcon. He had a hundred horses in his stable, a theatre and a company of musicians, the latter rivalling that of the Prince de Condé at Chantilly. Then came eight or nine great families of ancient lineage, with considerable possessions, and, at a respectful distance, a numerous body of so-called "bourgeois aristocracy," who lived on their estates, some with, and some without, titles of nobility. When the revolutionary storm subsided, the Montrevels had disappeared, the last of the name having expiated his superiority of birth and wealth on the scaffold ; the bishop, who lived in the house of one of his old servants, was a dependant on the alms of his flock, but as serene and resigned in poverty as he had in prosperity been magnificent and generous. Of the great families, a few who had either not emigrated or had contrived to return in time, preserved a portion of their estates. But the smaller gentry escaped on much easier terms : even those whose sons had joined the army of Condé had managed, by remaining quiescent at home, to avert confiscation, for the most part sustaining no greater damage than a few months in prison ; and as the compulsory division of property had as yet hardly begun to work, feasting and entertaining went on very much as in old times—sumptuous dinners, in which the reputation of Burgundy for good cheer was fully sustained, were frequent throughout the winter, till interrupted by the more riotous gaiety of the carnival. And what the society of Mâcon had lost in brilliancy it gained in solidity. Dicing and gambling no longer flourished ; cards were looked on as a sacred relic of the past in some houses, while others kept up the old tradition of " le bel esprit."

Among these, the salon of the Comte de Lamartine,

though only frequented by the graver sex, held the foremost place. Although time and experience had very
sensibly modified his own politics, the host continued
faithful to the friendships of his youth, so that among his
guests were found men of independent views and of what
were called in those days "compromising antecedents."
Such was M. de Larnaux, who had belonged to the party
of the Gironde, and been the intimate friend of Roland
and Vergniaud. He used to put forward Alfieri's excuse ;
"I knew my own class ; I did not know the people. My
own fault, if it be a fault, is that I had too good an opinion
of my fellow-men." Others, more steadfast to their convictions, declined to offer any apology, but carefully
abstained from political discussions. In private they were
not so reticent, and from them Lamartine, without ceasing
to be an enthusiastic Royalist, imbibed a decided leaning
towards constitutional and personal liberty.

But, favourable as were his impressions of Mâcon society
when viewed through the prism of forty years' memories,
his letters show that at eighteen he looked on it in a very
different light, and his longing to free himself from the
trammels of provincial life and enter some active career was
gaining ground daily. At first he takes it as a matter of
course that, by vigorous self-assertion, he will be able to
sweep away all obstacles. Indeed, at one moment his father,
who, if left to himself, would never have objected to any
profession which promised an honourable, useful existence
to his son, seems, in the autumn of 1810, to have consented
to his studying for the bar at Dijon. But this sensible
proposition was violently opposed, both by the Comte de
Lamartine, whose liberal opinions did not diminish his

horror of the least approach to social equality, and by the other uncle and aunts, who, never having married, all looked on their nephew as their heir and future representative, to whom consequently nothing which would involve a public adhesion to the reigning dynasty or in any way derogate from the aristocratic traditions of the family could be permitted. So that not only was the place of auditor to the Council of State which had been offered to Lamartine declined, but the army, the diplomatic service, were successively tabooed ; and at last it was decided that Alphonse should continue to make his father's house his home, with a yearly allowance of two thousand francs, and the permission, grudgingly accorded, to spend a part of the winter at Lyons.

All other occupations being closed to him, he now turned his thoughts and energies to literature, studying eight hours daily, and reading every book he could lay hands on. From his remarkable talent for improvisation and the abundance and prodigality of his gifts, Lamartine has been sometimes spoken of as a heaven-born genius, owing nothing to cultivation. But, as M. Scherer points out in one of his admirable essays, this was not at all the case. His efforts may not have been sufficiently sustained, but there were lengthened periods in Lamartine's life when, as we shall see in the sequel, he took immense pains with himself.

" Work, work," he now writes to Aymon de Virieu ; " for the next four or five years there is nothing else for us to do. Work, that you may one day give back with usury the talent you have received ; work, that you may test your powers ; and work, so that at your last hour you may be able to say, ' My span of life has been short, but it has been sufficient. I have lived long enough to observe and to study the small portion of the globe which has been placed within my reach. In the pursuit of knowledge I have perhaps sacrificed some precarious favours of fortune, some pleasures of sense, something of the good opinion of certain circles. If I have gained reputation, so much the better ; if I have remained obscure, I am easily consoled, for at least I have been of use to myself. I have increased my stock of ideas, I have tasted of that which is the supreme good, and if I die on the roadside and am not followed to the grave by four beadles or by a host of greedy heirs, I shall have been loved, and shall be mourned by two or three friends who have shared my sorrows and my labours, and I shall render back my soul and my intellect to Him who created them, perfected as far as my powers sufficed.'"

But all these projects of study were not without a special purpose, for he confides to Virieu his determination, if all other prospects fail, to seek employment abroad, and with this in view devoted a good deal of time to acquiring foreign languages, especially English and Italian. For the former, there were plenty of facilities, Napoleon having detained all English subjects who chanced to be resident or travelling in France at the moment of the rupture of the Peace of Amiens, and who, being treated as prisoners of war, were interned on parole in the principal towns of France. Lamartine speedily found an English master, and made the acquaintance of some young Englishmen, with whom he used often to spend his evenings. One of these was a poet, and excited Lamartine's envy and admiration by reading to him a poem he had just addressed

to a Florentine lady. He tried to translate the lines,
but could not render to his satisfaction their incomparable harmony. As the refrain, "Pensez, pensez à moi," is
repeated in every stanza, it is pretty evident that our
ingenious countryman had quietly appropriated one of the
most popular of Moore's melodies. Another of the group,
Mr. Douglas, won Lamartine's heart by his enthusiastic
praise of his friend Virieu. "He speaks of you with a
mixture of respect, esteem, and affection which gives me
immeasurable pleasure." Evidently the impression made
by the English colony was favourable, for a little later, *à
propos* of Zimmermann's book on solitude, Lamartine
writes, "Let us honour the Germans for their good sense,
the English for their genius, their strength of soul, their
indifference to the accidents of fortune ; let us love them
and imitate them. Except the Swiss, they are the only
nation for whom, at present, I have the slightest respect."
And his progress in the language was satisfactory. After
he had been at Lyons two months, he could, he says,
translate the poets not too badly. He had, besides, worked
hard at Greek, read every book he could lay hands on, and
expected to complete at least one tragedy in the course of
the winter.

In spite of all the advice he gets from his friends at
home, he is resolute in keeping aloof from frivolous society.
His own chamber, his books, with an occasional evening
at the theatre, suffice him. He goes on to call Virieu's
attention to the admirable system of compensation which
governs life : "You are in Paris, but you are not free ; I
am as free as the air I breathe, but I am not in Paris. You
envy my lot and I yours. Let us, my friend, accept the

lesson. Thank Providence, and hope for better things. Experience is an inexorable but an excellent master. If I had been told two years ago what was before me, I should not have believed it, or I should have hung myself. Yet I am not only alive but I rather enjoy existence. What I like above all is the society of artists—people who are not sure of to-morrow's dinner, but who would not exchange their philosophical dreams, their pen, or their brush for heaps of gold. I talk to them of you ; I tell them you are able to appreciate them, to emulate them ; that you are, like me, an artist by sympathy, an artist in spirit. They know you just as they know and consult me. I am like a little Mæcenas among them, handed on from one to the other. Admire, and you will be admired. I might, if I chose, emphasize my assertion by translating a long passage from Pope to the same effect, but I spare you."

In his letters to M. Guichard de Bienassis there is less philosophy, but more poetry, with a considerable amount of prosaic detail thrown in. The money troubles which dogged Lamartine all through his life had already begun, partly from the impossibility of making his expenditure tally with his modest income of two thousand francs, partly from the kindness and generosity which kept his purse always at the disposal of his friends,—three or four, to whom he had lent money, his English master among the number, gave him little hope of seeing it again. A hundred-and-fifty-franc note bestowed on him by his uncle, the abbé, was not twenty-four hours in his possession before he passed it on to an old schoolfellow, in penurious circumstances, whom he stumbled against unexpectedly. " I do not know how it is," he writes, "but I am like the Wandering Jew who always has sixpence in his purse, but never a penny more. After all, if no worse befalls me, I may be thankful."

In hopes of replenishing his exchequer, by gaining some of the prizes given by various provincial academies or literary societies for poetic effusions, he now set to assiduously courting the muses, but without much success. However, he was unexpectedly made an honorary member of the Académie de Sâone-et-Loire, and, on his friend Virieu receiving a similar mark of honour, remarks, "It is a good omen. In one respect we resemble the officer who, when congratulated on receiving the Cross of St. Louis, replied, 'It is the more flattering, because I have never been under fire.'" However, not only Lamartine's fortunes, but likewise his spirits, were falling to a very low ebb. Towards the end of 1810 he begins to weary of studies there is so little prospect of ever turning to account, and looks forward with despair to the coming winter at Mâcon, among people with whom he has nothing in common, and who accuse him of fatuity and arrogance because he is too stupid to be able to please them.

But hardly had the gay season set in, when an entire change came over the current of his thoughts, and he was found assiduously frequenting all the fashionable reunions, and no longer complaining of their weary dulness. The reason is not far to seek. Lamartine, for the first time in his life, had fallen in love—with a beautiful girl of seventeen, Mademoiselle P——, whom, after an interval of forty years, he thus describes: "Her figure was the most exquisite and delicate any sculptor ever idealized in a sylph;

she danced as the dragon-fly skims the water, scarcely touching the ground;" and so on through several paragraphs. The P—— family, who belonged to the *bourgeois* section of the Mâcon fashionable world, were pleased at Lamartine's admiration of their daughter, and welcomed him to their house. However, the flirtation was conducted within the strict limits which French ideas of decorum imposes on the admired of young ladies; a gracious bow and smile at the afternoon promenade, with hope of a few minutes' conversation or the felicity of a dance accorded in the evening, was the limit of their intercourse. And even this was of short duration. The Lamartines, who would by no means have approved of the alliance, became alarmed, and Madame de Lamartine undertook to reason with her son. He replied to her remonstrances by declaring that never could he hope to find a girl more charming or more accomplished than Mademoiselle P——, and that the happiness of his life was at stake. With her usual loving tact and gentleness, she agreed with him as to the perfections of Mademoiselle P——, but pointed out that the obstacles to such an alliance would be insurmountable, and that he was far too young to think of settling in life. Though he listened respectfully, his passion was not extinguished, and he announced his intention of saving up his allowance till he had sufficient means to go to Paris and solicit a Government appointment. Meanwhile, anguish of mind brought on a low fever. He was sent to travel for a month, and returned home none the better in mind or body. Evidently a serious remedy was required, and it was decided in full family council to take advantage of an opportunity which happily occurred to give the impracticable and unreasonable young man entire change of air and scene. He was to go to Italy with a newly married cousin, M. de Roquemont-vassy, spending the autumn at Leghorn and the winter at Rome under the care and supervision of the young couple. The remedy worked wonders; the fascinations of Mademoiselle P—— faded at once into insignificance compared with the immortal charms of "la Bella Italia." With an amusing mixture of resignation and despair, he writes, "A delightful and unexpected opportunity has offered for me to go to Italy. Miserable as I am at the thought of parting from her I love, I mean to profit by it. To-night I go to announce my departure. What tears will flow! But not Armida herself could keep me back."

Once started, there are no more regrets; and when, a month later, Lamartine received the news of Mademoiselle P——'s approaching marriage, he was able to offer his congratulations with a light heart.

CHAPTER II.

1811–1815.

THE journey to Italy was an immense enjoyment to Lamartine. His letters to his friends at this period, though not very long or numerous, are extremely characteristic. He describes himself, when first descending the Alpine range, as in a state of excitement which hardly left him the power of seeing or of judging. The rapid journey by night across the Lombard plains ; the moon, "large as Roland's buckler, flooding the whole world with radiance ;" the grey, mysterious shadows of the ilex trees, gave him the impression of a glimpse into fairyland. At Milan he spent his time chiefly in the cathedral, but had leisure to note the marvellous beauty of the women, and the harmonious voices of the men, who seemed to him to speak the language of the gods. The party halted for three weeks at Florence, where attractions of society were added to those of nature and art ; the chief *salon* being that of the Countess of Albany, no longer beautiful as when she inspired Alfieri's heroic verse, but gracious, agreeable, and kindly.

As the De Vassys had to combine business with pleasure, they all went on to Leghorn, where Lamartine

threw himself vigorously into the study of the Italian
language, working, he says, "as he had never worked
before," making himself thoroughly acquainted with the
writings of Ariosto, Tasso, Alfieri, and others of the
Romantic school, as in those days Dante and the *tre-
centisti* were not much the fashion. And for Tasso especially
he kept up all through life a special affection, delighting to
tread the paths and visit the scenes hallowed by memories
of Leonora's hapless lover. At Rome he almost choked
with indignation at the custodian of Sant' Onofrio, who,
in order to point out the beauties of some wretched
painting, trod underfoot the poet's sacred ashes. And
almost the last page Lamartine ever wrote is a description
of the house of Tasso's sister at Sorrento, "to which, on
leaving Ferrara, he fled, disguised as an Abruzzi peasant.
Throwing off his dress, he made himself known, reappearing
once more as a poet and as a gentleman, and there he
regained, after some months' rest, the health and the
intelligence which his friends had feared were gone for
ever. I know," Lamartine goes on to say—"I know one
man who is even more unfortunate than Tasso, and more
calumniated by his fellow-men, who have repaid his devotion to the cause of humanity by cruel insult. Those who
thus outrage him to-day will be sorry when it is too late."

But to return to Leghorn and 1811. The summer
passed away pleasantly enough, and with October came
the time at which the party had intended to proceed to
Rome and Naples, when M. and Madame de Vassy unexpectedly received letters obliging them to return at once
to France. They were anxious Lamartine should do the
same ; but he demurred, and wrote instead a dutiful letter

home, explaining what had happened, and asking leave to continue his journey, applying himself at the same time with joyful haste to all needful preparations, so as to have started before the answer, which he feared would be a prohibition, could arrive. As his means did not allow of his travelling by *vetturino*, he took a place in the mail-car, which, resting at night in the mountain hostelries, reached Rome in four or five days.

His travelling companions were three in number, a young Roman duke and two singers. The journey was pleasant. On arriving at Rome his fellow-travellers urged him to stay with them at an hotel in the Via Condotti, frequented by French, German, and Swiss travellers. The duke, who was going on to Naples, presented Lamartine to his sister-in-law, " a princess of royal German blood, full of grace and goodness," and the *impresario* introduced him to some pleasant artists' society. But Rome was very desolate just then. The Pope was a prisoner at Savona, deprived even of pen and paper ; the Cardinals in exile or in poverty ; and the Eternal City, " like a western Thebes, sat mourning her departed oracles," so that sight-seeing was the only resource left to travellers. Although both Lamartine's journals and his letters to his mother are filled with glowing descriptions, yet it is plain that Rome failed to awaken in him the emotion it usually excites in poetic and cultivated minds. This is owing in part, probably, to his natural disposition, and partly to the deficiencies of his somewhat desultory education. He lacked the historic sense which made Byron realize so fully the dignity and pathos of antiquity, nor had he the exquisite perception which enabled Keats to reproduce the mystery and magic still

clinging to its outworn creeds. He is but faintly scandalized
when a fair Roman singer dances with twinkling feet on
the tomb of Cecilia Metella; and the procession of
Capuchin friars, singing vespers in the Capitol, which roused
the soul of Gibbon to immortal anger, in Lamartine's
mind only added to the scene the additional charm of
picturesqueness. Moreover, it is evident that the prevailing
gloom and melancholy depressed his spirits; and when, at
the end of a few weeks, a young Lyons merchant, whose
acquaintance he had made at the *table d'hôte* of the Hôtel
Condotti, offered him a seat in his carriage to Naples, he
joyfully accepted.

As night travelling was, on account of the brigands,
by no means safe, they slept at Terracina. During the
next day's journey, as they were passing through an olive
wood, they suddenly heard several shots fired. Soon after
they came on a half-burnt carriage lying across the road,
which proved to be the mail car between Rome and Naples.
Two corpses lay on the roadside, and a wounded horse
was being guarded by some soldiers, while others were
following the assassins, firing on them as they fled from
rock to rock of the surrounding mountains. Such a sight,
though by no means uncommon in those days, not unnaturally alarmed the travellers; and it was with considerable relief that at nightfall of the second day they found
themselves at Naples; which, from the noise and bustle of
the crowded thoroughfares, lit up by the countless lights in
the shop windows, or in the niches of the Madonna (it
must be remembered that in those days street lamps were
quite unknown), seemed to Lamartine the gayest city in
the world. They went to an hotel where his companion

was well known, and next morning were wakened by songs
sung in their honour by monks who had brought fruits and
other gifts from their convent at Castellamare.   Lamartine
rose early, and strolled through the town, with which he
was even more delighted than on the previous evening.
"Nature and man," he enthusiastically exclaims, "have
combined to produce this most perfect spot ; the Grotto
of Pausilippe, where you pass through utter darkness to
find on the other side the green plains of Pozzuoli and the
azure Bay of Baiæ ; Virgil's tomb, where the old poet
seems to sleep beneath his laurels to the lullaby of the sea-
waves ; the ten thousand villas which crowd the Chiaja ;
the never-ceasing noise and bustle of the Via di Toledo, the
theatre, the market-place, the different cries and costumes
of the men, women, and children selling fruit on the shore ;
the monasteries and church-steeples ; the religious habits
mingling with the peasants' dresses ; the beautiful summer
palace of Capo di China rising like a white phantom from
its surrounding groups of cypress and of stone pine ; that
of Queen Joanna jutting its brown walls into the sea ;
Vesuvius soaring over all with its light cloud of smoke, like
a priestess playing with the coals of her censer ; add to
this a cloudless sun and sky of the deepest ultramarine.
No city has ever produced such an effect on me.   Rome
was a monastery, Naples is the Garden of Eden."

In the house of M. de Chavannes, a relative of his
mother, Lamartine found a warm welcome.   A charming
little room, opening on a terrace whence there was a
glorious.view, including Capri, Sorrento, and Vesuvius, was
placed at his disposal.   Soon after, to his immense delight,
his friend Aymon de Virieu arrived, so, with excursions in

the neighourhood and social pleasures in the then gayest
city of Italy, the winter passed swiftly away. At the *table
d'hôte* of his hotel in Rome, Lamartine had made the
acquaintance of M. von Humboldt, the younger brother
of the renowned traveller, himself almost as devoted to
science as his brother, and a far more agreeable companion.
M. von Humboldt, who had already won some reputation as
a successful diplomatist, showed Lamartine much kindness,
and, on finding him again at Naples, received him cordially,
and proposed at once to carry him off on an expedition he
was going to make to Calabria, halting first at Vesuvius to
explore the volcano, which was thought to be threatening
an eruption. The offer was gladly accepted, and the next
morning saw M. von Humboldt and his young friend
driving at a quick pace on the road to Torre dell' Annunziata,
a pretty village built at the foot of the mountain. They
put up at a hostelry, and sent for guides and mules to take
them to the hermit cell, built on the highest habitable cone.

After two or three hours of fatiguing march, either over
cool and slippery lava or on hot ashes, they reached the
hermitage, only to find it deserted, for the owner, fearing
to be surprised in the night by a sudden outburst of the
volcano, did not venture to sleep there. However, he soon
arrived on his donkey, which carried besides a goodly provision of flasks of Lacrymæ Christi—the hermit having
catered for his guests as well as for himself, making them,
however, pay largely for the luxury. He seems to have
been a pleasant host, not belonging to any religious order,
but one of those wandering friars who used to attach themselves to certain localities, whence they derived the means
of subsistence. This good monk was of the order of

Vesuvius, changing his cell, which was a quiet and picturesque house of refreshment, as often as the eruption changed its course. M. von Humboldt's object was to gather all the information he could as to the mountain and the usual preludes of the eruptions. Lamartine was neither a *savant* nor a naturalist, but, his curiosity becoming excited, he resolved to study the phenomenon by going down into the crater, and sent two of the guides back to Torre dell' Annunziata to fetch cords for the purpose. M. von Humboldt laughed, and tried to dissuade him from so rash an enterprise, but this only had the effect of rather stimulating Lamartine, and all arrangements were made for the perilous descent on the following morning.

Vesuvius was silent during the night, and when the sun rose nothing was to be seen but puffs of yellow smoke belching out at intervals from the cone. The ascent was by no means easy. It was no longer walking, but scrambling; while stones and ashes fell around, almost blinding them. At last they reached the summit, where the frightful crater yawned. It had the shape of an inverted cone, its sides lined to windward by streams of lava, which, further on, took the form of huge, jagged rocks, still smoking, and here and there glittering stalactites that seemed to have petrified as they fell. Towards the middle of the crater dense clouds of sulphurous smoke wreathed upwards; behind them streamed forth rivers of flame, lighting up the depths of the abyss. The guides sat down philosophically at the edge of the crater, asking the not unnatural question, "You can see it all from here. What will you gain by going down?" "I shall have touched it," was the reply; and, passing his hands through the cords,

Lamartine began the descent, while the guides, hanging over the mouth of the basin, helped him as well as they could without risk to themselves. As he neared the burning furnace, the heat became intense. He strove to find a footing on such portions of the sulphur as had cooled a little, springing over the rushing torrents of liquid fire in hopes of reaching a more solid crust, but without much success ; while it became evident that, if the least change of the wind drove the flames in his direction, he would be suffocated at once. So, gathering hastily such specimens of the burning metal as were within his reach, he gave the signal to be drawn up. On reaching *terra firma* he found that, unlike Empedocles, he had saved his life, but lost his shoes, which had been completely burnt off his feet. His clothes likewise had suffered severely. Though M. von Humboldt forebore to rally him, goodnaturedly proceeding at once to examine the specimens he had brought up, neither his kindness nor the bountiful supply of Lacrymæ Christi provided by the hermit prevented Lamartine from seeing his attempt had been rather foolish, and he returned decidedly crestfallen, to repair his damaged wardrobe at Torre dell' Annunziata.

Meanwhile, the noise in the mountain increased, and the inhabitants of the neighbouring villages spent the day watching in mute despair from which side of Vesuvius the expected explosion would break out. Suddenly at nightfall a loud cry was heard, and streams of liquid fire were seen, from the windows of the little inn, pouring out from the southern cone, down the side of the mountain. M. von Humboldt and his companion watched its progress through the night, and, as soon as day broke, they joined the crowd at the mountain foot. The rolling torrent had made terrible progress, having already reached the houses and gardens in the upper part of the village of Annunziata. Some cottages, perched on a little crest of hilly ground to the left, were almost surrounded by the fiery stream ; the poor inhabitants, carrying with them all they could save from the flames, were flying for their lives—the men dragging great sacks of Indian corn ; the women carrying their children on their backs. The animals, shaking with terror, followed, driven by boys and girls. The very cocks and hens, with wings half burnt, were striving to hide themselves under the vines. It was heartrending to see the lava slowly but surely gaining on its prey. The vine leaves, as they shrivelled up, seemed to crackle and groan almost with human voices ; and then the branches, bare of foliage, became dry as tinder, and, taking up the fire in their turn, spread the raging element along the ground till not a living thing was spared. There was no need to court danger now. Had the wind veered, the same burning breath would have swallowed up every living soul. As it was, they ran at one time considerable risk, Lamartine's walking-stick shrivelling up in his hand like a straw. At last the stream of lava turned into a narrow valley which crossed the high road to Naples, and along which horse and foot passengers were hurrying at full speed. But, anxious to study the phenomenon thoroughly, M. von Humboldt, and Lamartine with him, remained in the neighbourhood as long as the eruption lasted. They then drove through a dense forest of oleanders to Sorrento, to visit Pæstum and La Cava. After a delightful fortnight, Lamartine rejoined his friend Virieu at Naples.

The gay season had now come to an end, and both the young men began to spend most of their time rambling in the country or watching the fishermen at work on the seashore. At the approach of spring the somewhat timid Neapolitan sailors, instead of merely cruising along the shore, began to venture out into the offing. Their slightly adventurous and not over-laborious life attracted Lamartine and his friend so much that they resolved, half in jest and half in earnest, to follow it for a time. Having arranged with a fisherman named Beppo that he should provide them with food and lodging for a few carlini and what profit he could make of their labour, they cast off their *habits de bourgeois*, and arrayed themselves in the costume —fortunately a becoming one—of the Ischian mariners. The experiment was thoroughly successful. Nothing could be more delightful than those nights spent under the canopy of heaven, a warm, soft breeze just sufficing to carry their little bark over the waveless sea, with no greater labour to themselves than that of occasionally stooping down to watch the nets filling with a plentiful harvest. The two friends, accustomed from their boyhood to out-door life, and to cordial intercourse with the peasants of their own country, found plenty of occupation and interest in the life and movement going on around them in Naples. Lamartine, whose love for the romantic and picturesque aspects of life was thoroughly gratified, many years later described some of the incidents of these *vacances d'un poëte* in the pathetic tale of " Graziella," which had at the time of its publication immense popularity in France.

But however pleasant it may have been, this idyllic life did not last long, for early in the same spring Lamartine was at Florence on his homeward journey. He there found letters from his family desiring him not to cross the frontier just yet, apparently in order to avoid the severe conscription which was then being levied in preparation for the Russian campaign. After lingering at Milan, where he lost a good deal at the gambling-tables, he proceeded to Lausanne, where, hiring a little carriage, he drove across the mountains to Mâcon. He was received by his mother with tears of joy ; by his father with a degree of kindness and affection he felt he hardly deserved. For he had not only considerably exceeded the sum of money intended originally to suffice for his expenses, but had left some debts behind him.

"I have had much sorrow on Alphonse's account," writes poor Madame de Lamartine in her diary. "Bills to a large amount have been sent in to us from Italy. His uncles and aunts, who think I indulged him too much, say I am to blame for it all, and reproach me severely. I have shed many bitter tears, for, alas, it is too true ! My son's faults are my faults. Why was I not more severe with him in his childhood ? He would now be afraid of displeasing me. But then, perhaps, he would not love me as he does, nor would the remorse he now feels for the pain he is causing me be to him as a second conscience. They are going to pay all, but, meanwhile, they are making me pay, by the reproaches I have to bear and the tears I shed —a heavy price for the thoughtlessness of my child."

While this little domestic storm lasted, the poor prodigal passed a somewhat dreary time, chiefly alone at Milly. In his letters to Virieu he bewails his position, his health, the impossibility of finding congenial occupation. His uncles

want him to marry and settle down in the country, with a
little farm and the bringing up of a family as his sole
interests in life. Against this he manfully rebels. Ultimately he got permission to spend the winter in Paris,
where he hoped thoroughly to enjoy himself; but it was the
winter of 1812–13, and the gloom of the Russian disasters
overclouded everything, though the Parisians were the last
to know of them. The way in which Napoleon succeeded
in keeping in check the love of news in the modern Athens
is curiously exemplified in a letter written from Paris by
Lamartine to Virieu, asking his friend to tell him all he
can learn of public affairs, as if the little which could be
ascertained was smuggled across the frontier.

Early in May, Lamartine's stay in Paris came abruptly
to an end. He had been recommended to the care and
good offices of M. de Pansy, a councillor of State, whose
widowed niece, a cousin of his father, kept house for him.
They had received the young man with cordiality, and at
first much of his time was spent with them. However,
M. de Pansy, though a clever, agreeable man of the world,
was elderly, and his circle probably a trifle dull, so that
Lamartine came gradually to pass most of his evenings at
the house of a M. de Livry, where the play was high and late
hours were kept. M. de Larmand, the Comte de Lamartine's
Girondist friend, who lived in the same hotel as Lamartine,
thought the young man's health, as well as his purse, was
likely to suffer, especially as, after sitting through the night,
he studied incessantly all day ; and wrote a somewhat
exaggerated account of his proceedings to his family,
urging them to send for Alphonse without delay. When
the letter arrived, the Chevalier was absent from home, and

Madame de Lamartine, not sorry to ward off what might be a painful scene between father and son, started at once for Paris with her daughter Eugenie. The journey was long and wearisome, and in order to prepare herself as well as she could for the meeting with her son, the anxious mother went first to an hotel in the Rue de Richelieu, and thence wrote a confidential letter to Madame de Larmand, asking her to call. In painful suspense the poor lady lay down on a sofa to rest, her heart beating with fear lest she should find her son as sadly altered in appearance as M. de Larmand's letter led her to fear, and, above all, lest he should not be willing, as heretofore, to submit to her authority. Suddenly Eugenie, who was sitting at the window, watching the gay throng below with the curiosity of a country mouse, cried out, "Mamma, come quick! I am sure I see Alphonse!"

He was driving a very smart cabriolet, with a friend by his side, looking particularly well and animated. The cabriolet was probably the one alluded to in a poetic epistle addressed by Lamartine to his friend Jussieu, in terms not calculated to inspire much confidence in the driver—

> " Un char léger, par ton ami conduit,
> Dans le séjour du tumulte et du bruit
> A retenti sur le pavé glissant. . . .
> Déjà ma main maladroite et timide
> Contient à peine un coursier frémissant."

However, at the sight of her son's bright, happy face, all Madame de Lamartine's fears vanished. She felt sure that he was still unchanged, and went to rest with a light heart.

Early next morning the prodigal arrived, but there did not seem to be much need for penitence. He was overjoyed

to see his mother, deeply touched by the step she had
taken, and at once agreed to return home with her at the
end of a week. The interval was pleasantly passed in sight-
seeing and in visiting old friends of the family, all delighted
to see and make much of Madame de Lamartine and her
pretty daughter. One day they all drove in the famous
cabriolet to St. Cloud, the mother almost feeling as if her
girlhood had returned, as she walked with her children
through its stately avenues, showing them her old favourite
haunts and spots redolent with tender memories of her
happy youth.

This little episode, as it is described in Madame de
Lamartine's journal, gives a pleasant impression of the
affection and confidence which united mother and son, and
was a bright spot in both their lives; but the return home
did not pass off so smoothly.

"The family," writes Madame de Lamartine, "received
me very affectionately, but Alphonse very coldly. We
returned to Milly, where he reads, writes, studies almost all
day in his own room. At night we sit round the fire, and
our neighbours come in to talk over the terrible misfortunes
Bonaparte's folly is bringing on France. All Europe is
rising up against him. What will become of France if she
is invaded by those countless armies? How dearly nations
have to pay for the hollow glory of conquest! All the
unmarried men have been called out; taxes are enormously
increased, and are to be raised still higher. We have had
to sell our horse."

On the 31st of December there is a still more anxious
entry. "We have taken refuge in Mâcon. Every day we
are told the enemies are upon us; they are said to have

certainly passed Geneva. I went yesterday to Milly, to buy a little corn, as a last resource, should things come to the worst."

The change which had come over the political situation of France was too great and too disastrous to be any longer a secret. After the Russian campaign all the *prestige* of Napoleon's triumphs barely sufficed to uphold his authority, and now, when he returned defeated from Leipzig, it was evident the empire was tottering to its fall. His consummate military skill and the devotion of his veterans enabled him to keep his enemies at bay for a few weeks in the northern provinces, but to the south the Austrians under Bellegarde poured in across the sparsely guarded frontier. Augereau, who had under his command at Lyons a handful of soldiers lately returned from Spain, made an effort to repel them ; and the inhabitants of the province, with the natural instinct of a brave nation, notwithstanding their weariness of the Imperial yoke, seconded him to the utmost. For the moment, political differences were forgotten, and Lamartine was deputed by the préfet of the department to keep order in the villages round Milly. Without donning the Imperial uniform, he contrived to take part in some skirmishes on the neighbouring hills, once advancing so far into the lines of the Hungarian grenadiers that his horse was shot under him. But it was very soon shown that resistance was useless ; Mâcon was taken, and the country laid under contribution. Then came the news of the emperor's abdication and the proclamation of Louis XVIII. Lamartine describes the empire as crumbling into dust amid confused cries of wounded patriotism and self-love, mingled with anticipations of liberty and peace ;

still, until Paris had declared herself, the future of France
trembled in the balance.

At Lyons, whither he had hurried to take part in the
struggle of opinions, though the Bonapartists had disappeared as completely as if they had never existed, the
Republic had many adherents ; but the Royalists, with
delirious and contagious enthusiasm, speedily carried all
before them. The white flag floated everywhere in
triumph, and the streets resounded with cries of " Vive le
Roi ! "

Eager to forward the cause, Lamartine, with his friend
the Chevalier de Pierreclos, started early one morning with
white scarfs fastened to their shoulders, to reconnoitre the
land. They reached towards afternoon the little town of
Cluny, and rode into the market-place shouting " Vive le
Roi ! " The crowd of peasants and traders, who had
gathered to discuss the exciting events of the times, hesitated a moment, then responded with a somewhat faint
cheer. However, at the end of a couple of hours the zeal
and eloquence of the two young missionaries bore down
all opposition, and Cluny rallied definitely to the King.

Much elated by their success, they rode on to the house
of the Chevalier de Commartin, where they found a large
gathering of gentlemen of the province. Here there was
no conflict of opinions. After a joyous evening meal the
hall rang with toasts to the King and to liberty. It may
excite surprise that toasts so apparently opposite should have
been thus coupled, but it must be remembered that, both
with gentle and simple, the prevailing feeling was that of
deliverance from a heavy yoke ; and that, moreover, lovers
of liberty in France had found by experience Republican

and Imperial rule far more oppressive than that of the last Bourbon King. It is not unlikely that had the Royalist party kept steadily to the watchword, " For the King and for liberty," France would never have seen another Revolution.

Early in the May following, the Chevalier de Lamartine went to Paris with a deputation sent by the *conseil général* of the department to do homage to the new sovereign. Alphonse, who accompanied him, describes with pride his father's still handsome face and dignified bearing, and the warmth with which he was greeted by his old friends and companions-at-arms. In common with all the officers who at the fall of the monarchy had resigned their commissions rather than take an oath contrary to their first allegiance, the Chevalier de Lamartine was entitled to increased rank with a corresponding pension ; but he would not apply for it, giving as a reason that, having some means of his own, he ought not to add to the already heavy burdens of the State : and the only recompense he asked for his services was that his son might be enrolled in the Gardes du Corps, which was at once granted.

A few weeks later, father and son attended the *levée* of the commandant of the corps, the Prince de Poix, who, we are given to understand, expressed the most flattering approval of the external qualifications of the young recruit ; for Lamartine, as his portraits and the unanimous verdict of his contemporaries prove, had inherited from his father a conspicuous share of good looks, and doubtless in his twentieth year did credit to the brilliant uniform of the Royal Guard.

Whether from the chance of service, or, perhaps, because

the Prince de Poix had mentioned his name, Lamartine received orders two days later to attend the King on his first visit to the Louvre. It was an occasion of some political significance. The magnificent treasures of art which then adorned the galleries were, for the most part, trophies of Napoleon's victories, and in recognizing them as national glories Louis XVIII. wished at once to soothe the bitterly chafed feelings of the Imperialists, and to conciliate the distinguished artists to whom Napoleon had given the direction of the National Museum ; the visit was therefore conducted with a degree of pomp and circumstance which deeply impressed the fervid imagination of the young Garde du Corps. His duty was to walk with drawn sword on the left side of the easy-chair, pushed by two footmen, in which the King's infirmities obliged him to make his progress.

At first, Lamartine tells us, he was so impressed by the regal pomp of the *cortége*, that he could see nothing but the majestic figure of the King, dominating by his incomparable dignity the crowd of ministers, marshals of France, and artists who surrounded him ; hear nothing save the measured tread of the courtiers of two dynasties walking in long procession side by side ; and when at last a voice, at once clear and harmonious, broke the silence, he felt as if he were " listening to some far-off voice of the past, deepened and mellowed by adversity, yet speaking as if from a throne."

Some people may be inclined to consider this a theatrical and foolish outburst, only to be excused by the youth and provincial upbringing of the writer : but fifty years ago even very advanced thinkers had by no means

E

shaken off all belief in the divinity of kings ; and a good
deal later in the century so cool-headed an intellectual
giant as Goethe wrote, after an interview with that very
unimposing potentate, Louis I. of Bavaria, " It was no
slight matter to work out the powerful impression of the
king's presence, to assimilate it internally. It is difficult
under such circumstances to keep one's balance, and not to
lose one's head." So that it may fairly be counted creditable in Lamartine that he assimilated his emotions rapidly
enough to become, during the remainder of the royal
progress, an attentive and intelligent observer.

At first M. de Blacas walked next the king's chair,
occasionally pointing out some picture, but apparently with
more of the tact of a courtier than of the discernment of
a connoisseur, for, after a little, Louis XVIII. said, " Let us,
messieurs, pause for an instant. I have not come here as
to a rapid military review, but to see and to admire what
you have had the privilege of seeing often before. Then
turning to MM. Denon and de Forbin, the two presidents
of the Imperial Finè Arts Committee, who, probably from
the consciousness that it was to the late emperor they owed
their position, had discreetly effaced themselves, the king
asked them to point out the best pictures, adding graciously :
" Be sure you do not omit any, for I cherish all glory which
reflects on France. Talent is a dynasty which has no
usurpers."

M. Denon was the first to come forward, but he spoke
indistinctly, and whether from nervousness or stupidity,
was unable to answer the king's first question as to the
authorship of a picture.

Louis XVIII. then turned to M. de Forbin, who, besides

having been one of the most accomplished courtiers of the empire, was an artist of considerable merit, and able to satisfy the royal curiosity on all points. The King kept him by his side, listening to his observations with evident pleasure, yet was still careful not to neglect any of his *entourage.* Even the young Garde du Corps, who, being on duty, had to maintain the attitude of an automaton, yet felt that his royal master knew all about him, and looked at him from time to time with kindly and approving interest. " More than once nature and loyalty combined were stronger than etiquette, and an almost imperceptible movement of the eyes or lips betrayed admiration I could not altogether conceal, and which probably pleased the King the more because it was involuntary. Years afterwards, when my name came before him as that of a not unsuccessful author, he sent me a complete edition of the Greek and Roman poets, with a gracious allusion to my day of service in the Louvre, which he perfectly remembered."

As long as he was quartered in Paris, Lamartine's duties threw him in the way of learning a good deal of the habits of the court, and of the characters of the several members of the royal family. The Comte d'Artois, whom he praises for his personal qualities, was too much impressed with respect for the divine right of kings ; the Duc d'Angoulême was unpopular from his excessive reserve ; while the Duc de Berri, gay, kindly, and confiding, erred in the opposite extreme. The conversation at the royal table was lively and agreeable. Lamartine takes some pains to defend the King against the accusation of gluttony so frequently brought against him, whereas he was only a delicate and discriminating eater; and, certainly, if Louis XVIII. had ever been habitually self-indulgent, he would hardly have possessed the fortitude to discharge as he did his regal duties, and to conform unflinchingly to the rigorous prescriptions of etiquette through a painful and mortal illness, playfully replying to those who implored of him to give himself some indulgence, "The Kings of France die, but they are never ill."

After his turn of waiting had ended, Lamartine went into garrison at Beauvais. According to the custom of French officers, he did not live in the barracks, but took a lodging in the house of an elderly widow in the Faubourg d'Amiens. He was determined not to imitate the frivolous lives most of his brother-officers lived, and had provided himself with a good supply of solid reading. To avoid the distractions of the *table d'hôte*, he arranged with his land-lady that she should furnish his simple meals, and thus the modest allowance of fifty pounds made him by his father and his pay sufficed for all his wants. He rose at five, and went to the riding-school, which his love of horses made the pleasantest exercise of the day. When that and a certain amount of drill and musketry instruction were accomplished, his time was his own. Much of it was spent in somewhat desultory reading, chiefly in a little seques-tered vineyard he had discovered at a short distance from the town and quietly taken possession of; for in that country the vines, carefully pruned and tended once a year are not touched at other times, so that he never came in collision with the rightful owner. Here he could at least enjoy sunshine, silence, and the tender recollections of child-hood, the faint sweet perfume of the vines which had first attracted him to the spot reminding him of Milly; and before very long he found among his comrades some whom his studious habits had interested, and gradually a little society was formed, meeting usually in Lamartine's rooms, where literature, poetry, and philosophy were discussed.

After three months of garrison life at Beauvais, Lamartine returned home on leave, proud of his military· apprenticeship, and still more of his brilliant uniform. He confesses to some pleasure at finding himself the object of general attention at Mâcon, where he "touched a few hearts." On the other hand, he was hurt and astonished to hear mutterings of opposition against the reigning dynasty, and to find that the officers of the Imperial army were more popular in the *cafés* and with the crowd than even the Gardes du Corps. However, there seemed no reason to fear any serious troubles, and these slight mortifications did not hinder him from thoroughly enjoying the gay season which was drawing pleasantly to its close when, in the midst of festivities, and without any previous warning, came the news that Napoleon had left Elba.

There was great surprise, but not at first much anxiety; the universal verdict was that the ex-emperor had made a mistake, that he was already so completely forgotten that even the army had ceased to care for him. It was expected that, disconcerted by his reception, he would probably join Murat, and that if a battle was fought it would be in the Milanese plain. But when the news came that Marshal Macdonald's army had refused to obey his orders, that, at a single word from their old master, they had thrown away the white cockade, and that Napoleon, at the head of a rapidly growing army, was marching on Lyons,

Lamartine and his comrade, the Chevalier de Pierreclos, without waiting for orders, started for Paris on horseback. A few miles from Mâcon they met an old friend, Colonel Dulnat, aide-de-camp to Suchet. He stopped them, and asked anxiously, " Well, where is he ? "

" At Lyons, and marching on Paris," was the desponding answer.

" On Paris ? Well done ! " the colonel exclaimed with irrepressible delight ; and, digging the spurs into his horse, he galloped off to Mâcon, shouting, " Vive l'Empereur ! "

The only further incident was a sword-thrust inflicted by Lamartine on a Pole whom they found corrupting the troops, and whom he not unjustifiably reproached with meddling with matters which, as a foreigner, did not concern him. At Nemours they were joined by several other officers of the household troops, and being all enthusiastic and of one mind, reached Paris in high spirits. On their arrival they found the rest of the regiment equally zealous and hopeful, and were told that enthusiasm for the royal cause was universal. The King had just been in state to the Chambers, and the streets through which he had passed were still echoing with loyal acclamations. The working-men were among the most eager to fight in the cause of peace and justice. Even the students of the Lycées were being armed under the direction of M. Odillon-Barrot. A great battle was to be fought in the plain of Villejuif with the King's household troops. The musketeers and the whole population of Paris resolved either to drive away the usurper or to perish in the ruins of their city. Meanwhile, with all this enthusiasm, the royal cause had neither soldiers nor leaders, and Napoleon was advancing with rapidly increasing forces. The soldiers were deserting in masses, and the people, paralyzed with terror, began to yield to force, and to join the general defection.

On the day named for the battle of Villejuif the Court was secretly preparing for retreat. The Gardes du Corps passed the night armed in their quarters, expecting every hour orders which never came. At twelve next day they were sent to the Champ de Mars, at six brought back to the Place de la Concorde, where they remained till ten at night, when they were ordered to move quietly into the Boulevard. During the night the King's carriage passed through their ranks in the direction of Lille, and at early dawn the troops were marched out on the same road. "When the people," writes Lamartine, "saw through the glimmering darkness the last defenders of the throne leaving the city, nothing can picture their despair. The women brought out wine and bread, while curses on the emperor echoed from house to house. The soldiers, silent with consternation, knew not whither they were going."

The first ray of daylight showed them that Marmont and a staff of some twenty general officers, were riding at the head of the column, and with the princes. Wearily and sadly they marched on through the heavy mud of the Flanders road, and under the drizzling March rain. The marshal rode on doggedly, hardly concealing his disdainful indifference. The Comte d'Artois and the Duc d'Angoulême wrapped themselves silently in their cloaks, but the Duc de Berri went up and down the ranks with kindly and grateful words for all. At every village they passed the peasants stood weeping at their doors.

On approaching Lille, Mortier, who commanded the

garrison of twelve thousand men, still hesitating between
loyalty and defection, sent word he could not answer for
the consequences if the body-guard followed the King into
the citadel. On hearing this, Louis XVIII. resolved to
retire to Belgium. The royal troops, surrounded on all
sides by Excelman's cavalry, whose orders were to keep
them in sight without fighting, were marched into the little
fortress of Béthune, the only spot in France where the
white flag now floated. Here they received the parting
thanks and acknowledgments of the Princes, and a proclamation was issued, announcing that in virtue of a convention entered into by the generals on both sides, they
were to remain for three days in possession of Béthune,
and then were to be disbanded and to return unharmed to
their homes.

The prospect of a long journey with an almost exhausted purse, and in a uniform which had the stigma of
defeat, would have been gloomy indeed but for the unexpected kindness of an officer of Excelman's army, who
was a distant relative of Madame de Lamartine. He came
into Béthune under cover of the darkness, and insisted on
his young kinsman accepting a horse, a civilian dress, and
the loan of a sum of money for the journey to Paris, where
he advised him to remain quietly for a time. However,
finding the prevailing temper of the fickle populace little to
his taste, Lamartine at the end of a week decided to push
on to his uncle, the Abbé de Lamartine. To reach the
secluded château of Montculot, near Dijon, he took the
least frequented roads ; but the people were far less Royalist
than in the western provinces, and he often met with
menacing looks and provocations to insult. Once, near

Châtillon sur Sâone, he lost his temper, and drew his sword on some peasants who hooted him, whereupon they all took to flight, and hid in the vineyards.

After this exploit Lamartine rode on to the town, and had just sat down to dinner when the captain of the National Guard, to whom the incident had been reported, came to call him to account. However, on hearing his name, he treated him kindly, and saw him safely out of Châtillon. From this point onward the country was familiar to him, and, striking off the road at Pont de Parny, he followed a narrow path through a woodland gorge which brought him at nightfall to his uncle's house. Here he found a warm welcome, and his father, who had come from Mâcon to meet him. A merry supper made him forget the troubles he had gone through and the misfortunes of his country, which his elders, inured to revolutions, treated somewhat philosophically.

After a few days, father and son returned together to Mâcon; but here the news met them that the Arrière-Ban of the conscription was being levied with unsparing severity, and that the terms of the capitulation of Béthune were not likely to be observed. To avoid serving the emperor it was safest for Lamartine to remain in concealment for some time longer. Accordingly, he threw himself on the hospitality of an old family friend, M. de Maizod, an *emigré* of Condé's army, who lived in the Jura mountains, wending his way on foot with no other baggage than he could carry on his back. To his host, who, on seeing him approach, rushed out joyfully to welcome him, Lamartine made a pathetic little speech—" I come to you, like a bird poising himself on the last branch of the last tree in the forest, uncertain whether to stay or to take his flight across the fields of liberty at the appearance of the fowler."

M. de Maizod, who, though still a staunch Royalist, was more disposed to enjoy life tranquilly than to trouble himself about dynastic changes, was probably amused by this exordium ; he was one of those charming persons who suit themselves to people of all ages, and made his young friend thoroughly happy.

It so happened that the Lamartine family had before the Revolution a good deal of property in Franche-Comté, and were still affectionately remembered by the older inhabitants ; some of them used in Lamartine's childhood to send little offerings of butter, fruit, and honey, to his mother. One of these old retainers, Léonard Chaveriat, came at once to the Château de Maizod to welcome Lamartine, and, being a keen sportsman, accompanied him in many long excursions. After about a month had passed, Léonard brought one evening the unwelcome news that war having been declared, and the Emperor being in great need of men, the préfets and sous-préfets had special orders to find out all the young men who had served in the King's household regiments, and compel them to join the Imperial army ; and as Lamartine was resolved rather to die than to change his allegiance, not a moment was to be lost. He took a hasty leave of his kind host, and started off with Léonard, who offered to guide him to the Swiss frontier. Each carrying a gun, as a pretext for departure, they started at nightfall, taking the least frequented paths through the gloomy forest. The dawn of day brought them to the frontier. Léonard pointed out to his companion a hollow path, which led up the hill to a shelving bank,

which was the boundary line, while he himself remained
below, in order to divert the attention of the custom-house
officers. Lamartine was fortunate enough to cross unperceived, and walked on with a lightened heart to St. Cergues,
where lived a M. Reboul, who had served as guide to
Mathieu de Montmorenci, Benjamin Constant, and other
distinguished fugitives, and to whom his late host had
given him a letter which procured him the kindest of
receptions ; and he was able to pass the next three months
on the shores of the Lake of Geneva, without much
anxiety as to his personal security, but sorely troubled for
his country and those he had left there, till the news, at
once welcome and humiliating, of Napoleon's defeat at
Waterloo reopened the gates of France to all Royalist
exiles.

CHAPTER III.

1815–1821.

ON the return of the Bourbons, Lamartine rejoined his regiment for a short time. But it was evident that any prospect of either active service or of promotion was more remote than ever; and as neither his pay nor his private means allowed of his remaining, like some of his comrades, simply to enjoy the social advantages of being a " Garde du Corps," without thought for the future, he received the permission of his family to resign his commission and seek some more active career. But this last was no easy task. " Alphonse is trying," writes his mother, " to get into the diplomatic service, but we have not interest enough to force open the doors. I had hoped so much from the return of the Bourbons, and to see him again without a profession cuts me to the heart."

Lamartine now began to take interest in politics, which, since the Charter had established representative government, had become the chief subject of conversation in Paris, where he was whiling away his time. He wrote articles for the daily papers in the sense of conciliation and moderate Liberalism. In a long and rather amusing letter he confides to his uncle, the Comte de Lamartine, that some papers on questions of the day which he had written for his own amusement were much approved of by distinguished persons, who advised him to print them, and that one publisher had offered very advantageous terms ; but, finding it would be practically impossible to keep the authorship a secret, and that his reflections might cause some scandal to many, who, though they agreed with him, thought that at the present moment " toute vérité n'est pas bonne à dire," he had deemed it best to suppress them though the sum offered would have been extremely useful ; a hint which we must hope was not lost on the uncle.

Later in the year he spent some months in Savoy with an old schoolfellow, Louis de Vignet, where he found himself in totally new surroundings. Vignet, whom Lamartine describes as possessing one of the finest and most powerful intellects he had ever known, belonged to an exceptionally talented family. At the College of Bellay, where he had posed as somewhat of a freethinker and a democrat, he was feared rather than loved, both by his masters and his companions, and between him and Lamartine, who was frequently his closest competitor for prizes, there had been more rivalry than friendship. On leaving college, Vignet, who, though of very high birth, had but a slender fortune, gave up all he possessed to his mother and sister, and went to study for the bar at Grenoble, leading a life of heroic privation and severe labour. At the end of two years he was summoned to the death-bed of the mother he so passionately loved. Her death entirely changed his character ; he became fervently devout, gave up all his ambitions, and, in order to make a home for his orphan sister, settled down at the little demesne of Servolet near Chambéry, which was his sole remaining possession, to lead the life of an agriculturist.

An accidental meeting with his old schoolfellow laid the foundation of a devoted friendship. Some of the happiest periods of Lamartine's youth had been spent at Servolet, and this year, probably wearying of Paris and of his fruitless search for employment, he returned thither with renewed zest. Vignet's mother had been a De Maistre, her brothers lived at Chambéry, or in the environs, and in their houses Lamartine was received almost as a son. The head of the family, Count Joseph de Maistre, had lately returned from St. Petersburg, where for many years he had acted as the representative of Louis XVIII., and exercised considerable social and literary influence. His brothers, the Colonel and the Abbé de Maistre, if less celebrated than their elder, were equally agreeable, and far more tolerant of opposite opinions. All joined to Italian liveliness and *finesse* a large measure of cisalpine solidity and vigour. Lamartine has gratefully acknowledged that he owed much to their society, in which he became emancipated from the prejudices of the petty provincial *coteries* in which most of his life had been spent. With an audacity of metaphor which would have surprised his hosts, he compares the family gatherings under the pines which clothe the steep sides of the Montagne du Chat to the conversations of Boccaccio and his friends in their Florentine villa. In the winter evenings, the Comte de Maistre read out portions of his " Soirées de St. Péters-bourg," then preparing for publication—a book which, despite its many blemishes and paradoxes, is certainly the most powerful production of the religious and royalist

reactionary school, in which its author was among the
leaders ; and if its arguments were not irrefragable, they
seemed irresistible when repeated by the beautiful lips of
the youngest daughter of the house, "a *Corinne chrétienne*
as enthusiastic and far more fascinating than her prototype
at Coppet." However, Lamartine seems to have kept a
certain liberty of spirit on political matters, for early in
January, 1816, we find him in Paris deeply lamenting the
changes in the ministry by which the moderate element
was almost destroyed.

Owing to some losses sustained by his father, sufficient
funds were not forthcoming to allow of Lamartine remaining in Paris. He had, much against his will, to get through
the spring at Mâcon, and the summer at Milly, with no
other company than an old servant, his horse, and his dog,
the rest of the family being on a lengthened visit to their
uncle the abbé. Writing of these months of solitude,
Lamartine endeavours to throw over them a sort of poetic
glamour, describing himself as delighting in the utter
silence around him, unbroken save by the tinkling of the
distant flocks grazing on the mountain slopes, the happy
voices of the village children, or the monotonous cadence
of the flails on the threshing-floor. As summer advanced,
and the green tints of the landscape turned to ashy grey
under the scorching rays of the sun, which withered up all
vegetation, the sense of solitude deepened, and the deserted
house seemed like a sepulchre, in which his melancholy
thoughts wrapped him as it were in a shroud. It is pretty
evident that Lamartine was not suited for a life of such
unbroken solitude, nor is it surprising that he was per-
emptorily ordered by the family doctor to the not very

distant watering-place of Aix. Here he found himself in
comparatively lively society, and made some pleasant
acquaintances ; among others, that of M. and Madame
C——. The former had attained some celebrity as a
scientific man, and received at his house in Paris most of
the remarkable people of the day. Madame C——, who
is described as most beautiful and interesting, hopelessly
ill of consumption, has been immortalized by Lamartine ;
to her, under the name of "Elvire," some of his most
striking and best known poems are addressed.

When the season at Aix came to an end, he was most
anxious to rejoin the C——s in Paris, but the state of his
finances made this impossible. In his despair he hit on
an ingenious expedient. "Write quickly," he implores
a friend in Paris, "telling me you have hopes of a good
sous-préfecture ; it might induce my father to give me some
money for the journey." Apparently the plot was successful, for soon after we find Lamartine in Paris, sharing an
apartment with M. de Virieu, dividing his days, he says,
between study and poetry, spending his evenings with the
C——s. Madame C——, though her health was failing
rapidly, was still strong enough to enjoy society, and her
friends continued to gather round her sofa almost to the
last. It was at her house that Lamartine made the acquaintance of M. de Bonald, to whom he afterwards
addressed one of his finest odes. The veteran author
showed him much kindness, presenting him with a copy
of his own works, and introducing him in some of the best
salons.

The year 1818 marks the opening of what is, from
a social and intellectual point, a very brilliant epoch in

the chronicles of Paris. For the two centuries preceding the revolution, that beautiful city had been the unquestioned leader in literature, philosophy, and fashion, throughout the whole civilized world. Under the empire her position was reversed. She was, it is true, the military capital of Europe, but it would be difficult to find a society as devoid of light and leading, or even of gaiety and pleasure, as that described by Madame de Rémusat and other contemporary writers, alternately yawning and trembling under Imperial rule. At the return of the Bourbons there streamed in a throng of foreigners, mostly wealthy, highborn, and much inclined to amuse themselves, who by their lavish expenditure revived the material prosperity of the city ; but from them the higher classes of Parisians held aloof, and it was not until all traces of foreign occupation had gone that the great *hôtels* gradually threw open their portals, and what may be called the St. Martin's summer of the old *régime* began. Unquestionably, there were great changes since the days when brilliant courtiers and fascinating marquises thought the world was made for them alone, an oyster to be leisurely enjoyed at their *petits soupers;* still, if many pleasant things had been swept away, some remained, and others which had disappeared temporarily now returned again. Notwithstanding the enormous losses of privileges and of possessions which the aristocracy had suffered, they still retained great social power, which, it must be allowed, on the whole they used well.

The Faubourg St. Germain now conveys to most people the notion of a narrow, prudish, and bigoted *coterie*, chiefly remarkable for exclusiveness and dulness ; in those

F

days it was precisely the reverse. The Bonapartist ladies affected to be scandalized by its neglect of rules of etiquette which they carefully observed, by its frank, unconventional gaiety, and by the perfect equality only possible in a society of which the members were bound together by hereditary kinship, and in which no one tried to appear more or other than he or she really was. With wise discrimination, it admitted within its ranks those Paladins of the empire who, to borrow a famous phrase, "might count as ancestors," but the crowd of cringing and rapacious parasites enriched by plunder were rigidly excluded. Never, perhaps, has there been a society in which wealth and luxury were so little valued. People like Madame de Récamier and Madame de Luxembourg, whose means were of the slenderest, were the recognized leaders of fashion, and even in the great hôtels, of which the owners were rich enough to be able to resume the old habit of magnificence, it was so mellowed by antiquity as to have lost all trace of pomp or of parade. The repasts were excellent—for it was the golden age of French *cuisine*, to which gastronomers even now look back with regret—but served with simplicity. The master of the house used himself to carve, " avéc coquetterie et bonhomie," and took a personal concern in the comfort of his guests. And the unwritten sumptuary laws extended even to ladies' dress. Madame d'Abrantés has described, with amusing self-complacency, the impossibility of finding in her extensive wardrobe a single dress sufficiently plain to be worn on the occasion of her presentation to the Duchesse d'Angoulême ; the gorgeous court dresses of the empire, on many of which the gold embroidery alone weighed thirty or forty pounds, were not to be thought of, and she was obliged to confine herself to the unaccustomed simplicity of plain satin.

But if the claims of wealth did not count for much in those days, wit, intelligence, and talent of all kinds were very fully appreciated, partly, perhaps, in homage to the traditions of the *grand siècle*, and in rebuke of the Imperial dislike to "men with ideas," but in many cases from genuine sympathy and love of culture. Especially in the salons of the Duchesse de Duras, and of her daughter, Madame de Rauzun, in the Hôtels de Cayla and de la Rochefoucauld, intellectual superiority of all kinds was cordially appreciated, and the most distinguished men of the day were among the habitual guests.

Through the kindness of an old friend of his mother's, Madame de Raigemont, Lamartine had the *entrée* of all these houses, and soon began to make his mark. "Déjà en 1820," writes Madame d'Agoult, in her "Mémoires," "on commençait à beaucoup parler du jeune Lamartine." At Madame de Cayla's he came to know Sosthène de la Rochefoucauld, whose kindness he frequently alludes to in his letters. Even in the group of the "Droite passionée," which gathered in the Hôtel de la Trémouille, and affected to be more Royalist than the king, Lamartine made firm friends in MM. de Bonald and Marcellus, and the Prince de Polignac; while the Duc de Broglie, writing after the lapse of thirty years, recalls the deep impression Lamartine made when reading out of his poems to a brilliant circle in the Hôtel St. Aulaire.

It was probably the encouragement he now received which caused Lamartine to apply himself to poetical composition more seriously than he had hitherto done, and to outline sketches for compositions on a very large scale ; tragedies and epic poems are alluded to as mere trifles, while the sous-préfecture, the endeavour to obtain which had been the ostensible object of his stay in Paris, was relegated to a distant background.

The summer of 1818 he spent between Milly, Chambéry, and the Château de Grand-Lemps, where M. de Virieu, his mother, and sister made much of their guest. In the autumn he returned to Aix, but the C——s were not there ; all hope of Madame C——'s recovery had vanished, and her sufferings were so great that those who loved her could not wish her life to be prolonged. Many letters passed at this time between Lamartine and Mademoiselle Eleanore de Canorge, an intimate friend of the C——s, who kept him informed of the poor lady's state, and was the sympathizing confidante of his anxiety and sorrow.

It was during this sad autumn at Aix that Lamartine addressed to Madame C—— a poem entitled " Le Lac," written in a strain of the deepest melancholy. Faultless in expression and in style, it is usually considered the most perfect of his minor pieces. Before the year ended she died, and the last mention of " Elvire " is the dedication to her memory of the tragedy of " Saül," into the composition of which Lamartine, resolutely determined to conquer his grief, threw himself with unwonted energy. Early in May, the piece being completed, the next step was to have it acted, and Virieu was to do his best to get it read by Talma. But the prospect of success was at first very slight ; Virieu had to admit that several of those to whom he read it soon showed signs of weariness, and though full of enthusiasm in his friend's cause, he himself was evidently not very sanguine. But Lamartine, determined not to be baffled, writes to spur him on to further effort: "I know very well that to get a play of this kind accepted is, no easy task ; in addition to the ordinary difficulties, the religious and antiquated source from which the story is taken, and the simple, natural style in which it is treated, will be put forward as objections. All the same, I am convinced it ought to succeed ; and I think that you yourself, when you have read it a couple of times, will agree that, acted by Talma, interpreted as he and he alone can, it will have immense success. But if recited and acted indifferent what a total failure is inevitable. My uncle, who is not poenund by nature or easily moved, wept through it from beginning's to end, and takes the same view." Evidently this is not the terrible uncle, the head of the family, who prescribes mathematics and farming, but the kindly and amiable abbé, described by Lamartine as the St. Evremond of the family.

Apparently, M. de Virieu required still more urging, for a little later, after thanking him for his zeal, Lamartine returned to the charge : " Do not take any refusal till you have yourself read it to Talma. I had him in mind all through. I worked so entirely for him, that unless he takes the part of Saül I will not allow the piece to be acted. It is specially in such matters there is only one step from the sublime to the ridiculous. If he once sees what it really is, I am safe. After securing him, an actress must be found who can recite the lyrical parts in the third act with poetic inspiration ; then a high priest with some ardour; the rest may take its chance. Everything depends on Talma.

Let Jussieu and every one you know who knows him do their best, and, I implore of you, go yourself; go again and again till you have made him listen and understand. . . . Remember, there is really nothing humiliating in this, and, if there were, the humiliation would be honourable to you since you undergo it, not for yourself, but for your friend."

But the prospect remained doubtful; Virieu could not succeed in penetrating even to Talma's anti-chamber. Lamartine, feeling some more decisive step must be taken, resolved on going himself to Paris. He accordingly rode all Moulins, took the diligence there, and having alighted her ne Hôtel de Richelieu, spent a few days in reforming his wardrobe. This being done, he addressed to Talma a billet which he describes as " The best letter I have ever written. It touched him, and he asked me to call."

The interview passed off well, and Sunday was named for the day on which the fate of " Saül " was to be decided. Unfortunately the sentence was adverse. " The battle is lost. Talma was at first enthusiastic in his admiration of the verses, the style, the way in which the subject is treated. As I read on he threw himself about in his chair, repeating, ' But this is real tragedy.' He told me—indeed he did more, he let me see—that the part of Saül tempted him extremely ; that I was a poet—that some of the lines were among the finest he had ever read. But he went on to say that there were innovations which the Committee (of the Théâtre français) would never allow. The lyrical interludes he himself, naturally enough, objected to, and spent three or four hours in trying to get me to recast " Saül " in a way which, he himself admitted, would destroy all in it that is *grandiose* or original. I was inflexible. What grieves me most is that I see I shall never get the Committee to accept anything really good. To pass through those doors one must make one's-self very small."

However, notwithstanding this disappointment, the expedition to Paris seems to have had a salutary effect, both on Lamartine's health and on his spirits. He found himself warmly welcomed, and made much of by numerous friends. At a dinner at the St. Aulaires' he was presented to M. Decazes, already a person of much importance, who invited him to his house, and treated him in the kinde· way possible.

It was at this time that a romantic, though somewhat short-lived friendship sprang up between Lamartine and a young man of about his own age, whose career resembles that of an illustrious Englishman of our day, inasmuch as he began life as an officer in the Royal Guard, and rose to be a Cardinal Archbishop. Auguste, Duc de Rohan, has been described, even by antagonistic writers, as a singularly interesting and accomplished type of the aristocratic and æsthetic Churchman. After leaving the army he had married a charming and beautiful woman, to whom he was passionately attached, and had every prospect of a more than common share of happiness, when an awful tragedy dashed the cup from his lips. The Duchesse de Rohan, at the moment of starting for a ball at the Austrian Embassy, set fire to her dress, and, despite her husband's frantic efforts to save her, perished before his eyes. In his agonizing sorrow the Duke found consolation in fervent, almost mystical devotion, his greatest pleasure being to gather round him men of kindred minds, intellectual, cultivated, to whom religion was the one absorbing interest.

Into this circle, which included men so dissimilar in their future careers as Victor Hugo, L?.mennais, and Montalembert, Lamartine, with his enthusiastic and sympathetic temperament, was naturally drawn. The Duke took the utmost delight in his society, and seemed at one time hardly able to live without him. Towards the end of Lent he asked him to accompany him to his country place of Laroche-Guyon, where, in the Duke's private chapel, which, as if in imitation of the early Christians, was a subterranean crypt, the ceremonies of Holy Week were celebrated with the utmost solemnity and fervour. This atmosphere of prayer and mourning, of artistic splendour and rapt devotion inspired Lamartine's muse ; some of his most beautiful elegies are dated from Laroche-Guyon. But the sympathy between him and his host was not as complete as both believed it to be at the time.

In the Duc de Rohan was revived not only the charming and exquisite urbanity of the last century, but also its opinions and prejudices. "My intercourse with the Duc de Rohan," wrote Montalembert about the same time, "somehow embarrasses me. He has been most kind, and even shown me real affection and interest, yet there is something which keeps me aloof. Never could my heart yield itself to a Frenchman, to a priest in whose eyes constitutional liberty and equality are chimerical." However, Lamartine's political views were not at all so clearly defined as Montalembert's at that time ; it was very gradually, in his case, that the rift in the lute widened to absolute separation. And it is only fair to the Duc de Rohan to add that, if an ardent politician, he was before everything a Christian Bishop. At the time of the Revolution of 1830 he was besieged in his episcopal palace of Besançon by a furious mob, and driven out of the diocese with the utmost contumely. When the storm had subsided, he quietly resumed his pastoral labours, spent the remainder of his life and fortune in ministering to the wants of his diocese, then stricken by famine and pestilence, and died universally lamented by the flock among whom, three years before, his life had not been safe.

But the friends with whom Lamartine had the most unrestrained and pleasantest intercourse were the family of a lady already mentioned, whom he speaks of in his letters as " les incomparable Raigecourt." Madame de Raigecourt, who by rank and position was a very great lady, and to the end of her life remained the truest and most steadfast of Lamartine's friends, seems to have been a most interesting person. In her youth she had been the chosen friend of Louis XVI.'s angelic sister, Madame Elizabeth, and she continued ever after on terms of great intimacy with the Royal family. Her interest in Lamartine and her kindness to him were unceasing, and his letters show that his affection for her was almost that of a son. She was now full of sympathy for his disappointment at the rejection of " Saül," and insisted on his giving her the manuscript, that she might read it to the king. There was likewise much talk of obtaining for him a diplomatic appointment. An unpaid attachéship was offered, but, a salary being to him a matter of absolute necessity, he was obliged to decline it.

As spring advanced he returned to Milly. He now threw himself with hitherto unknown interest into agricultural pursuits, and became apparently disposed to think there is an indissoluble connection between wooden shoes and happiness. In his letters he still complains at times of his health, but is able to be out all day, frequently joining his neighbours at the "rendezvous de chasse," which, in Burgundy at least, are no trifling matters. Englishmen are apt to speak contemptuously of French sportsmen, but the hunting of wolves and bears, carried on as it was in those days, and is even now in the forest of Cluny, implies no small amount both of courage and of physical endurance. Lamartine mentions that he had to leave home at five in the morning, and ride hard in order to reach the *rendezvous* at seven, the hunt lasting nine or ten hours, and the quarry being pursued for the most part on foot.

But farming and hunting were by no means Lamartine's only occupations. Although he describes himself to Madame de Raigecourt as hardly able to string a few worthless stanzas together, he was writing a good deal of poetry, and in a strain superior to his former efforts. In the year previous, his thoughts had run exclusively on dramatic and epic subjects. He then wrote a " Médée," which has been published since his death ; two acts of " Zoraïde," and fragments of other plays. He also began an epic poem, " Clovis," in which the miraculous and supernatural were to abound, and to which he proposed to dedicate ten years of his life. But the failure of " Saül " disgusted him ; of the twenty projected cantos of " Clovis," only a fragment was ever written, and even a " Cæsar " was sacrificed. "Cæsar, my favourite hero, my king of men, half demi-god, half Henry IV., who was to have shown men that when they are hopelessly sunk in the corruption of egotism, a tyrant is their greatest benefactor, lies buried in the ashes of my grate." The loss is probably not to be regretted, especially as now, after many discouragements and disappointments, Lamartine developed a poetic style which, though it may have been suggested by verses of Bertin and of Parny, he made thoroughly his own, and carried to a very high point of perfection. "Sappho," "Le Golfe de Baiæ," "À Elvire," and other poems published in the "Méditations," belong to this period. He wrote them with the idea of immediate publication. "You will shortly see," he writes to Virieu, "a book of elegies in a certain style of my own ; they are just ready for the press." However, he changed his mind, because, he says, he thought, on reflection, that they did not do his powers full justice.

But this high and, as the sequel proved, perfectly just estimate of his poetic capabilities did not deter Lamartine from other speculations. We find him rather unexpectedly turning his thoughts to commerce and colonization. First, he made plans for going to America ; a little later, he proposes to M. de Virieu that they should obtain the concession of a little island near Leghorn, invest about sixty thousand francs in agricultural implements, and sow it with wheat. "The smallest profit would be a hundred per cent. the first year ; I have made the calculation with great care. By degrees, we could build modest habitations for ourselves and our friends. Let me know what you think of it, and how much you would be disposed to invest. I have already written to Florence about the concession." This reads like a joke, but, unfortunately, all through his life such speculations seemed to Lamartine at once serious and

simple matters, and in perfect good faith and honest conviction he was constantly trying to improve his fortunes in
every way save that of limiting his desires.

However, the Mediterranean island remained un-
colonized, and, with no further variety than a few weeks
spent in Paris, the year 1819 passed monotonously away;
nor did that of 1820, though destined to bring considerable
amelioration in Lamartine's position, begin more cheerfully.
"Alphonse is at Milly," writes his mother in January;
"calm, but very melancholy, living more than ever in his
books, studying and writing verses, which he shows to his
intimate friends, who speak to me enthusiastically of them.
But what use is this buried talent, even if it be real, to
a young man longing for an active career? I hoped that
his uncles would not now oppose his entering some profession, or that at any rate the princes we served and regretted
so long would have employed our son. But three years
have passed, and not a gleam of hope has been vouchsafed
us. Still, I can understand that they must be overwhelmed
with solicitations, and have no time to think of us poor
provincials."

Another painful disappointment now befell the poor
lady, her six daughters were successively growing up to
womanhood, and, according to French custom, marriages
ought to be arranged for them. They were pretty, amiable,
and well-educated, but besides these attractions it was
absolutely necessary each should have a dowry, and for this
the goodwill and co-operation of the aunts and uncles were
indispensable. The eldest, Cecile, had married the Comte
de Cessia, a few years her senior, but handsome and agreeable. The husband of Eugénie, the second, was a young

officer of good family, M. de Coppens ; and now the third,
Césarine, had made her *début.* Her mother describes her
as extremely beautiful. " People tell me she resembles,
feature for feature, a celebrated picture of Raphael, called
' The Fornarina.' She is warm-hearted, frank, and very
spirituelle. Every one praises her."

From her first appearance the young lady was passionately admired by a young man of much promise and of
very old family, M. de Parseval. Though he was not rich,
his suit was warmly approved by Madame de Lamartine,
who, seeing in him every quality likely to make her daughter
happy, encouraged their mutual liking. But the terrible
family council pronounced that M. de Parseval was not
a sufficiently brilliant match for the beautiful Césarine, and
the courtship was sternly ordered to be cut short—a cruel
blow to Madame de Lamartine, who had evidently looked
forward to seeing the romantic happiness of her own early
married life repeated in her daughter. " The proposed
marriage of my Césarine is entirely at an end. I had
myself to break it to the poor young man, and in doing so
could not restrain my own tears. He still persists in
hoping against hope ; but the family are inexorable.
Césarine is very sad, but touching in her submission,
fearing perhaps to bring some trouble on me. For miserable money considerations this marriage, which would
insure the happiness of two young lives, is disapproved !
Happily for me, my father and mother thought and agreed
differently. To their indulgence I owe a life of happiness."

Very shortly, a new suitor presented himself ; he, however, had secured beforehand the family approbation. M.
de Vignet was the elder brother of Lamartine's friend,

Louis de Vignet ; he had a good government appointment, and his reputation was deservedly high. But his home was in Savoy, and his intended mother-in-law did not think his appearance prepossessing, so it was with reluctance that she broached the subject to her daughter. To her surprise, she found the young lady not disinclined to the alliance. When urged by her brother not to do violence to her feelings, as he would shield her from any pressure on the part of the aunts and uncles, she replied that, though grateful to M. de Parseval for the attachment he had shown her, her feelings had not been engaged, and that she was quite ready to meet the wishes of her relatives and to marry, without the slightest repugnance, the estimable person they had selected. After this, the more romantic and impressionable mother could only say, " It seems she is as sensible as she is charming. Happy the man who will possess such a treasure ! " And all the remaining allusions to the subject are records of thankfulness for the happiness of her child, only the remembrance of the poor forsaken lover sometimes gave her pain ; however, she consoled him with such tenderness and tact that ever after he had for her almost filial affection, so that all ended well. Besides, the marriage of Césarine had indirectly a very happy influence on her brother's future.

Needless to say that, since he reached the age of twenty-five, Lamartine's marriage had been the subject of frequent and anxious discussion in his domestic circle. The young man himself felt, apparently, he must ultimately accept the inevitable lot, but endeavoured to postpone it as long as possible. The only reference to the subject in his letters is once when he tells M. de Virieu that he is shortly to propose for Mademoiselle D——, and that when she shall have refused him another young lady is in reserve. Nothing more is said of either, and Lamartine went, in the summer of 1819, to spend a few weeks with his newly married sister Césarine in Savoy.

It chanced that just at the time an English widow lady and her daughter were staying with the Marquise de la Pierre, who seems to have been the great lady of Chambéry. The De la Pierres had, during the emigration, received from Colonel and Mrs. Birch much hospitality and kindness, which they were now anxious to repay by showing every attention to their guests. Their house was a very gay one, and, as the Vignets were near neighbours and intimate friends, Lamartine had many opportunities, of which he eagerly availed himself, of meeting Miss Birch ; so that, before many weeks had elapsed, his mother heard from him, to her great surprise, not only that his happiness depended on his marrying a young English girl, but that they were already engaged ; "at least," she goes on in a qualifying tone, "as far as it is possible for two young people to be engaged without their parents' consent having as yet been given. Césarine, who knows the young lady very intimately, writes me word that, without being a regular beauty, she is pleasing, graceful, has a perfect figure, magnificent hair, and is extremely well educated, with many accomplishments and a superior understanding. Though not rich, her mother is sufficiently well off, and she is the only child. How thankful I should be," adds the poor lady, " if, instead of the brilliant career I once dreamt of for him, but of which now there is so little prospect, I could at least procure for him domestic happiness ! "

But the difficulties were many, and seemed insuperable ; the family did not approve of a foreigner, and still less of a Protestant connection. " However," adds the mother, " Césarine assures me that the young lady has confided to the Demoiselles de la Pierre that she has long felt an inclination to our religion, and would willingly embrace it, but for the pain it would give her mother. If this be really true, this difference might be got over. But what can be more contrary to the fixed, arbitrary notions of his uncles and aunts than this sort of romantic marriage with a foreigner ? And unless they help, nothing can be done. Love may suffice the young people themselves, but it is not they who draw up the contract."

Things turned out much as she had feared ; the family were inexorable, and when Lamartine, after spending a short time at home in fruitless endeavours to soften the hard hearts of his relatives, rejoined the De la Pierres and Birches at Aix, he could give but slender hopes of obtaining the necessary consents. Mrs. Birch, who at first encouraged his suit, naturally became alarmed for her daughter's happiness, and carried her off to Turin. However, the lovers would not give up all hope, and slightly scandalized Madame de Lamartine by keeping up a correspondence, or, as she carefully explains, " an occasional interchange of letters."

Lamartine was now more anxious than ever to obtain an appointment. For a time he had hopes of being named Secretary of Embassy to a German court, but, at the moment when all seemed settled, he received an intimation from the Foreign Office that it had lately been decided that such places were in future to be reserved for those

who had already gone through some period of service, but
that he could be attached to the legation without a salary,
and with the understanding that his period of probation
should be exceptionally short.   This, however, would not
suffice, and the disappointment was the greater because, as
he writes to Madame de Raigecourt, the fact of refusing
the post offered to him barred all further solicitation.
" My marriage is impossible for years, and though the
young lady is admirable in her constancy, it only serves
to make her persecuted and unhappy.   As to myself, I
am so accustomed to disappointment and sorrow that I
am almost resigned ; what cannot be cured must be endured.
My only project for the future is to wrap myself in solitude.
I am giving up all my correspondence save with three or
four old friends such as yourself.   Do not pity or trouble
yourself about my unlucky fate ; I am bearing it very well.
Nothing worries me much save my hopeless, interminable
money difficulties.   Once a man becomes early in life in-
volved in that terrible quicksand he never gets quite free."

Lamartine now found himself in much the same position
as the Heir of Linne in the old ballad, and, like him, it
was at the moment his fortunes had reached their lowest
ebb that his feet touched the first rung of the ladder which
was to lead to success.   He threw himself into poetic composition more earnestly than ever he had done before, and,
no longer hampered by the fear of injuring his official
prospects, he resolved to publish.   His letters to Virieu are
full of copies of verses sent for criticism or approval ; and,
at the end of a few months, with a roll of manuscript under
his arm, he began the round of the publishers.

He could afterwards afford to tell, with slightly malicious

G

pleasure, how the estimable M. Didot, then and justly the
head of the profession, received him with patronizing kindness, but told him that his poems were quite unlike anything he had ever read before, and advised him to try and
imitate the style of Delille, or Luce de Lancival, the then
popular poets of the day.   Happily, M. Nicolle, to whom
he next applied, was not so critical ; and early in 1820
appeared, in a slender anonymous volume, " Les Premières
Méditations."   Their   success   was   immediate   and   very
great ; the author, like Byron, awoke one morning to find
himself famous.

There are few things more difficult than to do justice
to the merits of the literature which has charmed and
influenced the generation immediately preceding our own.
So much that to them was original and striking is to us
trite and commonplace.   In the space of thirty years so
many illusions are dispelled, so many idols shattered, so
many mines worked out, so many new and apparently
inexhaustible ones opened, that dust is apt to accumulate
on volumes which, not many years ago, used to be read
and read again with passionate eagerness.   It is, therefore,
somewhat surprising to be told, in the preface written by
M. de Laprade for the volume of Lamartine's " Poésies
inédites," lately published for the first time, " Les adorateurs
de Lamartine composent une sorte d'église indestructible,
et qui survivra aux écoles les plus bruyantes et les plus
populaires.   Nos plus pures, nos plus hautes jouissances,
c'est à lui que nous les devons ; l'age lui-même n'émousse
pas la vivacité de ce sentiment, n'en altére pas la profondeur."

M. de Laprade was not a man to use such words lightly.
No doubt the little congregation still exists, that tapers are

burning at their shrine, and the air is heavy with incense ; but we suspect that each succeeding year visibly thins its ranks, and that the achievements of Lamartine's unquestioned genius are rather to be traced in results less direct, but also less perishable. For though a portion of his success may be ascribed to his possessing what the French call " the irresistible note of contemporaneity," the temperament at once receptive and sympathetic, which enabled him to feel keenly and to express forcibly the varying and conflicting influences which swayed his generation, it must be remembered that, if he reflected the spirit of his time, he likewise dominated it. " While still a very young man," writes Scherer, " Lamartine unquestionably gave the tone to French literature." Indeed, it is hardly too much to say that he was, for a time, the master of all who sang. As such he is hailed in Musset's beautiful ode, and his influence is plainly to be traced in the earlier poems of Victor Hugo. Doubtless the disciple is ranked higher than the master (at least, it would require much self-confidence now to hazard a contrary opinion), yet one may be permitted modestly to suggest that the fame of the younger poet would not have suffered had he retained longer the grace and simplicity of his first manner. Lamartine, though he belongs both by the date of his birth and by his intellectual sympathies to the modern period, never lost his respect for the dignity of style, for the consummate art, which had matured under the old *régime.* In his earliest days especially, he took much pains with his diction ; his natural good taste made him dislike the careless versification of which Voltaire set the fashion, and he strove to emulate the severity of the earlier traditions. He excels in the sustained

period which runs through ten or even twenty lines with
perfect clearness and harmony, yet is saved from monotony
by skilful use of the pause, or hemistich, so essential in
French verse, and which varies the rhythm without destroying it ; but he never learnt "the crowning art, the art to
blot." He is the troubadour of modern French poetry, his
verse trilling on like the song of a bird ; his composition an
improvisation, best described by his own simile :—

> " Mes fortes penseès,
> Au but de leurs desirs volant comme des traits,
> Chaque fois que mon sein respire, plus pressées
> Que les colombes des forêts.
> Montent, montent toujours, par d'autres remplacées,
> Et ne redescendent jamais ! "

In " L'Isolement," with which the first volume of " Les
Méditations " opens, the author, after the fashion of youthful bards, tells his readers that life is vanity, emptiness,
mirage ; that for him the summer sunshine has no reviving
warmth, the flying hours carry no message worth listening
to ; that he himself is but a seared leaf tossed by autumnal
gales :—

> " Quand la feuille des bois tombe dans la prairie,
> Le vent du soir s'élève et l'arrache aux vallons,
> Et moi, je suis semblable à la feuille flétrie,
> Emportez-moi comme elle, orageux aquilons ! "

The same note of suave and tender melancholy pervades
" Le Vallon," so well known from Gounod's beautiful
setting :—

> " Mon cœur, lassé de tout, même de l'espérance,
> N'ira plus de ses vœux importuner le sort ;
> Prêtez-moi seulement, vallons de mon enfance,
> Un asile d'un jour pour attendre la mort.
>
> *   *   *   *   *

" Repose-toi, mon âme, en ce dernier asile,
    Ainsi qu'un voyageur qui, le cœur plein d'espoir,
S'assied, avant d'entrer, aux portes de la ville,
    Et respire un moment l'air embaumé du soir.

" Comme lui, de nos pieds secouons la poussière ;
    L'homme par ce chemin ne repasse jamais,
Comme lui, respirons au bout de la carrière
    Ce calme avant-coureur de l'éternelle paix.

" Tes jours, sombres et courts comme des jours d'automne,
    Déclinent comme l'ombre au penchant des coteaux ;
L'amitié te trahit, la pitié t'abandonne,
    Et, seule, tu descends le sentier des tombeaux.

" Mais la nature est là qui t'invite et qui t'aime ;
    Plonge-toi dans son sein qu'elle t'ouvre toujours ;
Quand tout change pour toi, la nature est la même,
    Et le même soleil se lève sur tes jours.

" Suis le jour dans le ciel, suis l'ombre sur la terre ;
    Dans les plaines de l'air vole avec l'aquilon ;
Avec les doux rayons de l'astre de mystère
    Glisse à travers les bois dans l'ombre du vallon."

In the longer poems of this volume, " La Foi,"
" L'Immortalité," " Le Désespoir," religious and philosophical speculations are descanted on with perhaps more
fluency than power ; while, on the other hand, " Le Lac,"
written in the days of anguish which preceded the death of
Elvire, shows, in its more than wonted fulness of thought
and conciseness of expression, traces of strong though
carefully disciplined emotion. " The sense of the implacable
flight of time, the resistless passage of the hours " is perfectly given in the opening lines :—

" Ainsi, toujours poussés vers de nouveaux rivages,
    Dans la nuit éternelle emportés sans retour,
Ne pourrons nous jamais sur l'océan des âges
    Jeter l'ancre un seul jour ?

" Eternité, néant, passé, sombres abîmes,
Que faites vous des jours que vous engloutissez ?
Parlez ; nous rendrez-vous ces extases sublimes,
Que vous nous ravissez ?

The " Nouvelles Méditations," which appeared in the
course of the following year, are not so highly finished or
so self-contained as the first series ; they open on larger,
more luminous horizons.   In breadth of style, in fulness of
thought, Ste. Beuve considers them superior ; but they show
traces of more haste in the writing.   In " Les Étoiles " the
influence of Ossian, on whom Lamartine lavishes so much
praise, is clearly seen—the images are multiplied till the
poet finally loses himself in the mystic depths of the midnight skies.   " Les Préludes," in which, with rapid, flexible
fingers, Lamartine strikes every chord of his lyre, give full
utterance to the hopes, fears, and aspirations of a generation unsettled on all points, and without strong convictions,
nonchalant, indifferent, and yet eager for strife.   " Ischia,"
" Le Passé," " Les Consolations," Scherer reckons among
Lamartine's finest pieces.   " Bonaparte " has a clarion-like
note, and breathes a more generous spirit to the fallen foe
than was often found among Royalist writers of that period.
The rhythm and cadence are admirable :—

" Il est là ! . . . sous trois pas un enfant le mesure !
Son ombre ne rend pas même un léger murmure,
    Le pied de l'ennemi foule en paix son cercueil.
Sur ce front foudroyant le moucheron bourdonne,
Et son ombre n'entend que le bruit monotone,
    De la vague contre l'écueil.

" Les dieux étaient tombés, les trônes étaient vides ;
La victoire te prit sur ses ailes rapides ;
    D'un peuple de Brutus la gloire te fit roi !
Ce siècle dont l'écume entraînait dans sa course
Les mœurs, les rois, les dieux . . . refoulé vers sa source
    Recula d'un pas devant toi !

" Tu combattis l'erreur sans regarder le nombre ;
Pareil au fier Jacob tu luttas contre une ombre ;
  Le fantôme croula sous le poids d'un mortel
Et de tous ces grands noms profanateur sublime,
Tu jouas avec eux, comme la main du crime
  Avec les vases de l'autel.

  *   *   *   *   *

" Jamais, pour éclaircir ta royale tristesse,
La coupe des festins ne te versa l'ivresse,
  Tes yeux d'une autre pourpre aimaient à s'enivrer.
Comme un soldat debout qui veille sous ses armes,
Tu vis de la beauté le sourire ou les larmes,
  Sans sourire et sans soupirer.

" Tu grandis sans plaisir, tu tombas sans murmure,
Rien d'humain ne battais sous ton épaisse armure ;
  Sans haine et sans amour, tu vivais pour penser,
Comme l'aigle régnant dans un ciel solitaire,
Tu n'avais qu'un regard pour mesurer la terre,
  Et des serres pour l'embrasser !

" Être d'un siècle entier la pensée et la vie,
Émousser le poignard, décourager l'envie,
  Ébranler, raffermir, l'univers incertain ;
Aux sinistres clartés de ta foudre qui gronde
Vingt fois contre les dieux jouer le sort du monde,
  Quel rêve ! et ce fut ton destin !

" Tu mourus cependant de la mort du vulgaire,
Ainsi qu'un moissoneur va chercher son salaire,
  Et dort sur sa faucille avant d'être payé ;
De ton glaive sanglant tu t'armas en silence,
Et tu fus demander justice ou récompense
  Au Dieu qui t'avait envoyé.

  *   *   *   *   *

" Son cercueil est fermé ; Dieu l'a jugé. Silence !
Son crime et ses exploits pésent dans la balance ;
  Que de faibles mortels la main n'y touche plus !
Qui peut sonder, Seigneur, ta clémence infinie !
Et vous, fléau de Dieu, qui sait si le génie
  N'est pas une de vos vertus ? "

There is, however, a more enduring charm in the beautiful stanzas entitled, " Le Poëte Mourant."

" La coupe de mes jours s'est brisée encore pleine ;
Ma vie en long soupirs s'enfuit à chaque haleine,
     Ni larmes ni regrets ne peuvent l'arrêter ;
Et l'aile de la mort, sur l'airain qui me pleure,
En sons entrecoupés frappe ma dernière heure ;
     Faut-il gémir ? faut-il chanter ?

     *   *   *   *   *

" La lyre en se brisant jette un son plus sublime ;
La lampe qui s'éteint tout-à-coup se ranime,
     Et d'un éclat plus pur brille avant d'expirer ;
Le cygne voit le ciel à son heure dernière ;
L'homme seul, reportant ses regards en arrière,
     Compte ses jours pour les pleurer.

" Ma harpe fut souvent de larmes arrosée ;
Mais les pleurs sont pour nous la céleste rosée ;
     Sous un ciel toujours pur le cœur ne mûrit pas ;
Dans la coupe écrasé, le jus du pampre coule,
Et le baume flétri sous le pied qui le foule
     Répand ses parfume sous vos pas.

" Je jette un nom de plus à ces flots sans rivage ;
Au gré des vents, du ciel, qu'il s'abîme ou surnage,
     En serai-je plus grand ? Pourquoi ? ce n'est qu'un nom.
Le cygne qui s'envole aux voûtes éternelles,
Amis, s'informe-t-il si l'ombre de ses ailes
     Flotte encore sur un vil gazon ?

     *   *   *   *   *

" Brisez, livrez au vent, aux ondes, à la flamme,
Ce luth qui n'a qu'un son pour répondre à mon âme :
     Celui des Séraphins va frémir sous mes doigts.
Bientôt, vivant comme eux d'un immortel délire !
Je vais guider, peut-être, aux accords de ma lyre,
     Des cieux suspendus à ma voix.

" Bientôt. . . . Mais de la mort la main lourde et muette
Vient de toucher la corde, elles brise, et jette
     Un son plaintif et sourd dans le vague des airs ;
Mon luth glacé se tait. . . . Amis, prenez le vôtre ;
Et que mon âme encore passe d'un monde à l'autre
     Au bruit de vos sacrés concerts ! "

The "Harmonies poétiques et religieuses," which Lamartine wrote between the years 1825–1828, "established,"

Ste. Beuve tells us, "his claim to something more than popularity." From "the first 'Meditations,' to the 'Harmonies,' he goes on developing with progress, rising from the elegy to the hymn, from poetic expression to poetic thought. In the 'Novissima Verba,' is exhaled the poignant anguish which sometimes seizes on the noblest natures in their hour of triumph, and flings them prostrate in an icy sweat, asking for mercy." But the same poem is criticized by M. Planché for its needless prolixity. He compares it to Bernini's figures, crushed under the weight of their own draperies, and ranks it much higher than the "Jehovah," "passages of which leave on the memory a track of light." The "Hymne à la Douleur," shorter and more sustained throughout, contains some fine lines :—

> " Il est peut-être en moi quelque fibre sonore
> Qui peut sous ton regard se torturer encore,
> Comme un serpent coupé sur le chemin gisant,
> Dont le tronçon se tord sous le pied du passant.
>   *   *   *   *
>   Il n'est pas dans mon cœur,
> Une fibre qui n'ait résonné sa douleur !
> Pas un cheveu blanchi de ma tête penchée
> Qui n'ait été broyé comme une herbe fauchée !
> Pas un amour en moi qui n'ait été frappé,
> Un espoir, un desir, qui n'ait péri trompé !
> Tu fais l'homme, ô Douleur ! oui, l'homme tout entier,
> Comme le creuset l'or, et la flamme l'acier,
> Comme le grès noirci des débris qu'il enlève,
> En déchirant le fer, fait un tranchant au glaive ;
> Qui ne t'a pas connu, ne sait rien d'ici-bas,
> Il foule mollement la terre, il n'y vit pas ;
> Comme sur un nuage il flotte sur la vie ;
> Rien n'y marque pour lui la route en vain suivie ;
> Le sueur de son front n'y mouille pas sa main,
> Son pieds n'y heurte pas les cailloux du chemin,
> Il n'y sait pas, à l'heure où faiblissent ses armes !
> Retremper ses vertus aux flots brûlans des larmes,
> Il n'y sait point combattre avec son propre cœur,
> Ce combat douleureux dont gémit le vainqueru."

"La Source," and "Le Rossignol" are excellent ex-
amples of the charm—"vague, yet not without a power of
sweet coercion—of Lamartine's tender elegiac strain ; "
while " Milly, ou la terre natale," reveals, not so much the
genius of the poet, as the simple trustful nature of the man.
He yields to no temptation to gild the framing, or decorate
the picture of a place so dear to him ; its personal associations, the sweet and tender memories it evokes are
sufficient :—

> " Il est sur la terre une montagne aride
> Qui ne porte en ses flancs ni bois ni flot limpide,
> Un coteau qui décroit et, d'étage en étage,
> Porte, à l'abri des murs dont ils sont étayés,
> Quelques avares champs de nos sueurs payés,
> Quelques ceps dont les bras, cherchant en vain l'érable,
> Serpentent sur la terre ou rampent sur la sable ;
> Lieux que ni le doux bruit des caux pendant l'été,
> Ne le frémissement du feuillage agité,
> Ni l'hymne aérien du rossignol qui veille,
> Ne rappellent au cœur, n'enchantent pour l'oreille ;
> Mais que, sous les rayons d'un ciel toujours d'airain,
> La cigale assourdit de son cri souterrain.
> Il est dans ces deserts un toit rustique et sombre
> Que la montagne seule abrite de son ombre,
> Et dont les murs, battus par la pluie et les vents,
> Portent leur âge écrit sous la mousse des ans.
> Sur le seuil désuni de trois marches de pierre
> Le hazard a planté les racines d'un lierre
> Qui, redoublant cent fois ses nœuds entrelacés,
> Cache l'affront du temps sous ses bras élancés ;
> Un jardin qui descend au travers d'un coteau,
> Y présente au couchant son sable altéré d'eau ;
> La pierre sans ciment, que l'hiver a noircie
> En borne tristement l'enceinte rétrécie :
> La terre, que la bêche ouvre à chaque saison,
> Y montre à nu son sein sans ombre et sans gazon ;
> Ni tapis emaillés, ni cintres de verdure,
> Ni ruisseau sous des bois, ni fraîcheur, ni murmure ;
> Seulement sept tilleuls par le soc oubliés
> Protégeant un peu d'herbe étendue à leurs pieds,
> Y versent dans l'automne une ombre tiède et rare,
> D'autant plus douce au front sous un ciel plus avare ;

Arbres dont le sommeil et des songes si beaux,
Dans mon heureuse enfance habitaient les rameaux ;
Dans le champêtre enclos qui soupire après l'onde,
Un puits dans le rocher cache son eau profonde,
Où le vieillard qui puise, après de longs efforts,
Dépose en gémissant son urne sur les bords ;
Une aire ou le fléau sur l'argile étendue
Bat à coups cadencés la gerbe répandue ;
Où la blanche colombe et l'humble passereau
Se disputent l'épi qu'oublia le râteau ;
Et sur la terre épars des instruments rustiques,
Des jougs rompus, des chars dormant sous les portiques,
Des essieux dont l'ornière a brisé les rayons,
Et des socs émoussés qu'ont usés les sillons."

Many of Lamartine's poems are extremely religious in tone and feeling—a circumstance which has certainly contributed towards making their popularity widespread and enduring. For though most of the Latin hymns of the mediæval Church—the finest religious poetry that exists— were written by Frenchmen, there is very little good religious poetry in modern French, and to thousands it was a revelation to find in verse a vehicle for expressing their most exalted aspirations, nourishment for their most intense feelings. "Poetry," writes Amiel of Lamartine, " which raises you as this does, heavenwards, and fills you with divine emotion, which sings of love and death, of hope and sacrifice, and awakens the sense of the infinite." Some of Lamartine's religious verse is in the form of invocation ; as, for instance, his " Morning and Evening Hymns," and " Child's Morning Prayer ;" in others, he teaches the lesson of the world from the point of view of Catholic dogma ; of these the " Pensée des Morts," with its vivid realization of the Divine purity, its firm grasp of the communion of Christian souls, which no accident of life or death can affect, is perhaps the best known.

CHAPTER IV.

1821–1831.

"MY book," writes Lamartine to Virieu, "has a success which is astounding for poetry in these days. MM. Molé, Mounier, Pasquier, all the anti-poets are reading and quoting it. So you see you were a true prophet!" Even Talleyrand, whom no one would suspect of lyrical predilections, wrote to a lady who had lent him the volume, that he had sat up half the night reading it.

The author's friends profiting, as he modestly puts it, by the momentary celebrity of the "Méditations," made a last vigorous effort, and succeeded in obtaining for him the place of secretary to the French embassy at Naples— an appointment the more valued as it removed the only serious obstacle to his marriage. The offer was made by M. Pasquier in very flattering terms, and at the same time M. Simon, Minister of the Interior, sent him Didot's fine edition of the classics, with a gracious message from the King, who himself supplemented the paucity of the diplomatic salary with a pension of two thousand francs.

But lights and shadows were ever wont to alternate quickly in Lamartine's life. His mother, as she was rejoicing over his triumphs, received a letter summoning her hastily to Paris, where she found him stricken down by a severe attack of inflammation of the lungs. However, kind friends had been at his bedside from the first, and, though he lay for a time between life and death, he was finally pronounced convalescent. The knowledge that health, fortune, and happiness were all coming back to her beloved son, filled the mother's heart with joy. There is a touching passage in her journal telling how, on Easter Sunday evening, going to the Church of St. Roch, where she had often worshipped in her youth, her emotions of joy and gratitude well-nigh overwhelmed her. But it is evident from the letters in which Lamartine opens his mind unreservedly to Aymon de Virieu, that his convalescence was painful and trying enough : " I am only conscious that I live," he writes, " from the suffering I endure, and the feeling of affection for you and a few others. We shall surely meet again, my friend, here or elsewhere, most likely elsewhere. If I do recover, I shall marry Miss Birch this year. She is indeed the woman whose price is beyond rubies ; in everything she has been perfect. It is you and she I should regret most to leave. I shall write often, but only a few lines."

However, Lamartine's return to health, if slow, was complete, for in April we find him at Aix in the character of an engaged lover. His letters show a serious sense of the importance of the step he is about to take. " The time has come," he writes to Virieu, " to regulate a hitherto wasted life according to the established laws, whether they be human or Divine ; according to my view, if human, then of necessity Divine. Time flies, half the allotted span has already passed away ; let us find a clear and definite aim for the portion that yet remains, and let that aim be the most exalted of all, the wish to please God."

Nor was his mind quite free from minor preoccupations. His means were limited, and he went through extreme mortification at not being able to add to the *corbeille de noce*, which in France is offered by the bridegroom, a gift of jewels. Happily a remittance arrived unexpectedly, at the eleventh hour, and he rushed off to Geneva, where he procured a lovely *parure*, which was received with the most gratifying rapture. But, though he does not mention it, we learn from another source that the present most valued by the somewhat romantic young English lady was a manuscript copy of the " Méditations," in the delicate, aristocratic handwriting of the author.

On the 6th of June following, the marriage was solemnised in the private chapel of the Governor of Chambéry. "My daughter-in-law," writes Madame de Lamartine, " was dressed in the most suitable way possible ; she wore a very beautiful gown of embroidered muslin, and a superb lace veil, which covered her almost entirely from head to foot. Nothing could have been more graceful and dignified than her demeanour, or more touching than her piety. Words cannot express all I felt in seeing my son at this most important moment of his life. What adequate tribute of praise and thanksgiving can a mother find to offer when such a blessing is vouchsafed ? Having seen the happiness of her child thus secured, she may well feel her earthly task is accomplished."

At Geneva, the marriage according to the Protestant rite was solemnized, and the bridal party, including Madame de Lamartine's mother, Mrs. Birch, started for Naples, halting at Turin, Florence, and Rome on the way.

Lamartine's marriage was productive of much happiness, and may be considered one of the most fortunate events of his life. His wife, who seems to have combined all the good qualities of both English and French women, was devotedly attached to him, yet had plenty of individuality of character, and was thoroughly suited for a position which, judging from some recent biographies, would seem to be the most difficult of all, that of the wife of a man of genius—accepting the trials, burdens, and responsibilities thereto pertaining, with unfailing and enthusiastic self-devotion. It is remarkable that Lamartine, who was certainly not reticent in discoursing about his belongings, and repeatedly gave the world minute personal details as to his parents, relations, and friends, never alluded to his wife in any of his published writings, save incidentally in his travels, when it could not have been avoided without affectation, but even then always in a way which proved he respected her English reserve. His letters to his friends, in his early married life, show that her unselfishness and quiet discipline of character made a deep impression on him. He is constantly urging them to follow his example without delay, and, above all, not to select some young, unlessoned girl, but, like himself, a helpmate with formed and cultivated mind. Writing many years after his marriage, he speaks more fully, and with less reserve, as to his conjugal happiness. His wife had brought him, he says, virtue, wit, amiability, attractiveness, love, and fortune. The beautiful lyric inserted in " Les Préludes," beginning—

> " L'onde qui baise ce rivage,
> De quoi se plaint-elle à ses bords,"

was inspired by Madame de Lamartine.

The travellers journeyed in two comfortable post-chaises,

halting frequently on the road, after the pleasant and leisurely fashion of the time. The first stage was to Turin, where M. Aymon de Virieu was secretary of embassy, and some happy days were spent in his company. At Florence, Madame d'Albany, whom Lamartine had known on his former visit, gave them a gracious reception. M. de Fontenay, the French minister, was charming, and Madame de Lamartine fully shared her husband's enthusiasm for Dante's "beautiful sheepfold."

The first shadow that crossed the newly married couple's path was the news that "the Revolution" (it used to be the fashion to speak as if it were an epidemic) had broken out at Naples, making the roads unsafe for travellers, so Lamartine had to hurry on to his post, leaving his wife and mother-in-law in Rome. At the end of a month he was able to return and escort them to a house he had secured, overlooking the gardens of the Villa Reale on one side; on the other was a foreground of orange and fig groves, with Pausilipo in the distance. But as the heat was still oppressive at Naples, the autumn was passed in a châlet at Ischia. Here all the emotions and feelings of the spring-time of his life, when he first "saw Naples and lived," came back to Lamartine with renewed force, and brought fuel to the flame of his more cultivated and exercised genius : many of his most pleasing and popular poems were, if not written, at least inspired at this time ; for what Tivoli was to Horace, the Bay of Naples was to Lamartine.

"There are not ten days in the whole French summer," he writes to Virieu, "worth these autumnal ones ; one inhales life, sunshine, love, genius, with every breath. I think of you when, stepping out on my balcony in the early morning, I look down on the glittering sea that lies beneath me, fringed by the orange groves of Pausilipo, all incomparably more lovely than it even seemed to memory. Come and see. We have a room which is called yours." He goes on in a more prosaic strain : "Neapolitan politics are a curious study, even for such *connoisseurs* as we Frenchmen are in revolutions and constitutions. Can you fancy a Committee sitting round Virgil's tomb, and clubs of Carbonari in the temples of Baiæ and Pozzuoli? However, the crisis seems to have passed over peaceably, and even Sicily is settling down. The rebels, indeed, are fortifying Palermo, and troops are to be sent out from here to act against them, but both parties appear to waste as much time looking at each other as ever did Homer's heroes."

At the time of his entrance into diplomacy Lamartine was most fortunate in his chiefs. M. de Narbonne, whom he found at Naples, possessed a charm of conversation and manner which is a matter of history, and in private life was kindly, sensible, and easy to live with. He liked letter-writing, and transacted almost all the diplomatic business of the embassy himself, an arrangement of which Lamartine highly approved. After a few months M. de Narbonne was succeeded by M. de Fontenay, who at Florence had been simply charming, but is now described as the "rigid yet amiable Fontenay." He did not share M. de Narbonne's views as to the uses of *attachés*, but kept his occasionally for two days successively at their desks. However, this was accepted with good grace by Lamartine, who was pleased to find that he could work both hard and well, and

H

cherished the prospect of soon rising a step higher, with an increase of income.

He was now in his thirtieth year, and it seemed as if domestic happiness, literary celebrity, an assured position, and a profession he liked were all firmly secured to him, when an unexpected blow dashed his hopes; a severe attack of illness struck him down, and, after six weeks of acute suffering, left him quite unfit to resume his duties. Immediate change of air was imperative. M. de Fontenay obtained for him an indefinite leave of absence; and the early days of January, 1821, found him in the Via Barberini, Rome. His sufferings were still very great. He describes himself as bruised, crushed, shattered in every nerve; the disappointment caused by the alteration in his prospects very considerable; yet he writes, "Still I bless God, and am happy; such is the change a kind, tender, amiable, adorable companion has wrought in my life."

And we find in his mother's journal of about the same date: "Alphonse writes to me that he is completely happy. Such language from him is so unusual that it must be sincere. He sends me a sum of money for his old master, the Abbé Dumont, who is ill and in great poverty. I am touched by this recollection of one whom he might easily have forgotten amid the pre-occupations of his present life."

A little later she goes on to say, "On the 8th of May, at Rome, my daughter-in-law gave birth to a son. Alphonse writes he is beautiful as an angel, and is called Alphonse, after him. He was baptized in St. Peter's; his godfather is an Italian, the Marquis Pagliati, his godmother the Princess Oginski, a Pole. This news makes me very happy. The child, they say, resembles me, so I picture him to myself exactly as his father was at the same age. They will come here when she is strong enough to travel."

But the young mother's health did not allow of this visit being made for some time. The summer was spent at Aix-le-Bains, where both the invalids, by dint of taking asses' milk and living out of doors, were tolerably restored. Still it was evident that fresh air and a temperate climate and a country life were absolutely necessary for Lamartine and his wife ; and they decided to give up the prospect of any immediate advancement in diplomacy, and, for a time at least, to settle down at St. Point, which had been given to him by his father on his marriage, and where all these could be found. The château had not been occupied for some years, and to make it habitable with the very limited means at the young couple's disposal was not an easy task.

" There are *entr'actes* in life," he writes to Virieu, " if, indeed, the whole of life be not itself merely an *entr'acte*. I am, at any rate, passing through one at this moment. All my faculties are concentrated on bricklayers' bills and farm accounts. Let us hope that minds, after a period of hibernation, make a doubly vigorous spring growth. I write from my mountain lair, which is being got into order as quickly as may be. My wife and my mother-in-law are beginning to be satisfied. I shall have a good, substantial house, more substantial than its owner. You know St. Point is the twin-brother of Pupetières ; they are two nests of similar construction, prepared for two birds of like plumage. You will find here your towers and passages, your lime-trees of Henry IV., your woods, and fields, and brooks ; only St. Point is somewhat the larger, and while

I restore with one hand I destroy with the other, to bring
the house into proportion with my means and my tastes.
I long to be settled here."

But for various reasons the installation was delayed.
In May, 1822, a daughter was born at Mâcon, and the
end of the summer found the Lamartines in London,
living at 4, Great Cumberland Street. Lamartine seems
at first not to have been able quite to make up his mind
as to "questo dubbio paese,"—"The sky is gloomy, the
earth *dolce e lieto*, the houses extremely small, and
smoked outside, but the interiors are enchanting; here
is the apotheosis of physical existence embellished and
ennobled by elegance. Life is, on the whole, cheaper here
than in Paris ; house rent and provisions very much so,
only everything that requires manual labour is dear. I
like the people better than I expected ; all our connections
are excellent, noble, grave, and amiable. Since I have
been here I have done a good deal of sightseeing, and
mean to do more ; it is a beautiful country, and worthy of
many visits. Our richest Gothic conceptions are fully
realized ; I have acquired a passion, a mania, for this style,
and am in despair at having put a stone to St. Point before
my eyes were opened. Remember my words, and beware
of doing anything to Pupetières until yours are." Unfortunately this, Lamartine's longest visit to England, was
darkened by a great sorrow ; his little boy was taken ill,
and remained some time between life and death. His
father, who writes with great bitterness of the "miserable
and murderous English medical practice," clung to the
hope that French air and French treatment might cure
him, and, when he could be moved, the poor little sufferer

was brought to Paris, but only to die. The blow was a cruel one, and is sadly alluded to in the few letters written at this period.

Having taken their apartment for the winter, the Lamartines remained in Paris, living in great retirement, and seeing only " les incomparables et invariables Raige-court," and a few equally intimate friends. Louis de Vignet was there, but " absorbed by Duchesses." " Just as it should be," writes Lamartine, with his usual indulgence ; " he is quite right to try his wings." In the spring, Lamartine went out himself a little more, frequently spending a part of the evening in the *salon* of Madame de la Tré-moille—" whose noble and simple manners take us back to another and a better century. There is no one to compare with her." Politics were a good deal discussed at this time ; but Lamartine does not as yet seem to take much interest in public affairs, and is displeased at the change of ministry, chiefly because it has the result of reducing his salary to half-pay. However, the King came forward generously, and bestowed on him an additional pension of two thousand francs ; and a second volume of " Méditations," without having quite the success of the first, was well received, and realized fourteen thousand francs, which removed some anxiety as to the feasibility of completing the restoration of St. Point.

The next two or three years passed uneventfully, and on the whole happily, though not without some portion of sorrow. The restoration of St. Point, like most such undertakings, considerably exceeding the original estimate of cost, plans of visiting Paris had to be given up, and the winter months, during which the cold was very severe at

St. Point, were spent at Mâcon. Meanwhile, Lamartine, absorbed by masons and gardeners, did not find as much time for writing as might have been expected ; he brought out one poem on the death of Socrates, which, though he alludes to it complacently in his letters, as "what I have done best in the style *méditatif,*" would not now-a-days be read with much pleasure. The writer never possessed the power of divining or reproducing the thoughts or feelings of any epoch but his own.

The year 1824 was a specially sad one for the whole family. In February the beautiful Césarine de Vignet, with the Fornarina face, died in her far-away home in Savoy, too suddenly for any of her family to be summoned ; and, almost at the same time, her younger sister, Suzanne, who had married a Burgundian gentleman, M. de Mon-therot, was pronounced to be dying of consumption. The illness was long and trying. In a few pages written imme-diately after the death of this beloved daughter, Madame de Lamartine pathetically recalls each detail of those months of suffering, borne with angelic patience, and the last sad closing scene, "so edifying, so touching, so full of consolation for all true Christians, but heartrending to her mother. Throughout all," she writes, "Alphonse was of the utmost help and comfort ;" and when the end had come, and, according to the strange custom then usual in France, father, mother, and husband left the house of death, he stayed to fulfil the last sad offices, and then rejoined the rest of the family at St. Point. Here they all remained for some months, Lamartine devoting himself, with almost feminine tenderness, to console his mother, and his wife doing her utmost to supply the place of the daughter she had lost.

In November, 1824, a vacancy occurring in the Académie

française, Lamartine was strongly pressed by his friends in Paris to offer himself as a candidate. His first impulse was to refuse; but as this was vehemently opposed by his father and mother, he started, though reluctantly, on the quest. The business of candidature is not a very pleasant one for sensitive temperaments. The first obligation imposed on an aspirant, which consists in clothing himself from head to foot in ceremonious black, and, thus arrayed, presenting himself to each of the thirty-nine, asking him for his vote, is sarcastically described by Prosper Mérimée, in his "Letters à une Inconnue:" "In the mean time I conscientiously make visits; I find every one extremely civil, accustomed to his part, and taking it very seriously. I do my best, also, to take mine gravely, but it is difficult. Does it not seem ridiculous to say to a man, 'Monsieur, I think myself one of the forty cleverest men in France. At any rate I am as good as you,' and such like facetiæ? I have to express this in terms of politeness graduated according to the importance of the persons."

However, an amusing gloss on this irreverent satire is to be found in another correspondence of the period, that of M. Ximenes Doudan: "The election of M. Ste. Beuve and Prosper Mérimée has been an exciting campaign. To begin with, both, as they candidly acknowledged, were intensely eager to get in. M. Mérimée consulted Homer, opening the volume at random, and considering the first line of each page as prophetic. Since his election all the lines are proved to have been clearly in his favour. M. de Ste. Beuve was withering away so visibly with fear and expectation, that to refuse him a vote would have required a heart of steel."

At first Lamartine, in his confidential letters to M. de
Virieu, speaks of the distinction of belonging to the " Flock
of Immortals " quite as disparagingly, and let us hope with
more sincerity than M. Prosper Mérimée. But once fairly
launched in the campaign, he became, as is the case with
most candidates, anxious to succeed. His earlier bulletins
were trumpet-notes of triumph. " All goes," he writes, " on
four wheels. Roger has assured me of his devotion. Villemain says he is free, and that he admires me. Daru
received me gushingly, and Raynouard also very well.
Look after Lacretelle and Campenon, who alone are hostile.
Augier, too, is not with me ; he let me see it. I have just
seen M. Laine ; he was charming. L'Abbé Frayssinous has
promised my cousin that he will vote for me, and he brings
others with him."

Two days later the prospect had entirely changed :
" Alas ! and alas ! this diabolical journey ! I was in
perfect ignorance that the Academic flock follows blindly
a cabal of five or six bell-wethers, and I fell into the
trap. And who do you think is my rival ? A perfectly
unknown individual called Droz, who is the creature of
MM. Auger, Campenon, Lacretelle et Co.! The Liberals
are all with him, and five Royalists also support him. So
I am shelved there, without a hope of breaking the bundle
of faggots. I have gone too far to withdraw, and must do
my best to make my defeat honourable and dignified,
which is the utmost I can hope for ; two days more of this
ordeal still remains to be gone through. Every one is
most kind. M. de Châteaubriand, with whom I have every
reason to be pleased, Michaud, Villemain, and *tutti quanti*
are zealous, but feel themselves beaten. The only chance

would be if a third candidate offered himself, and so broke
the hostile coalition. . . . I have seen Prévot, and learnt
from him that I may look forward within a year to
Florence and eight thousand francs as a compensation, if
I like to avail myself of it. . . . I spent last evening
pleasantly, as in times of yore, at Madame de Montcalm's,
with MM. Molé, Pasquier, etc.   There is still some wit to
be found in that *salon*."

In September, 1825, the Lamartines started for Florence,
where he had been appointed secretary of embassy, not
altogether without regret. "It is an exile, and I ask myself
what it is I go for.   There will be less comfort than I can
command here, less·solitude, less leisure, fewer old associations and habits.   But my wife's health, and her still very
vivid imagination, have weighed the balance down, so
I follow the path Providence seems to have marked out
for me."

But, as so often happens, what was anticipated did not
occur. The years of Lamartine's Florentine mission, far
from being a period of exile, were perhaps the happiest,
certainly the least troubled of his life. At the end of a
few weeks he had settled his family comfortably, close to
the Poggio Imperiale.   The *hôtel*, of which they occupied
half, had lovely terraced gardens ; cypresses for shade and
coolness, enchanting views, only bounded by the distant
southern hills. A few weeks later, and, to their great joy,
the Virieus arrived for the winter ; then the St. Aulaires,
Castellanes, and Valences ; forming a circle which even
in Paris would have been deemed delightful.

In Florentine society the Lamartines were appreciated
and liked ; though, in the early days of 1826, an incident

occurred which might have had serious consequences. His
arrival there as secretary of the French embassy naturally
caused his poems to be sought for and read with curiosity.
Speaking generally, it would be difficult to find an author
whose works would bear so close a scrutiny as Lamartine's ; but, unfortunately, the death of Byron, his favourite
hero, inspired a lyric effusion, hastily written off. The
modern Italians are very unfavourably contrasted with the
Greeks, in a passage which ends with the lines—

> " Je cherche ailleurs (pardon, ô ombre romaine),
> Des hommes, et non pas la poussière humaine."

The poem was about the most uninteresting Lamartine
ever wrote, and one would think no 'one of the present
generation would have the patience to read it through, but
that it was lately asserted, in a recent *cause célèbre*, that
from it the sculptor of the Byron memorial in Hamilton
Gardens derived his inspiration. At the time of its publication, Lamartine had no thought of going to Italy, and the
lines passed quite unnoticed ; but when read and circulated
in Florence, they caused great indignation, shown in ways
which threatened to make his position very difficult. The
appearance of a *brochure* by a Neapolitan exile, Colonel
Pepe, in which his poetry was savagely criticized and his
personal character maligned, brought matters to a crisis.
Lamartine, though suffering severely from the effects of
a kick from a horse, at once sent the author a challenge,
which was accepted with the suggestion that the duel
should be postponed until Lamartine had completely
recovered. But, fearing that the Tuscan police might
interfere to prevent the meeting, Lamartine insisted on its
taking place at once ; his seconds being the Comte de

Villamella and M. de Virieu. After a few sword-thrusts had been exchanged, Lamartine was severely wounded in the arm. Colonel Pepe at once offered him an apology, and a cordial reconciliation ensued. The incident naturally caused some sensation. Colonel Pepe was arrested and put on his trial; but on Lamartine's taking all the blame on himself, his adversary, at the instance of the French minister, was honourably acquitted. This, together with Lamartine's bearing throughout, caused a reaction in Florentine feeling; the Grand Duke took an opportunity to express his appreciation of M. de Lamartine's conduct, and his former popularity came back to him with interest.

During the years 1826-1827, Lamartine inherited from his uncles, the Abbé and the Comte de Lamartine, a considerable amount of property; he had, however, to give large annuities to his surviving aunts, besides heavy charges made in favour of his sisters and their children. In his confidential letters he complains of having to combine the responsibilities of the *chef de famille* under the old *régime*, with the disadvantages of the modern system of division. Still, the immediate addition to his income was· very welcome, enabling him for the first, perhaps the only time in his life, to live according to his tastes, unhampered by anxieties or debts. Then the absence of his chief, the Marquis de la Maisonfort, who for nearly two years remained away on leave, gave Lamartine all the pleasant privileges of the head of a legation, or, according to the somewhat grandiloquent French phrase for the diplomatic rank immediately below that of ambassador, of "Minister plenipotentiary." To entertain frequently became at once

a duty and a pleasure ; the cordial and graceful hospitality
of the Lamartines soon made the French Embassy a social
centre, while their kindness and consideration for the
hitherto somewhat neglected French colony in Florence
were inexhaustible.

Decidedly, Lamartine's lines had fallen in pleasant
places ; the Court of Tuscany was, at the time, the most
brilliant and attractive in Italy. The Grand Duke, young,
handsome, and affable, had already gained much of the
personal popularity which, even in the darkest days for
Italian sovereignty, he never altogether lost. The Duchess,
a charming and accomplished Saxon, shared his wish to
maintain the intellectual supremacy of Florence, where
a literary reputation, far from being, as in France, a drawback to an aspiring diplomatist, was rather an advantage.
Lady Burghersh, the wife of the English minister, wrote
graceful verses. M. de Marcellus, *chargé d'affaires* at the
neighbouring Court of Lucca, was a successful author.
Encouraged by their example, Lamartine was only too
glad to beguile his leisure hours by exercising his poetic
faculty more seriously than he had done for some years.
Most of the lyrics afterwards published under the title of
" Harmonies poétiques et réligieuses " were written at this
time, and, though not published in France for some years,
found at once in Florence an appreciative audience. The
Grand Duchess, who from the first showed a cordial liking
for Madame de Lamartine, was an enthusiastic admirer of
poetry, and specially, as was natural in a German, of *l'école
romantique.* Accompanied by her sister, Princess Amelia
of Saxony, she often spent the afternoon at the Lamartines'
villa, where, after a little graceful reluctance, their host

would read to them his latest effusion. " I was not Tasso," he writes deprecatingly, " nor was she Leonora ; " but it is evident the similarity of situation did not displease him.

However, Lamartine's correspondence shows that, if not insensible to social successes and literary triumphs, his real interests and affections ever centred in his own home circle. " Alphonse has now almost recovered," writes his mother in her diary, " and all goes on well. He is occupying his leisure hours in the composition of some poems full of religious thought and feeling, which he calls 'Harmonies.' From time to time he sends me fragments which delight me. This is the use to which I have always wished he would end by turning his talents." And a little later : " Alphonse is now the King's *chargé d'affaires* for Tuscany, Lucca, and Parma ; his superiors are pleased with him, and he likes his position. The only drawback is that he represents his country perhaps a little too expensively, but Providence will watch over him. All my anxieties on his account are past ; it is now he who gives me back a thousand-fold in affection, and in solicitude for all my little difficulties, any sorrows and sacrifices his youthful mistakes and errors ever cost me."

Lamartine's own letters breathe a like strain of cheerfulness and content. Beyond all other sources of happiness he puts that which he is beginning to derive from his daughter. He writes to Madame de Raigecourt: " Julia leaves me nothing to wish for ; she has health, intelligence, beauty, and warm affections ; always gentle, tender, caressing, she winds herself more and more round my heart. I used to repine because my son was taken from me, but Heaven knows better than we do what is best for us."

And thus nearly three years passed away without much change or incident, save that to the number of Lamartine's friends was added the new English minister at Florence, Lord Normanby, whom, after a long interval, he was to meet again in 1848, amid very different surroundings. Towards the end of 1827 we find Lamartine much occupied by the purchase of the Casino Viviani, which, though situated almost in the heart of Florence, between the Boulevard and the Church of Santa Maria Novella, possessed a *jardin anglais*, and, stretching out behind, a little domain, comprising a large kitchen garden, olive and lemon groves, grazing for three cows, and a field of maize. The house, something between a cottage and a convent, was rearranged and decorated by a M. Sylvestris, who at first seemed to be a phœnix ; but finally, like the majority of architects, sent in a bill threefold his original estimate. " I paid it," writes Lamartine, " with a smile on my face, but with rage in my heart. That is how one must do here. But never again shall I be caught employing an architect to build as much as a chimney. Sylvestris' charming manners and amiable expression of countenance inspire confidence ; they only make him the more dangerous." However, the villa, furnished from England for comfort, from France for elegance, and decorated with artistic treasures such as Italy only could produce, was the admiration of Florence, and the source of much pleasure to its owners.

But hardly were they settled, when the death of the Marquis de la Maisonfort changed all their plans. His successor, M. de Vitrolles, was to arrive in a few months, and for Lamartine to go back to a subordinate position after having been supreme so long would have been impossible. The post of first secretary of embassy at Berne or Brussels was offered to him, and M. de Damas urged him to accept the latter. But save at Rome or Constantinople, Lamartine did not now care to be merely secretary; he thought his services and abilities entitled him to something better : he therefore elected to take an eight months' leave, with the intention, *in petto*, of resigning if nothing more suitable was offered to him ; and, having let the Casino Viviani to Princess Galitzin, he and his wife began, not without a pang, their preparations for departure.

"I hope soon," Lamartine wrote to Madame de Raigecourt, "to find myself in what is to me the great attraction of Paris, your delightful and much-loved *salon*. But we are sorrowful at leaving this beautiful country, and especially the Court—the most agreeable, the most virtuous, the most cordially kind to be found anywhere ; every possible mark of friendship and affection has been showered on us."

To his own family the return of Lamartine, after a three years' absence, was an immense joy.

"At last," writes his mother, under the date of September 28, 1828, "at last Alphonse has come, and with him his wife, his mother-in-law, and his sweet little girl ; all, thank God, seem well. He has grown very thin, which grieves me, but I must be satisfied. The time has been a very happy one, full of joyful emotion, and of much occupation. At my age all agitation is somewhat trying, but when the heart is at ease, one recovers quickly. It would be difficult to find a child of Julia's age lovelier or more winning. She

is indeed a treasure, and admirably brought up. Her
mother, too, grows in perfection ; pious, without affectation ;
fulfilling every duty with simplicity ; cultivating her talents.
She paints admirably, and has brought me some charming
sketches—among others, Julia's portrait."

At Montculot, the property inherited from the Abbé
de Lamartine, the new owners were received with cordial
respect and affection ; while at St. Point the reception was
enthusiastic. At a distance of three miles from the château,
they were met, Lamartine tells M. de Virieu, " by three municipal bodies, all wearing white scarfs ; a hundred notables
from the neighbouring parishes, all in their best clothes
and carrying arms. Two batteries thundered at intervals
from the hilltops ; volleys were fired off at every hundred
paces by the National Guard. The fifes, tambours, trumpets,
laurel crowns, flags, and devices were innumerable. Groups
of people, stationed all along the road, held their hands out
to us as we passed,—altogether a sight as touching and
gratifying as ever a November sun shone on. When we
reached the house, I replied to all the speeches in a single
harangue, in praise of Providence, religion, and all good
people. Two hogsheads of wine ready broached made my
eloquence doubly effective. Then came a dinner, to which
two hundred sat down. Nothing had been suggested or
inspired, it was all spontaneous. This sort of thing it is
that attaches one to a place ; let it not be said that kindness and consideration do not bring their reward. Some
of my friends rode with me ; I would have given a good
deal to have had you of the number."

Nor had Lamartine reason to complain, even in the
busy world of Paris, where three years bring many changes,

of forgetfulness or neglect. The King, from whom he had
a very long audience, received him with great kindness.
" His majesty expressed his complete satisfaction with my
services, and said he used to read my despatches himself
with lively interest. He then went on to discuss several
important matters with perfect openness and confidence.
M. de la Ferronnays was also most cordial and friendly;
he regretted that I would not stay on at Florence, where I
had so much influence and experience, but admitted my
claim to promotion. He promised me the post of secretary
of embassy in London within six months, adding, ' Even
if I should not then be myself in office, I shall have
arranged it with my successor.' I have every reason to
be more than satisfied ; I am on the high-road to promotion,
and shall be minister within a year at most. As for France,
I fear things do not look well ; now that I am in the midst
of the hurly-burly I cannot see anything very distinctly,
but where formerly I hoped I now fear."

It was at this moment of unwonted prosperity, with
every reasonable wish satisfied, and a successful career he
thoroughly liked opening before him, that a blow fell on
Lamartine causing him greater suffering than any trial he
had previously endured. These pages have sufficiently
indicated how strong and tender was his mother's love for
him, and his for her, all through his youth and early manhood. How powerless all the cares and distractions of
maturer life were to weaken his filial devotion, or the
burden of increasing years to deaden her maternal feeling,
a few more extracts from her diary will show.

" *November 7*, 1828.—Alphonse has just returned from
Paris, where he was admirably received, and especially by

I

the King. He brought me a beautiful chandelier for my *salon* at Mâcon, and a considerable sum of money, which he guessed by intuition I needed, to avoid troubling his father with matters of business. He also gave me some charming verses, which touch me because they express so exactly my own thoughts. There are many things I realize and feel very deeply without being able to put my thoughts into words. I thank God that He has bestowed this gift on my son."

A little later she records a visit to Paris : " Thanks to my son, it was one of perfect and unbroken enjoyment. It was a great pleasure to me to see once more the city in which my early years were passed, and where now, among the people most distinguished by merit and by position, my son numbers so many friends. Madame Récamier, whom some people say I resemble, received me with incomparable grace. In her *salon* I heard M. de Châteaubriand read his tragedy ' Moïse.' I was more interested in him than in his verses ; he had the majestic bearing of a king surrounded by his court. For though I really prefer the natural, unpretending manners of many men of great name and great talent who were also there, a reputation such as his has for me an immense prestige."

" *Milly, October* 21, 1829.—To-day is the anniversary of my son's birth. I am here alone, and have spent much of the day in reflections, which will, I hope, prepare me for and sustain me in death. How often at different dates of my life have I paced to and fro in this *allée de méditation*, sometimes saying my rosary, sometimes in silent prayer. Alas ! what would have become of me amid the many trials of life, if the Divine mercy had not sustained me, putting into my mind holy, strengthening thoughts. The love of silence and solitude is itself a great grace. I felt it to-day as I walked up and down the *allée*, and my whole life seemed to pass in vision before me, as it certainly will pass, on the day when I shall stand before my Creator to be judged. May He then be merciful to me! I saw myself, as it were yesterday, a child playing in the leafy avenue of St. Cloud; then a young *chanoinesse* chanting in the chapel at Galles, undecided as to whether I should, like my companions, take the final vows, and consecrate my whole life to singing the praises of God in that quiet haven. Then I saw my husband, young, handsome, in his rich uniform, visiting his sister, Madame de Villars, under whose special care I had been placed. Gradually it dawned upon me how frequent his visits became, and how he sought every opportunity of speaking to me, and, at the same time, how frank and manly was his air, how winning and noble the proud expression that always softened when he looked at me. Then came the message, conveyed to me by his sister, if his asking me in marriage of my parents would be displeasing to me; then the long negotiations, and all the difficulties which arose, all my tears and prayers through those three years of uncertainty; then the sudden and wonderful sweeping away of all obstacles; our first year of happiness in this poor little cottage of Milly; his danger in the terrible days of August; his being cast into prison; and the months of misery during which, with my child in my arms, I went to and fro to Dijon and to Lyons, trying to touch the hearts of those representatives of the people on whose slightest word hung life or death; the fall of Robespierre; our return hither; the births of my six other

children, their education, their marriages, the passing away
from earth of those two angels for whose loss not even
those left to me ever brought me consolation. . . . And
now, after all these labours, rest has come, and with rest
old age. For whatever others may say, I feel old. The
trees my own hands planted, the ivy grown from seed I
sowed, now covering the whole house, the cedar which,
when my little Sophy was four years old, just measured
her height, and under whose branches I am now sitting, all
tell me I have grown old. The graves of the peasants I
remember as young men and women now lie across my
path as I go into the house of God. All these, too, tell me
this is not my abiding dwelling-place, that another more
lasting will soon be prepared for me. And I weep when
I think of all I shall leave behind me : my poor husband,
older in years than I, not, indeed, weak in health, but
needing me by his side in days of sorrow as he used in
days of happiness. And my children, my dear children !
Alphonse, and his wife, who is to me as another daughter ;
Cecile and her dear little children,—a third generation of
loved and loving ones. And those I miss, whose spirits
seem to be with me as I walk up and down this solitary
path : my Césarine, my pride and joy for her wondrous
beauty, now sleeping far away from us behind that range
of snowy Alps, which never has ceased to remind me of
her ; Suzanne, who even in life seemed to mirror in her
eyes the light and purity of heaven. Alas ! to-day all are
absent or dead, and I am left alone, like a tree whose fruits
have been carried away by the Divine Husbandman. How
sad the thoughts which come on me, pressing me down
even to the ground ! Have I not, too, my 'Mount of

Olives'? Be still, sad heart. Have we not, each of us, our Gethsemane? And is not mine the dearer to me from its very desolation? Even when I miss the white dresses of my children, the joyous echo of their voices, must I not ask myself, What had I ever done for God that He should have given me this little piece of ground for my own possession, this house which, if it has sometimes caused me a false shame from its smallness and humility, has been a safe and secure nest wherein to rear my brood? May He be blest for His gracious gifts! . . . And now I hear the belfry of Bussières ringing the Angelus. It is better to pray than to write; I will repeat once more that prayer in which the little voices of my children used to mingle with mine, . . . but without undue emotion. Grief, the Scriptures tell us, weakens the heart of man, and to fulfil one's duties to the last all our strength is needed. As long as life is left to us, we have with it to gain heaven. As I close this book, I ask once more of God to pour forth on me and mine His choicest blessings. May He bless me in my children, in my friends, in all who love me or whom I have loved!"

With these tender words of blessing ends the last volume of Madame de Lamartine's diary. But the presentiment of approaching death which seems to have dictated them was never mentioned by her, nor suspected by those who loved her. Though now past sixty, she bore the burden of her years with such sweet autumnal grace, she went through the arduous works of charity which, now that her children were no longer with her, made the occupation and solace of her leisure hours, with such untiring energy and regularity, that her friends might well laughingly assure her "she was

not old;" and when, in the November following, her son
left her to spend a few weeks in Paris, the thought that the
parting was a final one never crossed his mind. The
catastrophe which cut short her life was as unexpected as
it was terrible. Only a few days before that he had named
for his return, Madame de Lamartine rose early to attend,
as was her daily custom, the service celebrated at daybreak
and therefore called "la messe des servantes." She then
took a bath, and, it was supposed, turned on the hot water
so that it struck her full in the chest with such force that
she for the moment lost consciousness. Before help came
she was fearfully scalded, and, after a day and a half of
suffering, borne with angelic patience, her spirit passed
peacefully away. Her only lamentation had been over the
pain it would give her son not to have been with her at the
last moment. "Tell Alphonse," were her last words—
"tell him I am not suffering now; I am very happy. My
God! Thou hast been true to Thy promises! I am very
happy."

In a most touching letter, Lamartine's wife implored
M. de Virieu, who was in Paris with her husband, to break
the cruel news to him. M. de Virieu performed his task
with utmost kindness, but the blow was terrible. Lamartine started at once for Mâcon. Travelling night and day,
he reached home the third day after his mother's death,
hoping to have at least the consolation of gazing once more
on that beloved face. But the inflexible rule of custom in
France allows of little delay. The elder M. de Lamartine
was utterly prostrated and helpless, and those to whom it
fell to make the final arrangements, singularly indifferent
to the feelings of the family, so hurried matters that when

Lamartine arrived he found the snow already lying on his mother's grave in the common cemetery of Mâcon. To him, who remembered well how often from his earliest childhood his mother used to point out the spot, now further consecrated by the grave of his little son, where she hoped one day to rest, it was intolerable to find her feelings disregarded, and her dear dust mingling with that of strangers ; and he resolved that, despite all difficulties and obstacles, it should not be.

Two nights later, he went to the churchyard, and, with the assistance of Philiberte, the faithful maid who had tended his mother to the last, was able to find the un-marked spot. After an hour of sorrowful watching, a band of stalwart peasants, summoned secretly from Milly, came in silently one by one, to bear home the remains of their beloved mistress. At midnight they started. Though the night was bitterly cold, the snow deep on the ground, and the number asked to attend strictly limited to the bearers, yet all along the road, long before they drew near to Milly, a long procession had formed, swelled by old men, women, and children clad in such poor mourning as they could afford, the silence of the night broken only by their stifled sobs and by the heavy tread of the *sabots* on the frozen snow.

After some three hours' march, they left the high-road to follow the narrow, paved way which leads up the mountain-side to the hamlet. There, at the door of each cottage was suspended a little copper lamp, a humble but pathetic token of respect. When the house was reached, the bearers laid their burden down in the vestibule where for so many years Madame de Lamartine used every

morning to receive all who came to her, whether sick,
sorrowful, or suffering, herself dressing their sores, pre-
scribing for their ailments, giving them help, advice, kind
words of consolation ; the oak benches on which these
poor people used to sit waiting their turn now served as
trestles for her coffin. Seeing this, old and young wept
aloud ; then, coming one by one, according to the pious
custom of their country, they walked round the coffin,
sprinkling holy water on it as they passed. Her son,
meanwhile, sat bowed down with grief in the adjoining
room.

At the first streak of dawn they set off again, in order
to traverse the difficult and dangerous path which led
across the mountain to St. Point by daylight. In many
places the road lay across deep ravines, now filled up with
snow, so that the only landmarks were the giant trunks of
chestnut-trees. But for the courage and devotion of the
robust men of Milly, the task could never have been
accomplished As it was, the journey took seven hours.
Evening had almost closed in before the Château of St.
Point was reached. After a second night of sorrowful vigil
the last rites were solemnized at break of day, and the
gentle lady laid to rest among her own people. " She is
never alone," Lamartine writes to Virieu. " Night and day
prayers rise up to heaven from around her grave. As for
me, I am happier now she is here, in the church she prayed
in so often and loved so dearly."

Three days later he returned to Mâcon on foot, for the
snow was still deep on the ground. Here fresh cares and
complications awaited him. As his father was no longer
able to manage his property single-handed, it was decided

in family council to carry out at once the division which at his death would be compulsory. In order to secure to the old man the undisturbed possession of the family house at Mâcon, Lamartine had it included in his own share ; consequently Milly fell to the widower of his sister Suzanne, M. de Montherot. This was to Lamartine a cruel trial. More than once he alludes in his letters to the pain it gave him to feel that the cradle of his childhood, endeared to him by a thousand memories, would pass into the hands of strangers. Finally, an arrangement was made by which Lamartine purchased from his brother-in-law all the property that had belonged to his father ; but at a considerable sacrifice of income, for he had to raise money at a high rate ; it thus began the gradual wasting away of his fortune.

The winter was spent at Mâcon in sorrow and seclusion. It was at this time he wrote the poem, " Le Tombeau d'une mère," beginning with the lines—

> " Là, dorment soixante ans d'une seule pensée !
>
>   *   *   *   *
>
> Tant de nuits sans sommeil pour veiller la souffrance,
> Tant de pain retranché pour nourrir l'indigence,
> Tant de pleurs toujours prêts a s'unir à des pleurs,
> Tant de soupirs brûlans vers une autre patrie ;
> Et tant de patience à porter une vie
>   Dont la couronne était ailleurs ! "

But though Lamartine, like other mourners, found solace in clothing his grief in verse, his was no transient sorrow, no passionate indulgence in a short-lived emotion. Years afterwards, amid the interest and excitement of a long-planned journey to the East, he writes as if his loss had been but of yesterday : " The only person who, had she been spared, would now at this moment completely share my happiness is my mother. In all that happens to me,

whether of joy or sorrow, my thoughts turn undeviatingly
to her, and one on whom our thoughts are constantly fixed
is never really absent. That which lives within us so
powerfully, so completely, is not dead. It was my habit
in her lifetime to communicate to her every impression
I received, and find it again in fresh colours, vivified, embellished, in her sparkling imagination. I see her now in the
peaceful solitude of Milly, where, when the accidents of life
separated us, she sat watching and waiting ; I see her
receiving, reading, commenting on my letters, carried away
even more completely than I am myself by the current of
my thoughts. Alas ! 'tis but a vision ! The world we inhabit
is one of realities ; to her our fleeting dreams are no longer
anything. Yet her spirit is with us—following, protecting
us ; in the region of eternity we may yet converse." Of
Lamartine it may with truth be said that "all the lapse
of years, all the events of his life, however strongly they
might move or affect him, never could remove that sainted
image from his heart, or banish that blessed love from its
sanctuary."

   In March, 1830, the Lamartines came for three months
to Paris. The time was one of great political tension. A
cabal of the Extreme Left, by joining the Ultras unexpectedly, on a not very important division, had driven
M. de Martignac from office. Short as it was, his administration has historical interest, as one during which Frenchmen enjoyed more civil and religious liberty than at any
subsequent period of the present century, and its fall was
deeply deplored by Lamartine on public grounds, although
the new premier, Prince Jules de Polignac, was eager to
show him the utmost kindness and favour ; treating him,

notwithstanding the difference in their ages and positions, rather as a friend than as a subordinate. All through the month of March, Lamartine was constantly sent for to the palace, and kept for hours in confidential conversation. But as to the subject of these interviews, Lamartine's correspondence is discreetly silent.

However, the business which brought him to Paris was literary rather than political. It will be remembered that in 1824 he had offered himself as a candidate for the chair then vacant in the Académie française, and was defeated, as he believed, by the intrigues of a petty cabal. Whatever the reason of the rejection, the Academy repented of it and paid him, in 1829, the very unusual compliment of nominating him, without any fresh canvassing on his part, and by an overwhelming majority.

Owing to his recent bereavement, the reception was postponed till the April following, when ·it was the most stirring incident of the season in Paris. For whatever difference of opinion there may be as to the literary dis-tinction conferred, there can be no doubt that the ceremony of reception is a social event of the highest importance. All class, all political differences are forgotten in the anxiety to obtain tickets of admission. In Lamartine's case there were additional elements stimulating expecta-tion. His political and personal popularity, his reputation for eloquence, his good looks and distinguished bearing, probably counted for something ; but, above all, the cir-cumstance that he was the first writer of the romantic school to whom the Academy had opened its classic portals, made the occasion one of exceptional interest.

The speech of Baron Cuvier, to whom it fell to welcome

Lamartine in the name of his colleagues, was of course extremely laudatory, and well turned, though certainly more personal than would be thought good taste on similar occasions in England, in its allusions to Lamartine's recent sorrow, and to the amiable character and brilliant career which silenced criticism and baffled envy. He also emphasized the religious character of Lamartine's lyrics, perhaps a little maliciously, for in his closing paragraph— " But you do not, of course, Monsieur, flatter yourself that you have said quite the last word on subjects which, when discussed at some length more than three thousand years ago in the Idumean desert, caused a momentary coolness between Job and his friends ; and on which, in our days, Leibnitz, Clarke, and Newton are not agreed,"—M. Cuvier certainly shows the cloven foot of the scientific rationalist.

Lamartine's *discours de réception* opened, according to the unvarying formula, with the panegyric of his predecessor, M. Daru. It had been Napoleon's custom, on annexing a new province, to send there at once some French man of letters, whose task it was to ransack the archives, and put together in the form of a history everything that could throw discredit on the former Government, and, in most cases (as was done by Llorente at Madrid), to burn all the papers which told in the contrary direction. M. Daru discharged his task with more talent and judgment than most of his fellow-labourers ; and, unfortunately for Venice, his history remained for three parts of a century the unchallenged authority on all matters appertaining to Venetian institutions and history, till the lifelong researches of Mr. Rawdon Browne and the eloquent indignation of Mr. Ruskin made his untrustworthiness known. That the

historiographer of Napoleon was not likely to be a favourite
in the society of the Restoration was only an additional
motive for Lamartine to make his panegyric as glowing as
possible. Then, having done full justice to this portion of
his subject, he went on to survey the present condition of
France in language for which his august audience were by
no means prepared. Phrases such as, "The development
of the human intellect, no longer stifled and confined in
narrow channels ; " "the influence and freedom of the press,
a blessing bestowed by Providence to renew the youth of
nations ;" "reason and liberty working together for the
happiness of mankind," leading up to a brilliant climax
about the Monarchy "to which France owes everything,
even the golden fruits of liberty." . . . from the lips of
the poet of religion and romance, the recognized favourite
of Prince Polignac, and on such an occasion, produced
much the effect of a shower of rockets.

When all was over, and Lamartine passed out through
the crowded ranks of his friends, reproaches were audibly
mingled with the usual congratulations. "You have gone
over to the enemy, disappointed all our hopes, ruined your
career," was the passionate exclamation of the Cardinal
Duc de Rohan. But the event proved that these prophets
of evil were "more Royalist than the King."

A few days later Charles X. received the new Acade-
mician with his accustomed kindness ; even Prince Polignac,
whether from the generosity of a temperament not prone
to take offence or from an utter blindness to the fact that
the course he was preparing to follow was in any way
opposed to liberty or to the Charter, showed no difference
in his demeanour, and renewed once more an offer he had

made to appoint Lamartine as his immediate subordinate
in the Foreign Office, which, as the Prince's time was now
almost entirely engrossed by home politics, would have
made him virtually Minister of Foreign Affairs. Lamartine
fully appreciated the generosity of the offer ; but, much as
he personally liked and admired Prince Polignac, he saw
that his policy was detaching the Crown from the people
"as completely as the axe of the woodman severs the bark
from the tree," and persisted in his refusal. "I could not
go against my convictions," he wrote to M. de Virieu, "and
so declined to have any hand in a work sure to end in an
explosion."

In the last days of May, Lamartine returned with his
wife to Burgundy, where, by taking into his own hands all
the property that had hitherto been his father's, he had
added considerably to his cares, and, as he was never inclined
to do things by halves, undertook agricultural improvements
on a large scale, giving employment to a hundred labourers.
"I planted six thousand trees before breakfast this morning," he writes, "and shall be most of the week laying out
a new road." But the burden of his still recent sorrow
weighed too heavily on him for enjoyment in his work ; he
felt, he says, like one maimed or paralyzed, unable to take
interest in anything. His health, too, had suffered, and
the Baths of Aix gave him no relief. Even the news that
he was named as the *chargé d'affaires* to the new Court
of Athens, one of his most cherished ambitions, left him
doubtful as to whether he was pleased or not. Practically,
he saw for France no future but chaos. " We are going
down the road which leads to Avernus, and there is nothing
to stop us. Our only hope is in heaven and in the strength

of the instinct of self-preservation. Do you ask if France
is ill? To me she seems as one dying, or at least in a
convulsion which resembles death. Who told you I was
on the wrong side? I am against fools certainly; but
there happily still are honest and God-fearing Royalists,
men who march under a very different banner from
that of MM. Barthier, Vitrolles, etc. I am neither with
Paul nor with Cephas; but with common sense, with the
monarchy, with fidelity to the dynasty. Alas! I fear, at
the rate things are going, we shall soon have to prove our
loyalty by deeds rather than by words. Let us lift up our
hands thither whence help can come, for here there is no
help. The redemption of France is not in a government
of remorses and repentances; nor in one of memories,
whether aristocratic, autocratic, or theocratic: it is in the
union of all interests and of all intelligences in a broad and
righteous way; in hopes which date, not from the empire,
not from an older and more worn-out order, but from the
Restoration."

The morning papers of the 29th of July brought to Aix
the news of the publication of the *Ordonnances*. A letter
of a little later date, from M. de Virieu, told of the abdication of Charles X.

"Nothing in your letter surprises me," was Lamartine's
answer, "unless it be the swiftness of it all. Anarchy is at
our gates; there is nothing between it and us but an improvised Government." For a moment it seemed as if, in
the provinces at least, anarchy was inevitable. Rumours
were circulated among the peasantry that the châteaux
were to be pillaged; bands of thieves and vagabonds wandering about created terror, though the mass of the people

were quiet and well-disposed. Lamartine had reason to be pleased with the loyalty of his tenants, those of Milly especially, who got ready to rise *en masse* with two other communes to defend the château, if necessary. To reward them he spent the winter there. It was a sad time enough. "I have been suffering beyond measure," he writes in the early spring. "Now I ride for four hours every day, and then return to my books."

It will be remembered that Lamartine had been nominated as minister at Athens, and he was making preparation to start at the moment when the Revolution broke out. The policy of Louis Philippe's Government was to retain in office all who gave in their adhesion to the new dynasty. This, however, Lamartine did not deem it consistent with his personal dignity to do, and he sent in, through Count Molé a letter, couched in respectful terms, tendering an absolute resignation of his diplomatic rank. But his correspondence shows that he refused to rally to the Irreconcilables, who would hardly allow that any civic duty remained binding, since the monarch they adhered to had been exiled. He, on the contrary, stoutly maintained that the extreme danger of lapsing into utter anarchy made it an obligation incumbent on all Frenchmen to take part in public affairs. Accordingly, when at the approach of the general election of June, 1831, he received an invitation from the Royalists and the Moderate Liberals of the electors of Bergues, he accepted at once. From the circumstance of his sister Eugénie having married a neighbouring landowner, M. Coppens d'Hondschoote, he was well known to his constituents, and, for a time, was sanguine of success. But, two days before the poll, the Liberals unexpectedly required him to sign a paper expressing personal devotion to the reigning dynasty, which he felt would be to pledge himself to the exclusion of the elder branch—a simple impossibility.   Even after his refusal the contest was close, and he polled 181 votes against 188.

Notwithstanding his defeat, the election was of use in showing the interest he took in politics.   Soon after he published a *brochure*, which, though too moderate in tone to have much success at the moment, was not without effect on public opinion, and defined clearly his political standpoint of combining with unchanging personal attachment to the elder branch of the House of France, respectful submission to the Government, and conscientious acceptance of all civic duties and responsibilities.

CHAPTER V.

1832–1833.

THE year 1832 found the Lamartines preparing to carry out a long cherished project of visiting the Holy Land. They had intended to start early in the spring, but the terrible epidemic of cholera which then swept over France delayed them. It had appeared suddenly in Paris in the beginning of March. Among its victims was Madame de Montcalm, one of Lamartine's kindest and most constant friends of the elder generation. On the 20th of April, still apparently in perfect health, she wrote to Lamartine that she hoped the cholera might release her from the many cares and burdens pressing her; two days later the deliverance had come. To him, her loss was a real sorrow. " I hardly realized," he writes, " till she was gone how strong the tie of friendship between us."

From Paris the plague spread rapidly through the northern provinces. The Lamartines remained quietly at St. Point, " waiting for it to come." As *président du conseil départemental*, Lamartine was able to do much to alleviate the sufferings it caused : he appointed a sanitary commission and worked hard on it himself, organizing and distributing relief three days in the week at Mâcon, the other days in the country; apparently with success, for by the end of June he felt free to leave home.

In those days steam-yachts were not thought of; but Lamartine hired a large sailing vessel of 250 tons, the *Alceste*, and had her fitted up with every possible comfort and convenience. The party included, besides Madame de Lamartine and her daughter, two friends, MM. de Capmas and Perseval, a doctor and six faithful servants, who, after the hardships and possible perils awaiting them had been fully pointed out, eagerly asked to be allowed to accompany their master and mistress.

The record of the journey, which occupied about a year and a half, was published later by Lamartine, under the title of "Un Voyage en Orient." The novelty of the undertaking is shown by his thinking it necessary to devote several pages of his work to enumerating the causes which impelled him "to leave a loved and peaceful home, rendered more delightful by perfect domestic happiness, and embark on a vast ocean for unknown shores and an uncertain future." One was the wish to nourish his imagination with fresh ideas and images. From his youth he had longed to visit the scenes of the Biblical drama, made familiar to him in his mother's earliest teachings. He had dreamt of such a journey as of a great act in the meditative life; it seemed to him that by it all the doubts and cavils of the mind would be set at rest, all the problems and difficulties of religious belief solved. Then came the wish to break loose from those political questions now become so painful. " A younger generation is rising up amongst us, to whom our prejudices, our fears, our recriminations are as things of a distant past; they can press forward full of pure enthusiasm to seize with energy the glorious career before them. Let us make way for such!" He winds up with a touching invocation to his departed mother, "to watch over the pilgrim band, to place herself as a saving providence between them and all dangers, to bless an expedition with which her own ardent soul would so deeply have sympathized, and if there were anything of imprudence in undertaking it, to plead for forgiveness and avert all evil consequences"—a prayer, which in the letter, was unhappily not granted.

After some delay from contrary winds, the *Alceste* sailed out of the port of Marseilles on the 13th of July, and, after coasting Africa, reached Malta on the 22nd. They remained for some days at La Valette, meeting everywhere a degree of hospitality which at once gratified and surprised Lamartine. "The English," he writes, "are a great people morally; but, speaking generally, they are not a social people. Concentrated in the sweet and sacred intimacy of their home life, when they leave 'tis usually not to amuse themselves or to communicate their thoughts and sentiments, but either from custom or from vanity. In the colonies it seems to be otherwise; there is something really chivalrous in the brilliant and generous hospitality which, unsought and unexpected, has been heaped on strangers like ourselves." He was particularly touched by the kindness of Captain Lyons, commanding H.M.S. *Madagascar*, who, on Madame de Lamartine's expressing some anxiety, rather on her daughter's account than her own, about the long sea-voyage to Greece, obligingly delayed his ship's departure for some days, in order to give the *Alceste* the advantage of her escort, offering even

to take her in tow if she was unable to keep up with the
frigate. The proposition was gratefully accepted, and the
two vessels set sail on the 1st of August.

A few hours after leaving the port they were becalmed,
and lay for several days " on a sea as glittering and smooth
as a mirror, above them a heaven as of molten brass ; " it
was not till the 6th that they saw at daybreak the unequal
summits of the mountains of Greece rising over the horizon.
That evening, as they were sailing before the wind between
Cape Matapan and the Island of Cerigo, an incident
occurred which recalls vividly what were the perils of the
deep even fifty years ago. The English frigate, having
sighted a suspicious-looking vessel, went out of her course
to reconnoitre, and was separated from the *Alceste* by
a distance of several miles, when a Greek pirate came
bearing down from the opposite direction in full sail.
Without a moment's delay the crew and passengers of the
Alceste, numbering twenty-five well-armed men, were in
their places on deck. Twice the pirate came so near that
they could see distinctly the villainous faces of her crew ;
some in Albanian costume, some in tattered European
garments, all armed to the teeth. But finding them so
well prepared, the pirates passed on, leaving the *Alceste*
unmolested.

The period of Lamartine's journey was one of great
disorder and anarchy in Greece ; the murder of Capo
d'Istria was of recent date, Missolonghi had just been
sacked, and every courier coming from inland brought
news of the burning of a town or of the massacre of
a population. At Nauplia, where they stayed two nights,
no one could venture outside the gates without a strong

escort. Prince Karadja offered a troop of Palikars to take
the travellers to the tomb of Agamemnon ; but Lamartine
replied that he did not care sufficiently about Agamemnon
to risk a single human life on his account. Indeed,
although Lamartine's descriptions of the scenery and
monuments of Greece are at once eloquent and graphic,
there are considerable limitations to his enthusiasm. The
impression made on him by the modern Greeks was most
unfavourable. "No language," he says, "can give an idea
of the horrible convulsions by which the Greeks are bringing shame and disgrace on themselves, and ruin on their
country ; but for the presence of the French and English
squadrons they would tear each other in pieces. As it is,
unless the Bavarian Prince come quickly, he will not find
a house standing to shelter him."

It was characteristic of Lamartine to generalize quickly
and positively from any fact passing before his eyes ;
and his youthful ardour for the Greek cause now gave
place to a strong preference for their former masters,
which he retained through life, and which, in later years,
influenced his views on the Eastern question. Even a
fortnight spent at Athens, enjoying delightful hospitality
with a perfect *cicerone* in M. Gropius, did not sensibly
modify his impressions. "In the Parthenon, Pericles yet
lives ; in the temple of Theseus the gods of Greece will be
for ever worshipped ;" but still all seemed to him dis-
appointingly small and circumscribed, and the emotions he
anticipated were not awakened.

It had been the Lamartines' intention to go from
Athens to Constantinople, then through Syria, travelling
slowly, and halting at all places of interest. But the

increasing delicacy of their daughter Julia, whose health had for two years caused them uneasiness, modified their plans; it was evident the hardships and fatigues of such a journey would outweigh the benefits the doctors had anticipated from the soft climate of the East, and it was decided to go straight from Athens to Beyrout, which was to be the winter residence for Madame de Lamartine and her daughter, for Lamartine and his two friends a starting-point for various excursions into the interiors of Syria and Palestine.

The sea-voyage was accomplished prosperously, but to find a suitable house at Beyrout was no easy task; however, at last, at a distance of a few hundred yards from the town, a group of buildings was secured, which the skill of the Arab carpenters transformed into a comfortable abode, not unlike the villas which are found in the neighbourhoods of Lucca or Leghorn. Divans were scattered about, book-shelves quickly improvised, pretty trifles strewn about on the quaint inlaid sweet-scented tables, even the walls were brightened up with frescoes from Madame de Lamartine's skilful brush; and so was made, out of most unpromising materials, an abode at once homelike and picturesque. The views and surrounding scenery were most beautiful; Lamartine, who preferred the charms of nature to those of either antiquity or art, dilates on them in pages of glowing and poetic description. As soon as his wife and daughter were comfortably settled, and had formed in the foreign colony at Beyrout some pleasant social relations, he, with M. Capmas and some other friends, began to explore the interior.

One incident on which Lamartine dwells at considerable

length, and to which he was afterwards fond of referring, was a visit he was permitted to pay Lady Hester Stanhope. He prefaces his account of it by a slight sketch of the Oriental life of this remarkable woman, describing the state and pomp with which she was at first surrounded. When fairly conversant with the customs, habits, and language of the country, she organized a large caravan, loaded a long file of camels with costly presents wherewith to propitiate the various tribes, and travelled over the whole of Syria, staying for some time sucessively at Jerusalem, Damascus, Aleppo, Baalbec, and Palmyra. At the last-named place, the Arabs gathered round her to the number of forty or fifty thousand, proclaimed her queen of Palmyra, and engaged themselves by a treaty, said to have been observed as long as she lived, to allow any European protected by her to visit with perfect security the desert and ruins of Palmyra, on payment of a tax of a thousand piastres. When, after many hairbreadth escapes, she became weary of wandering, Lady Hester, he goes on to say, settled herself on an almost inaccessible solitude on the flank of a mountain of the Lebanon range, near Said, the ancient Sidon, and dwelt there for some years in Oriental splendour, surrounded by a large retinue of European and Asiatic domestics. She was treated with the utmost respect by the Pasha of Acre, and entertained political relations with the Porte, with the ruler of the Lebanon, Emir Beschir, and with the Arab sheikhs of Syria and of the country round Bagdad.

After dwelling, with perhaps a touch of unconscious exaggeration, on this part of Lady Hester's career, Lamartine goes on to give, with still deeper respect and sympathy, the record of her later years. Improvidence, extravagance, probably treachery, had impaired her fortune ; most of the attendants who had at first surrounded her had either died or deserted ; the friendship of the Arabs, which always requires to be nourished by presents, grew cold. But neither poverty, isolation, nor even personal danger could subdue that undaunted spirit. She never for a moment dreamt of retracing her steps ; she wasted no regrets on the world or on the past ; she shrank not under her forlorn condition, her misfortunes, nor even from the prospect of an old age of oblivion and neglect. Without books or newspapers, without letters, without friends, without even servants attached to her person, attended solely by some black slaves, with a few Arab peasants to cultivate her gardens, once rivalling those of Semiramis, she lived on, resolute and undaunted. It was said, and Lamartine himself inclined to the belief, that her preternatural strength of mind was due partly, indeed, to her personal character, but still more to her religious theories, in which the teachings of Christianity were almost obscured by strange accretions of Oriental mysticism, and by a firm belief in the occult influences of the celestial bodies.

To European visitors, those of her own nation especially, her doors were known to be closed ; but feeling a strong desire to see her, and remembering the gracious reception she had accorded years before to his friend, M. de Marcellus, Lamartine, finding himself in Lady Hester's neighbourhood, resolved at least to make the attempt, and despatched an Arab messenger with a note in which, after describing himself as too sensible of the charms of solitude and of the value of liberty not to shrink from intruding on her secluded life, he yet asked to be allowed not to leave the East without seeing a lady who was herself one of the wonders of that land of mystery. The letter proved an open sesame ; a messenger came with an order to convey him and his party to Dgioum, where, on the day following, they arrived.

Lamartine devotes several pages to describing this mysterious and romantic abode; the atmosphere of dignified simplicity which pervaded it ; the mild, grave, majestic traits of the pale figure draped in Oriental costume, worn with the freedom and grace as of one who for years had never known any other. Lady Hester rose to receive him, extending her hand, which he kissed with deep respect. An interview beginning thus was not likely to turn on commonplace civilities ; it merged into a dialogue befitting a poet and a prophetess. During the two days Lamartine spent at Dgioum he and his hostess discussed, amid clouds of fragrant smoke, many mystical and metaphysical themes —happily in harmonious acquiescence, though Lady Hester would not hold her guest altogether free from the reproach of being one of those who place too strong a reliance on human will, from insufficient belief in the inscrutable forces of destiny. He was much struck by the strength and vividness of her intellect, and especially by the perspicacity of the judgments she passed on people with whom he, too, was personally acquainted. It was evidently a mortification to find that his own name was totally unknown to her, but his note had pleased her, and she believed him to be one who had a work to perform in the future. Before he left she insisted on casting his horoscope ; as the result, she was able to congratulate him on being born under fortunate

stars and gifted with corresponding powers ; one was certainly Mercury, "who gives clearness and colour to the
mind and tongue. The sun has also much influence over
your destinies. Be thankful ; there are not many to whom
the stars are as propitious." These, and other prophecies
equally flattering, Lamartine records with becoming
modesty, giving his readers to understand that, although
not himself a believer in Lady Hester's supernatural
powers, he was convinced both of her sincerity and her
sanity.

From Dgioum the travellers pushed on to the country
of the Druses and Maronites, and were hospitably entertained by the Emir Beschir at Dëir-el-Kammar, where
they spent some days in the society of the most high-bred
and cultivated Syrians, which Lamartine, who possessed in
an eminent degree the happy and gracious flexibility of
nature which has a fascination for Orientals, found delightful.
His descriptions of Dëir-el-Kammar and its inmates recall
Tancred's visit to the castle of Canobbia, as the guest of
another Emir of the House of Shehaab. Indeed, there is
more than one passage in Disraeli's Eastern romance which
seems to have been suggested by the "Voyage en Orient."

Finding on his return to Beyrout his wife and daughter
cheerful and well, he resolved to lose no time in visiting
the goal of all Christian pilgrims in Syria, and on the 8th
of October the caravan of eighteen horsemen started afresh,
following the road which, by a graduated ascent, leads over
the amphitheatre of hills encircling Beyrout. When they
arrived at the summit, a long line of coast stretched out
beneath them. Far away in the distance they were shown
the group of crumbling ruins marking the spot which once

was Tyre, recalling to Lamartine's memory some lines of
one of his earlier poems :—

> " Je n'ai pas entendu sous les cèdres antiques
> Les cris des nations monter et retentir,
> Ni vu du noir Liban les aigles prophétiques
> Descendre, au doigt de Dieu, sur les palais de Tyr."

The "black Lebanon" lay before him ; but the vultures
which, according to prophecy, were to come down unceasingly from the hills in order to feed or to seek their food in
the accursed city, where were they? Hardly, he tells us,
had the doubting thought passed through his mind, when
his eye fell on what seemed to be five formless, motionless,
statues of black marble, crowning the summit of an
adjacent peak. As the travellers drew near, the dark
masses were seen to move. They concluded it must be
a group of wandering Bedouins. But as they came closer
still, five huge eagles, slowly lifting their heavy wings,
raised themselves a few yards in the air. They did not
show signs of fear, nor move away to a distance, but
hovered over the doomed city as if it were theirs by divine
right. One of the Arab guides, lifting his rifle, fired at
them twice, still they did not seem to heed, but sailed
round majestically, as if they would say, "You cannot
harm us ; we are the eagles of God."

Turning inland, the travellers camped on the second
day at Solomon's Wells ; then, crossing the plain of Acre
they again began to ascend. It was not, as is the case
with most Europeans, from the rocky path leading from
Jaffa to Jerusalem, whence only a dwarfed and circumscribed landscape can be discerned, but from the heights
of the Galilean hills that Lamartine first viewed the Holy

Land. Far as eye could see it lay stretched before him,
"as of old beneath the failing vision of Moses. To the
left the rugged range of Lebanon rose against the dark
blue of the morning sky; below lay the plain of Zabulon,
the soft shores of the Galilean Lake, once the garden of
Palestine; and, far as eye could reach, a perspective of
mountains and valleys, hills and ravines, glistening as the
mists lifted in the bright Eastern sunshine;—a landscape
one may well believe to have been designed by the hand
of the Creator as the dwelling-place of His chosen people."

"On this day," he goes on to say, "new impressions
sprang up in my mind. Hitherto in travel, my eyes, my
thoughts, my imagination had been interested and occupied; but now, setting foot in this land of prophecy and of
mystery, the land of Jehovah and of Christ, the land whose
name I had lisped in childhood, the land where first were
revealed those sweet and sacred teachings which, at a later
period, roused my inmost soul, I felt as if springs long ice-
bound had melted before a summer sun, as if feelings
paralyzed for years had been vivified and restored; my
heart and my soul were touched to their very depths. As
one whose feet have led him unawares out of the busy
street to the silence of a sanctuary, this land of the
Scripture, whose sacred earth my feet are now treading,
is to me the Temple of God. Silently and alone, I lifted
my soul up to Him in prayer; I gave Him thanks for per-
mitting me to visit this His sanctuary. And from that day,
as I journeyed on through the hills of Judea and by the
shores of Galilee, an ever-deepening impression of tenderness
and reverence dominated all others. Here travel becomes
a prayer. With thoughts such as these in my mind,

I rode slowly on, till, having crossed a ridge of hills, I saw, nestling down in the valley, the white houses of Nazareth. In another moment, I found myself kneeling prostrate in the dust, unable to utter any words save 'Et Verbum caro factum est, et habitavit in nobis.' With deep emotion I kissed in silence, I moistened with tears of repentance, love, and hope the ground which had brought forth a Saviour."

After spending a few days in the Latin convent at Nazareth, they went on to Mount Tabor, called, from a tradition dating from the days of St. Jerome, the Mountain of the Transfiguration. This, however, Lamartine was inclined to doubt, as there is evidence that, at the period referred to, Tabor was a citadel, garrisoned by the Romans. Crossing the Jordan, and following the low line of volcanic hills that border the lake of Galilee, they returned by Cana to Nazareth, the state of the country making it impossible to go direct to Jerusalem. The Egyptian troops under Ibrahim Pasha had lately defeated the Turks, and taken St. Jean d'Acre, which they had reduced almost to ruins. War had been followed by pestilence, and a rigorous quarantine cut off the Holy City, where the plague was said to be lingering, from intercourse with the outer world. However, Lamartine was provided with powerful letters of introduction, one written in Mahomet Ali's own hand to his son Ibrahim, by means of which he procured, through a courier, an order from Ibrahim to the governor of Jaffa, desiring him to provide the Frankish travellers with all they needed, and troops, if necessary, for their protection.

From Nazareth, therefore, the little caravan journeyed on to Jaffa, receiving at the various places where they halted generous hospitality from the rich Greek and the Frankish merchants. All this took time, so that it was not till the 28th of October that, resolved, despite the entreaties of their friends, to see Jerusalem, they started from Jaffa. The Turkish-Egyptian governor had also warned them of their danger; but Lamartine's reply, " If it be the will of God that we die of the plague, we shall be no safer at Jaffa than at Jerusalem," was to a Moslem unanswerable. Admiring his submission to the will of Allah, the governor replied that he still could not allow a guest so recommended to him by Ibrahim Pasha to be exposed to any dangers that could be avoided, and that he would select from among the garrison a guard of the bravest and most reliable men to preserve him and his friends from the treachery of the Bedouins, and from contact with the plague-stricken.

The day following was fixed on for their departure, and they started at early dawn, accompanied as far as Ramleh by their Jaffa friends. Lamartine himself organized the troop: two horsemen, acting as scouts, rode fifty paces in front; the rest followed one by one in file, to diminish as much as possible the dangers incident to passing any infected caravan, a strong body of Egyptian soldiers bringing up the rear. Thanks to the admirable discipline of the soldiers, this order was kept during twenty-five days' march without break or interruption, the result being perfect immunity from plague.

But there were other dangers ahead. The cities of Palestine might have Turkish or Egyptian garrisons, but the open country was, even more than it is now, in the hands of the Bedouins, a large party of whom on the third

day were seen advancing in martial order. It was a
considerable relief to find that, far from being hostile, they
were sent from Abougoush, the most powerful of the Arab
chiefs, to inquire if Lamartine was the Frankish lord in
whose name Lady Hester Stanhope had lately sent him a
robe of honour, desiring that he should be treated as her
friend. On being answered in the affirmative, they were
invited to visit Jeremiah, where the tribe was then encamped, received with much honour, and provided with an
escort commanded by Abougoush's nephew and heir. But
the account given by the Bedouins of the state of Jerusalem
was even worse than what they had heard at Jaffa. The
plague was increasing in violence, the deaths numbering
sixty to seventy in the day ; all the convents and hospices
were closed. After much parleying, it was finally arranged
that the party should camp outside the walls of Jerusalem,
visit its sacred places and those situated in the country
adjoining, and return to the camp each night. It was on
the 29th of October that Lamartine and his companions
entered Jerusalem. They were met at the Bethlehem Gate
by a guard sent by the Pasha to escort them through the
streets, that they might be saved all contact with the
funeral processions which alone disturbed its solitude.

The terrible and exceptional circumstances of Lamartine's visit to the Holy Sepulchre added much to its
impressiveness. There was no noise or confusion of a busy
city to interfere with devotion, no throng of pushing
pilgrims to turn worship into a scuffle. At his earnest
request, a privilege hardly any have enjoyed was conceded
to him : he was allowed more than once to enter unaccom-
panied the Inner Sanctuary, and worship in solitude and

silence at that most hallowed spot. And, in truth, Lamartine needed all the strength and consolation religion could
give ; for, on his return to Beyrout, the crowning sorrow
of his life awaited him. Of the motives which had brought
the Lamartines to Syria, the most pressing was the hope
of benefiting the health of their daughter Julia, which
during the last two years had often caused them anxiety.
The physicians they consulted thought that a prolonged
residence in the soft climate of the East would ward off
any possible danger of consumption, and at first there
seemed every reason to hope the experiment was successful. All her father's earlier letters describe Julia as
enchanted by the journey, entering with a degree of intelligence far beyond her years into the thoughts and
interests of her parents, helping her mother to arrange and
decorate their Syrian home ; but delighting, above all, in
accompanying her father, to whom she was passionately
attached, in his walks and rides. Her health seemed so
much improved and strengthened that almost all anxiety
on her account had passed away ; and it was Lamartine's
intention to journey on from Jerusalem to Egypt, and
spend some weeks there before returning to Beyrout.

While encamped outside Jerusalem, he received, on his
return from an excursion to Jericho, a packet of letters
forwarded by his wife, in which she described her daughter
as perfectly well and happy. But at the foot of the letter
was a postscript in Julia's own writing, imploring her father
not to stay away longer. This pathetic little appeal,
probably dictated by anxiety for his safety, determined
Lamartine to start at once on the return journey, and he
reached Beyrout on the 6th of November. His daughter

L

greeted him with more than usual delight; nothing seemed now wanting to her happiness.

A few days later, she accompanied him on a long ride over the hills surrounding Beyrout, resting for their midday halt on a plateau which commands perhaps the most beautiful view in the world. Beneath their feet lay the Mediterranean, with its wonderfully varied coast-line ; while eastward rose the snow-clad peaks of Lebanon, and in the further distance lay the plains of Palestine, bathed in the soft autumnal sunshine, rich in gorgeous and glowing colouring, but still more in their thousand associations and memories.

They did not return until the sun was already setting behind the great pine forest of the Emir Fakredeen. Julia, who had, unlike her wont, remained a long time silent, turned to her father, saying, with girlish rapture, " Tell me, father, is not this the longest and the most beautiful ride we have ever taken ? Is there anything in the world that can be compared with it ? How good God is," she went on, " to allow a girl like me to see such wonders ! "

It was not only the longest and most beautiful ride the poor girl had ever taken, it was also to be the last. A few days later, she was stricken down by fever, and, on the 20th of December, Lamartine wrote to Virieu that he was childless. " After five days' illness our angel has been taken from us. There is no need to tell you how it is with us. It seems as if life were but a dream of transient happiness, followed by despair. All its joy and hope, all its zest and interest, are gone for ever. The reason of it God only can make plain. I came back from a six weeks' tour, and found her apparently full of life and strength ; loving, joyous, caressing, yet already almost a woman in intelligence. I had taken every possible precaution to strengthen her chest, which for two years had given us uneasiness ; daily she rode out, generally with me. At the first change of weather, she began to cough, inflammation came on, and in five days she was taken from us, despite all the care and skill of two French physicians and an excellent English one. All was in vain ! But, at least, save for a few hours, she did not suffer. We are crushed and stupefied, unable to return home till spring, for the sea-voyage has too many dangers. I shall then leave my wife in Italy, and return home alone. What a home-coming it will be ! "

Of the sad months that followed, passed in crushing grief at Beyrout, neither letters nor journal give any record. At last M. and Madame de Lamartine each felt that for the other's sake some change was to be desired, and in April they started from Beyrout to visit Baalbec and Damascus. The first night they spent at Hammanna, where rooms had been prepared for them by order of the Druse sheikh, in a castle said to be built by the crusaders, which, from the beauty of its architecture, recalled and rivalled those which are the glory of Touraine. The day following they were the guests of the Greek Bishop at Zakle, whence they reached Baalbec, where they remained for some days, entertained by the Emir, whose horsemen escorted them to the gates of Damascus, at that time a hotbed of Moslem fanaticism. No traveller or agent of any Christian power was admitted within its walls. But for the kindness of M. Baudin—a French merchant who, by adopting the dress and habits of the Moslems, had managed during the last ten years to remain on sufferance in order to guard the interests of his countrymen, and whom they had met at Beyrout—the Lamartines and their friends could never have penetrated within its walls. As it was, they were obliged completely to disguise themselves. The gentlemen of the party already had assumed the Eastern dress, and before they approached Damascus Madame de Lamartine and her maid were swathed from head to foot in white drapery, after the manner of Asiatic women. At the city gate a guide, who was watching for them, came forward, and silently directed them, away from the well-ordered gardens and sparkling fountains which have made Damascus famous, through narrow streets, to the Armenian quarter, where they stopped before a door so mean and narrow that they could hardly get through. Thence a dingy corridor led to a court, where, as if by enchantment, rose up a palace. They were received with Eastern magnificence, happily blended with European refinements, by M. Baudin and his family. With these kind friends some weeks were spent. Lamartine, in his Eastern dress, associated with the Armenians, who numbered thirty thousand, and about whom he gives, in his published travels, a good many interesting details.

It was on the return journey that an incident occurred which ultimately gave a fresh direction to Lamartine's life. The caravan had left Hammanna at early dawn. For the first two hours the sun's rays did not pierce the welcome screen of mist rising from the valley. All sign of human habitation had been left behind; hardly could the tower of some lonely monastery or the belfry minaret of some isolated village be discerned in the furthest distance. At the place selected for the noonday halt, the eyes ranged over a boundless horizon of solitude, unbroken save on the line which marks the great highway to Damascus, crossed at long intervals by groups of horsemen. From one of these a solitary rider detached himself to follow the track they had themselves made. It proved to be a courier sent from Beyrout with a packet of letters lately arrived from Europe, one of which announced to Lamartine that he had been elected as deputy by the arrondissement of Bergues, which, it will be remembered, he contested unsuccessfully two years before. His first impulse was to send the messenger back with an unqualified refusal; a life of action had now no attraction for him. His wish, as far as he had one, was to retire to St. Point, and there cherish in silence and isolation the memories which were more to him than all the world besides. But, happily, wiser counsels prevailed. His friends asked him at least to defer his answer, and their arguments, strengthened by his wife's earnest entreaty, prevailed on him not to add to the regrets of life that of opportunities neglected and talents wasted. He accepted the post, with the condition that he was not expected to undertake its duties till the following autumn.

On returning to Beyrout, the preparations for leaving Syria were begun. The original plan had been that the *Alceste*, which had been laid up at Marseilles during the winter, should call back in May, and, after a protracted cruise among the Isles of Greece and along the shores of the Bosphorus, take them home to France. But all was now changed. Julia, when she felt life ebbing away, had earnestly prayed that she might at least be buried at

St. Point. To spare his wife an additional pang, Lamartine chartered another vessel, the *Sophie*, in which the party were to start on their homeward journey, while the *Alceste* sailed straight back to France "with her sad freight—a vanished life."

It was with heavy hearts that they went on board the *Sophie*, leaving behind them, short as had been their stay in Syria, many sympathizing friends. After going through the sufferings and dangers of a terrible hurricane, and resting for short intervals at Rhodes, Cyprus, and Smyrna, they reached Constantinople on May 29th. Here, but a short time before, the European quarter of Pera had been almost entirely destroyed by fire; neither an hotel nor even a private house in which it was possible to find a lodging was left standing. However, Eastern hospitality speedily made up for the deficiency. M. Truqui, the Sardinian consul-general, on hearing of the arrival of the Lamartines, went at once on board the *Sophie*, to put his country house at their disposal. A few hours later, the French ambassador, Admiral Roussin, invited them to his hôtel at Therapia. The first offer was gratefully accepted, and they had no reason to regret it. Partly from gratitude for the kindness of their host, partly to give the friends who had been faithful to them during so many sad and dreary months some opportunity of enjoyment; perhaps, also, because each dreaded for the other the sad home-coming, the Lamartines agreed to remain at Constantinople for a longer time than they had originally intended.

The time was put to account by Lamartine to inform himself as much as possible on Eastern affairs, which were then threatening to become a serious question in European politics. Nor, despite his grief, could he fail to be deeply impressed by the many wonders of the beautiful city, then so little known to Europeans. In describing his visit to the Seraglio, which, since the massacre of the Mamelukes, had been deserted by Sultan Mahmoud, he mentions that he was the only European who had crossed its threshold since Lady Mary Wortley Montagu. He had also the good fortune to be allowed to accompany Admiral Roussin in the one visit which each newly arrived foreign ambassador is allowed to make to the Mosque of Saint Sophia, which, with its columns taken from the Temple of Ephesus, its gigantic figures of the Apostles plainly visible through the crumbling plaster of the Arabic ornaments that had once concealed them, he calls, in poetic phrase, " le grand caravansérail de Dieu."

Nor could he be otherwise than interested in much that was going on in the social and political world of Constantinople. The Russian fleet, which had been help-ing the Sultan to curb the power of the Viceroy of Egypt, now lay at anchor in the Bosphorus, under the walls of Therapia, and a detachment of Russian troops occupied an entrenched camp on the Asiatic shore. Would they, their task being now completed, stay or go? was the question asked on all sides with the keenest anxiety. Lamartine had the satisfaction of being one of the first enlightened, Count Orloff having shown him an autograph letter from the Czar, couched in about these terms :—

" MY DEAR ORLOFF,

" When Providence makes a man the ruler of forty millions of other men, it is in order that he may give

the world an example of the highest probity. I wish to
be worthy of the mission I have received. As soon as the
difficulties between the Grand Seignior are ended, bring my
fleet and my army back at once."

He therefore unhesitatingly expressed his confidence in
the good faith of Russia, and was justified by the result.
Early in July, her troops and fleet departed. " They now
know the way to Constantinople," he remarks, "and the
Turks have become used to seeing them here. The
opportunity was admirably used ; the language of the Czar
is noble and worthy of him. But Constantinople will not
fly away."

A few days later, Lamartine met at dinner the Prince
Royal of Bavaria, whom he describes as extremely cultivated, delighting in good conversation, and himself an
admirable talker. He had been staying with his brother,
King Otho, and consulted Lamartine as to the future
capital of Greece. The latter pleaded eagerly for Athens.
"Greece has risen from the dead. The form she assumes
must be that in which she is known to men. Her individuality must be unchanged. But for Athens, she would
be but a scantily peopled wilderness."

By this time they had reached the end of July. Even
at their seaside villa, the heat was becoming oppressive.
Having decided to return to France overland, Lamartine
arranged with a carriage owner in Stamboul to provide
five *arabas*, each drawn by six horses, to take him, his wife,
and M. de Capmas, with their servants, in twenty-five days'
march, to Belgrade. To these were added a train of mules
to carry beds, cooking utensils, and such luggage as was

needed on the journey, and six riding horses, in case the roads proved too hard of transit. They started late in July, at two a.m., from a trysting-place in the suburb of Eyoub, to avoid the confusion of passing through the streets of Constantinople.

The first stages of the journey were pleasant enough. Lamartine, having got letters from the Grand Vizier and other powerful personages, was able to send forward each day his interpreter and two Tartar horsemen to prepare rooms, generally in the house of some Greek or Armenian merchant ; their food was procured and prepared by their own cooks. At Philippopolis, a young Greek, M. Mauridis, insisted on their coming to his house as guests, and remaining for some days. Two days after this welcome rest, they came to Tatar Bazir, where a son of the Grand Vizier, who was governor, placed at their disposal a charming country house just outside the town.

After leaving Tatar, the aspect of the country changed ; the roads became so bad that it was only on men's shoulders the carriages could be got over difficult places, and the nightly bivouac was generally in some miserable village. At one of these Lamartine sickened with fever, and lay for twenty days between life and death on the floor of a mud-walled cabin. He ascribes his recovery to his wife's promptitude in sending men at once to search the swamps of the whole country side for leeches. After much trouble they were procured, and gave him immediate relief. Still, he had little hope or desire to live, and entrusted M. de Capmas with his last wishes, telling him the exact spot where he wished to be buried, under a spreading tree he had noticed by the roadside.

Nothing could exceed the desolation and helplessness of his devoted nurses, M. de Capmas and Madame de Lamartine. They knew not where to turn for help, when on the sixth day, their late host, M. Mauridi, rode up, bringing with him an excellent doctor, and every comfort the most thoughtful kindness could suggest. He had heard casually that a Frankish traveller was fever-stricken at Yenisiki, and guessing at once it must be Lamartine, started that night at ten o'clock, and rode without interruption night and day to bring relief. His kindness was itself a restorative, the danger gradually diminished, and by the end of a fortnight the invalid had sufficiently recovered to resume the journey.

The inhabitants of Yenisiki were Bulgarians. Though poor and half civilized, they had given many proofs of kindness and sympathy. The remainder of the route lay across Servia. Travelling by short stages and with frequent halts, Lamartine had opportunities of becoming acquainted with the Christian populations of northern Turkey, and, notwithstanding his predilections for the Ottomans, it was to these subject races he trusted for the future regeneration of European Turkey. The Bulgarians he seems personally to have liked the best, but their gentleness and simplicity, which he attributes to their partial enfranchisement, made him, perhaps, underrate their tenacity and martial spirit as compared with their neighbours, the Servians, whom he looked on as the nucleus of a great Slav Empire, to be established at no very distant date. To accept an invitation from Prince Milosch to spend some weeks with him at Belgrade was an attraction, but the health of M. de Capmas was causing some anxiety, and it was thought better, on reaching the Danube, to proceed at once by boat to Vienna. Some weeks later, Lamartine, leaving his wife with friends at Geneva, went on alone to Marseilles, and brought his daughter's remains thence to St. Point.

CHAPTER VI.

1833–1836.

IN September, Lamartine and his wife returned to their desolate home, where, in mourning and sadness, they passed the autumn. Fortunately, Lamartine's position as deputy obliged him to be in Paris during the winter, and, painful as was the change, both husband and wife benefited by it. From the moment Lamartine took his seat he concentrated his thoughts and energies on acquiring a ready and facile elocution, not at all underrating the difficulties of the task, which he calculated would take three or four years, during which he was prepared to endure failure with equanimity. "Even ridicule, harder to bear than the thrust of a dagger," should not deter him. Never in his life, he writes, did he work so hard. His first speech was on January 4, 1834. Four days later he spoke again, and found his audience tolerably attentive. By the end of the month he tried his hand at improvisation. Then he went down to Burgundy, and at the Conseil-General of the department spoke at every opportunity, and on every subject. His success surprised him, as he admits with amusing *naïveté:* "I am delighted to find I am master of my instrument ; the most spontaneous improvisation. the

clearest, the most crushing reply, are equally easy to me."
"I have spoken nine times in seven successive debates,"
he wrote in 1836, "and each time the Chamber has been
silent, attentive, sometimes even enthusiastic. . . . I have
reduced lawyers, peers, and deputies to mute astonishment.
It amuses me extremely. I feel like a schoolboy who has
been a long time studying a new language and suddenly
finds he knows it."

In a speech delivered on July 3, 1839, when a vote of
supply was asked for the augmentation of the French fleet
in the Mediterranean, Lamartine seems to have produced
a great impression. Royer Collard, in a somewhat theatrical
apostrophe, told him he was the most eloquent orator of
the nation, and prophesied still greater triumphs. "Your
poetic past has been glorious ; I venture to predict your
political future will be greater still." And all through the
following years his reputation rose, till at last, if we may
believe his bitterest enemies, the time came when one
phrase from Lamartine's lips would have sufficed to uphold
a throne and reinstate a dynasty.

But this is to anticipate very considerably. In 1834,
though taking his Parliamentary career seriously, Lamartine
speaks of it as merely an interlude, which is to last three
or four years at most, after which he proposed devoting
himself to forwarding by his pen the development of
notions and theories already fermenting in his brain.
There is a project of a political *Review* to be started in
company with Ballanche, Pagès, Lamennais, and others
but this was put an end to by the publication of Lamennais' "Paroles d'un croyant," from which Lamartine tried
in vain to dissuade him.

Meanwhile, there hangs over the house the shadow of a great sorrow, which kind friends do all they can to soften. Madame de Lamartine, still suffering in health, was quietly taking up the threads of her former daily occupations· "My wife," writes Lamartine, "employs herself in her household duties, in visiting the poor, and writing letters. She is the better for it, but very little. As for me, I rise early, thus gaining a few quiet hours for study, prayer, and sorrow. Towards noon, I ride for a couple of hours ; at three I go to the Chamber till five or six, and in the evenings our friends, knowing they will find us at home, never leave us quite to ourselves."

In the autumn of 1835 the Lamartines settled themselves in No. 82, Rue de l'Université, which was their town residence for many succeeding years. In those days, for the modest rent of six thousand francs, it was possible to get what is described as "une installation de grand seigneur"—a long suite of rooms on the first floor, looking on the one side across a spacious courtyard, opening on the other into one of the large shady gardens which even now are found here and there among the secluded streets of the Faubourg St. Germain. The flat, by an arrangement not usual in French houses, had its separate staircase, and was entirely cut off from the rest of the house, securing, much to the satisfaction of Madame de Lamartine, something of the privacy of an English home. On the left of the ante-chamber was a large dining-room ; then came the *salon*, to which Turkish hangings gave an oriental character uncommon in those days. Beyond the *salon* was Madame de Lamartine's own sitting-room. The rooms specially allotted to the master of the house were laid out after

much the same fashion.   To the right of the ante-chamber
was a library; beyond, a tiny study, in which, at early
dawn, or in winter by lamplight, Lamartine worked assiduously.   Here he received his intimate friends.   One
of the special features of the house was that, unless on
exceptionally fine days, clear, bright fires burnt continuously
in all the rooms—a luxury rather unusual in thrifty Parisian
households.

   Still mourning the loss of their daughter, the Lamartines saw little company save old and dear friends.
By his family connections, and by the majority of his
personal friendships, Lamartine belonged socially to the
Faubourg in which he had pitched his tent; politically his
position was still, and from choice, undefined.   By his resignation, on Louis Philippe's accession, of the post of Minister
at Athens, and his withdrawal from the career of diplomacy,
he had proved his loyal attachment to the elder branch of
the Bourbons; on the other hand, his refusal in 1830 to
endorse the policy of Prince Polignac, and still more the
independent tone of his first speeches, showed he had
separated himself from the hot-headed fanatics who now
claimed to represent the Legitimist cause.   Besides,
Royalist though he was, Lamartine had been cradled, so
to speak, in the very trough of the revolutionary wave,
and there had passed into his spirit something of that
weird and thrilling epoch, inclining him to look on great
social cataclysms as inevitable crises of civilization, and
to put some rather Utopian theories as to the progress of
humanity, the redressing of inequalities and restrictions,
the development of civil and religious liberty, before any
interests of dynasty or creed.   This tendency was very

manifest in a debate on the " Law of Association," in which
Lamartine, while strenuously pleading for the utmost
possible protection of individual liberty, supported the
Government in their endeavours to uphold order and
strengthen authority.   This line of conduct being directly
opposed to that followed by the Legitimist members, he
was violently denounced in the lower class of their
newspapers.   But the leaders of the party, anxious not to
lose so valuable an ally, were more moderate; the *Gazette*
de France, edited by Lamartine's personal friend, the Abbé
de Genoude, offered him its columns wherein to refute his
assailants; and in December, 1834, he was formally
invited to join a conference held at the house of a M.
Hennequin, in which the line of the party during the
winter session was to be discussed.   But this was already
a foregone conclusion, it being well known that the policy
resolved on was that of determined and continued opposition to every act and measure of the Government, and to
all the other parties in the Chamber except the extreme
Radicals, or " Republican Left."   To a scheme of conduct
so unpatriotic, so demoralizing, and, as the event proved,
so entirely mistaken, Lamartine absolutely refused his
adhesion.   He put forth all his powers of argument and
of language to show how fatally shortsighted such tactics
were.   " I made them feel," he writes to Virieu, " the
absurdity of political congregationalism at a time when,
entering the new Chamber, as they now are, perfectly free
from tie or fetter, they might as individuals join the most
conscientious and patriotic sections ; if they persisted in
this latter course they would one day find themselves very
strong.   They admitted I was right, but respect of persons

and the clamour of their own newspapers are forces they
have not courage to resist."

A few days later he tells the same correspondent how,
when dining with Prince Talleyrand, the sincerity of his
professions of independence was put to a severer test.
Towards the end of the evening, his host, with a solemnity
of manner which rather amused Lamartine, drew him aside
to a sofa at the furthest end of the room, and cere-
moniously congratulated him on his admirable entry into
les affaires, an expression which generally implies official
employment.

"You are laughing at me, Prince," replied Lamartine.
" I have nothing to do with *les affaires*. I am altogether
an outsider."

" 'Do not be falsely modest. You have made a better
start in public life than any man since 1830. You have
shown more depth, more intelligence, more initiative than
any one.' And thereupon," continues Lamartine, "he went
on for nearly an hour, unrolling before me the plan of
campaign I ought to follow, exactly as I had arranged in
my own mind. What do you think of that for a man of
eighty-two ? "

One gathers from this anecdote some insight into the
secret of Talleyrand's success as a diplomatist, but in this
instance, beyond charming his auditor, no ulterior gain was
achieved. Lamartine, in spite of all blandishments, kept
steadily to the line of conduct he had laid out for a period
much longer than the residue of Talleyrand's life, and when
at last he passed beyond, it was from causes and convictions
neither he nor any one else could in those early days have
anticipated.

M

When, in August, 1834, the new Parliament met for the first time, the result of the election was seen to be extremely favourable to Government. The Republicans had been almost everywhere defeated ; seventy members of their party in the last Chamber had now lost their seats ; twelve others had retired from the contest. Consequently the *juste-milieu*, as the supporters of the Ministry were called, mustered no less than 320 votes out of 460 ; the irreconcilable Opposition, counting both Royalists and Republicans, amounted only to 90, while the intermediate party, among whom Lamartine was included, was reckoned at 50.

The Legitimists, though only 15 in number, had considerable influence, owing partly to their historic past and to the powerful interests they represented, partly to the eloquence of their leader, Berryer. Tall, and of commanding presence, singularly graceful and dignified in gesture, however displeasing the matter of his speeches might be to the majority of his hearers, the very first tones of his perfectly modulated voice never failed to arrest attention. His style was pure and correct ; he treated his subject habitually from a lofty moral standpoint, seldom forgetting the respect due to himself and to his audience ; but when occasion required, he was scathing in his denunciations, unsurpassed in the swiftness of his crushing retort. While adhering with rare fidelity to the cause he had espoused, he always kept a certain independence of attitude. His personal friends were of all camps ; and at the bar, where his greatest triumphs were won, he was the defender, without distinction of creed or party, of all who were unfortunate, friendless, or oppressed. The only fault his bitterest foes could fasten on Berryer was, that, while holding himself aloof from all unworthy tactics, he did not attempt to exact similar forbearance from the rank and file of his party. Probably if he had tried to do so he would have failed.

The extreme Left, likewise not very numerous in the Chamber, had as leaders Garnier-Pagès and Armand-Carrel, men of character and intellect. Garnier-Pagès especially was as remarkable for his habitual urbanity and charm of manner as for his unflinching resolution on all critical occasions; both perhaps most fortunate in that death cut them off before the theories they advocated with eloquent enthusiasm came to be put in practice, and the spirits rashly evoked became masters instead of servants. But the strength of this party lay not so much in its leaders as in the stern, unbending phalanx of Republicans outside the Chamber, fired with the bitterest hatred for those who had, as they conceived, filched from them the fruits of the "three glorious days." Subdued for the moment by the failure of the April insurrections, they now began to apply themselves the more earnestly to undermine the existing social order with a network of secret societies.

The supporters of the Ministry filled the centre benches, forming a majority far too large to allow the opposition any hope of outvoting it, but, from its very numbers, unwieldy and liable to break up at any moment into hostile factions. The Prime Minister, Marshal Soult, had been brought into office by the Conservative reaction which followed the suppression of the insurrection of 1833, and for several months carried on the Government success-fully, though with a somewhat high hand. But the debate opening the session of 1834 showed that he had enemies in his household, and, on being outvoted in Council on the question of replacing the military governor of Algeria by a civilian, Marshal Soult resigned.

His successor, Marshal Gérard, was personally popular, and became still more so by at once pledging himself to reductions in expenditure, always opposed by Soult, and now loudly called for throughout the country. But he allowed himself to be led by the flatteries of the group called the Third Party, of which M. Dupin was the leader, into a democratic line of policy to which the other ministers were opposed, and which he had not sufficient personal weight to carry out single-handed, so that by the end of three months he could save his dignity only by resigning. The King then sent for Count Molé, who endeavoured to form a cabinet, but failed, owing to the intrigues of the Third Party, and there was for some weeks an interregnum.

The remaining members of the Ministry now resolved to foil their enemies by leaving them to bear the burden of the day. Accordingly they resigned in a body, and M. Dupin was summoned to the Tuileries. He prudently abstained from taking office himself, but selected among his friends a Ministerial list which, when published in the *Moniteur*, was received with incredulity, followed by peals of laughter. The unfortunate ministers, lacking courage to face the storm of ridicule before them, resigned at the end of three days, which the Parisian wits, parodying the famous " Journée des Dupes " of Mazarin's time, called " Les Journées des Dupins." To avoid a deadlock in public business, an arrangement was made by which the former Cabinet resumed their places, with Marshal Mortier as President of the Council, instead of Marshal Gérard. But Mortier, a brave, loyal soldier, had neither experience in the conduct of affairs nor the faculty of public speaking, and his incapacity for the post soon became, as he was himself the first to acknowledge, painfully manifest.

It was felt that after such a series of misadventures, no fresh combination should be tried until a premier had been found with character and position sufficiently commanding to restore the respect Ministerial Government had almost forfeited, and all eyes turned to the head of an historic house in which great talents have been for centuries as hereditary as great possessions. Equally attached to the Throne and to the Charter, the Duc de Broglie had dreaded and disliked the Revolution of July, but, once it was accomplished, he had loyally done his best to uphold the dignity and authority of the Crown, and, though personally averse to public life, could always be relied upon at those times "when no wise man will seek office, and no honourable man refuse it." With him as President of the Council, and MM. Guizot and Thiers holding the portfolios of foreign affairs and of public instruction, the "Ministry of October, 1832," returned to office.

Lamartine, though not personally affected by these Ministerial complications, watched them with interest. "Although," he writes to M. de Bienassis, "I try to keep philosophically aloof from the political movements of the hour, I am drawn into them against my will. Watch me from afar, and if you will not come down into the plain, at least pray for me on the mountain-top. But in these days every one ought to be among the combatants."

In the debate of January, 1835, on the question of

amnesty, which Lamartine considered desirable both on political and on moral grounds, he was for the first time in decided opposition to the Government, and had with M. Guizot a somewhat sharp altercation. A fortnight later, in a discussion on the Polish question, he approved their policy, and would have spoken on their side, but was prevented by his Legitimist friends, "who," he writes, "by tactics well known in the Chamber, but impossible to explain to outsiders," kept him out of the rostrum, notwithstanding his repeated efforts, during the six hours the debate lasted.

But a little later an opportunity came. In March, 1834, the Duc de Broglie had resigned office on account of a hostile vote of the Chambers, refusing him a credit of twenty-five million francs admittedly due by France to the United States for losses sustained by American subjects in consequence of the Milan decrees of Napoleon. The question had been postponed for the time, but in April, 1835, a direct and haughty interpellation from President Jackson revived it with urgency. An angry debate ensued, in which the Opposition, posing as champions of national pride and patriotism, were for refusing payment. Lamartine, who had on the previous occasion voted in the minority upholding the Duc de Broglie's policy, now, in an eloquent and exhaustive speech, argued that to fulfil strictly and to the letter the obligations incurred was the really patriotic course, and the only one open to a sensitive and honourable people. "The true dignity of nations lies in acting justly." With remarkable simplicity and clearness of language he went through the history of the question, proved that the justice of the American claim had never

been disputed ; pointed out the misery which provoking
a war, or even leaving the question undecided would bring
on the industrious populations of the west coast, "to whom,
as they had proved a thousand times by their readiness to
shed their blood for their country, the honour of France
was as dear as to any deputy in the Chamber, but who
had a right to ask that the fruit of their labours, the bread
of their families, should not be sacrificed to the unreal
sensitiveness of political animosities." The vote, on which
the Duc de Broglie had a second time staked the duration
of his Ministry, was passed by the Chamber.

A few weeks later, the diabolical attempt of Fieschi to
destroy the Throne and its supporters by a wholesale
massacre brought about a strong reaction. For the first
time since 1830, Legitimists and Republicans passed together through the portals of the Tuileries, vying in eagerness to congratulate the Sovereign on his escape, and show
their abhorrence of the crime. The necessity of strengthening the hands of the Executive, and of repressing the
scurrilous publications which had so long with impunity
encouraged crime of all kinds, was denied by none. Three
measures, intended to meet the evil, were brought forward
by the Ministry, and submitted to the Chamber, which, not
content with passing them by a large majority, added very
considerably to their stringency. Of these enactments two
were reasonable enough. The first introduced various
alterations and abbreviations in the form of procedure
against press offences ; the second authorized juries to
convict by a majority of eight or seven, and enjoined
secrecy as to the votes given. But the third clause was
extremely drastic ; by it an offence against the person

of the Sovereign or the monarchical principle was to be
summarily punished by heavy fines ; no engraving, emblem,
or drawing was to be exposed for sale without the sanction
of the censors ; the caution money to be found by journalists
was increased to the amount of £4000 in cash.

However, such was the indignation Fieschi's crime had
excited throughout the country, that, severe as were these
enactments, but few voices were raised in opposition. The
most forcible was that of Lamartine, who, in words which
recall a famous passage in English literature, protested at
once against those who would give to licence the sacred
name of liberty, and against those others who would stifle
all expression of thought. "If," he went on to say, " I
thought freedom of the press an insuperable obstacle to
the exercise of authority, I should be the first to say,
'Muzzle the press;' but it is not so. With a free press,
government may be difficult ; without it, 'tis impossible.
And have you not, in the awful crime which has been
committed, better security against future outrage or law-
lessness than any laws of repression, however severe, could
give you? Has it not already borne fruit? From the
office of Deputy to that of the humblest councillor, do
we not see the popular voice unanimous in electing none
but men of property and of good repute? Do we not
see the churches, so lately desecrated and pillaged, now
filled with worshippers, who recognize but one origin
for religion and for monarchy? Do we not see Royalty,
so recently insulted and attacked, now honoured and
applauded ? The corpses strewn about your streets, the
funeral procession followed by a mourning people,—these
solemn lessons of an overruling Providence, appealing in

living language to the emotions of the multitude, have
had effects more powerful and more lasting than your laws
of a day will ever produce."

But so strong was the feeling that the evils devastating
society were mainly due to the action of the press, that
the coercive laws, known as the "laws of September," were
passed by enormous majorities, after which the Chambers
were prorogued.

The session of 1836 opened under favourable auspices ;
the King was able to make the prosperity of the country
the principal theme of his speech. But there were tokens
that the Ministry did not feel their position one of absolute
security. M. de Broglie, in a recent speech, had said,
" Dangers are passing away, and with dangers the remembrance of them, for we live in times when impressions are
very evanescent. As order is being gradually restored,
the exalted posts we occupy become more and more the
goal of honourable ambition ; in quiet times changes of
administration are no longer looked upon as dangerous to
public safety. Then, men wear out quickly in office. Do
you want to know the result of our work? It will be to
have prepared, perhaps to have hastened, the advent of our
successors. Be it so ; we joyfully accept the omen."

But the hour for the actual accomplishment of this
prediction came somewhat unexpectedly. On the 15th of
January, M. Humann, minister of finance, in bringing
forward the Budget, ventured, without consulting his
colleagues, to suggest that the moment was favourable for
the reduction of the interest on the National Debt. This
caused the utmost embarrassment to the Ministry ; the
question, first brought forward, in 1824, by M. de Villele,

was always a crucial one for French administrations. It would have been wiser not to make it a Cabinet question ; but M. de Broglie, with characteristic indifference to results, stood up at once, and stated plainly that the Government had no present intention of bringing forward such a measure ; as to what they might do or not do at any future period, he refused to pledge himself. Whereupon M. Humann, who had perhaps expected to force his colleagues' hands (though Guizot acquits him of any such treachery) resigned.   But angry passions had been roused, many interests affected, and the Finance Committee of the Chamber passed a resolution in favour of conversion, which would certainly have alleviated the ratepayers, but at the expense of the stockholders.

Lamartine, who felt very strongly on the question, made two effective speeches in the course of the debate which ensued.   He dwelt forcibly on the injustice of applying such a measure to existing debtors, the rate of interest having been settled partly as a compensation to the original holders of Government stock, who, in 1797, agreed to a reduction of two-thirds of the value of their stock, with the express understanding that the compromise was to be final ; then on its cruelty, the holders of stock being chiefly old men, widows, and orphans, who in troublous times invested their little all in Government securities ; and, lastly, on the improvidence, not to say dishonour, of taking advantage of a perhaps transient gleam of prosperity to shake the foundations of national credit. He, however, allowed that in all future loans the State should reserve the power of paying off its creditors at par.

The result of the debate was that the Ministry found

themselves in a minority of two, and resigned. It was a matter of universal surprise that a question which cropped up as if by chance should have provoked such a cata-. strophe ; as if a minute grain of sand had stopped a machine which to all appearance was working smoothly. There had been, however, hostile influences at work, the most powerful being that of M. de Talleyrand, who was irritated by the Duc de Broglie's adherence to the English alliance, for which he was anxious to substitute that of Russia. Sharp criticisms, in the guise of oracles issuing from the Hôtel St. Florentin, were circulated in political coteries. Such as "M. de Broglie's vocation is not the Foreign Office," or, "I do not know how it is, but M. de Broglie has contrived to make himself hated equally and simultaneously at St. Petersburgh, London, and Vienna." As to London, the statement was quite without foundation, but none the less effective.

The immediate result of the Ministerial defeat was to break up the coalition of M. de Broglie, Thiers, and Guizot, which, during the six years it had lasted, though resting on a somewhat insecure basis, had been efficient and fruitful for good. The Duc de Broglie, though he continued to the end of his life to support all causes which seemed to him just ones, held himself henceforth aloof from all combinations of party. With M. Guizot it was different. His inclinations and his ambition made him at once accept the position of leader of the Conservatives, or Right Centre ; while M. Thiers' course remained for the moment undecided.

The King found difficulty in forming a fresh Cabinet. Marshal Gérard, Count Molé, M. Dupin, were successively applied to in vain. Meanwhile, Talleyrand, putting forth

all his influence in behalf of M. Thiers, was gradually
gaining for him the support of the foreign ministers of the
other continental powers, by pointing out how opposed
Thiers had always been to the Anglo-French alliance
favoured by the Duc de Broglie. To those who objected
to the obscure antecedents of his *protégé*, he had the reply
ready, " M. Thiers n'est pas parvenu, il est arrivé." Whether
he was cognizant or not of these manœuvres, M. Thiers'
own conduct was irreproachable. To all overtures he
opposed a firm refusal to replace his former colleagues,
save with their full consent. This the King undertook to
procure from M. de Broglie, who gave it at once.

Lamartine had been deeply interested and concerned
throughout the whole crisis. The side he had espoused as
to the " question des rentes " was the unpopular one ; and
as his speeches, reprinted in the form of a pamphlet, had
attracted considerable notice and influenced several votes,
he was severely censured in the papers. For this he cared
little, but he regretted the accession to power of M. Thiers,
whom he admired as a writer, yet disliked and distrusted
as a politician. However, the beginnings of the new
Ministry were better than had been anticipated. As their
predecessors had been overthrown on the "question des
rentes," it was expected they would at once bring in a
measure in harmony with the view so emphatically expressed by the Chamber ; but, to the general surprise, the
matter was suffered to drop, with the formality of adjourn-
ing it to the next session.

Thiers, at that time, was in many ways rather a puzzle
to his contemporaries. From the early days of the July
monarchy he had been manifestly eager to take a pro-

minent part in politics ; it was only a question to which
side he would definitively give the benefit of his brilliant
talents. At first his friendship with such men as Odillon-
Barrot, Armand-Carrel, and Lafitte seemed to point to a
union with the Republicans ; but, in the debate on the
hereditary peerage, he unexpectedly gave the Conservatives
his warm support, thus taking his place in the ranks
of the "politique de résistance," to which, in 1836, he
still apparently continued to belong. During the first
few months of his tenure of power, he steered with much
skill and success. By the mere force of his oratory he
allayed a storm provoked by a considerable excess in
the estimates, and got a vote for a large sum of secret-
service money passed, contrary to all expectations, by a
majority of two hundred, the extreme Left supporting him
in a body ; while, by paying off the last instalment of the
United States claim, and by joining Russia and England
in guaranteeing a Greek loan, he gained favour abroad.
But these successes had the unfortunate effect of making
him too confident. Always disposed to the aggressive line
of policy known as *Chauvinism*, M. Thiers became fired
by the desire of effecting a French intervention in Spain.
To this Louis Philippe was strongly opposed, and a
Ministerial crisis ensued, which resulted in the resignation
of M. Thiers and his Cabinet, and the appointment, in
September, 1836, of a new Ministry under the leadership
of Count Molé, who was supported by M. Guizot and the
doctrinaires.

From the date of the fall of the Broglie Ministry, to the
end of the session of 1836, Lamartine did not take much
part in purely political debates, but he spoke frequently on

other topics. On the question of the revenue derived from licensing gambling tables, he had a sharp encounter with the President of the Council (M. Thiers), who endeavoured to stop any discussion of the subject. Lamartine put forward, though without producing any result beyond momentary applause, the trite argument that no fiscal advantage could counterbalance the moral injury of giving legal sanction to a vice which was ruining thousands. " The most avaricious of the Roman emperors," he concluded, " said indeed that gold, no matter whence it came, was sweet to his nostrils. A free and a noble people is more scrupulous. To the money thus acquired clings the evil odour of corruption and misery. To this Chamber, to the whole French nation, it is therefore repugnant."

Again, on the question of free trade, the theories Lamartine propounded, though startling to the majority of his hearers, were those which have since found universal acceptance. In the name of five millions of vine cultivators, he pleaded for the removal of prohibitive laws which hindered France from being the richest of commercial nations ; in the name of thirty-three millions of bread-consumers, for the repeal of enactments protecting the interests of three millions of bread-producers. " Light duties and customs," he allowed, " are, considered as items of the national revenue, legitimate enough ; but when they amount to commercial restrictions, to hateful mono-polies, tending to keep up between the industrial and agricultural classes of various nations a state of hatred, envy, and ill-will, they work infinite mischief, and tend more than anything else to bring about the wholesale murder which is dignified by the name of war. Sweep away all arbitrary lines of demarcation, let nations mingle freely for their common advantage, let the surplus produce of one country be the daily food of another, 'and you diminish enormously the chances, the probabilities, the possibilities of war. What, for example, would be the incentive to aggression or to conquest between France, Belgium, and Germany, if there were no customs? There would be community of national life, free exchange, uniform commercial legislation. What could tempt any one of these nations to attack the other, knowing that by so doing it would injure itself, lose a market for its goods, restrict the sphere of its own activity? It is evident nations would quickly learn to look upon one another as members of one universal Fatherland, united under various flags and sovereignties.

After this somewhat bold flight of prophecy, Lamartine had to defend himself against an accusation of unpatriotic conduct, brought against him by a M. Jaubert, inasmuch as he had assisted an English apostle of free trade, Mr. Bowring, to obtain information as to the principal manufacturing and agricultural industries of France,—" conduct," it was said, "the more reprehensible because it was well known that any Frenchman, venturing on such a mission into cruel and perfidious Albion, would immediately have been stoned." To which Lamartine replied that the mission of Mr. Bowring was fully as much in the interest of France as in that of England ; and that, to allay the susceptibilities of the honourable member, he need only recall the generous hospitality and total absence of jealousy with which the illustrious and unfortunate Jacquemont had been permitted by English officials to explore India.

Again, when, a few weeks later, in a discussion on the
Budget of Foreign Affairs, the English alliance was violently
attacked, Lamartine repudiated the obsolete prejudices of
past generations, and showed that the friendship of England was to France, not merely an advantage, but almost
a necessity. "Sometimes," he writes at this time, "I bring
before the House opinions which are called advanced, ideal,
even revolutionary, and yet which I believe to be eminently
Conservative. For I hold that nothing is so revolutionary
as an abuse that is allowed to endure; nothing so subversive
as an iniquity left unpunished"—a phrase which shows
how closely he followed the best traditions of English
eloquence.

CHAPTER VII

1836–1840.

WITH winters and springs absorbed in the social and political turmoil of Paris, alternated summers and autumns whiled away more leisurely on the pleasant Burgundian uplands. The principal seat of the Lamartine family was Monceau, which Lamartine had, in 1827, inherited from his uncle. It was a mansion of some pretensions, approached from the high-road by a long avenue of walnut-trees, at the entrance of which, at Madame de Lamartine's suggestion, a lodge and gate in *le style anglais* had been built. The stately *façade* of the dwelling-house, flanked at the east end by a low pavilion, had been begun in the reign of the Grand Monarque, but was decorated in the lighter and more frivolous style which takes its name from his successor. Within, all was brightness and comfort ; the long suite of reception rooms opened on a gallery fitted up in semi-oriental style, which was the favourite resort of the family. With the exception of a wood of magnificent chestnut-trees at the back of the house, the surrounding ground was mostly laid out in vineyards, and wanting in interest ; but from the terraced front the eye ranges across the rich valley of the Sâone, over the low vine-clad hills

N

of Beaujolais, to where can be seen, on clear days, the
chain of the Savoy Alps, crowned by the snowy peak of
Mont Blanc. When the Lamartines were residing at
Monceau, the guest-chambers were seldom empty. They
both liked to see around them bright young faces, and
these the numerous families of his sisters amply supplied.
There went also innumerable cousins of Madame de
Lamartine's, both English and Irish ; bright-eyed, lively
girls, described as being all fearless riders, astonishing
their Burgundian companions by their originality and
independence. Among the other guests were some who
could almost be counted as members of the family circle—
M. de Champeaux, who for many years was Lamartine's
secretary ; M. and Madame Dargaud, the former a Burgundian settler in Paris, and author of a "History of Religious
Liberty" which made some stir in its day; his wife a charming woman and devoted helpmate, both sincerely attached
to Lamartine,—M. Dargaud would, it is said, had his life
been spared, have written Lamartine's biography, a work
for which he was eminently fitted ; M. A. Salamon, the
sculptor, whose wife, like her hostess, gave her time chiefly
to works of charity ; M. Louis Ronchaud, counted by
Lamartine among "the few elect souls who live only to be
consumed like incense before the sacred shrine of art ; "
Edgar Quinet, and his German wife, of whom Longfellow
wrote, " She is the most beautiful and interesting woman I
have ever met ; " the Abbé Cœur, a distinguished preacher,
in whose conversation Lamartine took particular pleasure.
Besides this inner circle of friends, whose visits were of
yearly recurrence, there were other frequent but more
erratic guests ; young men of talent, who, attracted at first

by Lamartine's genius, eagerly sought his society. Among these, MM. A. de Tocqueville, Beaumont, Carné, Courcelles, became ultimately the best known. Lamartine, whose most earnest wish it was to kindle in the rising generation a strong faith in social progress rather than in political reforms, took great pleasure in their society, and was tolerant of their failings. Some of his letters to them, showing the keenest interest in their welfare, are admirable. As years rolled on, the ever-widening circle of guests came to include almost every name of note in literature or in society—the Girardins, the La Granges, A. de Vigny, Laprade, the two Dumas, Liszt, Veuillot, George Sand, Victor Hugo, the Ecksteins, the D'Esgrignys, etc.

The most ceremonious receptions at Monceau were the gathering together of provincial notabilities during the sittings of the *Conseil général du département*, an institution which has some resemblance to our grand jury, and of which Lamartine was for many years president. Until the time when he became absorbed by politics, these meetings of the *Conseil général* were a great interest to Lamartine. He was personally much liked, and his oratorical gifts gave him exceptional influence, which he took every legitimate means of increasing. Among his diplomatic experiences he had learnt the importance of a well-kept table, and spared no trouble to secure it. On one occasion, when everything had passed off to his satisfaction, he was enthusiastic in his praise of a cook, whom he passed on to a friend as " Le roi des hommes, et fort bon cuisinier ; l'honnêteté, l'économie même. Faites qu'il sache le témoignage que je me plais à lui rendre." Frugal as he was, and almost a vegetarian, Lamartine had a French-

man's amiable weakness for sweets ; one of his letters, after
a serious dissertation on the politics of the day, ends with
the imperative request, " Send me ten pounds of chocolate
pastilles as quickly as possible." He was fond, too, of
talking about cookery, and had a recipe for the salting
of hams, to which he attached immense importance ; not
Dumas himself could have been more sententious on a
subject entirely out of his line. "I invented it myself,"
he used to say ; "it will outlive my greatest works. It is
exquisite, and contains six poisons, one of which was given
me by Lady Hester Stanhope ; another ingredient is that
of which Mithridates used to partake so freely—however, it
is now proved to be entirely harmless."

But the two summers following their return from the
East, as well as considerable portions of all succeeding
years, the Lamartines spent at St. Point, preferred by them
on account of the beauty of the surrounding country,
and for its many associations. During the thirty years
which had elapsed since the elder Madame de Lamartine,
somewhat alarmed by its decay and dilapidation, took
possession of it with her little brood, the château of
St. Point had undergone much transformation. Though
of no great size, it was now a comfortable, as well as
picturesque abode : the windows had been altered so as to
keep the wind out and let the sun into the tastefully
furnished rooms ; the latest improvement, a slender Gothic
clock tower, if a trifle too *flamboyant* in style, gave variety
to the outline ; the lichen-encrusted stone of the balustrades
was enlivened by the brilliant plumage of peacocks ; and
though there was no regular flower garden, masses of
flowering shrubs, cultivated chiefly for their fragrance,
brightened every available spot.

The routine of life at St. Point was simple enough. Lamartine invariably rose at five ; he did not, however, disturb his household, but, passing into his study, lit the fire, and made himself a cup of tea. Then, seated at the large black table, which was almost the only furniture of the room, he worked for hours, rapidly covering sheets of paper of unusual dimensions with the fine, clear writing which remained to the last unchanged. When the bell rang for the eleven o'clock *déjeuner*, he would proceed to complete his toilet, and come in towards the end of the meal, followed by the two or three dogs which were his constant companions. Fido, the eldest and most favoured, was a personage of importance in the household ; it was of him that Lamartine wrote lines among the most beautiful his race, beloved of poets, has ever inspired. Most of Lamartine's time at breakfast was taken up in feeding these humble friends, for he treated meals cavalierly, and a dish of vegetables, with a dessert of fruit, met all his requirements.

Then followed the task of visiting the horses, almost as great favourites as the dogs. The long range of stabling had seldom a stall empty ; but, except a white Arab named Saphir, well known in '48 in the streets of Paris, and a pair of English carriage horses, there were none of much value. But to their master's eye all were unrivalled ; any addition to his stud was to him an immense delight; and at once credited with all the perfections of Mahomet's mare.

After the stables had been passed in review, other outdoor occupations, more seriously engrossing, had their turn. On the owner of St. Point and Monceau devolved

the management of extensive vineyards, and the care and
skill required to produce the high-class Burgundian wines
are not trifling. All through the vintage, which began early
in September, Lamartine was on horseback from noon to
nightfall, going to and fro between Milly, Monceau, and
St. Point, taking his share of the labour, and sometimes
(but not often) rewarded by success. As he used to say,
" A vineyard is a *tapis vert*, presided over by two inexorable
croupiers, Sun and Rain, who distribute ruin more freely
than riches."

The evening meal was usually gay and sociable, visitors
from Mâcon and the neighbourhood dropping in. But,
save on very special occasions, Lamartine would take his
candle at the stroke of nine, and retire to his own room ;
Madame de Lamartine and her nieces lingering on for
another hour, after which the guests were left to solace
themselves with cigars, or, as one enthusiastic disciple
writes, " with the thought that under the same roof some
inspired verse was perhaps at that very moment flashing
into light."

M. Henri Lacretelle, in an article contributed in 1872
to *La Cloche*, then edited by an earnest admirer of Lamartine, Louis Ulbach, described his first visit to St. Point,
whither he was taken by his father soon after the Lamartines' return from the East. The elder Lacretelle was that
member of the Académie française who, in 1825, opposed
Lamartine's candidature so vehemently, but, afterwards
repenting his injustice, energetically supported him. He
was an influential member of the Liberal party at Mâcon,
and, not knowing that Lamartine was one of those
people, even now but rarely found in France, who do

not allow their politics to interfere with their friendships, had been rather surprised at receiving a warm invitation from the Légitimist owner of St. Point to visit him whenever he passed that way. However, he gladly availed himself of it, and, one pleasant afternoon in September, a ten-mile ride across the hills brought father and son to where St. Point, despite its sombre setting of sentinel mountains, lay bathed in the autumn sunshine.

They found Madame de Lamartine, still clad in deep mourning for her daughter Julie, but always gracious and hospitable, seated at a table formed of a single block of stone, and said to have been used for the same purpose by Abelard. Before her was a pile of newspapers, from which she was making selections for her husband's use. This lady, whose kindness and simple goodness impressed all who came in contact with her, had now been married some years, and had become "as much a Frenchwoman," writes M. de Lacretelle, "as was possible in one not so born." Her mastery of the language was perfect; she spelt better than her husband (the spelling of even the best-educated French people is sometimes curiously faulty), and was accustomed to correct his proofs. But Madame de Lamartine was quite free from literary pedantry. Her favourite occupations were painting, for which she had considerable talent, and works of charity, in which much of her time was spent. The only fault at which M. de Lacretelle even hints was too fervent piety. "She had thrown herself," he says, "with all the zeal of a neophyte into all the beliefs and practices of the faith she had espoused,"—in the eyes of a French Liberal, an almost unpardonable sin. But he allows—and from him the concession is immense—that her zeal was tempered with charity, and that she was still more attached to the spirit than to the letter of her creed. At a later period, when he recalled her bearing with unsubdued spirit the heaviest trials, unswerving in her love, faith, and devotion, he wrote, forgetting his shibboleths: " I think of her as a saint and a martyr."

After a few minutes' conversation with their hostess, they were joined by Lamartine, who brought with him some other guests, Aime Martin, a rather dull *littérateur*, the curé of a neighbouring village, and Edgar Quinet, who had just published his famous romance, "Ahasuerus." In this weird tale, the ocean, Mont Blanc, and the coloured glass windows of Cologne Cathedral all figure as actual personages ; but there was nothing uncanny in Quinet's conversation. He had brought the last news, political and social, with him from Paris, and had lately been spending some evenings, rather out of his usual element, in the *salon* of Madame Récamier, where Chateaubriand was persuaded to read aloud portions of his " Mémoires d'Outre-tombe," after which M. Quinet extracted from him some indiscreet revelations of the terrible dulness of the Court circle at Prague, where the Duc d'Angoulême was reigning under the name of Charles XI. This did not please Madame de Lamartine, an ardent Légitimiste, and when, later, the conversation turned on religious topics, and the elder M. de Lacretelle aired some very advanced opinions, M. Quinet, anxious to regain her good graces, unexpectedly took up the challenge, and, probably for the only time in his life, broke a lance as the champion of orthodoxy. After this, an apparently safe subject, the ruins of the neighbouring Abbey of Cluny were discussed. Here M. de Lacretelle, an enthusiastic antiquarian, was in his element, and, having every reason to think himself on perfectly safe ground, dilated eloquently on the marvels of that once-majestic centre of mediæval light and learning, winding up with a diatribe against the Vandalism which, in 1810, had destroyed what the Revolution left untouched. To his dismay, Madame de Lamartine suddenly looked excessively disconcerted, the curé, who sat opposite, plunged his face into his plate, and Lamartine, abruptly cutting M. de Lacretelle short, began a lively description of a visit he had once made to the Abbey of Monte Cassino in company with a Roman prince and two lovely daughters. The narrative, evidently improvised, lasted to the end of the meal.

When the guests began to disperse, M. de Lacretelle took an opportunity to draw his host aside, saying, " I see I was guilty of some terrible blunder, but have not the remotest conception in what it consisted."

" A thousand pardons, *mon cher confrère*," replied Lamartine, "but M. le Curé, your *vis-à-vis*, was one of the demolishers of Cluny."

How this could have been is a problem left unexplained by M. de Lacretelle ; but the anecdote shows how extremely difficult conversation must be among French people who happen to hold opposite opinions.

Sometimes, when the company consisted only of very intimate friends, the afternoon was spent at Milly. The first time M. Henri de Lacretelle was admitted to this privilege, it was arranged that Madame de Lamartine and the other ladies should drive thither, and be met by

Lamartine and M. de Lacretelle, who were to ride by a much shorter path across the hills. The young man, to whom the prospect of a *tête-à-tête* ride with Lamartine was delightful, was rather surprised at the moment of starting to see his host, who, on humanitarian grounds, abhorred shooting, take a gun, the explanation being that it was in case of meeting a mad dog. Fortunately, no such encounter interrupted the delightful flow of conversation in which old memories, present interests, and future projects all had their share. As they passed a somewhat secluded field, Lamartine observed, " I once fought a duel here."

M. de Lacretelle ventured to ask with whom.

Lamartine replied, " With a Pole."

Feeling it might be indiscreet to question further, Lacretelle casually asked, " Have you fought many duels ? "

" Yes ; no one who drew breath in the eighteenth century could escape the infection ; especially in the early years of this, when one could hardly sit down in a *café* without being challenged by some of Napoleon's officers on half-pay. The wisest plan was to go out, and say nothing about it. My duel with Pepe was the only one I was concerned in which had any notoriety. I was wrong in bringing a general indictment against a nation. The nation was avenged by a brave man, who put three inches of steel into me. Afterwards we became fast friends. But I always liked fencing, sword play, and military matters generally. I think if I had been a soldier I should have made my mark. I have often felt a longing to influence large masses of men, and feel that I have missed my vocation."

Lacretelle, who, besides not having been born in the

eighteenth century, had imbibed the neo-humanitarian
ideas of the nineteenth, was somewhat scandalized, and
did not know how to answer. As they drew near Milly,
the many beautiful lines inspired by the poet's birthplace
rushed in on his mind. He felt " as if approaching a
sanctuary, upheld, like that of Loretto, by the hands of
angels." This ecstatic state was followed by a terrible
reaction, when he saw before him the humble, unpretending
abode, *mesquin* in its surroundings, without even the life
and animation of a farmhouse; for, since the death of
Lamartine's mother, Milly had remained untenanted and
dismantled. Even the little *salon*, in which the ladies of
the party, who had arrived before them, sat shivering,
looked commonplace and dreary.

But when Lamartine entered all was changed. He
took his guests from room to room, recalling the traditions,
the memories, the anecdotes attached to each. At the
touch of the magician's wand, the vanished past came back ;
they saw the imposing figure of Lamartine's father, seated
in his favourite chair, getting his gun ready for use; his
mother, loving and beautiful as of old, filled the room with
her gracious presence ; his sisters, in their girlish loveliness,
each with her triumphs, her trials, her innocent romance,
swept smiling by. Milly, glorified, transfigured, justified
all the love, all the poetry lavished on it. But to Lamartine
the best moment of the day was when a very old man,
without going through the ceremony of touching his hat,
came up to him, and said, " Bonjour, Alphonse."

In the years following his return from the East,
Lamartine got through a great deal of literary work. His
first task was to complete, from notes made during the

journey, his "Voyage en Orient." Undertaken from practical motives, to repair the breach the journey had made in
his finances, the book gave him little satisfaction, save that
of knowing his publishers recouped themselves amply for
the £5000 they paid him in advance. It was, however,
translated into English and most other European languages,
and held its own for many years as a standard work on
the Holy Land.

With his next publication, "Jocelyn," the case was
reversed. The writing of it gave him immense pleasure.
For years he had meditated on the plan of a great epic
poem which was to illustrate each principal period of
history, from the dawn of Creation to the Day of Judgment,
and to bring its author immortality. Hitherto he had
produced only incomplete fragments; now he set seriously
to work, and in the years 1844–1845 wrote "Jocelyn,"
which is certainly the most important, and perhaps the
most beautiful of his poems. Into it he worked much of
his own inner life, the illusions, hopes, despairs, of his
youth ; the struggles, doubts, and forebodings of his manhood. It did not at first achieve the success of his earlier
poems. There were in it passages enthusiastic in their piety
which displeased freethinkers ; philosophical questioning
which puzzled the orthodox ; solutions of problems best
left unanswered. But before many years had elapsed,
every one with a taste for poetry could repeat hundreds of
lines out of "Jocelyn," and now its place among the
classics of French literature is uncontested.

The hero is an ecclesiastical student who, driven from
the seminary by the Revolution before he had completed his
studies, falls in love with Laurence, a young girl whose dying

father had left her in his charge, and is on the eve of
marrying her when the aged Bishop who had been his
teacher sends for him to the prison where he lies condemned to death, and imperiously requires Jocelyn to
receive Orders that he may be able to administer to him
the last rites of the Church. After a terrible struggle the
young man consents, takes the vows which cut him off
from all human ties, and, after fulfilling the task imposed
on him, goes forth broken-hearted to his lonely ministry.
Laurence, whom his desertion has driven to despair, he
never meets after their agonized parting till he is summoned
by an aged man to her death-bed, assures her of the pardon
of heaven, and receives hers.

The story is cumbrous and far-fetched, and Lamartine
lacked the dramatic power needed to give it the semblance
of probability. The personages, though drawn gracefully,
are too vague in outline ; but the poem abounds in striking
thoughts and noble sentiments, and many of the descriptions are admirable,—those specially of the communion of
the proscribed priest, and of the presbytery of Valneige are
so frequently cited as to have become classic pieces in
French literature. But modern readers will probably take
more pleasure in the pictures of rural life. Lamartine's
talent as a painter of landscape is unquestioned, and he is
considered by many to have been the founder of the
modern French descriptive school. Unlike his successors, he
spiritualizes all he touches ; the trees and fields and woods
are very beautiful in his eyes : he has the artist's perception
of detail, and the poet's phrase to clothe it in ; but what he
values most is the Divine origin of which they bear the
trace, the tender human memories they enshrine.

> " Le vent, l'épine en fleurs, l'herbe verte ou flétrie,
> Le soc dans le sillon, l'onde dans la prairie
> Tout me parle une langue aux intimes accents."

Unfortunately, though " Jocelyn," perhaps more than any of Lamartine's poems, abounds in vivid and graceful pictures, it is not easy, from the author's incorrigible aversion to correcting or condensing his verse, to find many passages of sustained beauty. The description of the advent of spring in the Alpine solitudes, in the fourth canto, may be worth quoting :—

> " Il est des jours de luxe et de saison choisie
> Que sont comme les fleurs précoces de la vie,
> Tout bleus, tout nuancés d'éclatantes couleurs,
> Tout trempés de rosée et tout fragrans d'odeurs,
> Que d'un nuit d'orage on voit parfois éclore,
> Qu'on savoure un instant, qu'on respire une aurore.
>
>   *   *   *   *   *
>
> Tout ce que l'air touchait s'éveillait pour verdir,
> La feuille du matin, sous l'œil semblait grandir ;
> Comme s'il n'avait eu pour été qu'une aurore,
> Il hâtait tout du souffle, il pressait tout d'éclore,
> Et les herbes, les fleurs, les lianes des bois
> S'étendaient en tapis, s'arrondissaient en toits,
> S'entrelaçaient aux troncs, se suspendaient aux roches,
> Sortaient de terre en grappe, en dentelles, en cloches,
> Entravaient nos sentiers par des réseaux de fleurs,
> Et nos yeux éblouis dans des flots de couleurs !
> La sève débordant d'abondance et de force,
> Coulait en gommes d'or des fentes de l'écorce,
> Suspendait aux rameaux des pampres étrangers,
> Des filets de feuillage et des tissus légers,
> Où les merles siffleurs, les geais, les tourterelles,
> En fuyant sous la feuille, embarrassaient leurs ailes ;
>
>   *   *   *   *   *
>
> Tous ces dômes des bois, qui frémissaient aux vents,
> Ondoyaient comme un lac aux flots verts et mouvans ;
> Chaque fois que nos pieds tombaient dans la verdure
> Les herbes nous montaient jusques à la ceinture,
> Des flots d'air embaumés se répandaient sur nous,
> Des nuages ailés partaient de nos genoux,

> Tous semblaient se hâter d'épuiser à l'envie
> Leur coupe de bonheur et leur goutte de vie,
> Et l'air qu'ils animaient de leurs frémissemens
> N'était que mélodie et que bourdonnemens."

But perhaps the most pleasing pictures are to be found in the interlude of "Les Laboureurs," which Mr. Hamerton quotes in his "Sylvan Year" as one of the most perfect specimens of the idyl in modern literature. It is a very real description of a day of toil—not, however, real in the sense of realistic : there is no deepening of lines, no accentuation of impressions ; the incidents are portrayed simply as they are :—

> " Laissant souffler ses bœufs, le jeune homme s'appuie
> Debout, au tronc d'un chêne, et de sa main essuie
> La sueur du sentier sur son front mâle et doux,
> La femme et les enfans tout petits, à genoux
> Devant les bœufs privés baissant leur corne à terre,
> Leur cassent des rejets de frêne et de fougère
> Et jettent devant eux en verdoyans monceaux
> Les feuilles que leurs mains émondent des rameaux ;
> Ils ruminent en paix, pendant que l'ombre obscure,
> Sous le soleil montant, se replie à mesure,
> Et laissant de la glèbe attiédir la froideur,
> Vient mourir et border les pieds du laboureur.
> Il rattache le joug, sous la forte courroie,
> Aux cornes qu'en pesant sa main robuste ploie ;
> Les enfans vont cueillir des rameaux découpés,
> Des gouttes de rosée encore tout trempés,
> Au joug avec la feuille en verts festons les nouent,
> Que sur leurs fronts voilés les fiers taureaux secouent,
> Pour que leur flanc qui bat et leur poitrail poudreux
> Portent sous le soleil un peu d'ombre avec eux ;
> Au joug de bois poli le timon s'équilibre,
> Sous l'essieu gémissant le soc se dresse et vibre,
> L'homme saisit le manche, et sous le coin tranchant
> Pour ouvrir le sillon le guide au bout du champ.
>
>   *   *   *   *   *
>
> Un travail est fini, l'autre aussitôt commence ;
> Voilà partout la terre ouverte à la semence ;

> Aux corbeilles de jonc puisant à pleine main
> En nuage poudreux la femme épand le grain ;
> Le froment répandu, l'homme attèle la herse,
> Le sillon raboteux la cadote et la berce ;
> En groupe sur ce char les enfans réunis
> Effacent sous leur poids les sillons aplanis ;
> Le jour tombe, et le soir sur les herbes s'essuie ;
> Et les vents chauds d'automme améneront la pluie,
> Et les neiges d'hiver sous leur tiède tapis
> Couvriront d'un manteau le duvet des épis ;
> Et les soleils dorés en jauniront les herbes,
> Et les filles des champs viendront nouer les gerbes,
> Et tressant sur leurs fronts les bluets, les pavots,
> Iront danser en chœur autour des tas nouveaux ;
> Et la meule broîra le froment sous les pierres ;
> Et choisissant la fleur, la femme des chaumières,
> Levée avant le jour pour battre le levain,
> De ses petits enfans aura pétri le pain ;
> Et les oiseaux du ciel, le chien, le misérable
> Ramasseront en paix les miettes de la table,
> Et tous béniront Dieu dont les fécondes mains
> Au festin de la terre appellent les humains ! "

This is no graceful idyl in the Strephon and Chlorinda style. The toil is severe and unremitting, the guerdon the bare means of subsistence ; the peasant, for all we know, may be as grasping, mean, and miserly as his comrades in the terrible sketches of Israels or of Balzac. But the sympathy of the poet is so true and strong that a generous glow of enthusiasm and faith floods the picture with a golden light. There is a justly famous passage in ancient literature, so frequently quoted and translated as to have become familiar to all, describing a character so well balanced that no adverse stroke of fate can ruffle its sublime calm :—

> " Against whose sphere-like surface, free of fault,
> Fortune falls baffled after each assault."

This is unquestionably very fine, but does not convey

much of hope or solace to suffering humanity. Lamartine's hero neither repels his sorrow nor struggles against it ; he bears it hidden in his bosom till, purified and transformed, it has become a perennial spring of strength and sweetness.

> " J'ai trouvé quelquefois, parmi les plus beaux arbres
> De ces monts où le bois est dur comme les marbres,
> De grands chênes blessés, mais où les bûcherons
> Vaincus, avaient laissé leur hache dans les troncs,
> Le chêne dans son nœud la retenant de force,
> Et recouvrant le fer de son bourlet d'écorce,
> Grandissait, élevant vers le ciel, dans son cœur,
> L'instrument de sa mort, dont il vivait vainqueur !
> C'est ainsi que ce juste élevait dans son âme,
> Comme une hache au cœur, ce souvenir de femme ! "

It will be seen that the versification is more careless in "Jocelyn" than in Lamartine's earlier poems, the rule of alternating masculine and feminine rhymes is frequently transgressed, and there are repetitions which show that the time was approaching when he would not even read over what he had written, but left the task of correction to other and very inferior hands. Yet, despite of many blemishes, it may be considered his most characteristic and interesting achievement in verse, and that on which, in conjunction with the "Harmonies," his poetic reputation most surely rests.

Still, despite the success of "Jocelyn," the mind of the author was, at the time of its publication, centred in politics. Readers of the elder generation will remember how Coningsby, when, in the winter of 1837, he came fresh from his Oxford honours to Paris, eagerly inquired of Sidonia, " This Prince, of whom one hears so much in all countries, and at all hours, on whose existence we are told the tranquillity, almost the civilization of Europe depends,

yet of whom the accounts are so conflicting and so contradictory, tell me, you who can tell me, what he is ? "

" I have," was the reply, "a theory of mine own that
the great characters of antiquity are at times reproduced
for our instruction and for our guidance. Nature, wearied
with mediocrity, pours the warm metal into an heroic
mould. When circumstances placed me in the presence of
the King of France, I recognized Ulysses ! "

Lord Beaconsfield lived probably to regret not having
remembered the advice of Solon before committing to print
so high-flown a panegyric of the monarch who, by the
way, always styled himself King of the French. But his
opinion as a young man, though not (to quote him again)
of great importance, is of some value as showing the favourable estimate intelligent contemporaries formed of Louis
Philippe's talents as a ruler, and of the chances of his
dynasty. So secure did he himself deem his possession of
the throne, that when, in 1836, Prince Louis Napoleon
made his abortive attempt at Strasburg to shake the
allegiance of the army, the King good-naturedly pardoned
him at once. It was, however, thought necessary to punish
the other persons implicated. As to their guilt there was
no question, but the sympathies of the Alsatian jury were
Bonapartist, and, in the face of the strongest evidence, the
prisoners were acquitted,—the first link in the long chain
of events which has brought to that unhappy province such
lasting misery.

After this startling proof of the impossibility of entrust-
ing civilian juries with the trial of military offenders in
political cases, the Ministry, early in the session of 1837,
brought forward a Bill by which civilians were to be tried

as heretofore, in ordinary jury courts, but military men before courts-martial, in the case of offences committed by them in common. This measure, called "the Law of Disjunction," was violently opposed by a coalition of the Extreme Right with the Extreme Left; most of the speakers judging the case, not as on its merits, but as they thought most advantageous to the interests of their party. Lamartine spoke in defence of the measure with eloquence greater than he had ever before displayed—plainly discerning that to oppose it was to imperil the constitutional liberties of France.

"Is there," he asked, "any parity of situation between a simple citizen invested with no powers, charged with no responsibilities, and a military commander who can, by a word, dispose of thousands of bayonets, and at once overturn a Government, pillage a city, violate all the sanctities of private life ; who can, by displacing a battery, cause the loss of thousands of men, or, as at Strasburg, seduce his soldiers to violate all laws, trample under foot all oaths, and light the fires of civil war in a peaceful land. There is no parity in the cases—there should be none between the courts that try them. The military man to the crime of the civilian has added one of far deeper dye which is exclusively his own ; a crime against military honour and subordination, stigmatized by the common consent of all nations. The proposed disjunction of the trials is therefore justified by the still more marked disproportion between the crimes, emphasized by the difference which the nature of things has established between them."

But the occasion was one on which eloquence and argument alike availed little ; it was really a trial of strength

between the Ministers and the Opposition, which resulted
in the Bill being thrown out in committee. The three
Ministerial members protested indignantly, but in vain ;
especially as the chairman, M. Dupin, though he had
accepted the support of the Ministry in his election as
President of the Chamber, now, at the eleventh and crucial
hour, turned against them. At the reading of the address
to the Throne, the excitement was indescribable ; the
debate which followed has become historical as the most
magnificent tournament of oratory ever known in the
French Chamber.

The attack was opened by speeches from the leaders of
the Centre and of the Left Centre, impeaching the Ministry
on entirely opposite grounds. " What use have you made
of your powers ? " thundered M. Guizot. " Where are our
liberties ? " shrieked M. Thiers, careless if their missiles
crossed, provided they were aimed at the common foe. In
point of eloquence the finest speech of the whole debate
was that of Berryer, whose tremendous indictment of Count
Molé's administration (which might, however, have been
launched with equal fitness at either of the ex-Ministers on
whose side he was fighting) so thrilled the Chamber that
at its close all the members rose in homage to his magnificent talent, and the sitting was suspended " in order to
give the deputies time to recover from their emotion."

Against these, and a score of other minor but yet able
speakers, Count Molé had to contend almost single-handed.
His colleagues, though men of talent and of character,
were unequal to weathering such a storm. M. de Montalivet, when striving to reply to a terrible onslaught, actually
fainted on the tribune. During twelve sittings, M. Molé

spoke seventeen times, facing democratic violence and party intrigue with a courage as undaunted as that with which, two centuries before, his famous ancestor had defended the privileges of Parliament against the encroachments of the Crown. His eloquence was not of the highest order, but it was reasoned and sustained ; when his enemies were literally raging against him he never lost his temper for a moment, and his replies were sometimes singularly felicitous. When M. Guizot tried to apply to him the phrase of Tacitus, " Omnia serviliter pro dominatione," Count Molé quickly interposed, " Quand Tacite disait cela, il parlait non pas des courtisans, mais des ambitieux." A retort felt to be so happy that it elicited applause even from the ranks of the Opposition,—M. Royer Collard, who entirely disapproved the course taken by his former pupil, literally beaming with delight.

Still, despite the spirit and steadfastness of the President of the Council, the fight was an uphill one, and could probably indeed hardly have been carried on, but for the unexpected and vigorous aid rendered him by Lamartine. During the earlier period of the debate, the member for Mâcon had remained silent, but a feeling of respect and sympathy for Count Molé, joined with the belief that the administration now so pitilessly lampooned was the very best France could hope for under the circumstances, moved him to throw himself into the fray with all the chivalry of his nature, and to identify himself as completely with an evidently hopeless cause as if he were a member of the Cabinet. As was a matter of course, he drew on himself the bitterest hatred of the coalition, and was interrupted and insulted every moment. On one occasion M. Thiers

was so outrageous and so persistent in his interpella-
tions, that the President, sold to the coalition as he was,
threatened to suspend the sitting.   At last the strife
drew to a close ; the Ministers winning so far the honours
of the fray as to succeed in passing a series of resolutions
which entirely changed the character of the Address which
the coalition were endeavouring to force on them, though
by infinitesimal majorities ; at the last division they.won
by 222 votes against 208.*

Satisfied at being able to retire with honour, Count
Molé resigned.   Now was seen the hollowness of the
coalition.   Marshal Soult, with whom all parties were
willing to act, was asked by the King to form a Ministry,
but, after spending some days in trying every variety of
combination, he had to give up the task.   On this the
King made a strong personal appeal to Count Molé to
resume the reins at least provisionally, and appeal to the
country, which he was convinced would show its disap-
probation of the coalition as plainly as the mercantile
classes had done.   A Council was held at the Hôtel Molé,
at which Lamartine was invited to attend.   He threw the
whole weight of his eloquence and influence against the
dissolution, which he foresaw would have the effect of
making M. Thiers master of the situation.   " Not," he
writes, " that I wished to yield weakly to M. Thiers, but
because a combination was still possible by which he
would have been constitutionally defeated."   But the
King's entreaties prevailed, and, against his own judgment,
which coincided with that of Lamartine, Count Molé
dissolved the Chamber.

* Karl Hildebrandt, "Geschichte Frankreichs," 1830–1871, vol. ii. p. 317.

The distinguished part sustained by Lamartine during this crisis added much to his influence. His speech of the 29th of January, with its famous climax, " La France, c'est une nation qui s'ennuie," had been, after that of Berryer, incomparably the most eloquent of the debate. To quote the picturesque phrase of an admirer, " Chaque matin, ses discours de la veille bondissaient sur toutes les dalles du pavé de Paris."

After the resignation of Count Molé, the 226 members who had supported him at the last, sent a deputation to Lamartine; asking him to become their leader ; and at the same time he received a message from the King, that, in the Ministerial combinations then going on at the Tuileries, any portfolio he liked was at his disposal. But despite these seductive offers, Lamartine adhered firmly to the line of conduct he had, from the time of his first entrance in political life, laid out for himself—that of keeping free from connection with any of the parties then existing. At times, in his letters, he gives expression to the hope of some day being the chief of a group of men with whose aid his political ideals should be realized. But when he goes on to explain that his desire was " to establish a social order which should embody at once liberty and authority ; combine a profound respect for human dignity with obedience to the dictates of morality, and apply the laws of nature, justice, and charity to political power, which was thus to become an expression of the Divine mind," we feel that this is only saying what any high-principled and sanguine public man would say in some form or other, and that a clearer definition is required for the creed of a party. But the position he achieved by his abstention was that which probably suited him far the best ; he became, as M. Scherer tells us, the *Ministre sans portefeuille de la haute opinion philosophique*, for a period far exceeding the duration of many Cabinets.

Lamartine's letters to M. de Virieu, in the beginning of 1839, throw a good deal of light on the situation.

"February 14, 1839.

"The dissolution which has been decided on is against my judgment. At the last Council (to which I was called confidentially and alone) I did my best. For a moment I made them waver; but they were not to be convinced. Now that it is done, there is no use in wasting time in regrets ; we must fight, else we may find ourselves plunged in a revolutionary whirlpool, with wars abroad and hopeless confusion at home. We can only hope that Providence and whatever fraction of good sense remains in the country may rescue us. I have received offers of election from twenty-two departments, many of them couched in enthusiastic language. I have refused all but two, the Nord and the Gironde, which I wish to keep in reserve, in case anything should go wrong at Mâcon. Hitherto I have succeeded in keeping within the bounds of a wise moderation. Two hundred and twenty-six deputies have asked me to be their leader. I have to speak two or three times at each of their daily meetings. I told them that, till the crisis is past, they may count on me, but that when it is over I shall retire, leaving, I trust, the germ of future confidence, and a well-established reputation of integrity. As to the rest, except Berryer, Suleau, and the fanatics of the Extreme Right, I am as pleased as possible with all your friends. The Faubourg St. Germain people, some of whom I meet every day, are perfect,—moral, conservative, and as indignant as you yourself are with *les tapageurs* in the Chamber. This gives hope of a reconciliation, in my opinion absolutely necessary, between the *juste-milieu* and the leaders of society, who are equally menaced. Meanwhile, I am very popular in the *ancien monde*. See how the wheel goes round! At the very moment I am doing my best to support the Government, the Duchesses and the *salons* applaud me!

"I often meet your sister. She hates and despises me. But she is charming, all the same, as she was in the old days at Lemps. I am just starting to dine with her. Adieu."

A few days later, he writes to the same correspondent: "I have just finished a campaign of fourteen days' hard fighting, during which I have had to speak twice every day, in the Chamber and at private meetings. I am fairly done up. Last night I had to fight Guizot, Thiers, Berryer, Barrot, Garnier-Pagès and Co. It was a hard struggle, but I gained my point—a majority sufficient to prevent Thiers from being King, and plunging us into a war with Belgium, just to serve his own ends at home."

As time passed on, the difficulties of forming a new Cabinet grew more and more evident. Between January and April, 1839, eight combinations were made and rejected. Once the carriages ordered to convey a batch of newly named Ministers to the Tuileries were seen by the expectant populace to drive to their houses and return empty. And this state of things, which was visibly undermining the respect for constitutional government throughout the country, might have gone on indefinitely, but for the insurrection headed by Barbès and Blanqui, which, though immediately quelled, drew attention to the fact that some steersman was needed at the helm. On the 13th of May an arrangement was come to by which MM. Thiers, Guizot, and Odillon-Barrot all agreed to stand aside and divide the portfolios among their respective followers, Marshal Soult being President of the Council. The only name of any eminence among the new ministers was that of M. Villemain, more distinguished, however, in literature than in politics. But the necessity of carrying on public business was so strongly felt, that they got in their nominee, M. Sauzet, as President of the Chamber, and passed all the measures they proposed without any difficulty.

The invasion of Syria by Ibrahim Pasha brought the Eastern question once more into prominence. On the 12th of July the Duc de Valmy, a leading Legitimist, opened the debate by blaming the Government for their policy, "which had weakened French influence in Constantinople without strengthening it at Alexandria." His sympathies and those of his party being with Turkey against Egypt, M. Carné, on the other side, pressed the Government to hail in Mahomet Ali the regenerator of the Arab race. To enthrone him, by the help of France, at Contantinople was, he insisted, the only way to maintain the integrity of the Ottoman empire and oppose a strong bulwark to Russian ambition ; while the Government inclined to maintaining the *status quo.*

Lamartine, following M. Carné at the *tribune*, expounded in a very powerful speech his own view—that of the division of the Ottoman empire among the European powers in the interests of civilization. The notion that either the Pasha of Egypt or the Sultan could preserve its integrity he utterly scouted. "Where," he asked, "are we to look for the Arab nationality? Is it among the incoherent, the monstrous agglomeration which is called Egypt, or the idolatrous Druses, or the Catholic Maronites, or the Bedouins of the desert? Mahomet Ali is spoken of as if he were the founder of an empire; but in a country in which there are neither institutions, nor a legal system, nor any political instincts—a country which has but one master and many slaves as its whole social hierarchy, can a great man be anything but a casual incident? Even if such an one there be, he will take away with him in dying the mantle of his genius, leaving an empty void behind."

Passing to the system advocated by the Government, of maintaining the *status quo*:—" I could have understood the system of *status quo* for the maintenance of the Turkish empire before the treaties of 1774, before the treaty of 1792,—even as late as 1815, say up to the destruction of the Turkish fleet, in a fit of insanity, by France and England for the benefit of Russia in 1829; but after the usurpation of the Crimea, the Russian protectorate in Wallachia and Moldavia, after the treaties of Adrianople, of Unkiar-Skelessi, of Katayia, after the despoiling of half the Ottoman empire by you, its protectors, the *status quo* is, allow me to say, as great a farce as the nationality of Poland. But if you really believe the maintenance of the Turkish empire necessary to the peace of Europe, be consistent,—instead of encouraging the revolt of Syria, strengthen the legitimate Sovereign in Constantinople. Lend your counsels, your engineers, your officers to help Mahmoud in his heroic efforts to civilize his people, to crush Ibrahim, to reconquer Egypt."

This speech, delivered at a time when Mahomet Ali was the hero of the hour, supports M. Scherer's view—that if Lamartine had not all the qualities required to make a great statesman, he had, at least, keen political insight. It was listened to with respect, but did not materially affect the division ; the Government received the eleven millions they asked for, and were supported in their policy of joining England in compelling Ibrahim Pasha to retire from Syria and confining Mahomet Ali to the Pashalic of Egypt. But before it could be carried out, the victory of Nezib, gained by Ibrahim, and the treacherous surrender by the Turkish Admiral of the Sultan's fleet to Egypt, completely changed the situation. The public opinion of France became enthusiastic for Mahomet Ali, and, by the end of February, 1840, Thiers was Prime Minister, had withdrawn from the English alliance, and thrown the influence of France on the side of Mahomet Ali.

During the leisure of the recess which followed, Lamartine was employed in writing, in the *Journal du Saône et Loire*, a series of articles on the Eastern question, of which the *Quarterly Review* said : " Some articles, lately published by M. de Lamartine in a prominent newspaper, have produced a great sensation, not only in France, but throughout Europe. This writer, by the elevation of his sentiments, by the enthusiastic yet practical nature of his views, by the honesty of his intention and the soundness of his reasoning, has immense influence, although from his indifference to political power he has party spirit of every shade and creed arrayed against him."

All through the session of 1840, Lamartine fought against the anti-English policy of Thiers, but, though listened to respectfully, he made little way. The Premier, supported enthusiastically by the press, fancied himself omnipotent, and, with a heart as light as that of M. Ollivier in 1870, was bringing France to the verge of an European war. " A majority of forty ambitious voices," writes Lamartine, " is oppressing the Crown, the peers, and the real majority of the Chamber. M. Thiers is no longer a Parliamentary Minister ; he has become a tyrant. The only future I can foresee (and many others think with me), is either the entire degradation of the Chamber, and internal troubles, or war with all its miseries and all its consequences."

As Thiers' tenure of office rested chiefly on his personal popularity, he left no stone unturned to increase it, and sought allies on all sides. Of the 226 supporters of Count Molé, whom Lamartine was striving to guide in the path of liberal progress, he detached fifty by tactics which the Parisians called "the system of individual annexation." He then tried to turn to account the tide of enthusiasm for the Napoleonic legend, which, under the spell of Béranger's songs and of his own History of the Empire, was rising rapidly, by the striking and unexpected proposition to bring over to France the ashes of the great Emperor. Having first privately assured himself of the consent of England, given through Lord Palmerston with a cordial grace which might well have disarmed enmity, Thiers proposed it in a speech of much eloquence and fire, which was received with unbounded enthusiasm.

Among the few warning voices was that of Lamartine.

Not that the author of the spirit-stirring "Ode à Napoléon" was moved by any feeling of personal or class hostility, but he saw clearly the danger that, beneath the laurels heaped on the conqueror's tomb, might be concealed daggers ready to strike at the heart of Liberty. "The lesson you are teaching is this—that nothing is really popular but military renown. Be great and do what you will. Win a battle, and you can then destroy the institutions of your country with as much impunity as if they were Chinese toys."

However, when the project was agreed to, Lamartine would not have it carried out in a parsimonious spirit, but voted in support of the large subsidy asked by the Government. And with all befitting state and dignity was the solemn pageant gone through ; the remains of Napoleon, brought to France by a Prince of the House of Bourbon, were received by the whole nation with an intense, passionate enthusiasm, such as never in the days of his greatest triumphs had greeted the conqueror laden with spoil. It seems hard to grudge the fulfilment of his last pathetic wish—" Je désire que mes cendres reposent sur les bords de la Seine, au milieu de ce peuple Français que j'ai tant aimé "—to one who, after the rancour of the enemies he crushed, after even the cynic candour of his own household have said their worst, still remains incomparably the most striking figure in modern history. But the sequel proved the truth of Lamartine's warning, "The ashes of Napoleon are not yet cold ; beware lest you kindle them to a devouring flame." Years afterwards, when Béranger, at once an ardent admirer of Napoleon and a fervent Republican, used to ask in angry excitement, "What is it, this Second Empire ?" "Why, Béranger," was Lamartine's reply, "is it not one of your songs?"

Meanwhile, Mahomet Ali was growing more powerful in the East, more popular in France, and Thiers' vaguely ambitious forecast seemed to be ripening into a definite policy. He easily got the supplies he wanted to strengthen the armed forces of France, sent Walewski on a mysterious mission to Alexandria, and declined with affectation any immediate action in concert with the other Powers. All this did not perhaps mean very much, but it produced an impression that any further delay in settling the Eastern question might give France the opportunity of working mischief, and so drew together Russia and England. Lord Palmerston, ever quick to secure an advantage to his own country, drew up an ultimatum, which, while guaranteeing to Mahomet Ali the hereditary Viceroyalty of Egypt, secured to Turkey all that it was yet possible to save for her, and was collectively signed by the Four Powers without waiting for France.

So palpable a check, coming at a moment when he thought himself scoring at every point, made Thiers furious. What he first began as a game of brag, he was now eager to follow up in earnest, regardless of consequences. On the meeting of the Chambers, in October, 1840, he prepared for the King a speech which amounted to a declaration of war to the rest of Europe. He had the support of the mob in every large town of France, and of the entire press ; M. Jules Janin offering to raise an army which should at once occupy the left bank of the Rhine: and if 1840 had been 1870, war was inevitable. But at the earlier date the Chamber of Deputies was very differently constituted ; its

members were returned by a body of electors not exceeding two hundred and sixty thousand in number, all belonging to the class sometimes described as that of "people
who have sixpence to lose." Neither the deputies nor their
constituents were disposed to change the course of policy
France had pursued successfully for twenty-five years, to
follow the *politique d'aventure* of any Premier, however
eloquent or persuasive he might be; and by one of
those happy inspirations which sometimes occur even to
Chambers of Deputies, they saw that to maintain peace
with honour the surest way was to entrust the foreign
policy of the country unreservedly to the Sovereign.
Therefore, when Louis Philippe refused to deliver the
speech prepared for him by M. Thiers, accepted his resignation, and summoned M. Guizot to his councils, the new
Ministry at once received the support of the Chamber;
and, known as the *Ministère du* 29 *Octobre*, proved the
longest lived of the reign.

During the formation of the new Cabinet, Lamartine
received flattering offers to join it. On his refusal,
M. Guizot pressed him warmly to accept one of the two
great embassies, London or Vienna; but though this last
offer had great temptations, he persisted in his refusal, pre-
ferring to keep his independence. Neither did the political
principles of M. Guizot, though he preferred him to
M. Thiers, altogether satisfy him. He thought him *mesquin*,
and mistrusted his earnestness in the causes of social progress and the development of political liberty, neither
could he altogether forgive him for having helped to bring
about the present humiliation of France by heading the
coalition against Count Molé. But though he declined to

join the Ministry of the 29th of October, Lamartine more than once did it good service.

The first trial of strength between the Ministry and the Chamber was in the debates of December, 1840, on the discussion of the Address in reply to the King's speech. The opening paragraph, on which the interest of the debate turned, and which was believed to have been written by the King himself, ran as follows : " The measures which the Emperor of Austria, the Queen of Great Britain, the King of Prussia, and the Emperor of Russia have taken in concert to regulate the respective positions of the Pasha of Egypt and of the Sultan have imposed on me serious duties. The dignity of our country is as dear to me as its peace and safety. By pursuing the moderate and con- ciliatory policy of which for the last ten years we have enjoyed the benefits, I have made France strong enough to face any contingency which the course of events in the East may bring about. The extraordinary credits which, from motives you appreciate, have been opened on this account, will be submitted to you, while I continue to hope that peace will remain unbroken. The preservation of it is necessary to the common interests of Europe, to the happiness of populations, to the progress of civilization. I count on you to assist me in sustaining it, as I count on you likewise, if the honour of France, the upholding of her rank among nations, require greater sacrifices."

Although the Chamber were really anxious for peace and grateful to the King for his exertions to maintain it, they were not generous enough to run the risk of impairing their own popularity by giving him their open and un- grudging support. Thiers opened the attack by accusing

P

the Ministry of ignominious concessions; and Berryer, following tactics which Lamartine stigmatized as "unworthy alike of his party and of himself," took the same line, with more than his wonted eloquence.

"I wish," wrote Lamartine, describing the scene to M. de Virieu—"I wish you had been in the House when I broke a lance with Berryer last week. It required all the courage I could muster to take up the gauntlet; he had been sublime in his vehemence, in his appeals to popular feeling. The Chamber was as if it were pulverized; no one would answer him. At last, when the Ministers and all the rest had refused, I stood up, and, with a passionate reply, made on the spur of the moment, took the Assembly by storm. I send it you. Do not be too severe on the style; remember all I had to contend against. At this moment I am the most unpopular and the best-abused man in France."

Finally, the Ministry carried the Address by a majority of eighty-six, a result to which Lamartine's speech, of which three thousand copies were sold in two days, had so visibly contributed, that he was once more besieged with offers of office; that of Minister-Plenipotentiary to a European congress supposed to be impending, tempted him for a moment; but no congress assembled, and the following month found him in direct conflict with Guizot on the question of the fortification of Paris.

This had always been a cherished project of Louis Philippe. Brought forward in 1833, it was then rejected by a large majority and allowed to drop. But the military spirit which animated the whole country in 1840, gave promise that it would now be popular; and by a bold

stroke of policy a credit of £40,000,000 was advanced by
Royal ordinance during the recess, to begin the works at
once ; and in February, 1841, the Chamber were asked to
ratify the loan. Lamartine was much excited by the
question. He spent November and December in studying
it at all points, reading up every work of military authority
he could lay hold of, and with a perfect arsenal of argument, opposed the motion in a speech of several hours'
duration.

As a rule, a speech delivered fifty years ago is not
better reading than a newspaper of the same date, but this
of Lamartine has something of the interest of fulfilled
prophecy, and is a curious instance of what he would have
called "the poet's gift of prescience." He describes what
would happen "if France, with an army of eight hundred
thousand men, had lost two or three of those great battles
that decide the *morale* of nations ; if her regular troops
were vanquished, dispersed, dismembered, demoralized to
the point of no longer presenting any solid obstacle to the
invasion of her territory. In such utter absence of all
resisting power, in such entire desertion of fortune, with
the enemy's *corps d'armée* of three or four hundred thousand men converging by different routes to a terrible
rendezvous under her walls, Paris could not save France ;
she could not save herself!

"You say Paris might gain time for France to rise up
and recompose her forces ; that a new army would be
recruited, and the siege of Paris raised. What ? Would
the crushed and severed limbs be able to accomplish that
which their united and unbroken strength had failed in ;
would a few isolated, dislocated fragments of an army

achieve that which the Marshals, the Government, the
whole organized strength of the country had not achieved?
" You talk of ' a flank manœuvre which would rally the
dispersed garrisons, and crush the enemy between their
bayonets and the walls of Paris.' But would not the enemy
have his own base of operations, leaving his rear and wings
free to occupy your fortified places—unless indeed you
suppose the enemy more weakened by victory than we
should be by defeat? Or is it that you want a battle to
be fought under the walls of Paris? But besides that
your armies are annihilated, has not Napoleon told you
that a battle-field without a base and with a town behind
it, which must be traversed before any new manœuvre
could be attempted, is a battle-field made for defeat?
Or do you want to shut up your army within the walls
of Paris? But Marshal Saxe has told you, and Napoleon
has repeated, that an army shut up in a town is useless
for fighting, and certain within a given time to succumb
to famine. Do you contemplate locking the Government
up in Paris? But a Government occupying an unfortified
house such as the Tuileries, surrounded by a population
of 1,500,000 souls, either starving or raging, what could
it do for France? There would be a 20 Juin every day!
Or if you intend the Government to leave Paris, the
morale of Paris would be destroyed, terror and despair
would take possession of the people. To separate Paris
from the Government of France is to separate soul and
body ; it would be to sign the death-warrant at once of
the Government and of the capital. I pass over the ruin
of Paris blockaded, and surrendered by the very nature
of things to the most violent and the most desperate

factions—imagination recoils before sounding such a gulf, —I reject this motion as an outrage on military science, whose fundamental principles it ignores ; as an outrage on public policy, for it subordinates all France to the fate of Paris, and Paris herself to the desperate domination of extreme factions ; an outrage on humanity, because it tramples on the recognized laws of warfare, by yielding up helpless old men, women, and children as victims to arson, famine, and assault ; and, finally, as an outrage on liberty, because Liberty cannot long subsist with cannon pointed at her breast. In the name of the common-sense, the dignity the humanity of my country, I reject this motion."

But from opposite motives the fortifying of Paris was strongly supported by two parties : the Government, who hoped the fortifications would serve as dykes to restrain popular licence ; and the Republicans, who saw in them weapons which could be advantageously turned against the Government. And the Bill was passed by a large majority, a result which many of those who voted for it had ample leisure to deplore, when transported, on the night of December 2, 1851, to the casemates for the construction of which they had so energetically worked.

CHAPTER VIII.

1840–1847.

ALL through the session of 1840–41 Lamartine was much occupied. He sat on several Committees ; that on the extension of copyright interested him specially, and brought him into collision with M. Emile de Girardin's paper, *La Presse*, without, however, interfering with their private friendship. He also spoke as the " representative of enlightened public opinion " on a number of questions. His position, as he wrote at this time to M. de Virieu, was all he could wish for : politically he was a power in the State ; among parliamentary orators he was in the first rank ; and idolized as a poet. The memoirs of people as unlike as Eugénie de Guérin, the La Ferronays, Renan, Madame d'Agoult, combine to show that his verses were household words in every refined home ; while of un-challenged respect and tender personal affection he had all heart could desire. Yet, thoroughly as Lamartine appreciated and enjoyed all these things, his burdens and sorrows were not few ; his health and strength barely sufficed for the demands made on them from all sides.

In the summer of 1840, change of air and scene being prescribed both for his wife and for himself, they went through the Pyrenees and the north of Spain, received everywhere with distinction, generally with enthusiasm. Yet Lamartine's health benefited but little. In August we hear of him at Hyères, suffering cruelly from neuralgia. He playfully asks Madame de la Grange to undertake a pilgrimage or some other of her many good works, to obtain the cure of at least one or two of those terrible nerves which made him, in this year of combat, incapable of anything but resignation.

From Hyères he was recalled by the news of his father's illness, and, after some weeks passed in anxious watching, the old man passed quietly away. The loss was inevitable, for M. de Lamartine had reached his ninetieth year, but was not the less deeply felt.

"It is," wrote his son to M. de Virieu, "as if half my own life were gone from me. I am as a tree severed from its root; lopped of its branches. Still God is over all ; in Him our lives will be renewed. I cannot now leave my wife, else I should go to you ; but her sorrow is as great as mine. Write to me, and, when you can, come and see me. The void around me makes me love you more and more."

A little later, after thanking M. de la Grange for his affectionate sympathy, Lamartine glances at politics. "You have chosen a bad time to visit your constituents. They do not know where they are. Thiers, with his fourteen newspapers, is scattering darkness abroad, and no one dares to contradict him. Yet I discern gleams of doubt, and suspect that the little man is beginning to inspire as much dread as admiration. For myself, I can do nothing. I cannot even read (but have to be read to), much less write. I just manage to dictate, but very little at a time. .

Even in this note, I have had to break off twice ; and yesterday I got twenty-eight letters ! Several Legitimist deputies
write to me, and seem inclined to join me in the hour of
peril. How will it all end ? That depends on Marshal
Soult, on the Duc d'Orleans, and, above all, on Providence.
Thence only comes our salvation. Adieu, let us love each
other."

In December, Lamartine had recovered sufficiently to
resume his seat in the Chamber, and to make another
speech on the question of the fortifications of Paris. According to his wont, he goes over the subject in his letters
to M. de Virieu, whose approbation he values far beyond
any windfalls of popular applause.

"I do not know how it is," he writes, "but of late years
we have come to be in unison on almost all questions. It
makes me very happy, and strengthens me in every way.
This letter, which I began last night, I close this morning,
1st of January, 1841, in order that I might end the old
year and begin the new one with you, my one, my only
friend."

This letter is almost the last of a correspondence which,
during the long span of thirty-five years, had been kept up
without a break. In the month of April following, M. de
Virieu died so suddenly that there was not even time for
Lamartine to be with him. The blow must have been
overwhelming. In the few letters written at that time,
Lamartine thanks his friends for their sympathy in brief
phrases, which show the subject was too painful to be
dwelt on. Only in one letter, written to M. de Virieu's
sister, does he speak of their common loss.

"What can I say of myself that will be anything but

an echo of what you are now feeling and suffering? Was he not to me also a brother, and much more than a brother? My loss is as great as yours; it includes my whole past, and all the affection, all the future promise of my life. Only in heaven and in memory do I now possess a friend. What you and M. de Miramon have told me of his last moments is consoling to us, who believe firmly in an eternal reunion. To die with this thought, so intensified by prayer that it has become a reality, is hardly to die; it is only to reach home a little before the rest. Like you, I rejoice at the grace vouchsafed; the remembrance of it will be our great support in the mournful path we have henceforth to tread alone. When Madame de Virieu has recovered sufficiently for you to speak to her for me, I entreat of you to do so. Assure her of my absolute devotion to his memory, to his affections, to his wishes, above all, to her and hers. My greatest happiness will be in proving to her that he whom she mourns has left a brother. Adieu, mademoiselle. During many years you were witness of a friendship death is powerless to destroy; be good enough to allow me sometimes to find it still living in the memory and in the affections of the two persons he most loved."

It is by the blank left in Lamartine's correspondence his loss and sorrow can best be gauged. The remaining letters, covering a span of twenty years, scarcely fill a volume, nor do we ever again find the unrestrained outpouring of thought and feeling, the certainty of sympathy which marked all those addressed to this beloved and familiar friend. And not only in Lamartine's affections is the place filled by M. de Virieu henceforth vacant, his death, occurring at a turning-point in Lamartine's life, influenced, as we shall see hereafter, its whole tenour.

A few weeks later, we find Lamartine again a mourner, and this time at the deathbed of one to whom he was bound by the double tie of affection and of kindred. The Chevalier de Pierreclos, Lamartine's old playfellow, after a brilliant but somewhat stormy youth, had died in early manhood. Towards his only son Lamartine acted as an affectionate and careful guardian.

Léon de Pierreclos evidently inherited his father's impetuous character. While quite a boy, he wrote to ask his guardian to take him away from school. Lamartine replied with much tact and kindness. He showed neither displeasure nor surprise ; but explained, at some length, to his young correspondent that the position of public affairs at the time made it difficult to find him a suitable career, and that it was really a matter of great good fortune to be able to postpone the decision a couple of years. "What is essential for the moment is for you, without troubling as to the future, to strengthen yourself in your studies as much as possible, and to prepare by varied acquirements, and by serious solidity of character, for whatever career the course of events may trace out for you. The stormier and more critical the period in which we live, the more necessary it is that our characters should be proportionately strengthened and elevated by study and by the assiduous exercise of self-control. It is this exercise which forms us to moral and political virtue, never more needed than now. But I do not pity you on that account. I prefer for you these revolutionary times, trying as they are, to the sloth and corruption of the last century. They infuse more strength in the soul; they make a man better able to discern, and better able to reach the one aim he has to strive for—self-devotion and virtue. Now is the time for you to study history; work at it during these final years of your school life. Remember that if a European war should break out, you would never have again the chance of making up for the time you would then lose. And remember, too, all this advice is only for your good. Tell me if there is anything that would be useful or pleasant to you in the way of books, masters, etc. Remember me to your mother, and ask her not to spoil you by too much indulgence. Adieu, my dear Léon. Never be afraid of tiring me by asking my advice or assistance in any way. I will keep my promise to your father by taking as much care of you as if you were my own son, until you are able to take care of yourself."

Not many people in Lamartine's position would have taken so much trouble in dealing with a refractory school-boy. But the trouble was evidently well repaid. His subsequent letters to Léon de Pierreclos are full of affectionate approval; the later ones are written as if to a friend of equal standing, with unrestrained confidence. M. Léon de Pierreclos seems to have entered the Civil Service. He was given, in 1840, an appointment in the south of France, which it was hoped would have proved a stepping-stone to promotion. But his health failed, and he had to return to his home in Burgundy, to be tenderly nursed by his wife, who was one of Lamartine's nieces. There is frequent mention of him in Lamartine's letters for some months; but gradually hope faded away. As the end drew near, he and his wife came to Mâcon to be within

reach of daily intercourse. M. de Pierreclos' last words
were of gratitude to his friend and guardian, to whom only
remained the sad task of bringing the poor widow back to
St. Point. "You have lost a friend, and I almost a son," he
writes to M. de Champeaux. "What you have written
under the impulse of a still fresh sorrow is worthy of him
and of you. He died as a just man should, seeing only
God in suffering, and immortality in death. In my
thoughts his pure and stainless memory will always abide
as a perfume, which will never lose its sweetness. And
you will always remain worthy of your friend, maturing in
heart and in mind. Thanks for having wept with us."

Besides the personal sorrows of this year, Lamartine
had at this time the additional trial of financial embarrassment. Though the estates he inherited from his uncles
were considerable in extent, they were encumbered with
charges in favour of their surviving sisters and nieces, and,
as he was loth to part with even a single acre, he had to
raise considerable sums on these accounts, as well as to
meet his own expenses, which, without much actual extravagance, were large. His hospitality was not ostentatious;
but he kept open house at St. Point and Monceau for
several months each year, and he was generous to a fault.
Finding himself seriously hampered, he contemplated for a
time resigning his seat in the Chamber, and living altogether
in the country ; but an unusually good vintage and a loan
raised, not without some difficulty, enabled him to tide
over the crisis.

"The man has come to look over my estates. He
examined them carefully, and found them very well tilled.
When he saw my vines and my vineyard labourers, with

their happy, well-housed families, he said he now realized the phrase he had heard somewhere, 'Lamartine, premier cultivateur de France.' You think it is a joke, but it was said with much solemnity. Whether he will lend the money I want on moral security is the question, and I shall not know for a month."

Apparently the answer was favourable, for we hear no more of Lamartine's resigning his seat, which would have been a considerable sacrifice; political life had become intensely interesting to him, and he felt himself the leading spirit in a forward movement, of which neither he, nor probably any one else, even vaguely foresaw the results.

It is the custom in the French Chamber for the President, whose position is, speaking generally, analogous to that of the Speaker of the English House of Commons, to be elected annually. At the opening of the session of 1841-42, Lamartine's was among the names proposed. His opponents described him as extremely desirous to succeed, and embittered by his defeat. But, in a confidential letter to M. Emile de Girardin, dated November 25, 1841, of which there is no reason to doubt the sincerity, Lamartine begs him not to waste his time in canvassing for him, as besides that his chance was a very slight one, he did not, for two categorical reasons, desire the presidency.

"It is a neutral position, and I like positive and combative positions. It is the decoration of a political career, not its strength; the purple on the garment, not its substance. Finally, to propose me as a candidate is to risk, on a successful or unsuccessful attitude in an arm-chair, the *prestige* of a name which already has some political

weight, and may one day be put to higher uses. He who
fills that place is not much increased thereby; when he
loses it, he may be much diminished. Therefore, let there
be no canvassing on my behalf; those who like to vote for
me, pay me a compliment by which I cannot but feel
flattered."

Ultimately, sixty-four votes were given for Lamartine,
against 193 for M. Sauzet, and it was to the former a
painful surprise to find that his supporters were all from
the Liberal section of the house, the Conservatives evidently mistrusting his ideas of progress. He did not,
however, move from his seat on the Right benches, nor
cease to support them on many occasions; but it is likely
that his hopes of enlisting their sympathies for the com-
prehensive measures of social amelioration, on which his
heart and soul were set, became much less sanguine.

The uncertainty of Lamartine's mental attitude was
illustrated in the debates of April, 1842, on the increase
of the electorate. The qualification was the payment of
200 francs of direct taxes, which gave only the obviously
inadequate number of 220,000 electors out of a population
of over thirty millions; and in 1839 M. Arago had proposed with much eloquence, but with a want of discretion
which deprived him of any serious support, a measure of
extension.

By 1842 the question had assumed such proportions
that it could no longer be safely postponed; all thinking
men had agreed that a change was necessary. The Duc
d'Orleans, who had Liberal opinions on many subjects, was
believed to favour it; and when it became known that a
solemn debate was to be held on the question in the

Council of State, a considerable increase of the electorate was reckoned on. But from the opening of the discussion it was seen that the King was strongly adverse to any change, he maintaining that the cry for reform was a malady of the age, which, if judiciously treated, would pass away. "Other monarchs preserve themselves by inspiring terror ; for my part I prefer the homœopathic method, and have found it successful."

M. Guizot followed in the same tone, describing the cry for reform as a fictitious one got up for party purposes, which, having no foundation on the real interests or permanent feelings of the country, might be put aside without endangering public tranquillity.

The expression of the Duc d'Orleans' views was now anxiously looked for, but probably out of respect for his father, for whom, although differing from him in opinion on many points, he always showed profound deference (or possibly at the instigation of M. Thiers, who, it was said, wished to reserve any electoral reform for his own administration), he silently acquiesced in the decision of the preceding speakers, and voted with the rest of the Council for resistance to any proposal for reform.

This decision was a severe blow to all enlightened and thoughtful men, and in April, 1842, two motions were brought forward by members anything but hostile to the Government. The first was to the effect that members of the Chamber of Deputies who were not office-bearers at the time of their election should be disqualified from receiving any appointment for a year after they continued to hold their seats. This measure, intended to lessen the influence of the Ministry on the Chamber, was opposed by

Lamartine on the ground that it would exclude from office the very men most fitted, by their position, talents, and experience, to do good service to the country.

After giving Government valuable help towards the rejection of this motion, Lamartine attacked them unsparingly in the debate on that which followed. M. Ducos, in order to obtain some extension of the electorate on perfectly safe and constitutional lines, proposed to give votes to all whose names were on the departmental list of jurymen. Moderate as was this demand, Guizot refused it in a long and carefully prepared speech, in which, putting forth all his powers of irony and of invective, he showed plainly his determination to reject even the slightest extension of popular power or privilege, his resolute hostility to Liberalism under any form.

In his reply, Lamartine, as was rather his custom, began by unfolding to his hearers the statistical aspects of the question, with a precision to which other speakers had not accustomed the Chamber. He gave a *résumé* of all the electoral bases which had successively prevailed in France since 1788, showing that the object of each had been gradually to increase the number of electors till it should include all who by their position or character were competent to exercise the duties of citizenship. He then went on to say, " In all countries and in all ages there have been men honourable, well-intentioned, but blinded by political passion, entrenched behind a numerical majority, shutting their eyes to all good, matured, even necessary changes. In vain have you served these men in their legitimate interests, in vain have you supported them in the struggles every Government has to maintain against factions, in vain have you stood forward to defend them or to perish with them. All is forgotten. Their esteem, indeed, they do not refuse you ; but from the hour when a measure of innovation, however wise, prudent, even conservative in its spirit, is suggested, from that moment they count you as an enemy. In saying this, I indulge in no personalities, I simply recount the history of all the great epochs, 1789, 1815, 1829, to the present time. It is in vain that the balance of power is altered, that the moral forces of the country are visibly corrupted ; men such as I have spoken of fear nothing, provide for nothing ; to shroud themselves in the immobility of despotism is their one resource. You have long inscribed on your banners, ' Resistance, eternal resistance.' At the period which immediately followed the Revolution of 1830 I can understand this being your watchword. During all that period resistance was the first duty of the Government, and you discharged it worthily, gloriously. But after 1834 the danger was over, the necessity for resistance existed no longer, and a variety of questions arose on which the ideas of our leading statesmen were not in accordance with the spirit of the age. I grieve to say it, there has come to France a period, not of national degradation—the nation never will be degraded,— but one in which important interests are strangled, just and passionate desires thwarted. If you value the country's welfare, do not now reject a proposition which, by infusing into the body of the electorate a living, patriotic force, will communicate new life to its decaying members, and make France strong to resist the coalition of Europe arrayed against her independence and her liberties."

One of the characteristics which made Lamartine so

Q

dangerous an opponent was his power of improvising some happy epithet, which caught the popular ear, and became at once a password. On this occasion he told Guizot that "if immobility is the one thing required of a Government, it is quite superfluous to have ministers ; boundary stones would suffice ;" and the nickname "*Les Conservateurs-bornes*" adhered to Guizot and his followers as long as the monarchy lasted. Another successful epigram was, "In France the Grand Elector is not the list of registered voters, it is public opinion." He wound up by a direct and impassioned appeal to Guizot himself, which seems for a moment to have pierced even his armour of imperturbability, "not to set aside lightly a proposal of which the certain result would be to give the electoral body a much needed supply of active, intelligent patriotism, and, by impulse to the political life of France, strengthen her against her enemies ; but rather to strike without fear the soil which would bring forth, not as in the classic legend, legions of armed men—France need never fear that in the day of battle her children will fail her,—but a strong and noble contingent of citizens who would bring back to the electoral body a fresh supply of the vitality it is so quickly losing, and, to the political institutions of the country, respect and love."

Needless to say his warning was entirely thrown away. Guizot persisted in that systematic opposition to any extension of popular power which has been regarded by many writers as the proximate cause of the Revolution of 1848, and the motion was lost.

But a few weeks later we find Lamartine speaking in support of a measure approved of by the Ambassadors of

the Four Great Powers, who met in London in December,
1841. A mutual right of search, instituted with the view
of stopping the slave trade, was agreed to. This mutual
right of search was totally different from that England had
claimed during the wars with Napoleon; it was established
on the base of complete reciprocity, without any claim on
England's part of superiority over any other Power, and it
was certain that without it the horrible traffic in human
flesh could never be abolished. Unfortunately, the recollection of Lord Palmerston's entire disregard of French
susceptibilities on the Eastern question during Thiers'
administration was still fresh, and the moment the terms
of the treaty were published in Paris in the *Moniteur*, a cry
of indignation rose up from one end of France to the other.
It was worse than Leipzic, more disgraceful than Waterloo;
a bowing of the neck to England for which no precedent
could be found in history; and when the subject came up
for discussion in the Chamber, M. Jacques Lefêvre proposed
an amendment which was practically a censure of the
Ministry.

Lamartine answered by showing that, even if French
susceptibilities had hardly been enough considered in
points of detail, nothing had been done which affected the
national honour, and, on behalf of the oppressed and
tortured slaves, pleaded eloquently for the ratification of
the treaty. Such, however, was the temper of the House,
that the question had to be withdrawn, and the Government, much weakened in *prestige* by what had occurred,
dissolved the Chamber.

In the election which followed, Lamartine had no
anxiety as to his own seat. At many successive elections

he had been returned by the town of Mâcon by increasing
majorities; this time with only sixty dissentient voices.
But he had to regret the absence from the Chamber of
several members whose places were but inadequately filled.
The general result was to give M. Guizot a decided
majority, but not a very large one ; while two of his most
distinguished supporters—MM. Rémusat and Duvergier
d'Hauranne passed to the Left Centre, and in the large
towns the increased strength of the Republicans was very
marked. They returned nine out of the twelve members
for Paris ; among whom were Michel (de Bourges), Marie,
and Henri Carnot, all Radicals of an advanced type. The
newly developed socialistic party was led by Ledru-Rollin
and Louis Blanc.

But a few weeks before the date fixed for the opening
of the new Chamber, all minor interests paled before the
overwhelming news that the Duc d'Orleans had been
thrown from his carriage on the road to Neuilly, and killed
on the spot. History has few pictures more pathetic than
that of the aged King and Queen following on foot, as a
last token of love and respect, the litter which brought
the dead body of their son back to the Tuileries. That
mournful train might almost be called the funeral procession of monarchy in France ; perhaps, indeed, of much
more. For if the Duc d'Orleans had lived to succeed
his father it can hardly be doubted that he would have
inherited his kingdom, and have bequeathed it, in his turn,
to his descendants. In him were united, in a remarkable
degree, all the qualities most valuable to a ruler of men—
a noble presence, high intelligence, conspicuous valour,
facile eloquence, and, it is said, a marvellous aptitude for

discerning the tendencies of the times. That the soldiers, whose privations he had shared through more than one African campaign, should have been strongly attached to him, was perhaps only natural ; but it is a strong proof of his superiority that even in Paris, where the habit of cease-less raillery makes it difficult for those occupying exalted positions to escape ridicule, the Duc d'Orleans was admired, and, in the best sense of the word, extremely popular.

There is, generally speaking, truth in the common saying that no one is really necessary ; but, to secure through another generation the peace of Europe, to main-tain intact the frontiers of France, experience has proved this Prince's life was necessary. Such seems, even at the time, to have been Lamartine's feeling ; for he writes from Marseilles : "We are cut to the heart; the more one reflects on this fatal news, the more terrible it seems. I have given up my journey to the South, as I must be in Paris for the opening of the Chambers. It is a matter of duty; absence would be impossible." The . task of drawing up the Deputies' address of condolence devolved on him, and was discharged with great eloquence, tact, and delicacy.

A few weeks later, the question of the Regency, in the not unlikely event of the King's decease before his grand-son should have reached his majority, came up for discus-sion. By the will of the late Duke, the Duchess was left guardian of the persons of her sons and of their private estates, the Duc de Nemours named as the future Regent of the kingdom. This second clause required the sanction of the legislature, and the Ministers brought forward a Bill, the principle of which was, that in default of a male heir of full age, the Regency should belong by right to the next

in succession to the throne, who in this instance was the
Duc de Nemours. To this M. Odillon-Barrot objected, on
the ground that not to the Chamber, but to the people
alone, it belonged to choose a Regent. Guizot made the
unanswerable rejoinder that the Chamber which had in the
person of Louis Philippe nominated a King, was surely
competent to select a Regent. Thiers followed on the
same side, while Berryer and his followers advocated
universal suffrage.

Contrary to expectation, Lamartine, after allowing that
his convictions were undecided, and describing the question
as a' choice of difficulties, stood forth, to quote his own
words, as the champion at once of the female sex and of
liberty, insisting that the proposed law was neither conservative nor dynastic, and that to banish a mother, the
natural guardian of her son, from his cradle, was a violation
alike of common sense and of justice. He showed that,
notwithstanding the Salic law, out of thirty-two Regents
in France twenty-six had been women ; to find an instance
in which the mother had been excluded they must go back
to times of barbarism. The circumstance that the Duchesse
d'Orleans was a Protestant, could, he argued, be no objec-
tion ; on the contrary, the principle of religious toleration,
embodied in the person of the ruler of the State, would
receive an additional guarantee.

With a Government majority of two hundred was
closed a debate on which a distinguished German writer,
Herr Hildebrandt, remarks : " Of a period rich in brilliant
debates this was the most brilliant, as if history wished to
teach us by a conspicuous example how uselessly talent,
emotion, and knowledge can be frittered away in Parlia-

mentary discussions; in all the political maxims, forms, and theories listened to, the actual facts were hardly glanced at ; it remains as a superb oratorical tournament, of which the prize was a Regency which never came into existence."

The autumn of 1842 was a busy one, both at Monceau and at St. Point. The sittings of the *Conseil général du département*, and of other local bodies ; friends coming and going ; increasing correspondence ; interruptions from all sides, left scarcely a moment of leisure. The great event of the season was the opening of the Royal College at Mâcon. During Louis Philippe's reign education was immensely developed all through France, and, both as a literary man and as a politician, Lamartine was interested in making Mâcon a centre of intelligence, and in obtaining for the town some share in the educational endowments which were being profusely distributed. For three years he had been working towards this end ; at one time his letters were full of indignation against the Minister of Education, M. Villemain, who, as he conceived, had deluded him with false hopes, and compromised him with his fellow-citizens. However, by perseverance Lamartine prevailed, and now, amid brilliant festivities, during which three hundred guests were received one day at Monceau, the College was inaugurated. At the opening *séance* all the speakers vied in expressing the gratitude of the province to Lamartine for his zeal and sustained efforts.

In his reply, he happily applied to himself the passage in which Cicero, writing from Rome to his friend Atticus, says, " While my name is here tossed about on every wind, a prey to Clodius and to Melibœus, I console myself with the thought that there is at Arpinum a tranquil haven where, untroubled by the noises of the market place, it abides in the love of my fellow-citizens ! "

About this time, an independent paper, *Le Bien public*, was founded at Mâcon under Lamartine's auspices. For many years he had been a frequent contributor to the principal newspaper of the department, *Le Journal du Saône et Loire;* but, gradually, political differences became apparent, and some of his articles having been accepted only on the condition of their being altered, Lamartine felt the need of an organ which would faithfully represent his views. For a moment there was question of purchasing a Parisian paper, *La Presse*, but the negotiation fell through. He then summoned to St. Point a group of literary friends, chiefly young men living in the neighbourhood, and rapidly exposed to them his ideas. "What," he asked, "is the signification of all our revolutions ? It is that France requires a National Government ; a Government which will call, without distinction of class, all the men most distinguished by intelligence or by character to the exercise of power ; a Government which will disperse its favours over the whole area of national life ; which will apply to the science of governing the principles of social charity. Until this goal is reached, the stream of revolution will follow its course ; sometimes troubled, sometimes outwardly calm, according to the facilities or the obstacles it may encounter. Let it be our task to construct a harbour in which ideas, not tumultuous but vivifying, may find secure shelter, and, like the fertilizing waters of the Nile, form a deposit which will bring forth a rich harvest of human liberty."

Passing to the practical side of the subject, Lamartine

explained to his auditors that the speculation was not likely to be a paying one ; their reward would rather lie in the consciousness they were helping a noble cause. This did not at all damp their enthusiasm, and the foundation of the paper was voted unanimously.

The editor was to be M. de Champvans, who had already some journalistic experience ; among the contributors were MM. de la Tour, Garnier, Charles Rolland, Laguerronnière, Pelletan, and Lacretelle. The last, writing in 1870 of the *Bien public*, says, " It formed a generation of citizens devoted to liberty in its purest sense, grouped round a master incomparable in genius and in kindness of heart. It was in this school M. Pelletan acquired the disinterested and unselfish policy which now gives him such authority in the Chamber ; M. de Laguerronnière the urbanity of style and perfection of manner which enabled him, even as a senator of the Empire, to be sympathetic to his opponents."

In striking contrast to most of the periodicals of the day, the *Bien public* was a model of the best and purest French ; Lamartine lavishing freely on its pages phrases as large and as luminous as those which thrilled his hearers in the Palais Bourbon. Its circulation was large, both at home and abroad, besides which, *Le Bien public* had the honour of furnishing matter to almost all the other papers. All the Parisian, and most of the provincial journals used to republish in full every article written by Lamartine, and many that were erroneously attributed to him ; but this compliment, though flattering, was not lucrative, so that, despite its success, Lamartine's launch into journalism must be reckoned as one among the causes of his financial difficulties. After about six years of provincial existence, the publishing offices of the *Bien public* were, in 1848, transferred to Paris. A little later it passed into other hands, and, with some variation in its politics, still exists. That the leaven of Republicanism was working in Lamartine's mind, and that he was likely to make a new departure in politics, was now pretty generally felt. " I am like Lamartine," writes the most delightful of correspondents, M. Doudan ; " I have a number of conflicting opinions on several subjects ;" while, with characteristic sententiousness, Humboldt delivered himself of the dictum, " M. de Lamartine is a comet whose orbit has not yet been determined." In his speech on the Address, after recapitulating the special points on which he had at different times opposed the Ministry, Lamartine ended by expressing the conviction that what he should henceforth oppose was the general drift of their policy, or, as he summed up in a phrase which at once became current, "their system." This declaration was hailed by the Liberals with fervour, which apparently surprised Lamartine.

. " Within three days," he writes, " I have received from all parts of France two hundred and fourteen letters, *tous fanatiques d'entraînement et d'enthousiasme.* The spark that fell from the tribune has, contrary to my expectations, lit up a conflagration such as you can hardly imagine. I did not think disaffection had made such progress, and it alarms me. If I meant, as some people seem to think, to direct and discipline the Left, I should indeed have a serious task before me, but I am thinking of nothing of the sort."

A few weeks later, we find him censuring the foreign

policy of the Ministry as severely as he had before censured
their home administration : especially the spirit of jealousy
and suspicion they were encouraging against England,
showing that the assumed incompatibility in the interests
of the two countries had no real foundation.   " It is false
that the earth and the sea are not wide enough to contain
these two great countries; false that the one or the other
must be sacrificed ; false that the constant aim of English
politicians is the humiliation of France.   It is England's
most vital interest that no one State should dominate the
Continent ; to avert this danger either the Russian or the
French alliance is necessary to her ; that of France on
many accounts preferable.   The common weal of these
two nations rests on foundations which are permanent ;
which will long outlive our blind and fleeting resentments.
On the alliance between France and England depends the
peace of the world."

In March, M. de Sade brought forward again his proposition to exclude all Government functionaries from the
Chamber.   Lamartine, in the debate which ensued, supported
the Ministry, taking occasion again to urge on them the
necessity of giving France that reality of representation
which he still hoped the pressure of public opinion might
gain by pacific means.   But M. Guizot and his majority
were more inflexible than ever, so that the transient phase
of reconciliation only led to a wider schism ; and at a
banquet given in June to Lamartine by the town of Mâcon,
he made a speech in which the sequence of cause and effect
which transformed the Royalist in 1829, the defender of
Count Molé in 1839, into the tribune of the people in 1848
is pretty clearly foreshadowed.

With the Government of July, Lamartine never had
any real sympathy. His historic sense and the kindness
he had received from Charles X. prevented his feeling any
personal loyalty save for the elder branch of the House of
Bourbon, and made him deeply regret the blow so thought-
lessly struck, in 1830, at the hereditary principle, to which
France owed her unity, her existence as a nation, and so
many centuries of greatness and of glory. Still he held
that, to a Frenchman, the interests of France must rank
before those of any dynasty, however august, and as long
as he believed that the Revolution of 1830 would, like
that of 1688 in England, lead to the further development
of civil liberty and of social progress, he allowed Louis
Philippe's claim on his allegiance, and gave, on all vital
occasions, his loyal support to the Crown. But now, he
held, the conditions had altered ; the stream of freedom,
instead of broadening down from precedent to precedent,
was ice-bound. In his words to Guizot, " France, if she
submits to the conditions you seek to impose on her, will
be France no longer." Still there was nothing factious
in his scheme of opposition. When at the Mâcon banquet
he was defining its outline a voice called out, " Like
O'Connell in Ireland," Lamartine at once replied, " I hear
O'Connell's name. No, gentlemen, there is nothing in
common between us and O'Connell." And he emphasized
his repudiation of the parallel in a pamphlet in which,
after expressing his deep admiration for O'Connell's earlier
career, he strongly censured the Repeal agitation, then at
its height, as indicating either aberration of intellect, or an
entire absence of moral sense in its promoters, "who must
know it to be as mischievous as it is useless." Again, in a

letter addressed about the same time to M. de Champvans
as to the line to be followed in editing *Le Bien public*, he
says : " Remember that one cannot break even the statue
of a saint without striking a blow at religion. The religion
of the Tuileries is the Royal prerogative ; we must perforce
come into pretty strong collision with it, but let it be done
respectfully."

It had always been Lamartine's hope that, for the policy
of abstention from public life, which, during the years
immediately following Charles X.'s abdication, had been
the most dignified and probably the wisest line of conduct for the Legitimists, there might, as time passed on,
be gradually substituted one of active support of all
such measures as were unquestionably for the public
welfare. He was convinced that if to the *prestige* of a
historic past, and of great territorial possessions, were
added enlightened patriotism, moderation, energy, and
good sense, this party, which alone had a living political
faith, firm religious convictions, and a distinct principle
to fight for, must, sooner or later, become masters of
the situation. Again and again he exerted his eloquence
to induce all who came within his influence to pursue
this course, and his correspondence shows that there
were times when he had hopes of success. And although
as early as 1834 he had plainly stated his intention of
following an independent path in politics, Lamartine never
failed to take pleasure in recording occasions on which
he found himself acting in concert with the party which
possessed the largest share of his sympathies. In 1837,
he thanks the editor of the *Moniteur de la Religion*
for some favourable judgments ; the year following he

repudiation of Guizot's saying—" Le Catholicisme, c'est la plus grande, la plus sainte école de respect qu'ait vue le monde."

This was particularly unfortunate at a time when the strained relations which, at the beginning of Louis Philippe's reign, existed between Church and State were undergoing considerable change. The Queen and the junior members of the Royal family were models of enlightened piety; the King, if not himself a religious man, was anxious to secure the support of the clergy; while M. Guizot, although a Protestant, had much more sympathy with their views and aims than most French statesmen, and was now endeavouring to pass a Bill which would have increased the influence of the Church over higher education. But half-measures did not satisfy the zeal of the editor of the *Univers*, nor of the group of pamphleteers he had rallied round his standard; and a broadside of abuse was poured out, sparing neither friend nor foe. In vain did the Archbishop of Paris, Mgr. Affre, exhaust admonition and persuasion in the endeavour to keep the zeal of the too ardent neophyte within bounds; and in a pastoral letter, of which the address was unmistakable, point out its inevitable results. "Bitterness alienates men's minds. How many hitherto peaceful spectators have become irritated, have descended into the arena to defend what they deem rights ruthlessly attacked! How often has not virulent personality reached the level of serious injustice?" But no rebuke (not even direct Papal censure) ever did more than silence M. Veuillot for the moment. His license of language and virulent personality grew more and more offensive, and among those who, in the words of the Archbishop of Paris,

"becoming irritated, descended into the arena," was
Lamartine, who, in a pamphlet headed " L'Église, l'État,
l'Enseignment," defended the University system. This
brought on him vials of wrath from the *Univers*, whereupon
the writers of the *Bien Public* took up their leader's cause
enthusiastically, and a duel of newspaper articles ensued.
Happily, Lamartine's temperament was too serene to allow
of his dwelling long in the heated atmosphere of con-
troversy. It rather amused him to find himself in the
course of a week, the same week, denounced by one paper
as a Jesuit in disguise, and by another as the enemy of all
religion, an atheist, and an infidel ! Nor was he, as is so
often the case with men of weaker minds, driven by unjust
aspersions into the enemy's camp, for he was among
the most eloquent opponents of Thiers' measure for the
expulsion of the Jesuits ; and we find in Mgr. Dupanloup's
memoirs, recently published, a letter from Lamartine
warmly congratulating the Bishop on a pamphlet which
he wrote a little later on the much-vexed " University
question." Still the incident was probably among the
causes which made Lamartine give up trying to turn the
Conservative element to any practical account as a hopeless
task, and led him to devote himself to literature more
seriously than he had done for many years.

"I am getting on," he writes in August, 1843, "with the
first book of ' Les Girondins.' I have never before written
anything in this style. Partly from uncertain health, and
partly from other causes, I cannot hope to have the volume
finished before the end of 1844. We are here for the
Conseil général du Departement. I was, in concert with
M. de Lacretelle, to have delivered a lecture on literature

R

at the College of Mâcon on the day of the distribution of prizes ; but the Recteur of Dijon has just arrived with counter-orders. Mâcon is thought to have been too loquacious of late, so we are to hold our peace. I am delighted ; the town very discontented. The musicians and the audience wished to absent themselves, but I have persuaded them not to humiliate an institution that has been successful, and of which we all are proud. I shall be present, but shall not speak."

" St. Point, September, 1843.

· "Your letter charmed me. I have no time for writing, for I work hard for four hours in the morning, and am on horseback all the rest of the day. Champeaux is working hard for the *Bien public ;* I occasionally suggest a paragraph to him, without accepting any responsibility. I know nothing as to how the affairs of the country are faring, being entirely engrossed by my own, which are not flourishing. To keep one's-self independent costs dear, but it is worth the price. I had rather go to Ste. Pelagie now, than to Turin or Madrid."

To the MARQUIS DE LAGRANGE.

" January, 1844.

" Thanks for your valuable details as to the anatomy of a corpse. What life could you expect to find in a Chamber capable of taking the grimaces of D. [Dupin ?] seriously ? Away with it, as unworthy our attention. I should like to be at my post, but my post is where the law of necessity keeps me. Happy the men 'who have straw in their boots '—I have only stones in mine. I pity you for having to sit out the debate on the Parliamentary address of 1844. But do not say this. Say, what after all is the truth, 'He is furious at not being here.'"

" Paris, February 10th.

"Great events are happening. The Opposition is going through the process of entire reconstruction. The Republicans have separated from the Extreme Left. MM. Thiers and Odillon-Barrot are reconciled. They are making me splendid offers to be the Mark Antony of their triumvirate. I am staying on account of Mâcon, which shall have her railroad, though I do not promise it before 1845."

" Paris, May, 1844.

" I am not working much in the Chamber this year. I do not care to appear mixed up in the little oppositions which begin again the little intrigues of 1840. I shall be home before the month is out."

" May 8, 1844.

" Here is a speech, and a famous one! as they say at Milly, on the prisons. Never was a greater or a more un-expected effect produced on the Chamber. My wife and Surigny were there. The law was lost, and I resuscitated it by inserting deportation, without which it would have been valueless. You must not judge by the newspaper reports, which are ridiculous. But the Chamber was more impressed than I have ever before seen it—friends and foes alike. I have had no sleep, and am thoroughly done up. The railroad is crushing me ; I doubt our carrying it this year. Nothing new in politics ; they are sleeping less heavily."

" Monceau, July 8th.

"Your letter was most welcome. It explains the incomprehensible mysteries of the marriage settlement [of
the Duc de Nemours]. The King and M. Guizot are ill-
advised ; it is a deplorable affair. I pity you for having
to breathe the air of Paris ; I am inhaling the perfume of
our vines. My wife is at St. Point, where I join her to-
morrow. I work every morning at my history ; my vines
flourish ; I am well and cheerful, and wish you were within
ten miles of us. Make up for the distance by your letters ;
yours are the only ones that have interest for me now.
Take us on your way from Bordeaux. My constituents
are full of gratitude for the new railway ; they welcomed
me with a hymn of praise. I am now forgetting their
existence, listening to the soughing of the wind among the
chestnut-trees. A thousand tender and respectful remem-
brances to Madame de Lagrange. When this volume of
my history is done, I will send her some verses, but ' bread
must go first to the oven ! ' "

To M. DARGAUD.

" Marseilles, August 5th.

"Your letter went to my heart. It is pleasant to be
understood, better still to be loved. We are at Marseilles—
my wife, Madame de Cessia, her son and daughter—and
to-morrow we start by steamer for Naples ; we go then to
Ischia, where we shall have the sea and the choice of
fourteen mineral springs. We stay there till the end of
September, returning to Monceau in October. I am taking
my books, and shall work for forty days at Ischia, then for
three months at Monceau. My year is full."

"Geneva, October 4th.

"Here we are at the end of our Odyssey of a thousand leagues ; we crossed the Simplon Alps amid thunder, rain, and snow, and are now resting for a few days at the house of an old friend. I have taken up my pen to ask you to Monceau, where a cosy chimney-corner awaits you. Come quickly; I hear the vintage has been good, and I have written a volume and a half on various topics. Champeaux, who joined us at Rome, is with me."

About this time, M. Villemain, Minister of Education, retired from office under circumstances peculiarly painful. Though a writer and lecturer of great ability, he had not the toughness of fibre necessary to statesmen in those days, and had felt deeply the way in which his Bill for the creation of a new scholastic system, which was to work under the direction of the University, had been received. The difficulty of reconciling the religious feeling of others with his own convictions on the subject of education, together with the violent attacks made on him by the party of which the *Univers* was the mouthpiece, so preyed upon him that his health gave way, and his reason became impaired. At the time of the foundation of the College of Mâcon, in 1843, Lamartine, who had reason to think himself unfairly treated by the Minister of Public Instruction, wrote of him with a very unusual amount of bitterness ; but, on hearing of his misfortune, forgot all former grievances.

"The news of Villemain saddens me beyond expression," he writes to M. de Lagrange. "If an intellect so full, a judgment so upright as his have failed, what are we ? Empty bubbles of renown, on whom God breathes and we cease to be. I pray to Him for this poor Villemain, once so kind to me. I pray for you, for myself, for all. As for the chaff of ambition to be harvested in the Salle des Conférences, you are right in despising it, as I do. What does it matter whether the puppet set up for the moment is called Molé, or Guizot, or Thiers, or Lamartine? Let it be our task to devote ourselves to distinct truths, to the organic ideas of our time, and let the rest pass by."

To M. DE LAGRANGE.

" Paris, January 22nd.

"Thanks to you and to Gizorne, the *Bien public* has a wonderful reputation ; nowhere else is political sense found. But as for politics, they are, as far as I am concerned, dead and buried long ago ; men succeed each other, but nothing is done. I myself am between a lawsuit and ruin. I think it will always be thus. God is good, and sorrow is the portion of His prophets. It seems as if He fights on the side of His enemies ! Do not hurry yourself ; there is nothing to be done here save to weep over Jeru-salem. No one is at this moment more popular in the Chamber than I am ; Guizot is abhorred ; but men sell themselves as in the open market. The Opposition is divided into four groups. M. Barrot tried a little while ago to bring about a fusion, which ended in a fresh break-up. Such is the bulletin of the political Waterloo. But at Waterloo blood flowed ; now it is honour which oozes at every pore."

" Monceau, May 24th, 1845.

"I have hardly time for a word. I have on hand (1) a great concert given by Liszt and Felicien David ;

(2) a procession combining music and patriotism, which is to come out here from Mâcon ; (3) to-morrow an improvised banquet with speeches—the country is enthusiastic."

"Monceau, May 26th.

"All has passed off well; music, festivities, Liszt, piano, speeches, toast ; a cordial fusion of working-men, aristocrats, *juste-milieu*, all one in heart and mind. We can only send you the dry bones of the speeches gathered up and put together next day by Gizorne, Lenormant, and me. At Monceau all goes on well. I have my dear nieces close to me. The weather is good ; the vines are growing and thriving."

To M. DE LAGRANGE.

"St. Point, August 22nd, 1845.

"I found your letter here among two hundred others, and hasten to answer it the first. I can see you in the middle of your installations, political and domestic. You are like the oak which throws its roots deep down among the rocks, and thus braves the storm with impunity. But your rock is at once firm and yielding ; you are one of those deputies who are not to be dislodged. Putting friendship aside, where else could they find your equal in name, in talent, in perfect independence, in capacity and sincerity of intention. That kind of grain does not grow under the feet of most electors. As for your domestic installation, I have passed half my life at that business. It has its pains and its pleasures ; it makes you feverish, but it is like the fever of public speaking—give it up, and you return to it unconsciously. I can see from here Madame de Lagrange's genius displaying itself in the

drapery of a curtain, and yours in the laying out of a
garden. Do it thoroughly and completely while you are
about it, is my advice !

"We have just come from the waters of Neris, which
have done us neither good nor harm. I have sold 'Les
Girondins' for 250,000 francs, but for ten years only. I
hope then to make as much more if—if—a great many
more 'ifs.' I shall have twenty more volumes of writings,
old and new, to sell in the next three years.

"As to quality, the vintage is bad, but we have quantity.
Yesterday evening, two stout brokers from the neighbourhood came up unexpectedly and bought the whole vintage
of Milly and Monceau from me on foot. Have I done well
or ill ? I don't know, but I stumbled on the opportunity,
and seized it at once.

"No one admires your friend, M. Thiers, more than I
do. To persevere in opposing him, I have to struggle
against a strong natural inclination, but instinct must be
overcome by logic. M. Thiers may be an excellent minister ;
he can neither be a leader nor even a member of the
Opposition after his fifteen years of triumphing over Liberal
principles. I am sorry to say you will see this opinion of
mine in print ; it has just been sent to a Mâcon paper,
whence it will probably be copied into the Parisian ones.
When Thiers and I have a common creed, I will profess it
with a joy as sincere as yours, but the Laws of September,
the Eastern Question, and the Fortifications have put
between me and him a political gulf no feeling of personal
liking is sufficient to bridge over. I am at present absorbed
in the study of the Revolution, and give but a side-glance
from time to time at the politics of the day. But I am

reading M. Thiers' fifth volume with serious admiration. If you see him, tell him this. He is mistaken if he counts me among his enemies ; I am only his adversary, and that with regret."

Lamartine did not take much part in the debates of the session of 1846. He had put his name down to speak against the annexation of Texas by the United States, foreseeing that it would lead to the extension of slavery, but gave way to M. Guizot, who spoke on the same side. On the 5th of July, he made a long speech in the sense of not allowing French influence in Syria to be overshadowed by that of Russia or of England, especially with the view of supporting the Emir Beschir, whose hospitality he had enjoyed in Syria.

To M. RONOT.

" Paris, April, 1846.

" Thanks, but the questions as to England and the Navy have been passed over. Now, nothing is talked of but the salt-tax, which, at the sound of my voice, crumbled away like the walls of Jericho. There has been nothing like it since August 6th, '90 (*la nuit des sacrifices*), the Chamber giving up forty-eight millions of taxes under the influence of a single voice. Paris is extraordinarily kind to me this year ; I hardly know how to respond to the enthusiasm which everywhere greets me. It is, alas, little merited, but genuine. As for Mâcon, I hear I am being undermined on all sides. The saying as to the prophets will stand good for eternity."

" St. Point, August, 1845.

" I have been returned for Mâcon with a calm, deliberate, and kindly unanimity, which is a miracle of wisdom on the part of the Progressive-Conservative party, which looked on me as a deserter in 1842. I, who care little for politics, am touched to the heart. I am here alone with my family, no longer troubled with rheumatism, and all day on horse-back. Three-fourths of the Milly vintage was destroyed by hail, but I shall still have twelve thousand *pièces de vin* for sale, I hope at seventy francs the piece."

To MADAME EMILE DE GIRARDIN.

"August, 1846.

" Banned be the carriage that played you false, and blessed the post-chaise that will bring you. You will find us alone, sad, but happy in having you under the humble rafters of St. Point. Write, that I may know when we are to meet you at Mâcon. But do not come unless you are prepared to vegetate all day and to go to roost with the chickens, and do not forget to bring ' Cléopatre.' *Mille tendres respects.*"

Madame de Girardin arrived in due course. Among the other guests were the Esgrignys, Lafon the actor and his pretty young daughter, Paul Delaroche, le docteur Pascal, M. Ronot, and Madame de Pierreclos, " still in deep mourning, but at times letting fall *reparties* which almost eclipsed Madame de Girardin," who herself was never more brilliant.

A few weeks later, Lamartine wrote to her : " Since you left I have not had a moment to myself—between the Conseil-général, the Académie de Mâcon, estate business, accounts, and festivities ; so I came here yesterday from Monceau, and am just beginning to draw breath. First, I must thank you for your charming letter to my wife, and for the enchanting *bonhomie* which made you as rustic as any of us at St. Point. There is a Latin line which says admirably, ' Omnis Aristipp decuit color ; ' in French, ' Tous les habits séyaient à Aristippe.' And in like manner everything you do suits your nature, at once strong and supple ; you wear with equal grace the buskin and the *sabot.*

"I am sending you one of two of my articles ; one of yesterday on wheat (*sur la crise des subsistances*), another of this morning, terribly severe on the Spanish marriages, but still courteous. The King's name is not mentioned. He does wrong in hating me ; no one else, while attacking his policy, speaks as well of him personally.

"My vintage is over, and it is scanty. We must live, and to live must write. Adieu. Love us, for here you are loved truly and sincerely."

To M. Dubois.

"Monceau, December, 1846.

"Thanks for your good news. As for politics, you know my opinions. The day on which the King put his signature to the Spanish marriage treaty, he signed the eventual abdication of his dynasty. I could prove this to you on ten different grounds, but have only time to assert it. *Adieu et attachment.* I finish ' Les Girondins ' this week, and go to Paris January 15th. There is nothing to be done save to wait. The King is a madman ; M. Guizot, a bladder inflated with vanity ; M. Thiers, a teetotum ; the Opposition, a woman who has lost her reputation ; the nation, Geronte.* But for many the farce will have a tragic ending."

* The allusion is to a character in Destouche's comedy, "Le Philosophe marié."

The correspondence of 1847 opens with a letter to a village labourer, who, having accidentally become possessed of the first volume of "Jocelyn," read it aloud to his family. Being too poor to purchase the second volume, he wrote to Lamartine, asking him for a copy.

"February, 1847.

"MONSIEUR,

"Your letter has touched me deeply. Never did any token of esteem for my poor work give me greater pleasure. To give comfort and intellectual food to a poor, isolated, and virtuous family; to be thus intimately linked with aspirations which arise from the village hearth to God ; to have a name among the memories and in the thanksgivings of an honest man to whom one is personally unknown, and by whom one is yet loved, this, to my mind, is true glory, and I owe it to you.

" I hasten to thank you, thinking that a letter written by my own hand will give you more pleasure than one dictated to a secretary, and I send you the second volume of 'Jocelyn,' to which I add my 'Voyage en Orient,' a work in prose, which may interest you in the winter evenings.

"Continue to refresh yourself after your manual labours by reading, and do not be unhappy because you are only a village labourer. Labour is the universal law. Ours is perhaps quite as hard as yours. The mind must sweat as well as the brow. God blesses both equally, and will in good time pay us our wages, without considering whether we wrote poems or ploughed furrows. I wish you a long life, virtuous children, and your daily bread.

"LAMARTINE."

In the March following, Lamartine's most important historical work, "Les Girondins," of which portions, appearing at intervals, had aroused general expectation, was published in four volumes. Three years previously, partly to sustain his literary reputation, partly to increase his intellectual capital as a politician and as an orator by thorough study of an important period in French history, Lamartine had agreed with a publisher to write within a given period a history of the Revolution ; but when he found how enormous was the amount of material to be studied, compared, sifted, he limited himself to a single episode—the history of the party of the Gironde,—and applied himself with the utmost ardour to the thorough fulfilment of his task. Besides much patient and conscientious labour among archives, papers, files, letters, he made himself familiar with the localities in which the scenes of the great drama had been enacted: the house of Madame Roland at Villefranche ; that of Charlotte Corday's aunt at Rouen ; the fetid dens where Marat lay in ambush ; Robespierre's neat *appartement* in the Rue St. Honoré,— and, despite the lapse of half a century, unearthed living witnesses of the events he wanted to describe, adding many strange figures to the circle of his acquaintances, as, for example, Danton's widow and an intimate friend of Fouquier Tinville, who, when questioned as to the personal characteristics of the "purveyor of the guillotine," replied with enthusiasm, " He was a charming fellow ; always in good spirits."

After these preliminary studies, Lamartine's pen sped swiftly over the paper. From the first the work delighted him, and thoroughly suited his personal predilections ; for,

notwithstanding many errors and some crimes, the Girondins represent, not unworthily, the ideal and intellectual
side of the Revolution. To illustrate it he concentrated
all his powers, and succeeded so perfectly as to have
created single-handed the " Legend of the Gironde." The
story, which opens at the deathbed of Mirabeau, and closes
at the scaffold of Robespierre, is told with great force
and effect, justifying the warm, but not very gratifying,
encomium of the elder Dumas : " You have raised history
to the level of romance ! " Lamartine possessed what
many would consider the first qualification of an historian
—the gift of telling a story with such animation and vividness that the events narrated seem to be passing before the
reader's eyes, and that in an admirable, flowing style, with
a due sense of proportion. In his judgments he was
generous, and certainly strove to be impartial. Republican
though he was, he never strives to minimize the crimes of
the democrats. His descriptions of the September massacres
and of the fiendish cruelties practised upon the unfortunate Royal family have not been surpassed in force.
He was bitterly reproached at the time for taking too
favourable a view of Robespierre's character, and with
passing over too lightly the sufferings and the heroism of
Marie Antoinette. Of this last accusation the following
passage, to which might be added many others too long
for quotation, may be considered a sufficient refutation.

" Marie Antoinette, whom her enemies describe on that
fatal night as a crowned fury, delirious in her excitement,
hysterical in her fear, showed no such weakness. She
behaved with simple, unaffected dignity, always and under
all circumstances what her sex, her rank, her position as

mother, as wife, as Queen required of her. She feared, she
hoped, she desponded, she hoped again ; but there was no
exultation in her hopes, no undignified tremor in her fears ;
her heart and her nerve alike bore unshrinkingly the severest
blows fate could inflict. When she wept, her tears flowed
from love, not from weakness ; when she shuddered, it was
not at her own fate, but at that of her children. But her
tears and her tremor were alike shrouded from her enemies ;
the respect shown to herself, to her Royal station, to her
mother's memory, was a veil, hiding from those who sat
and watched her every trace of emotion."

Perhaps Lamartine's most conspicuous fault is that
he is inclined to give too much importance to the group
from which his history takes its title. However, the
Girondins were, it cannot be denied, a party distinguished
by great talents, great courage, by the high personal
characters of the leaders. The austere probity of Roland,
the eloquence of Gensonné, of Guadet,—above all, that of
Vergniaud, enabled them to sway for a time the National
Assembly. And the gist of Lamartine's narrative is to
show that, had but their influence continued to prevail, the
purest, the most virtuous of Republics would have been
established ; but that the King's flight to Varennes, and
the insurrection of the 10th of August, ruined everything.
The Girondins had henceforth before them the scaffold of
Louis XVI., Danton and Robespierre pressing on them
from behind. Condemned to failure, they illuminated an
inevitable defeat by an heroic struggle. Driven from the
clubs by the invasion of the Montagne, from the muni-
cipalities by the defeat of Roland and his colleagues, from
the army by the treachery of Dumouriez, there remained

to them only the Convention ; and here they intrenched
themselves, fought courageously, and finally succumbed.
When, on the 31st of October, Vergniaud and his friends,
twenty-two in all, mounted the scaffold, chanting the
"Marseillaise," all that was spiritual and heroic in the
Revolution perished with them.   It henceforth became a
struggle between brutal force and feline cunning.

In consequence, perhaps, of the political action of "Les
Girondins," and of the poetry of its style, at once senti-
mental and picturesque, the fashion has been to allude to
the work as if it were a romance rather than a history, and
to overlook its more serious and abiding merits. Yet
Buckle, who assuredly was a good judge and one not likely
to be biased in the author's favour, considered "Les
Girondins" the best history of the French Revolution
extant in his day, and quoted it frequently. He selects
specially for approval "Lamartine's striking and beautiful
sketch of Madame Roland ; the thrilling account of the
September massacres ; that of the three days' interval
between the 31st of May and the 3rd of June, which was
the 10th of August of the Gironde." However, the minute
and persistent labours of two generations, harvested by
such writers as Sybel, Taine, and Hildebrandt, having at
their disposal documents inaccessible at an earlier date,
have diminished the value of "Les Girondins" from the
historical standpoint ; but the work has still value, as
showing in what light the Revolution appeared to men of
Lamartine's day,—to those who saw it, not as did the
generation which had gone through its terrible experience ;
not as we, to whom the inexorable logic of statistics has
unveiled what the Government of the Convention really

was, see it now—its cruelty, its exactions, above all, its incredible meanness, and the miseries it entailed on the classes it professed to benefit ; but viewed through the glamour of childish recollections, mingled with the confused rhapsodies of surviving actors, whose interest lay in depicting it as a great and beneficial event.

Financially, the success of " Les Girondins " has hardly a parallel in French literature. Lamartine, being pressed for money, sold the copyright for ten years to a company for £10,000 paid in advance. Within a week they wrote him word that no work ever had such a sale. Booksellers who had ordered ten copies, now sent for five hundred, so that all their men, working night and day, could not suffice to supply the demand. Within two months the sale had exceeded £20,000, and so continued. It would seem that the publishers then gave Lamartine some additional share in the profits, for M. de Lacretelle speaks of his having received £16,000 for the work.

From all sides congratulations poured in. The inhabitants of Mâcon, fired by the general enthusiasm, became eager to do honour to its most illustrious citizen, and asked Lamartine's permission to erect his statue. On his refusal, based on the ground that such an honour should be paid to no man during his lifetime, " La mort seule consacre," a second communication was forwarded, inviting him to a public banquet, which he accepted, with the condition that there was to be no advertising, no touting for subscriptions, no exclusion of persons of any shade of public opinion ; that it should be a simple expression of kindly feeling on the part of his fellow-citizens.

From the moment it was announced the banquet far

S

outgrew the original programme. Twenty neighbouring departments asked to be represented by delegates ; the number of guests was with difficulty limited to two thousand, exclusive of a numerous audience of ladies. A large open space on the right bank of the Saône was selected. There, on the 15th of July, were spread fifty tables, protected from the weather by tents and awnings, and surrounded by galleries, crowded with spectators, " forming, under a canvas dome measuring half an acre, a living, breathing Coliseum, the like of which was never seen in Greece or Rome." Besides its other attractions, this banquet to Lamartine is said to have been one of the last exhibitions of costumes of "Le Mâconnais" and "La Bresse." " For it the wives of rich farmers took out of their presses of aromatic walnut wood, blacker than ebony, silk gowns and lace head-gears, dating from the time of Marguerite de Savoie ; enamels of Bourg, gold crosses, and necklets were everywhere glittering in the sun. The *pêle-mêle* was at once confused and majestic. Journalists from Paris and from all points of the compass, priests in their soutanes, artisans in their Sunday suits, stray soldiers, English tourists, leaving their beaten tracks, were all fused as in a moving, shifting kaleidoscope ; a crowd tumultuous with eager expectation, yet restraining its own clamour, mingling deep reverence with almost delirious excitement."*

When the bell of the old Church of St. Etienne had rung out four o'clock, Lamartine appeared, escorted by the municipality, and received an enthusiastic welcome. The guests then sat down to the material portion of the banquet, which was admirably organized, the only untoward incident

* Henri de Lacretelle, " Lamartine et ses Amis."

being the serving at the principal table of a calf roasted whole. "It was Homeric, but, save in the Iliad, is not imposing." Meanwhile, as the feast was going on, the dazzling July sunshine became obscured by a canopy of thunder-clouds. Hardly had the Mayor of Mâcon, M. Rolland, proposed Lamartine's health amid frantic applause, when a terrific storm of thunder and lightning burst forth, affording to the superstitious a presage of the impending Revolution. But such was the *suspension des esprits* that, in the immense assembly, not a chair moved ; all were intent on catching the first accents of Lamartine's reply.

"You are, indeed," were his opening words, "the sons of those Gauls who said, were the firmament to fall, they would uphold it with their lances !" And for more than two hours, amid rolling peals of thunder and fiery forks of lightning, he continued to deliver an impassioned harangue, winding up, perhaps without being fully conscious of the effect of his words, with an apotheosis of Republicanism, and was finally escorted back to his hotel by a chorus of two hundred voices singing the " Marseillaise."

A few days later, he writes to M. Chamborre, one of his colleagues at the Académie française, who had, apparently, been somewhat scandalized by the newspaper report of the Mâcon banquet :—

" MONSIEUR ET CHER CONFRÈRE,

" I have read with pleasure the well-reasoned, well-expressed letter you have done me the honour of addressing to me.

" I am far from desiring a Revolution. In France a Revolution has only one lever—war. Do me the justice to remember that, alike in the ranks and out of the ranks, I have always striven to break this weapon in the hands of those who wield it. If I had wished for a Revolution in 1839 or in 1840, I needed but to join the coalition. Who sang the 'Marseillaise,' from the balcony of Neuilly in 1830? Was it not the King? Who faced unpopularity to snatch a declaration of war out of the weak hands of M. Thiers? Was it not I? Remember this. I admit with you that material progress is more secure in France with the Conservatives than with the Liberals. But there is an immense moral progress which it is necessary, obligatory to achieve, and of this progress the Throne and the Conservatives of to-day have alike shown themselves incapable. It is for this reason I think a more energetic impulse in the forces of Government is desirable, and that I resolutely run the risk, not of Revolution, but of Reform, in the organic working of opinion. When we are together at Charnay or at St. Point, I will tell you in what consists the moral and political progress for which a country like France must be ready when the prophetic hour strikes, to hasten the advent of which I think it my duty to fan with my weak breath the sacred fire of '89, of which the last lingering embers will speedily die out unless a few like-minded with me are found to cherish them. Do not fear any excess of energy in France—it is not there the danger now lies. Fear rather for her too heavy a sleep. And do not be anxious if a few men of good will venture to utter the words, 'Sursum corda.'

"With sincere attachment,

"LAMARTINE."

The autumn of 1847 was felt by many to be an anxious and critical time. " A strange disquietude," writes M. de Tocqueville to a friend in England, " is coming over men's minds ; not a ripple on the surface, yet many persons have a secret conviction that the existing order will suddenly and quickly collapse." New men, new interests, and new forces were surging on all sides ; people felt that the political hairsplitting, the changes of Ministries which had sufficed to occupy public attention for the last six years, were but a perpetual reshuffling of the same cards, in which the vital interests of the country had been overlooked, and that a fresh infusion of national life, and, above all, some barrier against the overweening influence of the middle class, now no longer balanced by a territorial aristocracy, was imperatively needed. Every year the inadequacy of the Parliament to represent the country was becoming more evident, and now the Opposition, though not numerically stronger than before, were more closely united. A general meeting of the Liberals took place, at which MM. Thiers and Odillon-Barrot, the leaders of the Dynastic Opposition, agreed to join the Republicans on the understanding that legal measures alone were to be adopted until the reforms demanded were achieved ; after that, each party was free to pursue its own course.

The next step was to organize, under the direction of the Committees constituted in 1845 to direct the elections, a series of public banquets in all the principal towns—a species of agitation which, not having been foreseen, was less hampered by legal restrictions than any other. The first banquet was held at Chateauroux, near Paris, under the presidency of M. de Lasteyrie—Odillon-Barrot and

Duvergier d'Hauranne making very violent speeches; and
was followed by seventy others in different parts of the
country. The excitement and enthusiasm steadily increased, those who at first stood aloof getting gradually
drawn into the vortex, especially as the general impression
was that the Government would not now allow the agitation
to go on unchecked, unless they intend ultimately to yield.
Lamartine, however, with what Herr Hildebrandt calls
"his wonderful, bard-like gift of second sight," judged
from the first that the movement would soon get beyond
the control of those who inaugurated it, and, always dis-
liking coalitions, refused to join this.

He and his wife spent the autumn in a villa on the
Mediterranean, where they were joined by his sisters and
their children. The welcome relief from pecuniary anxieties
which the success of his book procured, braced and
brightened his spirits, and he was able thoroughly to enjoy
the wave of popularity which came rippling to his feet.

The political horizon was clouded; but never had
Lamartine's own position been more assured or fuller of
promise.

CHAPTER IX.

WHEN the Chambers opened in December, 1847, many
and various were the rumours circulating in the *salle des
pas perdus*, the place where gossips congregate, and where
the Parisian deputies first make the acquaintance of their
provincial colleagues. Some said there would be a speedy
break-up of the Ministry, others prophesied an immediate
coup d'état. The King's speech increased the excitement.
Louis Philippe, at all times too much inclined to parade
his personal feelings, after alluding at unnecessary length
to his own advanced age and accumulated experience, went
on to speak of "an agitation fomented by blind and hostile
passions," and wound up by attributing disloyal, if not
traitorous designs to those who had been present at the
political demonstrations of the last months.

This was accepted, both by them and by their opponents,
as a direct attack on the Left. It was felt to be dangerous
as well as undignified for the King to have thus stigmatized
publicly proceedings which were avowedly not illegal, and
in the debate on the speech even the staunchest supporters
of the Government criticized severely the concluding paragraph. Still, such was the strength of the Governmental

majority, that an address which contained an echo of the obnoxious passage was carried, after three weeks of angry discussion, during which Thiers, Lamartine, and Odillon-Barrot all spoke with great force and effect, while it was remarked of Guizot that the wonderful oratorical power by which he had often triumphed over far greater trials now seemed to have deserted him—he never made an effective rally. And matters were made worse by a violent and indiscreet speech of the Minister of Justice, M. Hébert, who vehemently denied that the Constitution gave Frenchmen the right of free discussion; whereupon M. Odillon-Barrot shouted out, " Never would M. de Peyronnet have used such language ! " justifying his words by his own experience in the spring of 1830.

The position of the Liberal party was now a very difficult one. After the manner in which the right to convene public meetings, and the right to freedom of discussion, had been alluded to, it was impossible they should remain passive; yet they felt that if agitation were kept up too long, it might degenerate into a riot. After much consideration, the course resolved on was to persevere in the banquets; should their meetings be prevented by any display of force, not to resist, but to carry the question at once before the legal tribunals. Accordingly, a banquet, got up by the twelfth arrondissement of the city of Paris, was announced for Tuesday, the 22nd of February, and, to keep order, the National Guard were invited to line the streets in uniform, but unarmed.

This calling out of the National Guard was, not unnaturally, resented by the Government, which resolved to forbid the banquet, but delayed to make its intention

known until a sufficient number of troops were collected in
Paris to quench any outbreak which might occur. It was
not, therefore, till late on Monday night that the decision
was announced in the Chambers. The Opposition agreed,
after some discussion, not to hold the banquet, but to
impeach the Ministry.

On the morning of Tuesday, the walls of Paris were
placarded with copies of General Jacqueminot's order of
the day, desiring the National Guard not to take part in
the demonstration, and with a proclamation, signed by the
prefect of police, formally forbidding the banquet. This
excited much indignation, and the manifesto of the Opposition, posted underneath, declaring that, as the Government
had determined to suppress their meeting by force, they
would not expose the people to the consequences, had not
a soothing effect. Angry groups gathered, denouncing
them as traitors, and threatened to attack the Hôtel des
Affaires Étrangères, occupied by M. Guizot. They were,
however, easily dispersed by the military on duty, and the
city remained, on the whole, tolerably tranquil.

Still, those who remembered the Revolution of July,
1830, said it was very like the first day of that period.
And by the afternoon of Wednesday things wore a
threatening aspect. Barricades had sprung up in the
district between the Rue St. Martin and the Seine—always
the hot-bed of sedition. The troops were indeed fully
competent to settle matters ; but it was doubtful whether
they would act against the civic soldiers, should these take
the side of the populace, and much anxiety to avoid a collision
was shown. At twelve o'clock, the National Guard sent
a deputation of their officers to the Tuileries to say that

they would not help in putting down a popular demonstration against a Minister whom they detested, coupling the message with a demand for a change of Ministry. It was thought at first this would not be granted, but at five o'clock M. Guizot informed the Chambers that he only held office till Count Molé should have constructed a Cabinet.

This concession acted like oil on troubled waters : the funds rose at once ; many of the barricades were destroyed by the people themselves, and a considerable portion of Paris was spontaneously illuminated. But if the people were satisfied, the revolutionary leaders were not, and at the moment when tranquillity seemed to be restored, one of the inexplicable incidents which seem like the touch of destiny completely changed the face of affairs.

A group of about a hundred and fifty men, mostly armed, followed by a band of idlers, went about insisting that every house should illuminate. Having carried their point at the Ministry of Justice, they went on to the Hôtel des Affaires Étrangères, which M. Guizot had just vacated, and where, to preserve order, a troop of horse was stationed. Hardly had the mob reached the spot, when a shot, supposed to have been fired by a reprieved convict, named Lagrange, broke the leg of the horse of the officer commanding the troop, and brought the rider heavily to the ground. The soldiers, thinking they were attacked, levelled their muskets without waiting for orders, and a storm of bullets swept the Boulevard.

The crowd at once dispersed into the different quarters of Paris, shouting, " Treachery ! " " Vengeance ! " The corpses, placed on waggons, were paraded through the city ; and the populace, made to think they had been wantonly attacked, became violently excited, and from that moment determined to overthrow the monarchy. The barricades just demolished were reconstructed at once ; the trees of the Boulevards were cut down, and, together with cabs, omnibuses, and every object on which the mob could lay hands, converted into new ones. Orators moved from group to group, exciting the people to begin a fresh conflict. Parties were sent round to the houses of the National Guards, insisting that all arms should be given up—collecting in this manner a large provision from the terrified inmates.

Meanwhile, at the Tuileries no such energy was shown. Hour after hour was wasted in divided and contradictory councils. Late in the evening Count Molé came to announce that he had failed in forming a Cabinet, and advised the King to send for M. Thiers, who agreed to undertake the task, provided he were allowed to have M. Odillon-Barrot.

The next question was the disposal of the forces. Guizot's last act, the appointment of Marshal Bugeaud as commander-in-chief, had been a wise one. He was not popular, but was known to be courageous and prompt in action, and the troops were cheered by seeing him at their head. He at once made excellent military dispositions, and gave orders to prepare for an attack on the barricades. At two in the morning he received his final instructions from the King in person, and went out to the military head-quarters in the city. Here he found everything in confusion : very few officers in attendance, and no one knowing who was to command, and who to obey. Never

was seen more clearly what vigour and capacity, even in
the most terrible crisis, can achieve. As if by enchantment, everything was changed, order succeeded to chaos,
consecutive movement to vacillating direction. By early
dawn, four columns were in motion, rapidly advancing to
the points assigned to them. At seven, the Hôtel de Ville,
the Panthéon, and the whole centre of the city were strongly
occupied, without the troops left at the Tuileries and the
Hôtel de Ville being weakened. Twenty-five thousand
men had done the whole, and done it by the mere force of
advance, without firing a shot ; barricades were being
surmounted and levelled, the important posts occupied.
From a military point of view, Paris was secure and the
victory gained, when Marshal Bugeaud received an order,
signed by Thiers and Odillon-Barrot, to cease action and
withdraw the troops.

The reason of this extraordinary and calamitous change
was the overweening vanity of M. Thiers, who seems really
to have believed that the mere announcement of his advent
to the Ministry would of itself restore order without any
military intervention. Unfortunately, the King, always
averse to bloodshed, was only too ready to adopt a policy
of conciliation, and trust to the National Guard for the
defence of his throne and person. A proclamation to this
effect greeted the citizens when they rose on Thursday
morning, and was read by the quiet and law-abiding with
dismay, not lessened by the undisguised triumph of the
Revolutionists. So bitter was the indignation of the
troops when marched through the barricades they had just
carried by assault, that the rank and file threw away their
muskets, and many of the officers broke their swords. The

insurgents, though as yet few in number, became excited and encouraged, pressing on as the soldiers retired. The vacillating crowd, believing theirs the winning side, rapidly swelled the ranks, while the brave and loyal despaired of a cause its leaders had abandoned ; and, as might have been anticipated, by ten o'clock the mob was in possession of the whole of that portion of Paris which lies behind the Palais Royal and the Tuileries.

The Royal family, in perfect ignorance of the situation, were seated at breakfast, when MM. de Remusat and Duvergier Hauranne came in, and called the Duc de Montpensier aside. The King asked what had happened, and on being told that the populace and the few remaining dragoons were in conflict behind the palace, put on his uniform and went, accompanied by his two sons, to review the National Guard and the handful of troops stationed in the Place de la Concorde. His reception by the surrounding crowd was not encouraging ; the feeble cries of " Vive le Roi ! " were drowned in far louder ones of " Vive la Reforme ! " " À bas les Ministres ! " He returned to the palace much dispirited, and there met M. Thiers, who, having found, to his surprise, that his name had not sufficed to restore tranquillity, had come to advise the King to entrust everthing to M. Odillon-Barrot alone. As he was speaking, a sharp volley of musketry announced that an attack on the Château d'Eau was being made by the insurgents, which proved successful, notwithstanding the gallantry of the troops, who, it is said, perished to a man.

The people were now marching rapidly on the Tuileries, and among their ranks were to be seen several uniforms of the National Guard ! It was ascertained, later, that these were for the most part insurgents who had assumed the uniform, partly in order to save themselves from being fired on, partly to serve as decoy ducks to such as might be wavering in their allegiance, and that the majority of the Guard were sincerely attached to the King, and would gladly have fought in his defence, had they been properly led. But the effect which their apparent defection produced on Louis Philippe was deplorable ; he had counted blindly on the support of the *bourgeoisie,* to whom he owed his crown, and now, believing they had turned against him, he was ready to abdicate rather than provoke a sanguinary and doubtful contest. In vain the Queen, once so reluctant to accept the crown, now urged him to a more spirited course, saying, " Sire, n'abdiquez pas ! Mettez vous à la tête de vos troupes, et je prierais Dieu pour vous." Louis Philippe, broken by sorrow, age, and infirmity, unsupported, as a legitimate sovereign would have been, by the consciousness of a just cause, signed the act of abdication which terminated his reign.

Lamartine, wishing to have no hand either in destroying or in sustaining the existing order, had kept aloof from the political movement of the last three days, so that his precise view as to the Government most desirable for France was an enigma, the solution of which, from his position and influence, was of great importance. The Radicals had frequently made him offers of leadership, which he invariably rejected. At last, on the morning of the 25th of February, when the King's abdication was felt to be imminent, a group of deputies of the Left invited

him, as he was on his way to the Chamber, to a conference
they were holding in one of the private rooms of the Palais
Bourbon, and asked him definitely to explain his views.
Thus pressed, he answered unreservedly, that, at the
present crisis, a Regency without the support either of a
legitimacy or of popularity would have no stability. "A
Republic alone can save France from anarchy, civil war,
the overthrow of society, the invasion of the stranger. The
remedy is a heroic one, but there are occasions when the
only safe policy is one as extreme as the crisis. The
Republic alone can dominate anarchy, conquer Com-
munism, avert bloodshed. Therefore, in reason as in conscience, without fanaticism and without illusions, I repeat
that if the hour we are passing through brings forth a
revolution, I will not work for a semi-revolution ; I would
rather have a complete one. But, that such a crisis may
be averted, I am willing to accept a Republic, but will
have no hand in making one." With these words Lamartine
rose and left them.

When he reached the Chamber, all was tumult and
confusion. No business was going on, but the deputies,
broken up into groups, were talking eagerly and excitedly,
"not concealing," writes an eye-witness, "that they were,
for the most part, each far more occupied as to the effect
the march of events might have on his individual fortune,
than about the welfare of the nation." Some sensation
was caused by the arrival of M. Thiers, who rushed in with
the news of Louis Philippe's abdication and departure ;
then, throwing up his arms with an excited gesture, exclaimed, "The flood is rising !" and disappeared from the
scene. At about half-past one, an officer in uniform came

in, and whispered something in the president's ear. M. Sauzet then informed the Assembly that the Duchesse d'Orleans was on her way to the Chamber. A few minutes later the folding doors were thrown open, and the Duchess entered. The scene and her appearance are thus described by Lamartine :—

" A respectful silence immediately ensued, the deputies rising at once from their seats to receive the august Princess. She was dressed in mourning ; her half-raised veil partly disclosed a countenance in which the charm of youth and beauty was enhanced by emotion ; her pale cheeks bore traces of the widow's tears, of the mother's anxieties. No man could look unmoved on that countenance, a single glance sufficed to wipe away every feeling of resentment against the monarchy. For a moment the eyes of the Princess wandered over the hall, as if imploring aid. Her slight and fragile form trembled at the sounds of applause which greeted her ; a faint blush, the mark of reviving hope, tinged her cheek ; a smile of gratitude flitted for a moment on her lips : she felt she was surrounded by friends. At her right hand walked her eldest son, the Comte de Paris, with her left she led the little Duc de Chartres,— children to whom their own downfall was as a scene in a play ! Dressed alike in short suits of black velvet, they looked as if they had just stepped out of the canvas of Vandyck's portrait of the children of Charles I."

Yet, graceful, dignified, and interesting as was the deportment of the Duchesse d'Orleans, she wanted the one quality which alone at such a crisis would have appealed successfully to the national sympathies,—she was not a Frenchwoman. Moreover, it was to her brother-in-law,

the Duc de Nemours, who now accompanied her, that the
post of Regent legally belonged; but, probably on that
account, the enemies of the dynasty had done their utmost
to make him unpopular, accusing him of reactionary
tendencies. How entirely without foundation the accusation was he proved by the well-known letter, written in
1854, in which, when all his interests lay in the opposite
direction, he maintained the steadfast adherence of the
House of Orleans to the tricolor flag and the principles
of '89. And now, when it was suggested by MM. Dupin,
Odillon-Barrot, and other partisans of the dynasty, that
when the Crown was in jeopardy the Regency of the Duchess
was the more likely to be accepted, he, with the chivalrous
loyalty of a character to which Lamartine has done fuller
justice than perhaps any other writer, had come personally
to renounce his own claim, and to sustain that of his
brother's wife.

Unfortunately, a resolution, however noble, founded on
the consciousness of unpopularity, does not excite enthusiasm; and when M. Dupin proposed that a decree
should be registered by the Chamber proclaiming the
Duchesse d'Orleans Regent, he failed to produce the
hoped-for effect. The mention of the Duchess was received
with warm acclamations, but the deputies refused to vote
on the question. M. Marie, known as a veteran Republican,
then ascended the tribune: on which Lamartine, speaking
from his place, asked the president, "from the double
motive of respect to the representatives of the nation, and
of respect to the august Princess who is now honouring
the Assembly with her presence, to declare the sitting
suspended."

T

The Duchess, after a little hesitation, yielded so far to the advice of those who surrounded her as to retire to a higher place on the benches—a measure necessary for her personal security, as the lower part of the Chamber was being gradually invaded by the populace.

M. Marie then adjured the Assembly to nominate a Provisional Government. " In the present state of Paris," he urged, "the duty devolves on you of taking measures for public security, and you have not a moment to lose. You cannot create a new Regency to-day; the laws forbid it. I demand a Provisional Government, which may later take the question into consideration in conjunction with the Chambers." He was listened to, Lamartine tells us, without opposition; the ideas of Royalty and Regency seemed to have vanished like smoke.

M. Odillon-Barrot, whose Ministry had begun and ended with the passing hours of the day, spoke on the other side, supporting the establishment of the Regency for the sake of the real interests of the nation and of constitutional liberty. But, popular as he was, he could not command the attention of the House, and was followed by M. de Larochejaquelin, who, in a few impassioned phrases, dressed the Legitimist predilections he had inherited with his name in the garb of Republican declamation, telling the Chamber they were no longer anything, the people were all in all! And, as if by magic, the people responded to the call: while he was yet speaking, masses of insurgents, fresh from their triumph in the Tuileries, invaded the Chamber on every side.

Lamartine, who had hitherto remained in his place, his face buried in his hands, as if uncertain as to the course he should pursue, now went up to the tribune. His opening words were awaited with intense interest, for it was felt that, were he to declare himself in favour of the Regency, his eloquence might even now retrieve the fortune of the fallen dynasty. It was true that to his " Histoire des Girondins " was chiefly attributed the sudden and surprising revival in France of Republican sentiment ; yet how pathetic, how thrilling had been his sympathy for the noble and innocent victims of the Revolution ! and those who remembered the glowing peroration of the speech in which he had, in 1842, upheld almost single-handed the maternal rights of the Duchesse d'Orleans, could not now but hope that the sight of this young and heroic mother pleading for her children would kindle the imagination and secure the fealty of a nature at once so chivalrous and so impressionable.

Lamartine himself admits that such was the case, that words which might have carried for the moment the suffrages of his audience trembled on his lips, and that nothing but a deep, reasoned conviction of the hopelessness of achieving more than a momentary and therefore pernicious triumph kept him from leading the forlorn hope of a cause to which no element of pathos and poetry were lacking. This uncertainty impeded the ordinarily unembarrassed flow of his eloquence. It was not without some hesitation and circumlocution that he at length definitely pronounced in favour of a Provisional Executive, " which should to-day put a stop to anarchy and bloodshed ; to-morrow call into its councils the entire nation to decide what form the future Government of France should take. One word more," he was about to add,—but at this moment the doors of the Chamber were violently burst open, and a band of over three hundred excited, half-delirious men, led by Lagrange, rushed in.

A scene of indescribable confusion ensued. The attendants of the Duchess, in agony for her life, hurried her and her children away. The Assembly rose in the utmost agitation, while the foremost of the ringleaders, climbing up the benches, levelled their muskets at the deputies.

When the first panic was over, it was found that the President, M. Sauzet, had disappeared from the scene. Lamartine, who had kept his place at the tribune, then proposed that M. Dupont de l'Eure, a man whose patriarchal age and experience gave him pre-eminence, should occupy the chair. This having been done, cries for the proclamation of a Provisional Government broke forth from all parts of the House, mingled with calls to Lamartine to name the members who were to compose it. This he declined to do, but handed to M. Dupont a list of names to be accepted or refused by acclamation. They were read out as follows : " Dupont de l'Eure, Arago, Lamartine, Marie, Garnier-Pagès, Ledru-Rollin, Crémieux." As to the last, the story current was that the original list only contained six names, but that, amid the deafening clamour, poor old Dupont de l'Eure, when called on to read it, could not make his voice heard. He transferred the list to the person next him, who, having a weak voice, was equally inaudible. As it was important no time should be lost, the list was then handed to M. Crémieux, who was known to have stentorian lungs ; he added his own name, which was, amid the clamour, adopted with the others, and, by happy dexterity, he thus appropriated, one-seventh of absolute dominion over thirty-seven millions of people.

The form of an election having thus been gone through, it was suggested that the new rulers of France should adjourn to the Hôtel of the Ministry of the Interior, and there instal themselves. But rumours began to circulate that the Hôtel de Ville had been invaded by a lower stratum of the populace, and that there also a Provisional Government was being established. Lamartine, seeing at once the danger of allowing any rival authority to exist even for an hour, and, above all, in the head-quarters of former revolutions, the Aventine of Parisian sedition—where gathered instinctively in times of anarchy the surging masses of the surrounding Faubourgs, swarming with desperate, half-crazy fanatics, ever biding the time to revive the bloody scenes of '93,—urged his colleagues to immediate action. Giving to those nearest him the watchword, "À l'Hôtel de Ville!" which was quickly taken up by the people, he and Arago set out on foot, escorted by some officers of the National Guard, one of whom carried the tricolor flag, while Dupont de l'Eure, who was old and in failing health, followed in a carriage. The procession was not an imposing one, nor was the task its leaders were undertaking easy.

Lamartine, in his "Histoire de la Révolution de 1848," tells us that he and his colleagues felt keenly that their election to the supreme power by a handful of insurgents in a deserted Chamber was perfectly invalid. To those who might question their authority they could give no reply save by pointing to the empty throne, the dispersed Legislature, the public buildings in flames, the city in

possession of an armed and excited populace. Their
authority was that which every citizen possesses at the
moment of his country's peril, to extinguish conflagration,
to avert bloodshed, to save life ; and, cost them what it
might, they were resolved to exercise it.

Having crossed the Pont Neuf, they came to the
barricade of the Quai de la Megisserie. It was with great
difficulty that Dupont de l'Eure was lifted over this
formidable obstacle, and the passage was painful to all.
The pavement tinged with blood, the corpses strewn about,
the wounded yet uncared for, bore witness to the severity
of the recent struggle ; and from this point the advance
became at every fresh step more difficult. All the
approaches to the Place de la Grève, in which the Hôtel
de Ville stood, were blocked by a dense crowd, which knew
nothing of what had passed at the Chamber of Deputies,
and paid scant attention to the order, " Make way for the
Government ! " Indeed, when they realized that the little
group of deputies, preceded by a single officer carrying the
National flag, were about to become their rulers, the first
impulse was one of rage. Ominous cries of " Treason,
treason ! They want to have 1830 over again ! " were
heard. It was chiefly, Lamartine says, owing to the
respect felt for Dupont de l'Eure, who was personally
known to many of the crowd, that the Hôtel de Ville was
at length reached.

Here still greater difficulties awaited them : the mob
was in full possession of the building ; many of the rooms
were filled with the dead and dying of yesterday's combat ;
others served as bivouacs for the victors ; while at every
door and staircase excited crowds were swaying to and fro.

The members of the Government, sometimes violently separated, sometimes as unexpectedly flung together, unable to converse, to organize any plan or resolution, were almost overwhelmed by the hopelessness of their position.

The hours sped swiftly on, and still no human voice could hope to dominate the many and terrible sounds echoing through the vast pile of building,—the clatter of arms carried by unskilful hands, the shrieks of the wounded, the moans of the dying, the continual discharges of musketry going on all round, the clamour of a hundred thousand voices in the Place below. There seemed no prospect of obtaining an instant of silence ; not so much as a pen or a sheet of paper could be procured to enable the Provisional Government of France to give some sign of authority or even of existence. At last, when hope seemed idlest, an unexpected deliverance came. One of the clerks of the Préfecture, M. Flottard, having succeeded in reaching Lamartine, whispered to him that he had in his pocket the key of a room at the end of a secluded corridor, which might serve as a council chamber, if the passages leading to it were first quietly secured by the friends of the Government. The offer was taken advantage of at once, the long corridors garrisoned by men whose devotion could be relied on, and within half an hour Dupont de l'Eure, Lamartine, Arago, Crémieux, Ledru-Rollin, Garnier-Pagès, and Marie began their labours.

As the news spread through Paris that the Provisional Government was installed, the Hôtel de Ville became the rallying point of all the partisans of order. The mayors of the different quarters of Paris, deputies, leading citizens, civil and military officials, editors of newspapers beyond counting, came in from all sides. A graphic description of this first council is to be found in the "Histoire de '48," by Daniel Stern. Dupont de l'Eure and Arago sat together, thoughtful, anxious, obviously troubled by melancholy recollections and still more melancholy forebodings. Garnier-Pagès and Marie, who had all through striven hard for the Regency of the Duchesse d'Orleans, were yet more desponding. Ledru-Rollin, the representative of the intransigeant Republican party, sat somewhat apart from his colleagues, conversing with Louis Blanc. Albert and Flôcon, who having been, they announced, added by the popular voice to the members of the Provisional Government, made their entry in a very imperious fashion, but, after some parleying, consented to accept the post of Secretaries, with consultative voices. Crémieux seemed cheerful and eager to talk, but carefully avoided committing himself to anything positive. Lamartine alone was ready to face all possibilities with a serene and undaunted spirit, his courage and eloquence rising visibly with the occasion. Taking up a pen, he began to draft the proclamation by which the Government was to make the French nation aware of its existence and of its mission. It was not an easy task. Both the tidings brought by messengers from without and the loud cries rising from some sixty thousand voices, testified to the growing anxiety and impatience of the populace for the proclamation of a Republic. Nothing else, it was reported on all sides, would arrest anarchy, pillage, and massacre. But, with the exception of Ledru-Rollin, all the members of the Government were strongly opposed to this course, feeling that, elected as they had been at haphazard, they had no right to impose a constitution on the French nation. A brisk altercation ensued, in which Ledru-Rollin's views were warmly supported by Louis Blanc, Flôcon, and Marrast.

Meanwhile, the agitation was increasing every moment outside, as fresh relays of populace came pouring in from every avenue leading to the Hôtel de Ville. In order to restrain them, those in the Council Chamber had repeatedly to go out, and make speeches, exhorting them to calmness and silence, with repeated assurances that the Provisional Government had no object but the good and the safety of the people.

Only to Lamartine, however, would they listen at last. He seemed at once better liked and more trusted than any of his colleagues, though with the cries of "We want Lamartine," "Vive Lamartine!" that greeted him each time he came out, were mingled others of "He is an aristocrat! a royalist! a Girondin!" But he, calm and self-possessed, appeasing them by some happy phrase, never failed in changing the mood of the populace, and thus obtaining a momentary lull.

The proclamation, drafted amid such infinite difficulties, after a few high-flown phrases, in which the people of Paris were complimented on their admirable conduct during the past three days, ran as follows: "A Provisional Government, created with acclamation by the voice of the people and of the Deputies of the Departments in the sitting of the 24th of February, is momentarily entrusted with the office of securing and organizing the national victory. It is composed of MM. Dupont, Lamartine, Arago, Marie, Crémieux, Garnier-Pagès, Ledru-Rollin; and has for secretaries MM. Louis Blanc, Flôcon, Marrast, Albert."

But the most important phrase was that in which the form the future Government of France must be indicated. When first drafted by Lamartine, it stood thus: "Although the Provisional Government, acting solely in the name of the French people, prefer the Republican form, yet neither the people of Paris nor the Provisional Government assume to substitute their opinion for that of the citizens, who will be consulted as to the definite form of Government which the Sovereignty of the People shall assume."

This paragraph was considered too ambiguous, and for it was substituted, in M. Crémieux's writing: "The Provisional Government wish the Republic to be ratified by the people, who will be immediately consulted."

Thus altered, copies of the proclamation, hastily printed off in the bureaux of the Hôtel de Ville, were thrown out of the windows, to the exultation of the mob, which, dispersing for the moment, hastened to convey the news throughout Paris. Some approach to silence and order being thus obtained, the organization of the Executive began, and the principal portfolios were allotted. Dupont was made President of the Council, without holding any other office ; Arago had the navy ; Crémieux, the Ministry of Justice ; Lamartine, that of Foreign Affairs ; Ledru-Rollin, the Interior ; and Garnier-Pagès was named Mayor of Paris. There was some difficulty in filling the post of Minister of War. Generals Bedeau and Lamoricière, though they gave in their adhesion to the Provisional Government, respectfully declined to serve. It was then given to General Subervier, who had served under Napoleon, and was universally respected, but far too old for such a post.

It is hardly possible to give an idea of the labours and difficulties of the Provisional Government during these first days of its existence. "No sooner," writes Lamartine, "was one messenger despatched with an order or a decree scribbled in pencil on the corner of a scrap of paper, than another arrived with a similar note, announcing that the Tuileries was menaced with flames and devastation; another, that Versailles was surrounded by a raging mob, thirsting to devour the last relics of royalty; another, that Neuilly was already half-burnt; a fourth, that all the railway stations were destroyed, the bridges cut or burned. It was indispensable at once to re-establish the traffic on the roads by which a capital with a million of mouths was to be fed; then huge mountains of barricades had to be cut through in order to let the convoys pass when they did reach the streets. Crowds who had been for three days famishing were to be fed, the dead to be collected, the wounded tended, the soldiers protected against the people, the barracks evacuated, the arms and horses gathered together; the palaces, the museums protected from pillage; an insurgent populace, numbering three hundred thousand, were to be calmed, pacified, and, if possible, sent to their workshops; posts manned by the National Guards and volunteers established at all points, in order to prevent pillage. In a word, the things to be done were innumerable; it was hard to say where neglect would entail the most serious evils."

Meanwhile, the crowd in the Place du Grève, thinned for a moment by the distribution of the proclamation, soon became denser and more unmanageable than ever. With the unceasing flux and reflux of labourers and artisans,

inevitable in a great city in which for three days all industry had ceased, were mingled other and more dangerous
elements. Idlers and loafers, with perhaps no political
ideas in their heads, but rejoicing in revolution for the
excitement it afforded, were going about among the people,
inciting them to fresh demands and to renewed violence,
and, as neither the troops nor the National Guard had yet
given in their adhesion, the new Government were perfectly
powerless, and could only trust to the isolated efforts of
their friends, and to whatever personal ascendency they
could gain.

And as evening closed in, the crowd surrounding the
Hôtel de Ville became still more excited and menacing.
It had been largely recruited by men of dangerous types ;
combatants from the more distant barricades, dissatisfied
with the results of their victory. Conspirators, to whom
the rebellion against any authority was as the breath of
their nostrils, were moving about among the people, telling
them they were being deceived, betrayed, mocked ; spreading rumours that the King was returning with an armed
force, and the garrisons of the detached forts preparing
red-hot shot to rain down on the devoted city. These
rumours, absurd and contradictory as they were, so excited
the people, that, forming themselves into an improvised
and tumultuous Assembly, they began to pass decrees and
resolutions to meet the treachery they supposed was plan-
ning their destruction. Some asked to have the red flag
hoisted, as a symbol of the blood which should not cease
to flow until all the enemies of liberty were crushed ; others
that all who had not fought on the barricades should be
excluded from any share of power ; others that the Govern-

ment should deliberate only in the presence of delegates named and trusted by the people.

Detachment after detachment of ringleaders were sent up, threatening to throw all the occupants of the Council Chamber into the street, unless their demands were complied with. Each member of the Government, Lamartine tells us, went out in turn to appease the seething multitude, by appealing to their patriotism and to their sense of justice ; trying to banish their fears and disarm their passions. But all accounts concur in stating that he alone exercised the slightest influence. Seven times during that terrible night he went out, at first alone, then, as the danger became greater and greater, escorted by a little band of devoted friends, to harangue from the steps of the Hôtel de Ville the raging crowd. Received with imprecations and menaces ; having to fight his way through a barrier of sabres, pikes, bayonets, quivering in the unsteady hands of men maddened with rage and excitement ; with difficulty gaining a hearing ; but, once he was heard, subjugating by the irresistible force of his energy and eloquence, or by his ready wit turning execration into applause,—as once when the storm was at its wildest, and the furious multitude, threatening to break down all barriers, had directed a volley of firearms against the lower windows of the Hôtel de Ville, Lamartine came out, and was greeted with cries of " Down with Lamartine ! We will not hear him ! We want his head ! " But he, with an expression of mingled amusement and disdain, looking quietly at them, said, " You want my head ? Well, things would certainly go on better if you had it on your shoulders." At this the menacing cries turned to peals of laughter, and arms lifted to strike stretched out for a cordial handgrasp. Still the temper of the mob, continually reinforced by fresh comers, could not be counted on for an instant. "What do you calculate," asked Lamartine of Arago, the one of his colleagues with whom he had most in common, "are our chances of seeing the sun rise to-morrow?" "I fear," replied the illustrious astronomer, "the chances are decidedly the other way. But as long as there remains even a single chance of saving the nation, it is sufficient for us."

Nor were the historical associations of the Hôtel de Ville reassuring to those who occupied it at such a crisis. Here had been fought out the last terrible struggle of the Montagnards. In one of the rooms adjacent to that they were using as a council chamber, Robespierre had lain mangled till he was dragged forth to execution; Robespierre the younger and Henriot trying to escape from an adjoining window, were flung on the pavement and severely injured. To the historian of "Les Girondins" it specially recalled the 9th of September. "If there is a Barras waiting for us outside," he whispered to Dupont de l'Eure, who himself had sat in the Convention, "we are lost, for we are precisely in the position of the Commune on the 9th Thermidor, only our conspiracy is in the cause of peace and of order, against anarchy and bloodshed."

But the exigencies of the situation left little leisure for such reflections. Regardless of threats and interruptions, the Provisional Government went on with its work. Innumerable decrees, drawn up with the rapidity of thought and the absolute determination of will which alone at such a time could enforce obedience and command success, were sent by reliable messengers to the several public offices, and the machinery of administration, shattered by three days' anarchy, was beginning to work again.

How much suffering had been caused by the cutting off for three days of all supplies, may be guessed by the fact that the rulers of the most civilized and luxurious city in the world were themselves all but starved on their first accession to power. When at nightfall they asked for some refreshment, nothing could be procured but a loaf of black bread and half a bottle of wine, left accidentally in the guardroom. A bucket of water was fetched, and the rations divided, and, though insufficient for a party of men who had not tasted food for twelve hours, were partaken of with cheerfulness, Lamartine remarking that the feast augured well for the economy of their rule.

Long and trying as the day had been, it came to an end at last. By the time sixty-two proclamations of immediate necessity had been issued, the good sense of the people and Lamartine's influence had checked the evil efforts of the would-be disturbers of the peace ; weariness and lassitude did the rest, and at length all was so quiet that it was agreed the Council might break up, leaving Lamartine and Marie to guard the post of danger alternately through the night.

In order to reassure his wife, who had gone through terrible anxiety, Lamartine went home for a couple of hours, returning at daybreak rested and refreshed. When he went out first the people were going through a semblance of military discipline and duty ; fires had been lit in the Place du Grêve, round which were gathered groups of men told off for the duty of guarding the guns

which had been brought there the day before, and still
were loaded. Sentries were posted in many of the streets,
and volleys of small arms let off from time to time with
the object of warning the regular troops, whose dispositions
were not yet known, that the people were on the alert.
But on his return Lamartine found the streets far more
quiet and deserted; the camp-fires had gone out, the
sentries were sleeping at their posts; only from time to
time men, somewhat better dressed than ordinary artisans,
passed him in little groups of three or four, all of whom,
he noticed, had in their button-holes a tiny piece of red
ribbon—a circumstance to which he did not at the time
attach any importance.

Lamartine, whose " History of the Revolution of 1848 "
we are following substantially, though not exclusively,
before narrating the events of the 25th of February, pauses
to describe three groups into which he divides the principal
actors of the day.

First he puts what he styles the National and Liberal
party, composed of the friends of liberty and progress,
taken from all classes, without distinction of condition or
of fortune. This party, by its twenty years of opposition in the Chamber, by the agitation of the Reform
banquets, by its action in detaching the National Guard
from the King, had been the principal motor in the Revolution. To it Lamartine did not, strictly speaking, belong;
his position in the Chamber had always been independent
of party ties, and on several occasions he had worked
earnestly and successfully against them. But "great movements are oftenest led by brilliant outsiders;" and the
rush of events during the past twenty-four hours had trans-

formed him from a distinguished free lance into a recognized leader. And now, just as the National and Liberal
party thought they had successfully inaugurated, perhaps
established, an enlightened, almost ideal Republic, there
sprang forward unexpectedly two other factions preparing
to enter at the half-repaired breach, and rise on the necks
of their precursors to power.

One was that of the Socialists, whose schemes, however
impracticable, were not yet tainted with violence. Lamartine expressly says that at this stage of the Revolution
they were distinctly opposed to the Terrorists, with whom
they afterwards coalesced, and that their most trusted
leader, Louis Blanc, who was at the time acting as secretary
to the Provisional Government, honestly did his best to
support it.

Far more powerful was the Montagnard or Terrorist
party, consisting of men with no desire of progress,
no visions of political regeneration, unfettered by the
illusions of those who think that the social edifice can
be regenerated without first burying a generation beneath
its ruins; men without faith, without principles, full of
passion and violence, wishing for a state of society as
violent as themselves, whose theory of Government is a
prolonged Revolution; without justice, without law, without
principle, without morality. Lamartine goes on to describe
the Terrorists as the producers of the Revolutionary literature which sprang up during the Restoration, and flourished
all through Louis Philippe's reign; which endeavoured, by
heaping praise on the destroyers and contempt on the
victims, to reverse the verdict of history. In the vocabulary
of this party the Republic meant the violent triumph of

U

a faction over a nation, the substitution of tyranny from below for tyranny from above, its arbitrary will for law, fury for justice, and the scaffold for Government. The believers in this creed were mostly young men bleached in the shade of secret societies, poisoned from infancy by the classics of the Reign of Terror, accustomed to deify Danton for his audacity in slaughter, and St. Just for his pitiless cruelty ; to ascribe grandeur to actions that were merely atrocious ; ready to purchase notoriety at any price.

And all through the night of the 25th of February, when Lamartine and his colleagues, of necessity but imperfectly informed, believed all immediate danger of insurrection dispelled, these men, made desperate by their defeat on the preceding day, were up and at work, intriguing, combining, organizing another and far more terrible onslaught.

The Place de la Bastille, which was the centre of their operations, had the appearance of an armed camp ; there the sentries did not fall asleep at their posts, nor the watchfires die out. In the clubs of the adjoining *faubourgs,* orators were thrilling their audiences with denunciations of their new rulers : " These are not the men we want. A people in Revolution ask for leaders, not for moderators ; for men who will kindle their impulses, not for men who will suppress them. To moderate a Revolution is to betray it. Do not, for the sake of such men as these, let the wages of your blood be again filched from you at the Hôtel de Ville. Remember Lafayette ! And how do you know Lamartine is not another Lafayette ? If he is one of us, let him serve us as we wish, not as he wishes ; or if he will not, let him be replaced by a man chosen by ourselves out of our own

·anks. Let us be there when he and his colleagues consult
:ogether, so that the Government may really be a _plébiscite_,
vith the axe visibly suspended over the heads of those men
who would betray the people."

These and similar speeches wrought the famished, half-
delirious crowd to uncontrollable excitement. One body
of men set off before break of day to Vincennes, which they
·ansacked for ammunition ; another made their way to the
Invalides, where, however, a force, hastily despatched by
he Minister of Police, succeeded in keeping them at bay.
Meanwhile, all through the morning, little bands of men
vere quietly, almost imperceptibly, taking possession of
he Place du Grêve. They were mostly young, but to some
degree disciplined in their bearing, and accustomed to
:xercise authority over their fellows. They formed centres
·ound which others of a somewhat inferior class grouped
hemselves, till the whole space between the Bastille and
he Hôtel de Ville was one living, moving mass. Each of
hose who seemed to be leaders wore in his button-hole the
ittle red ribbon Lamartine had noticed on his way home
he preceding night, of which the significance now became
manifest. As the crowd grew more dense and more
hreatening, men, stationed evidently for the purpose, began
o distribute scarfs, sashes, and flags of the same hue. As
he excitement increased, yards of red material were torn
ip and cast in fragments among the crowd, snatched by
outstretched hands, till the signal ran like lightning through
he masses. The Members of the Government, from the
ralcony of the Hôtel de Ville, could see it flashing out like
he flaming cross of Gaelic warfare, as far as the eye could
·each. When from time to time a band of artisans paraded

the streets, as had been their wont for the last few days, carrying the tricolor banner, they were stopped, reasoned with by the Montagnards, who, tearing down the national flag of France, made them hoist instead the lurid symbol of the Terror.

The excitement of the crowd increased every moment. Urged by their leaders, they insisted on ransacking the Hôtel de Ville from cellar to attic under the pretext of searching for arms. The few defenders of the Provisional Government, consisting chiefly of students from the École Polytechnique, and of personal friends of the members, were driven back from post to post, till, pressed together in the narrow corridor leading to the Salle de Conseil, they held the foe at bay by sheer density. It seems as if the ringleaders hesitated at actual violence, for they had recourse to other, at first incomprehensible, tactics. Processions of men carrying the corpses of those who had perished at the barricades came in from all parts of the city, laying down their burdens in the courtyard of the Hôtel de Ville, which was literally piled up with these ghastly trophies, with the evident intention of exciting the people to madness, and also, it is supposed, to asphyxiate the Government if all other means of coercion failed.

From the overwhelmed members a decree guaranteeing employment to all was extorted ; then another bestowing on the combatants at the barricades the million of francs which it was very erroneously supposed would be saved to the civil list by the abolition of royalty. But these con- cessions merely whetted the appetites of the mob for further demands. Louder and more menacing grew the cries of " Le drapeau rouge ! Nous voulons le drapeau rouge ! "

At this undisguised call for mob tyranny and the reign of blood, the bravest hung back. Some members of the Government were for temporizing, and Louis Blanc vehemently urged immediate concession. Lamartine, who had been lying on the ground, utterly exhausted and worn out, on hearing this suggestion, sprang to his feet.

A writer, whose claim to speak with authority cannot be gainsaid, has attributed the misfortunes of France during the last century to the political influence exercised in that country by men of letters. Doubtless the habit of generalization has inclined minds, perhaps naturally not ungenerous, to regard the losses, the torturing anxieties, the ultimate ruin of thousands as the cheap price of Revolution; to accept even the crushing out of blameless lives, the shedding of innocent blood, as eternal commonplaces of human occasion. But—idealist as he was, and less conversant with the science of statesmanship than is desirable in those who undertake to be rulers of men—Lamartine's genius was of very different stamp. Far from deadening his sensibilities, it quickened them tenfold. Nor did it make him less prompt or decisive in action than men of rougher natures. With the courage of Bayard—with a courage Bayard himself might not have shown in civic contest—while others were hesitating or talking of compromise, he went out alone to withstand the multitude. Putting forth all his eloquence, he implored the people not thus to sully their victory.

" Yesterday," were the concluding words of a long and thrilling appeal—" yesterday you asked us to usurp, in the name of the people of Paris, the rights of thirty-five millions of our fellow-citizens by proclaiming the Republic without consulting France. And now you ask us for the red instead of the tricolour flag. Citizens, neither I nor a single member of the Government will ever consent to this. And I will tell you why. The tricolour has made the circuit of the world with the Republic and the Empire, with your liberties and with your triumphs. The red flag has only made the circuit of the Champ de Mars, drenched with the blood of Frenchmen!"

As to what passed immediately after this, there is some discrepancy of evidence, but it seems as if those within the range of Lamartine's eloquence were subjugated; but that in the next moment another column of insurgents, fiercer and more implacable than the last, poured in, drowning the cries of "Vive Lamartine! Vive le drapeau tricolor!" with those of "À bas Lamartine! Point de paroles! Le decret! ou le gouvernement de trâitres à la lanterne." Lamartine was standing on a low scaffolding in front of the great gate. The friends who had followed him out, striving to keep back the mob, were pressed in on all sides by a band of ruffians, who, with swords and bayonets, struck wildly at him. His voice could not be heard in the tumult; a pike-thrust had wounded one of his hands severely. Again and again he was implored to retreat, but this he refused to do, and for a time there seemed but a hair's-breadth between him and the fate of Foulon, when he was saved, as in no other place in Europe he would have been saved, by a man in the garb of a beggar, who rushed in between him and his assailants, invoked him as his father, his brother, the saviour of the people, embraced him, blessed him, till he obtained for him all he needed for his triumph—a hearing. Then the last detachment of the Terrorists was subdued, as the previous ones had been, amid cries of "Vive Lamartine ! Vive le Gouvernement Provisoire ! " The tricolor, which had been torn down, floated once more over the great gates. The mob, breaking up into columns, paraded the streets, singing the Marseillaise—the thrilling notes of that magnificent but terrible hymn bringing for once a message of peace.

Years afterwards, when friends were gathered round Lamartine's fireside, they asked him, "Did you not, at the sight of that raging crowd, shouting for your head, feel something akin to terror ? " "Yes," was his reply ; "for a moment I was afraid. But when I had laid my hand on the lion's mane, and felt it quiver beneath my touch, I knew I should conquer, and all fear passed away."

The struggle thus briefly narrated lasted for eight hours, and it was evening before the Provisional Government resumed their labours. This sitting Lamartine has described with much enthusiasm. Thrilled, he tells us, with patriotic emotion, each member of the Council sought in the depths of his heart and intelligence for some much-needed reform to be proposed ; for some hitherto untried remedy which should bring healing to the wounds of suffering humanity. The last vestiges of the slave laws yet lingering in the colonies were swept away ; the "laws of September," with their vexatious restrictions on liberty of speech and thought, repealed ; popular suffrage substituted for the unreasonably restricted franchise so long complained of ; all class distinctions abolished. It has been sarcastically said, parodying Lamartine's words, that their sweeping reforms "bore the stamp of impulse rather

than that of reason." But Lord Normanby, who certainly
had no Republican sympathies, writes, " Making allowance
for the difficulties under which they laboured, I think
many of the decrees of the Provisional Government do
great credit to their political capacities." And alluding to
the one abolishing the punishment of death for political
offences, which Lamartine, despite some reluctance on the
part of his colleagues, and furious resistance from without,
succeeded in passing, the same writer says, " I do not think
that in the history of the world there was ever such an
instance of the triumph of noble sentiments over the brute
instincts of the masses."

Those who, in the words of the old ballad, " live at
home at ease," can have a very faint notion of the anxieties
and tremors of peaceful citizens during a period of revolution. The journal of the English ambassador shows that
even those to whom the law of nations—not violated during
the worst periods of the first French Revolution—gave
comparative security, were not without anxieties. All
through the 24th and 25th of February the streets were
unsafe, and little was known of the state of affairs, save
that a Provisional Government was established ; of what
elements composed, it was impossible to conjecture. During
the night of the 25th, the firing slackened, but at early
dawn a lady who lived near the Embassy rushed in with
the news that her husband, who had been all night on
duty with the National Guard, had come to tell her that
a drunken, excited mob, fresh from the sack of Neuilly,
were setting fire to the Elysée. The report proved to be
perfectly correct. Torches had been applied to the palace
in several places, a high wind was blowing, and for a time

it seemed as if nothing could save the quarter. But already the exertions of the Government had begun to tell. A battalion of the National Guard, in which a couple of hundred men of the better classes had just enrolled themselves, turned out to oppose the incendiaries. They fixed bayonets and charged ; on which the mob, opposed for the first time since they sacked the Tuileries, soon gave way.

Still, all through the day the anxiety was extreme. Their personal influence was the only means of defence the Government possessed, and the pressure brought to bear on them was known to be terrific. So great was the danger of the inmates of the Embassy felt to be, that a deputation of Irish gentlemen, of whom Mr. John O'Connell was one, came to say they had procured arms, and that two hundred of their number were ready to garrison the building. And to the fear of incendiarism and of mob violence was added that of starvation. The barricades had completely impeded the free circulation towards the outskirts, and the frightful reports of the state of anarchy within the town deterred all those who usually supplied the city from attempting to reach the centre. From want of flour the bakers had ceased to supply bread, and closed their shops ; food of any kind could only be had at exorbitant prices. Pictures, statues, plate, apparel, all that people are accustomed to look on as valuable possessions, were beginning to be considered as useless lumber ; those who were seeking safety in flight trying in vain to raise a pittance on the costliest jewels. It seemed as if the most civilized city in the world was reduced to the primitive conditions of barter, when, according to the instincts of the savage state, the relative value of things is estimated according to their utility in preserving life.

But by evening the prospect brightened. Six thousand respectable citizens had been since daybreak guarding the Hôtel de Ville, armed to the teeth, and resolved to defend the newly constituted Government at all hazards. During the day the principal officers of the army and navy gave in their submission. Persons of eminence from all the camps into which France was divided—Legitimists, Orleanists, Republicans—alike rallied to the Government, recognizing that in the vigorous efforts it was making to moderate public excitement and restore order lay the only hope of salvation for society.

The Government, on the other hand, did not shrink from responsibility. Within a couple of hours after the proclamation of the abolition of capital punishment for political offences, twenty-four marauders, taken in the act of pillage, were sent to the nearest guard-house and shot. One of Lamartine's happiest creations, that of the Garde Mobile, dates from this time. From the first outbreak of the insurrection he had noticed numbers of youths, hardly more than schoolboys, drawn into the vortex by high spirits and love of excitement, tossed about like froth on the waves—raw material equally ready to be fashioned into destroyers or saviours of society. He resolved to make at least an effort to save them from the abyss into which they were visibly drifting, and issued a decree for the formation of a corps for the defence of the Executive, to be composed of those who had been most conspicuous for their courage and steadfastness on the barricades. The result amply justified the venture. The most ardent and ambitious of these youths eagerly filled up the *cadastre*, and the restraint of military discipline speedily changed them from the turbulent *gamins* into a band of resolute, steadfast soldiers. The Garde Mobile, which soon numbered four thousand, showed their fidelity to the State on more than one occasion by the ready sacrifice of their lives. In the June insurrection they are said to have proved more reliable than the National Guard, and as steadfast as the troops of the line—a result principally to be attributed to their enthusiastic devotion to Lamartine.

The proclamation of the Republic on the 27th of February was made the occasion of a national *fête*. The Members of the Provisional Government, attended by the principal ministers and officials, proceeded in state to the Colonne de Juillet, which commemorates the taking of the Bastille in July, 1789. Dupont de l'Eure, Crémieux, and Arago addressed the people, Lamartine effacing himself as much as possible. But everywhere he was greeted with acclamations, and on his return from the ceremony forty thousand citizens insisted on escorting him home with cries of "Vive Lamartine! premier consul." Hearing this, Lamartine turned round quickly and decisively, saying, "You all know perfectly I do not want this," on which they desisted.

But similar scenes repeated themselves again and again; indeed, it is hardly possible to give an idea of the enthusiastic admiration Lamartine's courage and conduct evoked, not in France alone, but throughout Europe, and especially in England. Perhaps the world was less selfish in those days than it is now, for there is ample evidence, both in the memoirs and correspondence of the time, that the

knowledge of the terrible crisis through which a neighbouring, even though alien, nation was passing, caused the
people of England almost insupportable anxiety, and when
it became known how terrific had been the struggle, how
doubtful the issue, how complete for the moment was the
victory, the news was received with rapture. And no
element of interest was wanting ; noble words had been
mated with noble deeds, and Lamartine's portrait, multiplied ten thousandfold, made the spell complete. "That
beautiful face," writes George Eliot, "worthy an aureole!"

But perhaps the strongest testimony to the estimation
in which Lamartine was held is that of a writer whose
position makes his opinion of exceptional value, and whose
judgments seldom err on the side of laudation. In the
third volume of the Greville memoirs we read : "In
all this great drama he (Lamartine) stands forth prominently as the principal character. How long it may
last God only knows, but a fortnight of such greatness the
world has hardly ever seen. For fame and glory it were
probably well for him to die now. His position is something superhuman at this moment ; the eyes of the universe
are on him, and he is not only the theme of general admiration, but on him almost alone the hopes of the world
are placed. He is the principal author of the Revolution.
They say that his book has been a prime cause of that
which he has now the glory of directing, moderating,
restraining. His labour has been stupendous, his eloquence
wonderful. When the new Government was surrounded
by thousands of armed rabble, shouting, bellowing for they
knew not what, he contrived to appease their rage, to soften,
control, and eventually master them. So great a trial of

eloquence was hardly ever heard of. Then from the beginning he has exhibited undaunted courage and consummate skill, proclaiming order, peace, humanity, respect for
persons and property. This improvised Cabinet, strangely
composed, has evinced the most curious, vigorous, activity
and wisdom ; they have forced everybody to respect them.
But Lamartine towers above them all, and is the presiding
genius of the new creation. He has acted like a man of
honour, and of feeling too. He offered the King an escort;
he wrote to Madame Guizot, and told her her son was
safe in England, and caused the report of this to be spread
about, that he might not be sought for, and, moreover, he
sent word to Guizot that, if he was not in safety, he might
come to his house. When he first proposed the abolition
of the punishment of death for political offences he was
overruled, but the next day he proposed it again, and
declared that if his colleagues did not consent he would
throw up office and quit the concern, and that they might
make him, if he pleased, the first victim of the law they
would not abolish. All this is very great."

It cannot be said that Lamartine wore his honours
altogether unconsciously. To his sympathetic nature and
vivid imagination this brimming draught of popularity was
even more delicious and exhilarating than it might have
been to colder spirits, and he certainly forgot that ele-
mentary teaching of history, that the triumphs of the
Gracchi are apt to be more evanescent than those of the
Cæsars. But in dignity of demeanour, in restraint of
conduct, he never failed.

When, after the 26th of February, he was repeatedly
pressed by all, including Dupont de l'Eure himself, to

assume the office of President, he as persistently refused. When urged to make the Tuileries the seat of the Provisional Government, he replied, " The citizens to whom power has been momentarily entrusted have no palaces save their own homes." And the unselfish consideration for others, of which Mr. Greville quotes instances, was with him a matter of course. At nightfall, on the 25th of February, after sixty hours of continuous strain and fatigue, he went, disguised and on foot, to the house of M. de Montalivet, known to be one of the most devoted adherents of the house of Orleans, to find out from him in what way it would be possible to assist those members of the Royal family who had not crossed the frontier. MM. Dargaud and de Chamborand were then sent on special missions for the purpose, while means were found to convey to M. Guizot, who was still in hiding, the sum of fifteen thousand francs.

CHAPTER X.

IT was not till several days after his assumption of office that Lamartine was able to give his attention to the department allotted to him, and take possession of the Hôtel des Affaires Étrangères. The apartments of M. Guizot seemed still tenanted by his shade. The room, the table scattered over with papers, showed how unexpected had been the departure of the minister who thought he was leaving his house but for a moment, when in reality he had left it for ever. Lamartine had asked a person in M. Guizot's confidence to accompany him, and to remove all the private documents and papers, as well as anything that could be of interest or value to M. Guizot or to any of his family, and, with characteristic delicacy of feeling, would not occupy any of the private apartments till this had been done at leisure, but had mattresses laid down in the reception rooms for himself and his attendants.

The greater part of the first night spent under a roof which hitherto had brought no good fortune to its inmates was passed, he tells us, in reflecting on the attitude the Government should take with regard to external relations. A warlike policy would much diminish the

present difficulties of the Government, and make them
very popular : but Lamartine had too strong a sense of the
horrors and losses of war to allow such a consideration to
weigh with him for an instant; his firm resolution was,
to do all in his power to preserve the peace of Europe
unbroken as long as the honour of France permitted
it. The difficulty lay in the fear and mistrust which
recollections of the first Republic revived in all the continental nations, at a moment when the strained, excited
state of public feeling in France was adding tenfold to the
national susceptibility.

The only foreign minister with whom Lamartine had
as yet any personal intercourse was the English ambassador,
with whom, ever since he had known him at Florence, he
had remained on terms of intimacy, and who, the day
before, had paid him an unofficial visit at his private
residence to congratulate him on the services he had
rendered to his country. Lamartine received Lord Normanby with much cordiality, and said at once frankly that
his first desire was the development of the English alliance,
that all his efforts would be directed to that object, for he
felt that in doing this he would be promoting the only true
interests of France. With reference to foreign politics,
Lamartine went on to say there had been at first much
excitement on the question of the frontiers, and the war of
1815, and that an idea had begun to prevail that a war of
revolutionary propagandism should now be undertaken.
This feeling he had succeeded in calming, and had been
careful to insert in the circular to the *corps diplomatique* he
was about to issue, a paragraph to the effect that the
position of France in Europe remained the same, though

the form of her internal government might change. He added they had no desire to attack any one, and that he was prepared to give any guarantee against such intention, but that if any weaker State be attacked they would feel it a duty to support it; otherwise they would look to the force of intelligence, not to the force of arms, for the progress of liberal ideas.

A few days later, Lamartine, who was anxious to obtain some outward expression of support from the English Government, saw Lord Normanby again. The diplomatic etiquette which made it impossible to accredit an ambassador to a Government which had neither the wish nor the pretension to be anything but provisional, created a difficulty which Lamartine regretted, not, he explained, as far as he himself was concerned, but because the French people always required something of show, and that any act which could have proved that the cordial co-operation of England was secured, would have been of immense value. Lord Normanby convinced Lamartine, " who," he remarks, " was very reasonable on the subject," that there was no difference between the two countries, save in the observance on the part of England of established forms, and that Lamartine could use in any way he pleased the fact that the sentiments of admiration for his conduct, and the desire to cultivate friendly relations with France expressed by the Prime Minister in the House of Commons, had been personally communicated to him by the ambassador.

On the 3rd of March, Lamartine brought Lord Normanby a summary of his circular to the European Powers, which had been discussed the previous day in

X

Council, expressing infinite regret at the allusion it contained to the treaties of 1815, allusions which he himself
had been anxious to omit. But the feeling which existed
on the subject in France was so strong as to make it
imperative for him not to pass over the manner in which
they had been violated at pleasure by the other Powers,
and to deny that France was bound, as a matter of right, to
observe them. This, however, was moderated by an accompanying expression of readiness to maintain the existing
territorial arrangements, laying down as a precept that
they were only to be modified by negotiation, and with the
consent of all parties. The conversation then turned on the
fate of the King, who was still weather-bound in concealment at Havre, and for whom Lamartine manifested much
concern. This led Lord Normanby to speak of the condition
of the Royal family, especially as regarded their property.

Lamartine replied at once that he was glad of the
opportunity of giving an assurance that if, at the first
moment of excitement, there had been question of confiscation, there did not really exist any such intention, especially
as regarded the private property of the House of Orleans.
All had been sequestrated for the present, with the view of
making a careful distinction as to what might be said to
belong to the State. Lamartine had even succeeded in
obtaining from his colleagues a written promise to place
a million of francs at once at the disposal of the King, but
before this could be carried out there was such increased
distress among all classes, mingled with fear that the commercial credit of France would be sensibly affected by the
unavoidable stoppage in public payments, that no one
could venture to send any money placed under official

charge out of the country ; the notice of such an incident in the papers would have upset the Government, while it was equally impossible to do it without publicity, and Lord Normanby, anxious as he was to do all in his power for the exiled Royalities, forbore to press it.

The circular just alluded to was published on the 6th of March, and received " by France with applause, by Europe with respect." Lamartine's next step was to reorganize the diplomatic corps so that it should fairly represent the new order. As it would have been a manifest contradiction for a Provisional Government to assume the state and authority of established ones, it was thought best to employ simple ministers instead of ambassadors, except at Rome, where, as a special mark of respect to the Supreme Pontiff, M. d'Harcourt, distinguished by his ancient lineage and great personal dignity, was sent as ambassador. In London, the acting secretary of legation, M. de Jarnac, was asked to continue at his post, but he, being honoured by the personal friendship of the exiled Princes, begged to be replaced, and M. de Talleney went in his stead. M. de Lesseps was sent to Madrid, M. Thiard to Berne ; but at Vienna and St. Petersburg, the two courts most unfriendly to the Republic, it was thought best to leave the post of minister vacant, the secretaries transacting all necessary business.

In all these appointments, Lamartine is allowed to have shown the tact and discretion of a man accomplished in diplomatic usage ; still it occasionally transpired that in his foreign policy he was not exempt from the weakness which diminishes his value as a historian—he was too ready to take on trust any report that attracted his sympathies. Of

this, M. de Circourt, sent by him as minister to Berlin,
gives an amusing illustration. In imparting his final
instructions, Lamartine outlined the tendencies of Prussian
diplomacy, and the courses the minister had better pursue.
The King was to be encouraged in his efforts to gain over
the minor States and detach them from Austria—the State
looked on as the most dangerous enemy of France. "The
most important person at the Court of Berlin," Lamartine
proceeded to explain, "is the wife of the heir to the Crown.
She is a charming brunette, vivacious, *spirituelle*, already
well-disposed to France. Make yourself agreeable to her.
It will be for the interest of France." M. de Circourt, a
brilliant type of the Parisian *jeunesse dorée*, set off well
pleased with his mission, and eager to behold this charming "Queen Mab of the Borussians." One can picture his
dismay when, at his first audience, he found himself in the
majestic presence of the great lady now styled the Empress
Augusta !

Another anecdote of Lamartine's official experiences
used to be afterwards repeated with much enjoyment in
M. Guizot's circle at Val Richer. When Lamartine was in
power, it was said, he used to jot down indiscriminately
hints for his poems and hints for his administration. On
a paper, containing among other things a list of Préfets,
was found the word David. The name appeared therefore
in the *Moniteur Officiel*, but as no one knew anything of
the newly appointed préfet, Lamartine's secretary came to
ask him for M. David's address. Lamartine was sorely
puzzled. The name was certainly in his writing, but how
it came there he could not tell. At last he recollected that
he had put it down as a memorandum of some allusion to

the Royal Prophet, to be introduced in a "Méditation." So another notice appeared in the *Moniteur*, nominating M. A. B——, in the place of M. David, "appelé à d'autres fonctions." For any friend of Lamartine to have recalled that his latest "Méditation" was written years before, would have been perfectly useless ; the story was far too good to be discredited on such trivial grounds.

Meanwhile, financial difficulties beset the Government on all sides. The panic caused by the Revolution, spreading throughout the country, had stopped traffic, save in the actual necessaries of life ; and even in these consumption was reduced to the lowest point possible, the *octroi* of Paris falling to nearly one-half. It seemed as if coin would soon cease to circulate. At first the difficulty was met by a decree postponing for a month the payment of all bills falling due between the 25th of February and the 15th of March, but as this raised a clamour among the holders of securities, it had to be followed by another anticipating the payment of Government bonds. This only made matters worse, and the Minister of Finance, M. Gondchaux, had to resign. He was replaced by Garnier-Pagès, who, seeing that the situation was becoming absolutely desperate, and that in a few days the Bank of France would be entirely drained of specie, stopped all cash payments, and issued notes to the amount of £18,000,000 sterling. At the same time the greatest efforts were made by the Government to sustain credit ; discount banks and loan banks were established all over the country, by means of which the Government advanced large sums. It was necessary to provide for this immense outlay, and as customs and export duties were almost unproductive, the only way in which money could be obtained was by raising the direct taxation forty-five per cent. ; thus causing a degree of disappointment and indignation of which it is difficult to convey a notion, especially as the chief burden fell on the peasant proprietors, who had hardly yet recovered from the distress caused by the bad seasons of 1846–1847. There was not, however, as would have been the case in many other countries, the least attempt at resistance. Many as had been the shiftings of political power in France, her internal administration, organized fifty years before by a master hand, centred in the capital, radiating to the utmost bounds, still retained its tremendous authority. A large accession of revenue was at once obtained, and a crisis, which would probably have resulted in anarchy, averted.

All was smooth on the surface, and, to outward seeming, the establishment of the Republic on a durable basis was becoming an accomplished fact. In his "Histoire de 1848," Lamartine describes in glowing colours those first sunny days "when the Republic had no enemies, hardly any unbelievers to contend with ; when those who had shuddered at her name were gazing in astonishment at the calm magnanimity, the harmony pervading everywhere. The first programme of the new Government, the voluntary respect of the people for authority, the patience of the working-men, the charity of the rich, the serenity of all, diffused over the first weeks of the Republic unclouded radiance. The suffering classes were content to wait, the affluent rejoiced in their unhoped-for security, opinions the most adverse were being reconciled on the large and common field of liberty, where all were welcome.

Even those who belonged to the vanquished party were grateful to the Government for the generosity with which recriminations were silenced, proscriptions blotted out, and the complete exercise of political rights thrown open to all." And others were hardly less sanguine. M. de Labonyale, writing of himself, says, " I looked forward with confidence to a general disarmament, to peaceful progress, and the coming triumph of liberty throughout the world. Lamartine seemed to be realizing the Utopia of poets and prophets, a new era in which Democracy would become established without violence or bloodshed as the result of a regular and apparently irresistible movement—

> " ' La paix descendait sur la terre,
> Semant de l'or, des fleurs, et des épis.' "

But this halcyon period was probably never as unclouded in its actual present as it seemed in restrospect, and was, even Lamartine admits, very brief. In summing up the causes which deprived the Republic of 1848 of the crowning grace of stability, he reckons first the intriguing, injudicious action of the Radical section of the Provisional Government, which the original defects of its constitution much facilitated. It was almost inevitable that in an Executive made up of men without administrative experience, without the habit—so rarely acquired in mature life—of acting in concert with others, each member should practically be supreme in his own department. The divergence of action which resulted, Lamartine gracefully veils in sonorous phrases. " Unis dans les grandes tendences d'ordre et de républicanisme, ils pouvaient diverger dans les détails ; chacun suivait son esprit et ne répondait qu'à sa conscience et au salut de son pays."

But conscience and the public welfare are words which
admit of very various interpretation, and it soon became
manifest that Ledru-Rollin's reading of them was different
to that of his colleagues. A week's exercise of the functions
of Minister of the Interior showed him that the proximate
election was likely to return a large majority of deputies
who would strongly oppose the Radical section of the
Government, of which he was the leader. Accordingly he
sent down to the provinces four hundred commissioners
with ample salaries, in order to bring the constituencies to
the desired way of thinking. He issued his instructions to
them in the form of a circular letter, telling them that the
elections were to be their work, that their powers were
unlimited, that the Assembly must be animated by a
revolutionary spirit, and that, to effect this, new men must
be sought among the workmen and artisans,—thus initiating
a degree of interference with the freedom of election which,
had it been attempted by any previous Government, he
would justly have called the worst of tyrannies, and which
was entirely opposed to the views of his colleagues, who
only became aware of his proceedings from the disquietude
and irritation they excited.

Lord Normanby says that it was from him Lamartine
first received a copy of the Ministerial circular of the 11th
of March. He was appalled by it, and, as he read, exclaimed repeatedly, " *Très mauvais !* *très mauvais !* He
wants to make Proconsuls, not Commissioners! It is the
creation of an Electoral Dictatorship."

" I could not help," Lord Normanby goes on to say,
" telling M. de Lamartine I thought there could be no
duty more pressing on the leading member of a Govern-

ment than not to allow such documents to go forth to the public without his sanction." To which Lamartine replied, "*Que voulez-vous ?* We have so much of such immediate urgency." But he added that for the future he would endeavour to watch these matters more closely, and that, as to this mistake, he would correct it as far as lay in his power. He could not, as a member of the Government, publish a counter-manifesto, but he would to-morrow write an address to his own department which should lay down very different principles, and impose very different duties on the electors.

A few days later Lord Normanby writes, "This Lamartine did ; and again, a few days later, when a deputation came to the Hôtel de Ville to express the consternation with which all sober citizens had been seized on reading the alarming circular, Lamartine replied, ' The Provisional Government has authorized no one to speak to the nation in its name, and least of all to speak in language which overrides the laws. The Government, recognizing freedom of opinion, repudiates that worst of corruption, intimidation. It has deliberately resolved not to interfere, either directly or indirectly, in the elections. I trust public opinion will be reassured, and not take in an alarming sense some words indiscriminately used by ministers who often attach their signatures in haste.' "

The effect produced by this energetic disclaimer was so great that it was at first thought impossible M. Ledru-Rollin could remain member of the Government. A report prevailed, during a part of the day, that he had resigned, and the funds at once rose four per cent. Unfortunately for his colleagues, M. Ledru-Rollin, if he had not many gifts, possessed that of accommodating himself to circumstances. He signed a paper prepared by Lamartine, pledging the Government to resist all unnecessary postponement of the elections, and remained at his post.

"An increased gloom," writes Lord Normanby, under the date of March 11th, "has, within the last three or four days, been gathering over the political horizon ; every one now talks with more despondency of the future, all speakers beginning with, 'If we reach the National Assembly?' One of the grounds of doubt certainly is the financial convulsion, which has been much aggravated by panic, though most serious in itself. Accumulating ruin is every day over-whelming thousands, and will, before many months are over, indirectly affect millions. This is, of course, calculated to increase the pressure and double the danger of any political crisis. The aspect of affairs is also threatening in this respect—there is a decided schism in the Provisional Government ; and yet, unless dissolved by some violent expulsion, they must continue nominally to work together till the National Assembly meets, being all equally sup-posed to owe their power to a spontaneous emanation of the popular will. The state of the case I take to be this : the moderate party in the Government, to which the great body of the nation are looking as their only safety, is led by M. de Lamartine, who, as yet, has been backed by the majority of the other members. The disposition of this majority is still supposed to be good, but there are doubts as to the courage of several, should the pressure from without become intense. The great point in dispute at this moment is whether or not the elections should be

postponed ; this step is strongly advocated by M. Ledru-
Rollin, M. Louis Blanc, and M. Albert. Ledru-Rollin, the
nominal head of this party, is a man of no great capacity,
and of not undoubted moral courage, but a regular mob
orator of ruined fortunes, who is desirous, as long as he
can, to retain his present power, and quite bold enough to
attempt anything, providing he feels himself backed by
a multitude. The Jacobin clubs and the Communists are
said to form a very small proportion of the people of Paris,
but they are armed and organized, and one cannot but fear
they would be joined in any demonstration by the many
thousands of workmen out of employment. The general
feeling of the country is sound, but there exists no combined object. They desire to resist what they dread, but
they have no rallying point. They cannot cordially support
a Government most of whose acts they disapprove ; and
they cannot conscientiously take for a leader a man who
himself is, though often unconsciously, a party to those
very acts. Lamartine is this very day prepared to resist
with energy the demand that will be made at the Hôtel de
Ville, by an overwhelming multitude, for the adjournment
of the elections, with the almost avowed purpose of .
arranging machinery to tyrannize over the provinces. He
will there probably prevail by his eloquence and by his
firmness, but he unfortunately has not all the qualities
required to trace out the underplots by which his colleagues
endeavour to circumvent him. All at this moment depends
on the spirit and the resolution of the National Guard. It
happens that the time of the annual election of the officers
was fixed for next Saturday. Arrangements have been
made which, in most of the legions, would have ensured

a very fair selection ; but the violent party wanted t(
swamp the original regiments with the recent admissions
and, in order that more of the working classes might enro
themselves, they have obtained four days' delay, nominall)
on the ground of giving time to fuse the flank companie;
which have been dissolved into the others.   The dissolutioi
of the flank companies was in reality an insidious design t(
destroy their efficiency, and the effect of this measure wa
not sufficiently foreseen by Lamartine, and has disguste(
four and twenty thousand of the best-disposed and mos
resolute men."

On the 16th of March, a large representative body o
the National Guard marched in procession to the Hôtel d(
Ville, in order to lay their grievances before the Govern
ment.   Many of the companies were intercepted on th(
quays by crowds of workmen partially armed, and oblige(
to turn back.   Those who made their way were addresse(
by M. Marrast, the Mayor of Paris, and subsequently b)
Lamartine, who told them their conduct would serve a
an encouragement to those who were endeavouring, b)
threatening demonstrations, to overawe the Government
and exhorted them to sacrifice their personal feelings t(
the vital interests of the country.   M. Maxime du Camp
who was serving as a private in the ranks, says this advice
which, in his opinion, amounted to an intimation that wha
was allowable in every one else was forbidden to a Nationa
Guard, was not well received.   Some ardent spirits propose(
that they should seize the Hôtel de Ville, and throw th(
Provisional Government out of the windows ; but coole
heads suggested an immediate return to the barracks, whicl
wiser counsel prevailed; and so ended the "manifestation o

the beavers," as, from the head-gear of the flank companies, it was facetiously called.

But the day following, March 17th, was one of real anxiety and danger. For some time a great demonstration had been in preparation, with the object of forcing on the Government laws equalizing the rate of wages, and pro- viding employment to all, which the Commission for the Organization of Labour, then sitting at the Luxembourg, had been for some time promising. With these demands were coupled others for the postponement of the elections, inspired by Louis Blanc, from the wish to see Socialism fully established before the National Assembly met; by Ledru-Rollin, because he feared that, without some great additional stimulus, the elections would result in the triumph of the reactionary party. But, unknown to these two leaders, other yet more reckless and ambitious spirits were purposing to take advantage of the projected move- ment; the clubs were at work, rousing the whole of the *prolétariat*, in order to effect a demonstration which might not merely coerce the Provisional Government, but com- pletely overthrow it.

From an early hour, crowds began to gather on the Boulevards and in the adjoining streets. By noon, a multi- tude, said to number over a hundred thousand men, was advancing towards the Hôtel de Ville, which was only defended by three battalions of the Civic Guard. Beyond closing the outer gates, no defence was attempted. When the heads of the columns were first seen from the upper windows of the Hôtel de Ville, Ledru-Rollin and Louis Blanc scarcely tried to conceal their triumph. "When I saw the people advancing," wrote the latter, "tears of

joy stood in my eyes." And Ledru-Rollin, in the excite
ment of approaching triumph, is said—though Lamartin
does not mention the incident—to have turned to hi
colleagues, exclaiming, " Do you know that your popularit
is as nothing compared to mine ? I have only to open thi
window, and call to the people, and you would all b
turned into the street. Do you wish me to try ?" Upo
this, Garnier-Pagès walked up to him, drew a pistol fror
his pocket, and placed it against Ledru-Rollin's breas
saying, " If you take one step towards that window, it sha
be your last." Ledru-Rollin looked daggers, paused
moment, and then sat down. A few minutes later, th
mob was thundering at the gate ; at first, admittance wa
refused, but after some parleying it was conceded to ;
limited number of delegates. The gate being openec
there rushed in sufficient numbers to fill the whole build
ing, the leaders making their way to the Council Chamber

The first glance at their faces entirely changed th
attitude of the Radical section of the Government. I
addition to the men they expected, and whom they knev
to be in their interest, Louis Blanc and Ledru-Rollin foun
themselves face to face with Blanqui, Cabet, Raspail, an
their followers, men personally unknown to them, bu
notorious from the violence of their opinions,—" Figure
inconnues," writes Louis Blanc, " et dont l'expression avai
quelque chose de sinistre."

It was evident that the demonstration was led by th
party of violence, and directed quite as much agains
Louis Blanc and Ledru-Rollin as against Lamartine an
Garnier-Pagès. Their demands, formulated by Blanqui
were—the postponement of the elections, the immediat

and final removal of all troops from Paris, the implicit
obedience of the Government to the voice of the people,
as expressed by the clubs—in short, entire surrender to
the scum of the Parisian populace, ending in an imperative
demand for an immediate answer, made more emphatic by
the menacing strains of the "Marseillaise" rising in chorus
from the court below, and by the band of powerful,
determined men, numbering some eight hundred, who
crowded the building from basement to *mansarde*, seemingly waiting for the signal to exterminate the Provisional
Government, who, unarmed and defenceless as they were,
constituted all that remained of political authority in
France. They, however, seeing their existence was at
stake, were firm ; a sense of common danger produced a
unanimity which surprised and disconcerted their foes.
Louis Blanc openly condemned the movement he himself
had originated; and Ledru-Rollin spoke yet more emphatically, and with ready, nervous elocution.

Lamartine's courage and eloquence were more than
equal to the occasion, and after some hours of angry discussion, the deputation, wearied and baffled, began to shift
their ground. "Be assured," said one of the speakers, "the
people have no other wish than to strengthen the Government." "I quite believe you," replied Lamartine ; "but
remember, demonstrations such as these, admirable as they
are, become dangerous ; the 18 Brumaire of the people
may lead to the 18 Brumaire of a despot, and neither you
nor I wish that."

These words told, and Sobrier and Cabet, who were to
some degree supported by Barbés, gave the signal of retreat,
to which Blanqui and his friends had reluctantly to submit,

not without taunts levelled at Louis Blanc, on whose oppo
sition to his colleagues they had counted. One of the
delegates, turning back, hissed out with a menacing
gesture, " So you, too, are a traitor ! "

A manifesto, drawn up by Lamartine, in which the
demands of the populace were decisively refused, was
unanimously signed and placarded, the mob, apparently
indifferent, quietly dispersing. But though, by their un-
looked-for union, the Government had surmounted any
immediate danger, the manifestation of the 17th of March
produced a deep impression on the public ; it was felt that
in the last three days a rapid retrogression towards anarchy
had been effected. " Encore un pas," writes Count Molé
"et nous sommes en plein '93." " And," added others, " in
the Convention there was indeed personal insecurity,
arising from capricious cruelty, but there was at any rate
a strong will which made a Government. Now all confidence is crumbling away, there is no credit, no employment, no money, no physical force anywhere save in the
masses."

No one felt this more deeply than Lamartine. Early
in the morning of the 18th of March, he tells us, he
returned home anxious and dejected ; for he saw clearly
that he and his colleagues had no longer to deal with the
turbulent and emotional multitude of the first previous
weeks, that had been swayed by his eloquence and disarmed by his self-devotion, but with an army of *prolétaires*,
disciplined and organized by able, unscrupulous leaders,
who, if they had for once been disconcerted by not meeting
the aid they had counted on within the citadel, would
quickly recruit their forces and return to the assault. Still,

he did not despair of the Republic. Many indications showed that, despite Ledru-Rollin's commissioners and circulars, the provinces might be relied on to return moderate members in sufficient numbers to outvote the Socialists of the town, and that their support would give to the Executive the strength of legality. The question was how to tide over the period intervening till the 4th of May, which, from the enormous labour required in preparing the lists of voters, was the earliest date at which the new Chamber could assemble.

The unfortunate concession made by Louis Philippe, in consenting to send away almost the entire garrison of Paris, could not easily be revoked by the Provisional Government. But Lamartine had done much to strengthen the army, and, acting as Minister of Foreign Affairs, insisted on the collecting of large forces on the Italian and Swiss frontiers ; the corps on which he relied chiefly being, however, massed round Lille under the command of General Negrier. Still anything likely to lead to a military despotism would have been in contradiction to Lamartine's whole previous career, certain not to be resorted to by him save in the last extremity. He based his hopes chiefly on the influence he was able to exercise on the people and on individuals.

As far as his position permitted, he was in communication with the leaders of all parties and all factions. Careless of personal danger, he laboured night and day to become known to those most bitterly opposed to him, and forced them, against their wills, to believe in his sincerity and patriotism. His ready eloquence and the singular charm of his manner were powerful auxiliaries, and if his success

was not always as great as his sanguine, sympathetic
temperament led him to suppose, it was sufficient to draw
on him the hatred of the Reds, "who bitterly denounced
him," writes Lord Normanby, "as 'the man whose egregiou
popularity, produced by his writings and power of publi
speaking, is no longer to be borne by those who valu
their liberties. Will you submit to him ? Do you expec
him to submit to you ? If not, what remains but to tak
his life ?' It is impossible," the ambassador goes on to say
"not to feel that the present position of M. de Lamartin
is now, and must remain for some weeks, one of grea
danger. He does not himself seem to expect deliberat
assassination, as the reaction would be dreaded ; but ther
is a plan to overpower the guard of the Hôtel des Affaire
Étrangères, and shut him up in one of the fortresses."

Of the other members of the Council, the most zealou
in the cause of order were MM. Marie and Marrast, wh
undertook to organize such elements of resistance as ther
were in the *bourgeoisie* and better class of artisans, and t
soothe the discontented spirits of the National Guard, whos
adhesion to the Government, after their recent rebuff, coulc
not be considered certain. , The Minister of the Interior
supposed to be the guardian of public safety, was, on th
contrary, growing more and more erratic in his line o
conduct. Elected by the department of Sarthe after th
premature death of the elder Garnier-Pagès in 1842, Ledru
Rollin, a man of vigorous physique, considerable fluenc
of speech, and untiring energy, had quickly risen to th
position of a leader in the second rank of the popula
movement. Lamartine had an amount of indulgence anc
liking for him which has always remained a problem

Probably Ledru-Rollin's immense capacity for work, coupled with a sort of good-humoured simplicity of character, and a readiness to repent which almost kept pace with his proneness to blunder, had something to do with it. When he first came to the Ministry of the Interior, he seemed, even more than his colleagues, absorbed in anxiety to bring his department at once back to ordinary working order. The first edict he sent forth, announcing that the Exhibition of Sculpture would open as usual on the 15th of April, caused some amusement. But, unused to power, he was susceptible to flattery, and speedily fell a victim to influences which might have turned a much stronger head.

At the first *tocsin* of the Revolution, Madame Georges Sand had hastened to Paris, and quickly became the central figure of a talented and powerful *coterie*, which had as its organ the weekly paper, *La Cause du Peuple.* M. Ledru-Rollin was among the frequenters of Madame Sand's circle, and very soon the documents emanating from the Ministère de l'Intérieur bore clear evidence of the style of the most accomplished writer of the day; while in the *milieu politique*, of which she held the threads, M. Ledru-Rollin was hailed as future President of the French Republic.

As far as the tangled web can now be unravelled, it appears that the Socialist leaders suggested to M. Ledru-Rollin the remodelling of the Executive, to which, as long as he believed himself sure of the post of leader, he did not object, and he accordingly—notwithstanding the severe lesson he had received in the demonstration of the 17th of March—paid little attention to the notices he received that a still larger one of the most dangerous kind was projected for the 16th of April. But at a meeting which took place on the night of the 14th, he found that he was expected to divide his power with Blanqui, who, it was known, would shrink at nothing—least of all at betraying a colleague Ledru-Rollin's courage failed him, and after spending the remainder of the night in agonies of indecision, he resolved to throw himself on Lamartine's mercy and reveal every thing. Accordingly he rushed into his room at break o day, exclaiming, " We are lost ! A hundred thousand men led by Blanqui, are marching on the Hôtel de Ville They are making use of my name, but I utterly renounce them, and am ready to fight against them by your side I am not, I have never been, a traitor ! "

" Then there is not a moment to lose," was Lamartine': reply ; and he at once suggested that Ledru-Rollin should order the *rappel* to beat for the muster of the Nationa Guard, while he himself started off to summon three battalions of the Garde Mobile, which he knew were ready for action, to defend the Hôtel de Ville.

Having done this, Lamartine, perhaps not altogether trusting his colleague, went himself to the head-quarters o the National Guard. General Courtais, who was in com mand, refused to believe in the danger or to beat the *rappel* In vain Lamartine stormed and threatened. At last, finding he was losing valuable time, he went to join Marrast at the Hôtel de Ville.

The situation was most critical. Already the insurgents were gathering in numbers, and twelve hundred Garde: Mobile were the only troops available. But a happy accident brought unexpected aid. General Changarnier who had just been appointed to a foreign mission, called that morning to receive his last instructions from Lamartine, and hearing from Madame de Lamartine, who was in terrible anxiety on her husband's account, of the critical state of things at the Hôtel de Ville, hastened there at once. He afterwards told Lord Normanby, that he found Marrast, as might be expected of a man who had only wielded pens all his life, as white as the paper he was in the habit of spoiling ; Lamartine, prepared for the worst, but perfectly cool and collected. Changarnier, when the situation was explained to him, joined Lamartine in persuading Marrast that it was his duty, as Mayor of Paris, to call out the National Guard when the safety of the town was threatened. Marrast acquiesced, and Changarnier then took the direction of the defence, wisely withdrawing his handful of troops within the building, which he strongly barricaded.

"If you can answer for three hours," Lamartine said to him, " we are safe."

" I can answer for seven hours," was Changarnier's reply.

At the end of about two hours the insurgents began to file into the Place du Grève in considerable numbers, and with an evident determination to proceed at once to extremities. Fortunately, before they could begin the attack, a body of volunteers, entering the Place on the opposite side, got between them and the building, and with great courage and determination kept them at bay. The odds were overwhelming, and for a moment it seemed as if all were lost, when the glitter of bayonets was seen on the quays, a strong detachment of the National Guard came down at a brisk run, hemming in one body of insurgents, and soon dispersing the rest. Their numbers

increasing every moment, they spread like an inundation
over the surrounding streets, and for a moment the triumph
of the party of order was complete.

Lamartine and Marrast received an ovation which
lasted for hours, during which they were rejoined by their
colleagues. Garnier-Pagès was cordial and sympathetic
Albert and Louis Blanc visibly disconcerted ; Crémieux
went to and fro, alternately condoling with them or con
gratulating Changarnier on the events of the day, while
Ledru-Rollin's happy temperament enabled him—though
really more to blame than any one—to rejoice unfeignedly
in his reconciliation with Lamartine, and forget all that
had passed.

The short space that intervened before the meeting
of the Assembly was got over smoothly ; the manifestation
of Conservative feeling which the late events evoked, was
taken advantage of by Lamartine to get the consent of the
other members of the Government to bring back as many
regular troops to Paris as would at least make a *coup de
main* on the part of the Socialists impossible. On the
20th of April, the distribution of the Republican colours to
the Garde Mobile and to the National Guard of Paris and
the surrounding towns was made the occasion of an
immense review. The march past the Arc de l'Étoile
where the Members of the Provisional Government had
taken their station, lasted from eight in the morning till
eleven at night, and fifty thousand men had to wait till the
morrow. Lamartine's description of the day, which he
looked on as one of the brightest of his life, is glowing
Contrary to the expectations of· many, the troops were
extremely well received by the populace ; the soldiers

bayonets were decorated with ribbons ; the touch-holes of the cannon wreathed with flowers ; joy and enthusiasm prevailed everywhere.

, The elections took place throughout the whole of France on Easter Day, and—save at Rouen, where, without much apparent reason, the troops shot fifty of the mob dead in a single volley—there was no disturbance. The difficulty seems to have been to get the working classes, whose enfranchisement had been the chief excuse for the Revolution, to take any interest in the matter. In many places the practical side of the French character was curiously illustrated. The peasants, who had been furnished with lists, took them to any neighbour they respected, to have the names of the richest candidates pointed out, as they wished to choose the people most likely to be useful to them. In other districts, the electors came in bands to the notary of the nearest village, asking to have lists made out for them, as they were going to exercise their new right of voting. On being asked what names should be put down, they replied they did not care in the least. In Paris, however, the electors showed themselves rather disposed to resist dictation. Louis Blanc and his friends prepared a list for the diffusion of Socialist principles, prefaced with the names of twenty-four working men. Of the thirty-six candidates they proposed, thirty-two were defeated.

Generally speaking, however, the towns returned men of extreme democratic opinions ; the provinces men of some local celebrity, who, though nominally Republicans, were known to be inclined to check the ultra-revolutionary movement,—thus establishing between the rural and urban

constituencies a line of demarcation which, if broadened
and deepened, must inevitably prove fatal to the Republic
Still the prevailing feeling was one of thankfulness that
the long period of suspense and anxiety was over, though
even to the eve of the day fixed for the opening of the
Assembly, warnings and letters came in to Lamartine from
all sides, telling him that blood would flow before the
National Assembly would be suffered to meet. As to his
own fate, it was said that hundreds of fanatics were pledged
to proclaim the triumph of Socialism over his corpse. " It
may be so," was his reply, " but at the present hour France
is safe. Her choice is made, the names of her representatives are known. If the present Government were over-
turned, these men will come from the provinces backed by
legality, escorted by millions of armed citizens, and will
easily crush the dictatorship of a Committee of Public
Safety. And what matters it if I die, since the future of
France is secure ? "

Fortunately, these sinister predictions were not verified,
and on the 4th of May—the anniversary of the meeting of
the States-General in 1789—the opening ceremony took
place.

" Never," writes Lamartine, " was the sovereign of a
great people installed with such majesty. The Government, assembled at an early hour at the Ministry of
Justice, went on foot, preceded by the General of the
National Guard and his staff, passing between ranks lined
by two hundred thousand men ; every roof and window of
the quarter filled with people ; the air ringing with cries
and plaudits. Never did any Government make its entry
into a capital, preceded by the enthusiastic hopes of a

people, with such echoing acclamations as this Government, which in another hour would no longer exist, received! Its faults, its weaknesses, its illegality, its insufficiency, were all forgotten; only its efforts and its disinterestedness remembered. There was no affectation of pomp or circumstance on the part of any of its members; they were citizens wearing the garb of everyday life, having the authority, but none of the accessories of sovereignty. People pointed out to each other Dupont de l'Eure in the post of honour; next to him Lamartine and Louis Blanc. They saw personified in Arago the homage due to science and political capacity; in Garnier-Pagès, antique probity and simplicity; Crémieux, Marie, Marrast, were respected for their services; Flocon, Albert, Ledru-Rollin, names dear to Republicans of the older school, 'whose hopes lay in their past and in their future.' "

Lord Normanby and M. Maxime du Camp, also eyewitnesses, are much more reserved, to say the least, in their descriptions, but they unite in speaking of Lamartine, whose striking personality and perfection of manner enabled him to fill the most difficult positions with self-possession and dignity, as the undisputed sovereign of the hour, the rallying point of all enthusiasm,—the cries of "Vive Lamartine!" far outnumbering those of "Vive la République."

As the former Chamber of Deputies was quite inadequate to receive the nine hundred members of the new Assembly, a temporary construction had been erected within the precincts of the Palais Bourbon, in which they now mustered. Even to the critical eye of the English ambassador, "the appearance of the deputies, as a body,

was highly respectable, though there were among them
some strange figures and wild countenances."

The Legitimists were represented by Berryer, Falloux,
Larochejaquelin, and a good many ecclesiastics ; with the
solitary exception of M. Thiers, all the former " Opposition
dynastique" had returned ; of the supporters of the last
administration only the most prominently unpopular were
missed. " France," writes Lamartine, " showed she had the
genius of transition, the supreme tact of circumstance ; nor
were they proscribed, but only postponed."

It had been decreed the deputies should wear a special
costume, of which a " gilet à la Robespierre " was the most
conspicuous part. But they had the good sense to disregard this injunction, and only Caussidière appeared in
the prescribed dress. ˙However, piquant contrasts, both
political and social, were not wanting. There was Barbés
sitting beside his former judges, mingling his voice with
the voices of those who had condemned him to death ; two
Bonapartes were in close proximity to Larochejaquelin ;
sons of regicides elbowed sons of crusaders ; the white robe
of the Dominican Lacordaire gleamed like a mediæval
vision beside the sombre garb of the Lutheran pastor,
Coquerel, and the black frock-coat of the Jew, Crémieux.

When, ushered in by a peal of cannon from the Invalides, the Provisional Government entered, the deputies
rose at once to receive them, and the cry, " Vive le Gouvernement Provisoire ! " echoed through the hall, proceeding,
according to some, from the whole Assembly, according to
others, only from the Left and the galleries.

After the speech with which they surrendered their
powers to the representatives of the nation had been read

by M. Dupont, Lamartine, speaking in his colleagues' name as well as his own, gave a detailed *compte rendu* of their internal administration and external policy. Alluding to the latter, he said with just pride, " We accept the whole responsibility of the situation, and congratulate ourselves at being able to appear before the representatives of the nation with the greatness of France unimpaired, her hands full of alliances, and unstained by human blood." He was listened to with extreme favour. His concluding phrase, " May the record of the three months which have elapsed between the fall of the monarchy and the enthronement of the Republic be deemed (though at an infinite distance from other more glorious epochs), yet not an unworthy page in the history of our beloved country, and may there be written on that page, not the obscure and forgotten names of men whose only merit is that they willingly efface themselves for the public welfare, but the name of the People that has established, and of God who has blessed the formation of the Republic," elicited enthusiastic applause.

The first serious business awaiting the Assembly was to make some arrangement for the government of the nation pending the formation of a new constitution. It was the general wish and expectation, after the experience of the evils of a divided executive, that a temporary dictatorship should be established ; nor was there any doubt that, in such case, Lamartine would be elected. But to this he strongly opposed himself, throwing the whole of his influence in favour of an Executive Commission of five members, which was reluctantly voted. When the members of this Commission came to be selected, a powerful political group, inspired by M. Marrast, and called, from the news-

paper which was his organ, " Le parti du National,"
determined to exclude Ledru-Rollin, and with the support
of the provincial deputies, to whom the promulgator of
the Electoral Circulars was extremely obnoxious, they felt
sure of success.

Late in the debate Lamartine unexpectedly rose and
vehemently opposed the motion, giving it to be understood
that, if the Commission were formed on the principle of
excluding any of the members of the late Provisional
Government, he would not belong to it. Lamartine carried
his point, but at the cost of his own political future, the
Conservatives regarding him as a deserter. Their hostility
was shown in the division on the election of the Commission, when his name came out fourth on the list.

" Causes of a very different character," writes Lord
Normanby, " combined to produce this result. Some of
the extreme party, who are opposed to the nomination of
a President in the future Republic, may have wished to
show there was no man whose pre-eminence pointed him
out peculiarly for the post ; but the principal cause of this
sudden fall was Lamartine's not having proved himself equal
to the occasion. . . . When, a few days ago, he volunteered
to speak confidentially to me of the course he meant to
pursue, though he did not then push the morbid sentiment
to the extent to which he subsequently put it in practice,
he talked of not making himself the instrument to undo his
colleagues. I told him frankly, as he mentioned this in
a manner to elicit an opinion, that whilst he must always
enjoy high favour from the varied exercise of his genius
which had made his name dear to all his contemporaries,
I could not but think at this moment that some portion of

his popularity was owing to the conviction that he would protect the country from those men whom all friends of order dreaded, and that any apparent collusion with them might shake the position which was so necessary to him in facing the immense difficulties with which he had to contend. M. de Lamartine seemed to feel, and to a certain extent he admitted, the danger."

That Lamartine, never deficient in political sense, should thus deliberately have laid out for himself, and despite all warnings, persevered in a line of conduct by which he could in no case have gained anything, and immediately lost so much, has been treated by many historians as at once a problem and a reproach. Yet his own explanation, of which subsequent events proved both the accuracy and the discernment, might well be deemed sufficient.*

The deputies returned by the provinces, mostly men of the wealthier middle class, though nominally Republicans, were avowedly anxious for the most Conservative form of Government that could be established, and formed a strong majority. But against them were arrayed the members for Paris, and the other large towns, all holding extreme, even violent Radical views, and these, if in a minority in the Chamber, had with them the clubs, the hundred thousand artisans in the Ateliers Nationaux, the Bonapartists, and the Terrorists. The exclusion of Ledru-Rollin and Marie, the only men they thoroughly trusted, would have driven them to desperation, and brought on at once a sanguinary struggle which the Party of Order was not yet prepared

---

* The suggestion, sometimes even now ignorantly repeated, that Ledru-Rollin had in his hands a document proving that Lamartine had received from Louis Philippe a considerable sum of money, is completely refuted in his " Lettre aux dix départements."

to meet, and out of which, whatever the issue, would have
emerged a Republic either mutilated or disgraced—not
Lamartine's ideal Republic, free from the stain of blood
and the bar sinister of proscription.

But it was soon seen that the advanced section of the
Republicans were very far from considering the inclusion
of Ledru-Rollin and Marie in the Government a sufficient
concession. The leaders of the clubs, Blanqui, Raspail, and
Cabet, furious at not getting seats in the Assembly, turned
their energies to effecting a coalition with Louis Blanc and
Albert, who were known to be chagrined by their own
exclusion from the Executive Commission. It was not
easy to find ground on which two parties, so entirely
opposed in principles as the Communists and the Socialists,
could act openly in common. However, the happy expedient was hit on of a joint petition in favour of the
independence of Poland, coupled with a demand for the
immediate declaration of war with Germany, which, they
proclaimed, was to be presented by a hundred thousand
working men. The Assembly, feeling that a petition thus
presented was, as Lamartine phrased it, "not a petition,
but a menace," refused to receive it ; whereupon the clubs
and their allies resolved on a great demonstration for the
15th of May, with the avowed design of terrifying the
Assembly into submission. To meet it, the means of
resistance the Government now had at their disposal were
amply sufficient ; to secure the Palais Bourbon against
attack it only required, in the opinion of competent military
men, to station a moderate number of troops in the Place
and the streets leading to it. The General in command
of Paris and the Préfet de Police were accordingly sent for

and desired to mass, on the morning of the 15th of May, twelve thousand troops round the palace, and place several strong detachments of the National Guard along the Boulevards.

Unfortunately, in order to keep the peace more easily, the Provisional Government had resorted to the plan which now figures as the last resource of civilization, but which our ancestors used to describe by the homelier phrase of " setting the wolves to guard the sheep." General Courtais and M. Caussidière's only claim to their respective posts lay in their great popularity, and in moments of emergency their chief care naturally was to avoid anything which would impair it. When the morning of the 15th of May came, Caussidière sent word to the Executive Commission that he was too ill to leave his house that day, but that there was nothing in the state of Paris to justify the slightest anxiety; and General Courtais duly posted his troops as directed round the Palais Bourbon, but, on receiving from the leaders of the demonstration the assurance that their intentions were purely pacific, he ordered the soldiers to unfix their bayonets and let the insurgents pass, to the number of fifteen thousand, through his lines.

When this became known in the Assembly, Lamartine went out in the hope of once more dispelling physical force by the power of his eloquence. But the spell no longer worked, and he was hooted down with cries of, " Assez joué de la lyre !" "Mort à Lamartine !" After some unsuccessful efforts to obtain a hearing, he was forced back to the second line of railings, where, with a group of friends, among whom M. de Morny was the most resolute, he tried to oppose a barrier to the rising flood. Seeing it was hope-

less, they returned to the Chamber, where the word wa
passed that all should keep their seats.

"The attitude of the members," writes an eye-witness
M. Maxime du Camp, "was admirable. They remained
perfectly calm during a tumult which baffles description
and lasted nearly four hours." The President, M. Buchez
did not sustain his part so well. Surrounded by a furiou
crowd, which threatened him with instant death unless he
signed an order forbidding the National Guard to act, h
resisted for a long time, but yielded at last. On this th
last vestige of order was lost. Barbés, forced into the
tribune, was desired to state the demands of the people
He began by announcing a tax of forty millions on the
rich. "You are wrong, Barbés," interrupted a chorus o
voices. "What we want is two hours' pillage." Wearied
at length with their own noise, the mob declared the
Assembly dissolved, and proceeded to nominate a new
Provisional Government, of which Louis Blanc, Raspail
and Cabet were the principal members.

Meanwhile, Lamartine had found means to despatch
messengers to those battalions of the National Guard
which could be most securely relied on, and, at four o'clock
the welcome sound of their drums was heard. Before they
reached the Palais Bourbon, its unwelcome occupants had
almost cleared out, and the Assembly resumed its sitting
Lamartine went to the tribune, and announced his intention
of going at once to the Hôtel de Ville to rescue it from the
usurpation of the mob; then, accompanied by Ledru-
Rollin, M. de Morny, and the Comte de Falloux (a
strangely assorted group), he rode down the quays, the
mob now cheering and shouting, "Vive Lamartine!" "Vive

l'Assemblée Nationale!" They were escorted by a battalion of the National Guard, which happened to number in its ranks several well-known members of Parisian society. Halting once for a moment, they were descried by a secretary of the Russian Embassy, who, recognizing some acquaintances, rushed up to them, pale and excited, with difficulty gasping out, "What about Poland?" It was not for a moment that those he addressed recollected that the independence of Poland had been the pretext for the events of the day; then they promptly replied, "Poland is dead. Blanqui and Raspail have strangled her."

The military anarchy was complete. General Courtais had been gagged and insulted by his own troops; General Tampor could not be found. But the insurgents had not time to organize any defence. A few battalions of the National Guard and a regiment of dragoons under General Goyon were sufficient to liberate the Hôtel de Ville, and secure some of the principal ringleaders, who were at once sent to Vincennes.

The events of the 15th of May, coming, as they did, immediately after the opening of the Assembly chosen by universal suffrage, and with great expectations, were, to all patriotic Frenchmen, cruelly humiliating. Still they produced indirectly some salutary effects. Coupled with similar incidents of the last three months, they fixed, in the minds of the most absorbed men of business, as well as of the idlest of Parisian *flaneurs*, the idea some very clever people still find it difficult to grasp, that, once the streets of a modern city are in possession of a mob less afraid of the authorities than the authorities are of them, the inhabitants are within a distance of pillage and arson perhaps as measurable as used to be the dwellers on the Celtic seaboard, when the Danish fleet was sighted in the offing. But the Parisian mind, if slow in taking in new and unpleasant ideas, is eminently practical. M. Maxime du Camp, calling one morning on an uncle who had made a large fortune by possessing the scent of an Iroquois for coming events, found his relative busily occupied, not at his desk, but in looking over his store of firearms, sub- situting for his ordinary *poudre de chasseur* a supply of English powder, the best procurable. On M. du Camp expressing his surprise, his uncle replied, "I am getting ready for the battle, and I advise you to do the same ;' and no doubt scores of old gentlemen were, at the same day and hour, similarly occupied.

At the seat of Government the anxiety was not less To leave Paris "with no garrison but the devotion and patriotism of her citizens," was indeed a graceful and effective phrase ; but events showed that the Nationa Guard, though, on the 18th of April, they supported the Government with unexpected loyalty, had, by the 15th of May, got weary of doing what was properly the work of the regular army, for the maintenance of which they were heavily taxed. Still, as the last act of the Monarchy had been to withdraw, at the request of the people, the troops from Paris, it was not an easy task for a Republican Executive Commission to re-garrison the town adequately without exciting a fresh insurrection. All that was possible was being done. The number of regular troops in the city exceeded twenty thousand, and, in place of Genera Courtais, Cavaignac, the bravest and most reliable of the Republican generals, had, at Lamartine's urgent request

been recalled from Algeria, and given the command of the
garrison. The *corps d'armée* in the surrounding provinces
were being massed and strengthened, and to secure the
triumph of order time only was needed. Unfortunately,
events marched rapidly. The arrest of Barbés angered the
mob ; the supplementary elections which took place in
June caused fresh excitement, increased by the unexpected
nomination of Louis Napoleon Bonaparte by three departments, and by the return of Thiers, who (so quickly had
events progressed) was now regarded as the chief of the
reactionary party.

But the question which finally brought about the
catastrophe was that of the National Workshops. In the
early days of the Revolution, when credit no longer existed,
and all industries had been paralyzed, the Government
had been obliged to assume the duty of providing some
sustenance for the thousands of destitute artisans and
labourers who would otherwise constitute a serious danger
to the city, and a decree was passed appointing giant
workshops, at which all who applied received two francs a
day. As it was always hoped that, when once the crisis
was over, industry would return to its natural channels, the
impossibility of providing profitable employment was not
at first recognized. The men, who were put to easy,
nominal tasks, practically spent most of their time in
lounging about in *cafés*, and, as the wages were above the
average, their number was increased by recruits from the
country, till the cost of their maintenance amounted to
£12,000 per day, at a time when the Minister of Finance
did not know how to meet the ordinary expenses of the
budget, and the country was weighed down by extra

taxation. The Parisian *bourgeoisie* grumbled under th
burden, abusing the Ateliers Nationaux freely. Still the
felt that to suppress them would be dangerous, so the evi
day was adjourned. But the provincial deputies were no
so long-suffering, and, before the Assembly had sat thre
weeks, a decree, striking off the names of all who had no
been for six months domiciled in Paris, and requiring al
between the ages of eighteen to twenty-six to enlist a
once in the regular army, was passed.

Whatever hesitation there might have been on the par
of the Government about bringing matters to a crisis, ther
was none on the part of the workmen. During the tw
nights following the 20th of June, all who were belated i
the streets met patrols of two or three thousand men, quie
noiseless, merely marching in military order, repeating th
monotonous refrain, " Bread or lead," " Bread or lead ; " anc
on the evening of the 22nd, began a conflict more desperat
and more sanguinary than any the streets of Paris ha
hitherto known. The organization of the insurgents wa
admirable, corresponding exactly to that of the brigade
of the National Workshops ; the whole under the abl
direction of the " Société des Droits de l'Homme," whicl
in defiance of the Government, had reconstituted itself o
the 11th of June. All through the night, men, women, an
children were working at the barricades with a degree c
rapidity, order, and consistency which revealed a long
matured plan. Before noon, that part of the city which lie
eastward of a line drawn from the Panthéon to the Châtea
d'Eau was an almost impregnable stronghold. Two grea
barricades had been erected, one at the Porte St. Deni:
the other at the Porte St. Martin ; one of stupendou

magnitude at the entry of the Faubourg St. Antoine; thirty
in the Île St. Denis—about 150 in all, defended by sharpshooters well provided with ammunition,—besides which
four large bodies of insurgents, supported by musketeers
and *tirailleurs,* were told off for the assault of the Hôtel de
Ville.

The forces of which the Government could dispose were
very inadequate to cope with such a movement. The
regular troops under Cavaignac did not exceed twenty-
three thousand, a mere handful in comparison to the masses
opposed to them. Not fully realizing the extent of the
danger at first, he had lost time in summoning the troops
scattered round the environs of Paris; and the camp of
twenty thousand men, so anxiously pressed for by Lamartine, had not yet been formed. The National Guard, too,
had shown themselves unexpectedly slack in answering the
rappel; and the Garde Mobile, recruited among the *gamins*
of Paris, who had taken active part in the days of February,
were hardly counted on seriously,—indeed, it was taken
almost for granted, though very mistakenly, that their
sympathies would be instinctively on the side of disorder.
It was not to be wondered at that Cavaignac, knowing the
hazard, from a military point of view, of risking an attack
with insufficient numbers in the narrow streets of a great
city, and sufficiently experienced in revolutions to fear the
result of exposing even an inconsiderable number of soldiers
to defeat and capture, refused to divide his forces or act on ·
any extended scale till reinforced. On the other hand, it
seems difficult to understand that any risk of defeat or,
within certain bounds, that any not useless loss of life
could counterbalance the disadvantage of allowing the first

erection of barricades, which gave the populace such de:
perate strength both in attack and in resistance, and whic
would ultimately have to be carried with an amount (
bloodshed terrible to contemplate. The latter view pr(
vailed among the party of resistance in Paris. On th
afternoon of Friday, Lamartine and Ledru-Rollin wer
insulted as traitors, because to them was attributed th
quiescence of the troops ; the fact being that the Executiv
Commission had been all through the day unanimous i
pressing on Cavaignac precisely the line of conduct the
were accused of neglecting.

M. Barthélémy thus describes what took place on th
morning of the 23rd : "Une dernière tentative fut fait
auprès du général. MM. Arago, Marie, Lamartine, Ledru
Rollin, avec M. Barthélémy St. Hilaire le pressèrent d
commencer l'attaque. Le général fut inflexible; les instance
dont il était l'objet irritant sa colère. ' Croyez vous,' dit i
' que je sois ici pour défendre vos Parisiens, votre Gard
Nationale ? qu'elle se défende elle-même, sa ville et s(
boutiques. Je ne veux pas disséminer mes troupes. J
me rappelle 1830 ; je me rappelle Février. Si une seule d
mes compagnies est desarmée, si nous subissons encore un
fois cet affront, je me brûle la cervelle, je ne survivrai pa
à ce déshonneur.' On eut beau représenter au général qu
son suicide ne remédierait à rien, qu'il s'agissait d'enleve
les barricades qu'il avait laissé former ; aucun argument n
put le décider à donner l'ordre d'attaque ; le moment décis
ne lui parût pas encore venu. On ajouta que les insurgé
gagnaient à tout instant du terrain. ' Que m'importe,' répon
dit le général, ' Eh bien, s'ils sont maîtres de Paris, je m
retirerai avec mon armée dans les plaines de St. Denis (

je leur livrerais bataille.' 'Oui,' dit M. Arago, 'mais ils ne vous y suiveront pas.'"

Perhaps the fairest allocation of praise and blame between the Executive Committee and General Cavaignac is to be found in the second volume of Lord Normanby's "Journal of a Year of Revolution," where, with full knowledge of the facts, he sums up the situation, and decides, with some reservation, in favour of the Executive. Meanwhile, from the military point of view, General Cavaignac's position was unassailable, and his tactics faultless. He massed his troops in the Tuileries, the Champs Elysées, the Place de la Concorde, and round the Palais du Luxembourg. The Hôtel de Ville was occupied by sixteen battalions under General Duvivier. To General Dumesne was given the command of the quarter of the Panthéon, and to General Lamoricière the charge of covering the whole left bank of the Seine, from the Château d'Eau to the Madeleine, which alone would have given sufficient work to an army. The first attack on the insurgents' lines was made on the afternoon of the 23rd. The barricades of the Porte St. Martin and of the Port St. Denis were carried, the latter only after a most desperate resistance. The troops being so few in number, Cavaignac was then disposed to let them rest; but on Lamartine's imploring him not to lose the hours of daylight yet remaining, it was decided to liberate the Faubourg du Temple, Cavaignac himself leading the attack. The first obstacle was a barricade of tremendous strength, on which three hours of incessant firing scarcely produced any effect. Four hundred soldiers and two generals were killed. Lamartine then brought up four more guns. At the end of another hour, the barrier was broken down, and the enemy either driven back or held at bay at all points, when nightfall brought a cessation of hostilities, though only till they broke out again with renewed desperation at early dawn. But by this time the reinforcements so eagerly looked for came pouring in ; a large train of ammunition arrived from Vincennes, another from Bourges ; the trains were steadily bringing up troops from Orleans and all the garrison towns within a day's journey of Paris, making the ultimate issue of the insurrection no longer doubtful.

But a fierce and deadly struggle was still inevitable, and it was felt that at such a crisis there should be no division of responsibility or of authority. By the almost unanimous vote of the Assembly, General Cavaignac was invested with absolute powers, under the title of Military Dictator. The Executive Committee then resigned, and Lamartine at once offered his services to Cavaignac, saying, with loyal frankness, " I am not one of those who, when they cease to hold office, join the Opposition. My earnest wish will be to support my successors as if my cause and theirs were one. You may count on me as fully to-morrow as to-day."

During these months of stormy vicissitude the position of Madame de Lamartine had been a very difficult one ; but her unfailing tact and goodness enabled her to escape the many pitfalls that beset her path, and to go through "three months of power" without making an enemy or losing a friend. All her personal predilections, all the traditions of the society into which she had been so warmly received in the early days of her married life, were anti-republican. Madame d'Agoult describes rather sarcastically how the great ladies of the Faubourg used to be seen, half *incognite*, ascending and descending the staircase leading to the private apartments of the Hôtel des Affaires Étrangères, to pour out to Madame de Lamartine's sympathetic ears their hopes and fears for the " lost cause and impossible allegiance " to which they still devoutly clung. But, on the other hand, we are told by the most ardent of Republicans, M. Henri de Lacretelle, that the strange and motley company which used in those days to invade Madame de Lamartine's fireside, were always received with the serene courtesy which was her unvarying attribute, and he is at a loss for words to describe his admiration for the courage and self-devotion shown by one so gentle and so feminine in the terrible " last days of June." " Wrapt up as she was in Lamartine, living only in his life, this woman, this foreigner, never attempted to keep him back from what, even after his personal responsibility had ceased, he held to be the post of duty." Probably nothing would have held him back, at any rate as long as the conflict lasted. Lamartine, surrounded by a little band of friends was night and day unsparing in his exertions and utterly regardless of personal danger, sometimes leading up to the attack a company of the Gardes Mobile so romantically devoted to him ; sometimes within the lines of the insurgents, appealing to their patriotism, justice, and humanity to put an end to this hopeless and fratricidal strife ; at times apparently successful for the moment, but never attaining any practical result.

One night scene he has described at some length in his " Portraits et Souvenirs." It was the evening of the second day of the insurrection. Lamartine was returning from

an attack on the barricades, accompanied by Prince Pierr
Bonaparte, then an ardent Republican, one of whose horse
had just been killed under him, and a young Nation
Guard named Lachaud, who, unknown to Lamartine, ha
attached himself to him as a body-guard. Full of anxiet
and grief at the desperate nature of the struggle, Lamartin
wished to judge for himself as to the disposition of th
masses thronging the Boulevards all along the line fror
the Faubourg du Temple to the Bastille. Passing throug
the line of troops employed in keeping off the multitud
at this latter point, he, with his three companions, rod
slowly down the carriage-way. The mob, pushed back o
the foot-way, was at first angry and astonished; the
recognizing Lamartine, surrounded him with almost franti
eagerness, so that their progress was seriously impede
they could hardly advance ten paces in a minute. Th
crowd did not, Lamartine says, consist of the rough u
washed idlers every revolutionary movement brings to th
surface; it was composed of the inhabitants of the quarte
of honest, hard-working artisans whose features wore
gentle, almost patient expression, though their lips no
trembled with emotion.

A confused eager murmur rose up from their rank
gradually formulating itself into distinct sounds, wit
intervals of comparative silence, in which could be hear
questions and answers such as these: " Who is riding th
black horse?" " Vive Lamartine!" " Let me shake h
hand!" " Let me touch his horse!" Other voices ar
swered, " Death to Lamartine! Vive la Republique Dem
cratique et Sociale!"—but these were quickly drowned b
angry hisses. Workmen in their blouses gathered in ii

creasing myriads round Lamartine, all speaking at once.
"Do not fear. Do not *you* fear, Lamartine ; we are not
assassins. We want neither blood nor plunder. We are
honest workmen, hating as you do those who fire on their
brethren. All we want is order, work, bread. Look at
our wives, our children ; see how they tremble, how they
weep ! See how pale, how thin, how scantily clothed they
are ! Do we look like a pampered, overfed people ? For
three months we have lived on rations for the sake of
Liberty. We don't regret it, we don't repent it ; but Liberty
must feed the people. . . . Send away the Assemblée
Nationale ! Down with the Assemblée Nationale. It does
nothing for us. It does not know what to do. Do *you*
govern us ! You *shall* govern us. Govern us yourself,
Lamartine. We have always obeyed you, and we always
will.

Lamartine. "What you ask is a crime. The Assembly
is France. Give it time ; a Government cannot be founded
in one sitting."

A thousand voices. "No, no, no ! it is doing nothing ;
it does not know us, nor understand us. Govern us by
yourself. We will obey you ; we have always obeyed you."

Thousands of voices along the line. "We do not want
blood. We do not want this insurrection. But send away
this Assembly of chatterers. Make the combat to cease ;
silence the cannon."

Lamartine. "Do you want us, then, to allow the destruction of Paris, of France, without defending them
against a handful of criminals ? "

Thousands of voices. " That is true ; that is true. We
don't take their part. We know nothing of them. They

are bad citizens. But make haste, or we cannot answer foi
ourselves. Send away the Assembly. Give us work
bread, peace ; but forgive the conquered. We have nc
enemies. Let there be no vengeance, no scaffold. Work
peace, bread, but spare the vanquished. We are al
Frenchmen ! "

In these words, taken down on the spot by the Nationa
Guard, Lachaud, Lamartine recognizes the voice, confused
piteous, but yet humane, of the true people of Paris.

But in reality the Boulevards were but the outskirts o
the movement. Within the terrible stronghold Seditior
had built for herself, the cry was one of vengeance, and o
blind, unreasoning hatred. In vain, when alike physicallɣ
and morally certain of the victory, did the Executivɩ
Government, and afterwards General Cavaignac, send ou
messenger after messenger with flags of truce ; they werɩ
first derided and insulted, then treacherously murdered
often, as in the case of General Bréa, cruelly mutilated
And finally, when the Archbishop of Paris, Mgr. Affre
horror-struck at the hopeless and apparently never-endinɡ
slaughter, went out " to give his life for his sheep," he, toɑ
was ruthlessly struck down.

Only at the eleventh hour, when their cause was entirelɣ
lost, did the insurgents offer to lay down their arms, bu
on the condition of absolute and unconditional amnesty
It was refused, and for this refusal Lamartine, who might
far more truthfully than Hugo, have said of himself—

> " Moi, qui pour tous les crimes veux tous les pardons,"

never forgave Cavaignac.

On the following morning, June 26th, both sides preparec

for a renewal of the conflict. At daybreak the combatants
stood to their arms ; barricades and windows were crowded
with sharpshooters, the gunners stood with lighted matches
beside their pieces, and, ere long, sounds were heard which
must have convinced the insurgents that further resistance was hopeless. A loud cannonade announced that
Lamoricière, having forced his way through the Faubourg,
was assailing them in the rear. Still they held out, and
ten o'clock, the period assigned for an unconditional surrender, having passed without any sign being made, the
combat recommenced. An immense shower of bombs
directed on the Faubourg, set it on fire in several places.
The troops then rushed on in three columns. All the
attacks were successful, and at last the insurgents capitu-
lated, thus ending a struggle in which "more generals were
slain than at Waterloo, more soldiers than in the bloodiest
of Napoleon's battles."* Of the wounded the number was
never known, but there was reason to fear that poisoned
missiles did among them the work hinted at in the mut-
tered sneers of the prisoners : "The dead are dead ; the
wounded will never recover."

* Alison, "History of Europe, 1815-1852."

CHAPTER XI.

1848–1853.

"THEY went out to battle, but they always fell," wrote Cæsar of the Gauls of his time, and, triumphant as are the annals of mediæval and modern France, there have been periods when something of their ancestors' fatality has seemed to follow Frenchmen. However, there are contests in which the vanquished share the glory with the victors ; where, as at Marignan and Waterloo and Gravelotte, much is lost, but not honour. And thus it was in the long struggle that had lasted from February to July; Lamartine had not desired the fall of the monarchy, but when the ship of the State was drifting swiftly to destruction, he went to the helm and steered into smooth waters, if not into port. In the three first days of the Provisional Government he had been, to quote a not too partial judge, "undoubtedly the man demanded by the crisis. During those sixty hours of 'fighting with the beasts' he acted with a courage worthy of Bayard." When the first lull came, he was the only member of the Government who realized his responsibilities. It was his energy, promptitude, and forethought that saved Paris from famine. Afterwards it was his determination and his influence that preserved the peace of Europe. Thirty years of aimless conscription and the memory of Napoleon's victories had made Frenchmen wild with restless ambition. Had Thiers been in Lamartine's place, he would, as he told Mr. Senior in 1852, at once have extended the frontier to Mayence. By his resolution in bringing up troops round Paris, Lamartine had mitigated and made abortive the insurrection of June. If he did not succeed in averting it, nor in establishing authority on a secure basis, it was because he shrank from the only possible means, the assumption of absolute power. For three months the Dictatorship lay within his hand. He might have had his 18 Brumaire or his 2 Decembre without striking a blow, perhaps without sacrificing a life. If he abstained from respect for or faith in Republican institutions, those who hold such belief to be superstition will be the last to condemn him.

During the weeks immediately following the events just narrated Lamartine remained in Paris, but took little part in politics. He saw plainly that the insurrection had seriously weakened, if it had not altogether destroyed, what remained in France of the Republican spirit. All the same, his dislike to repressive measures remained. Not even the rage and passion of actual conflict, so terribly exciting to those unused to it, could change a temperament still more abounding in mansuetude than in sympathy; his dominant feeling for the insurgents—would-be destroyers of the Republic though they were—was one of pity. There seems no reason to believe that the punishments meted by General Cavaignac were in any way excessive; but Lamartine, without blaming him, suffered with and for the vanquished, and did all that was in his power to shield

them, thankful that the sword and balance of justice we
in other hands. The only real pleasure he seems to ha'
found in that sorrowful time was in the strong affection
the friends who now gathered round him with increas(
devotion. The narrative of his conduct in the days
February was drawing towards him an electric curre:
of sympathy from all parts of France. Another source
satisfaction was the re-knitting of some ties of person
friendship which the misunderstandings incident to co
flicting political opinions had strained to the utmo:
This had been the case with the Girardins, who had rang(
themselves in opposition, and, always susceptible in tl
extreme, were indignant that their criticisms remain(
unheeded. Lamartine, though the bitterness of M. (
Girardin's writings gave him sufficient cause for irritatic
would gladly have passed it over in silence, but when tl
kindly intervention of Madame de Lamartine was mi
interpreted, he had felt it due to himself to remonstrate
a letter addressed to Madame de Girardin.

   "I am grieved that you should have misunderstoc
Madame de Lamartine, whose feeling for you is that of tl
tenderest interest. Neither you nor M. de Girardin s
things as they really are, nor do you know how hard y(
make it to save you from yourselves ; later, you will und(
stand better. The opposition M. de Girardin is carryil
on in such unsparing. terms is wrong in point of da'
When the Republic is settled on a solid base, he will fil
nothing to complain of. Ask him to wait. At tl
moment, opposition, whether at home or abroad, can ser
no useful purpose. Do not think that what I ask is til
for the Government. I speak, not as one in authority, b

as a friend, in the name of social peril and of special circumstances which you cannot know, but which are ser

The letter was apparently left unanswered, but
soon after Lamartine's resignation, M. de Girardin
arrested by Cavaignac's orders, the impracticable cou
must have seen they had done him an injustice. Ai,
article from Madame de Girardin's pen, which appeared
soon after, and was evidently intended as an *amende*,
touched and pleased Lamartine much. Nor did politics
ever again trouble the serenity of that long-lived and
sincere friendship.

To M. de Circourt, who feared that by the line of
conduct he had followed he might have given Lamartine
offence, the latter wrote about this time: "My opinions
never interfere with my friendships. And I take for
granted it is the same with you, so that there is no fear of
our present non-agreement disturbing our mutual relations.
You do not believe in the future of the Republic; I do,
though there is danger in the coalition of Thiers and
Cavaignac; and, being on the spot, I ought to be the best
judge. Read the English newspapers. You wish to uphold
social order; its surest bulwark is a moderate and conciliatory Republic. Your friends want to destroy it; then
the choice will lie between the Convention and a dictator."

However, in M. de Circourt's case the breach widened,
and for some years he and Lamartine did not speak.

In August the question of the formation of the Constitution brought Lamartine again to the front. On the
first point discussed—whether the Legislature should
consist of one or of two Chambers—he spoke with much
animation, laying down the axiom that an Upper Chamber,

2 A

formed on any basis but that of aristocracy, must alway
.:merical.

have been a witness," he said, "of the misfortune
:atastrophes which may befall nations governed b
.e Legislature, but I have seen the same under a govern
.nent resting on two. Between the situation of th
countries in which the latter form is permanently establishe
and that of our country, I see no identity. Has France a
aristocracy like England? And how are the elections (
the senators to be regulated? Are they to be chosen o
account of their fortunes or their age? In the first cas(
would they form an aristocracy in any sense of the word
Would they not rather be representatives of the banke1
and of the *Chaussée d'Antin?* They would be, n(
'Chevaliers de l'epée,' but 'Chevaliers de la bours(
Would you even be justified in laying down a certain a£
as an indispensable preliminary to an election to th
Upper Chamber? Could you say to Franklin or to Roy
Collard, 'Your years do not admit of your sitting in tl
junior Chamber; go to the Chamber of the elders, to tl
Luxembourg.'"

To which M. Odillon-Barrot, who, it will be remembere
had been the leader of the extreme Democratic par
during the last ten years, replied,—not denying Lamartin(
arguments, but on the ground of necessity, "All Democraci
have begun by establishing a single Legislature, but e
perience soon teaches them that a balance is indispensab
and that a power responsible to none must, if uncontrolle
fall from its own weight."

The Assembly having decided, by a sweeping majori1
in favour of a single Chamber, the next question was,]

whom should the President of the Chamber be appointed, and what were to be his powers as the recognized Chief Magistrate of the Republic? On these points opinion was divided between an election by the Assembly and a direct appeal to the people. Lamartine was in favour of the latter alternative. In his speech of the 5th of October, he says, "If you desire a President of the Republic, he must be elected by the Republic. Appointed by the Chamber, he would never be more than its delegate. Would he not of necessity be pledged to the majority which had elected him, a majority which might consist only of some twenty or thirty votes? What a phantom of authority would a President thus elected prove! What influence could he have, either in asserting externally the dignity of France, or in suppressing internal factions? Even supposing the people, impelled by a general and irresistible impulse, should fix their choice on some dangerous character, my decision would be the same—*alea jacta est;* let God and the people declare the result. We must leave something to Providence. Possibly we may perish in the undertaking; and I say this, not as menace, but as a title of glory. I hope better things of France; I hope for them firmly and confidently. But if it prove otherwise, and the people are deceived in their choice; if they show themselves determined to disavow their past and ours; if they are resolved to renounce the immense hopes which may legitimately be formed as to the results of popular rule; if they are determined to repudiate their safety, their future, their liberties; —on them the responsibility will rest, not on us whose glory it is that we have restored their liberties to them, leaving them only the easier task of guarding and protecting them.

But I repeat, if they are resolved to return to the conditio
of a monarchy, if to pursue some delusive meteor the
throw away the future which lies in their hands, they ai
their own masters ; they can do it, for they are sovereig
It is not for us to say to them, ' You shall go thus far, bi
no further ; here you may go, but not there.' If they ai
bent on their own ruin, we will say with the vanquished ·
Pharsalia, ' Victrix causa deis placuit, sed victa Catoni
and that protest, which will be the eternal reproach of
nation imprudent and abandoned enough to surrender i·
liberties, will be in the eyes of posterity our sufficiei
vindication."

The view thus enunciated by Lamartine was that ·
the majority of the Assembly, which, in the division th;
immediately followed, referred the choice of a President ·
the people.   To us, who judge the matter after the even
the election of Louis Napoleon appears a foregone coi
clusion ; but it is certain that Cavaignac was sanguir
to the last.   It has also been constantly asserted th;
Lamartine expected the choice of the people would fall o
him.   His published correspondence does not, howeve
confirm that opinion.   He wrote to M. Dargeau, the mo:
intimate of his surviving friends, " As for the election ·
the Presidency, my dislike to the notion of its falling o
me ·increases daily.   But I have no need for anxiety o
the subject ; it lies between Bonaparte and Cavaigna
And notwithstanding all the rumours, I do *not* believe i
Bonaparte.   If human stupidity reaches so far, we sha
want another Molière to write another ' Misanthrope.'   Bu
I do believe in Cavaignac, and approve the choice, thoug
I regret the turn of fortune which has created the situatio

and brought him to the post. But there he is, and that is enough for me. And I believe him to be a Republican. I shall have in my turn the votes of some honest artisans, not five hundred thousand in all."

That the number he actually got was only nineteen thousand must have been a discomfiture, but all personal feelings were swallowed up in indignation and anguish at the fall of the Republic, which he felt to be the inevitable result of Louis Napoleon's election. "France has gone mad," he writes. "A Republic to end in a *promenade de Franconi!* A cocked hat, and not even a head in it. I should have preferred that of Tell (of course he means Gessler). There will be no alternative left for a Frenchman but death or exile."

Thus ended, with its anxieties, its struggles, its meteoric brilliancy, its terrible disappointments, the year 1848.

Soon after the newly elected President had entered on his functions, Lamartine returned to Paris. His first speech that session was in a debate on Foreign Affairs, in the course of which M. Drouyn de Lhuys had alluded to the foreign policy of the Executive Commission as one which made loud professions of peace while endangering it every moment. Lamartine rose to reply, taking on himself the responsibility of every act of the administration. He entirely denied having, as was hinted, encouraged insurrection in either Germany, Belgium, or Poland, and, appealing to the testimony of the Envoys of all the foreign powers, he defied his adversaries to show a single word spoken, or letter written, either by a member of the Executive or by any of their agents, which would support such an accusation. He sat down amid applause. But

though his eloquence still commanded attention, h
prestige, in a country where nothing succeeds but succes
was much diminished; and he, who in the June election ha
been returned spontaneously by ten departments, was a
but excluded from the Chamber in the new Legislativ
Assembly. That this was not the case was owing to M
Louis de Cormenin, a young man of considerable literar
talent, but at the time quite unknown to Lamartine. A
the general election, M. de Cormenin lost, by a few vote
only, his seat as member for the Département du Loire
One of the members dying suddenly left a vacancy, an
his election was considered certain. He was possessed c
great ability, and had every reason to anticipate a brilliar
Parliamentary career, but such was his enthusiastic admira
tion for Lamartine that, surrendering his own prospects, h
addressed to the editor of the *Journal du Loiret* the followin
letter :—

"I have just heard of the death of M. Roger. I conside
it the duty of every other candidate to make way for M. d
Lamartine, whom a disgraceful ostracism has rejected
Genius has claims far beyond any considerations of party
The return of Lamartine will ennoble the Département d
Loiret, and I trust, sir, that you will join your voice t
mine to achieve this object. To name him is to honou
and to consecrate universal suffrage."

The appeal was fully responded to, and the Départemen
du Loiret unanimously returned Lamartine. M. Maxim
du Camp, who narrates the incident in his "Souvenirs,
adds, " M. de Cormenin, to whose generous initiative thi
was owing, never again had the chance of entering a caree
for which he showed exceptional aptitude. He doubtles

regretted not belonging to the Legislative Assembly of his country, but he never repented having given his place up to Lamartine."

This occurred early in July, but some time elapsed before Lamartine took his seat in the new Assembly. He had found himself a much poorer man at the end than at the beginning of his three months of power, and his only hope of meeting overwhelming liabilities lay in hard literary work, to which he devoted himself all through the autumn and early winter. After which a sharp attack of illness kept him at home till the beginning of January, 1850.

Even those who most mistrusted the sincerity of Louis Napoleon's republicanism, could not deny that, in the opening period of his presidency, his conduct was moderate and conciliatory. There are many who still think that, had his position been made agreeable, or even tolerable, he would have been content to remain, for some years at least, President of the Republic. But by one of those unaccountable revulsions apparently inherent to the loose and lurching cargo of universal suffrage, the electors who, in December, 1848, had chosen him as President by a majority of four million votes, returned in May, 1849, an Assembly in which his opponents were far more numerous than his supporters, and in which the Socialistic element was very strong. This time, again, the electors had gone further than they intended ; the funds fell considerably, and a second reaction in favour of the President set in. He was also able to count on the support of the coalition which called itself "the Party of Order," for such measures as were obviously necessary to uphold the social fabric,

but it was always given grudgingly, and, in unimportant
matters, sometimes capriciously withheld. Still his chief
dependence was necessarily on them, and his first Cabinet
included, not the chiefs of any party, but men trusted
by each ; Drouyn de Lhuys, Odillon-Barrot, and Passy
had been ministers under Louis Philippe ; Falloux was a
Legitimist, and Bixio a strong Republican. They were
however, dismissed by the President in the following
October, on a question of foreign policy. Thiers calls this
" an act of dishonesty, because they had served him conscientiously and well; " others say their conflicting opinions
made the whole machinery of government unworkable.

Still the President continued on friendly terms with the
Party of Order, of whom the five heads, Molé, Broglie
Thiers, Berryer, and Montalembert, were called, in allusion
to a new play of Victor Hugo, " Les Burgraves." Thiers
especially says he was much consulted by the President at
this time, and gives himself the credit of having suggested
all the measures which ultimately proved successful, but is
careful to explain that he always avoided being seen in the
President's company in public. Lamartine, on the contrary, though not in any private communication with Louis
Napoleon, was an occasional guest at the Elysée, and
certainly did not allow his personal dislike to influence his
conduct, for in the debate on the President's salary he was
indignant at the parsimony of the Assembly. " They are
disputing over a mess of pottage; I would give him *suprême
de volaille* every day." But a country which was paying
seven hundred deputies at the rate of a pound a day each,
could not afford to be very generous to the head of the
Executive, even though it was he who, in the eyes of

Europe, represented France. And the President was kept in a state of pecuniary dependence, which may be reckoned among the causes that drove him to the *coup d'état.*

In the debates on the army and navy budgets, the subventions for the State railway lines, and of the "Théâtre des Italiens," Lamartine supported the Government; in those on the laws restricting the liberty of the press, and the proposal to found a new penal colony in the Marquesas Islands, he was with the Radical opposition; and again with the Government, against the Conservatives, on the question of limitations of universal suffrage proposed and carried by the Conservative coalition.

His speeches on the two last questions were very powerful and of considerable length, delivered amid a storm of interruptions and insults from the Conservative benches, and especially from the Orleanists, who never forgave him his abstention on the occasion of proclaiming the Regency, after Louis Philippe's abdication. Yet the event might surely have shown them that no course would have been more fatal to their interests than that which would have for ever linked their cause with the sanguinary repression of the insurrection of June; for the stain of blood, though it only appears to add additional piquancy to the charms of the lady of the Phrygian cap, would be fatal to a Royalist banner.

In the summer of 1850 the Lamartines made a short excursion to Syria. Ever since the time of his first voyage in the East, the noble qualities of the Moslem, their generous hospitality to strangers, perhaps also their calm belief in destiny, had impressed Lamartine's vivid imagination. Both as a politician and as a writer, he had rendered considerable services to the Porte. That he himself would ever derive any benefit from the line of conduct he spontaneously followed, never crossed his mind It was with extreme surprise that he received, in the autumn of 1849, an official communication to the effect that the Sultan Abdul-Medjid had heard with regret that reverses of fortune had overtaken the illustrious friend of Turkey, and now placed at his disposal a large estate in Asia Minor. It seemed to Lamartine like a page out of the "Arabian Nights;" but, on practically ascertaining that the domain of Burghaz-eva really existed and was his property he was not sorry to absent himself for a few months from France, and judge of the capabilities of his new possession

The expedition was rather a hazardous one for people of the Lamartines' age, but they were accompanied by two friends—MM. de Chamborand and de Champeaux Lamartine, in the diary which he afterwards published under the title of "Second Voyage en Orient," describes them as follows : " M. de Chamborand was a young man o old family and chivalrous instincts. He had been brought up in strict Legitimist principles, which, though tempered by the moderate liberalism of the Charter, prevented him from serving under the Government of Louis Philippe The Revolution of '48 found him weary of forced inaction very foreign to his nature, and he gladly joined the party which, led by Lamartine, was striving to maintain peace and order. On the 15th of April, his company of the National Guard helped to defend the Assembly against the mob. His attachment to Lamartine soon became personal rather than political. His remarkable physica strength and activity, and his practical knowledge of agri

culture, made him a first-rate colonist, with the fervour of
an Eastern pilgrim superadded. M. de Champeaux (who,
it will be remembered, had been for years Lamartine's
private secretary) represented the more prosaic element of
the party. In his eyes the beauty of a landscape lay in its
suitability for human requirements far more than in its
history or associations ; all the romance of his Breton
temperament was concentrated in attachment to his friends ;
rather than separate from them he was ready to make any
sacrifice."

Early in July the party left Marseilles in the *Orontes*, a
merchant vessel, the captain of which agreed to take no
other passengers, and convey the large amount of luggage
and *impedimenta* necessary for such an expedition. They
stayed a couple of days at Leghorn. As the quarantine
was strictly enforced against all vessels coming from France,
they could only view from a distance places with which, in
the happy years of their residence in Florence, they had
been pleasantly familiar. The next halt was at Constantinople, where kind friends had made ready to receive
them. Lamartine was glad to give his wife a few days
rest after the long sea-voyage, but elected to remain himself
on board. A tent, intended for Eastern travel, was pitched
on deck, serving him at once as a *cabinet de travail* and as
a *salon* in which to receive his visitors. These were very
numerous. Besides the Pashas and other officials whose
acquaintance he had made at the time of his first visit to
Constantinople, many others, with whom he had been
thrown in contact during his diplomatic career, were there
to welcome him.

As we know, Lamartine had, at a time when all the

sentiment and poetry of Europe were strongly enlisted or
the side of the Greeks, expressed in his book of Eastern
travel sympathy for the Turks, to which he was later able
to give practical effect. In the debates on the Eastern
question, all through Louis Philippe's reign, he was their
constant champion, and it so happened that his own brief
tenure of power supervened at a moment when the Turks
had reason to fear a rupture with France, and almost his
first act of external policy had been to replace the
relations between the two countries on a thoroughly cordial
footing. Such obligations are not habitually remembered
when those who have conferred them experience great
reverses; but for what in the West is called misfortune
or disgrace, there is in the East no other name than fate
Had Lamartine come to Constantinople as the accredited
envoy of a great Power, his reception could not have been
more flattering or more cordial.

And what gave him, perhaps, still greater pleasure was
to find that he was even better known in Constantinople as
a poet than as a politician, his poems, as well as his travels
and speeches, having been repeatedly translated into both
Greek and Turkish. When, by the kindness of Reschid
Pasha, he was invited to a private and informal audience
with the Sultan, his progress through the streets, in the
Imperial carriage sent for him, was a perfect ovation. His
name, somewhat strangely metamorphosed, was echoed in
half a dozen dialects, and with especial enthusiasm by
groups of beautiful women—Greeks, Franks, and Armenians
who, in attitudes recalling the figures of some antique
frieze, crowded all the balconies. The audience is described
by Lamartine at considerable length, and in glowing

colours; for which his romantic sympathy for the East, his very natural gratitude for the flattering reception accorded to him, and a certain excitement of imagination roused by an interview with the ruler of forty millions of men, fully account. In the handsome, melancholy young prince of six and twenty, who received him with almost timid affability and kindness, he saw the promise of many Imperial qualities which Abdul-Medjid never developed in his long and disastrous reign.

Lamartine had been previously told by Reschid Pasha that, although Oriental etiquette required that everything said to the Sultan in a foreign tongue should be rendered by an interpreter into Turkish, yet that His Majesty understood French perfectly. Of this he received a pleasing confirmation; for before the interpreter had time to interfere, a gesture of gracious approbation greeted each pause in his carefully prepared oration. "Son visage prenait toutes les impressions de mon discours ; ses yeux calquaient mes paroles, fier quand j'étais fier, resigné quand j'étais resigné ; triste quand j'étais triste ; homme enfin à l'unison d'un autre homme." Then followed a conversation, in which the Sultan continued to show the same gracious flexibility. An allusion made by him to the difficulty of ruling with a single sceptre so many different races and nationalities was happily turned to account by Lamartine. "Other monarchs," he replied, "may not have sufficed for the task. But your Imperial Majesty is crowned with a double diadem : you rule first by power, and then by goodness." The audience ended, Lamartine withdrew. He was, however, at once followed by the Vizier, who conveyed to him Abdul-Medjid's wish that he should be present at a distribution of prizes his Majesty was about to make to the pupils of the École Polytechnique, accordingly he attended it, and carried away the most favourable impression of the rising generations of Turkey.

There was now nothing to detain the Lamartines at Constantinople, and the *Orontes* resumed her journey through the islands of the Greek Archipelago. Here, again Lamartine was enthusiastically welcomed. To him were applied the lines, written of one of their own poets, " Partout où a passé un des vers de ta lyre, ton pied peut passer La muse t'a ouvert la porte de chaque foyer." And the description of a feast given in his honour by a Greek merchant named Pinto reads like a page out of " Lothair."

A few days more brought the travellers to Smyrna where they provided themselves, with as little delay as possible, with the necessaries of Eastern life. The weather was oppressively hot, so it was at nightfall that the little caravan left Smyrna. First came a file of camels laden with tents, books, and household goods of various kinds ; next the Minmandhar, in command of the escort sent by the Pasha of Smyrna ; then M. and Madame de Lamartine, with their friends and their servants, all on horseback ; the procession being closed by a troop of fierce-looking horsemen, the principal inhabitants of the estate, who had come to do homage to their new lord, each carrying a yataghan and a pair of silver-mounted pistols. Passing down the long street of the Franks, they descended the slope of Mount Pagas ; then, leaving to the right the Castle of the Crusaders, they followed the valley road which leads to Tireh, reaching, while it yet was early morning, Tryanda. After resting there till the noonday heat had subsided, they started

again, and a couple of hours' march brought them to a
river, which proved to be one of the boundaries of the
estate. The village of Achmet-Sched, half hidden by trees,
lay before them, and the rising ground beyond was crowned
by a long line of buildings, about a century old, of which
Jacoub Pasha had been the last tenant ; a shady avenue
of trees led up to it.

There was not much time to lose in making preparation,
for already the fleeting Eastern twilight had set in ; the
kneeling camels were quickly relieved of their burdens, and
the great central hall soon resembled a Levantine bazaar,
from which every one carried off what was needed for his
or her room. After a few hours of hard labour, the Syrian
dwelling was transformed into a habitation, to which even
the Parisian fastidiousness of M. de Champeaux could not
deny comfort and elegance, the only unconcerned spectators of the noise and bustle being a family of storks
perched on the housetop. To them the ways of Easterns
and those of Europeans were equally familiar.

There was, naturally, plenty of occupation for many
days following. The house, which remained just as Jacoub
Pasha had left it, was altogether Eastern in its arrangements, the principal portion being divided into large and
lofty rooms. That which the Lamartines usually occupied
was an arcaded saloon, of which the lofty, unglazed windows
let in the sea-breezes, making it deliciously cool. But,
excepting the audience chamber of Jacoub Pasha, these
rooms had but little decoration ; while the secluded wing,
formerly occupied by the harem, was fitted up with
exquisite taste, both the rooms and the cloisters abounding in graceful, delicate arabesques.

The garden, laid out solely with a view to utility, ha
neither flowerbeds nor borders, not even a secluded alle
for poetic musings. Yet the luxuriant growth of vegetatio
gave it the charm of picturesqueness. Instead of wall
dense hedges of prickly pear kept out all intruders ; neithe
cows nor camels, not even the wild buffaloes ranging ɛ
will in the surrounding plains, could have forced a
entrance. In one portion the homely products of Europ
—beet-root, carrots, lettuce—were not unsuccessfully cult
vated ; but in the greater portion reigned a more attractiv
confusion—huge gourds and melons lay "like golde
nuggets on their giant leaves ; " cotton-plants, loaded wit
pods, scattered their snowy down on every passing breeze
tall stems of maize glittered like lighted torches in th
dazzling sunshine ; the mulberry trees were large as oak
in Europe, and far more gnarled and rugged ; even th
vines, instead of clinging with the feminine tenderness s
often sung by poets to their wedded poplars, seemed as
they were striving to drag them down in their huge, ropɛ
like coils. But even in this seemingly neglected medle
thin lines of trickling silver gave evidence of a careful an
ingenious system of irrigation.

The advent and installation at Achmet-Sched of
French owner, distinguished by the special favour an
protection of the Commander of the Faithful, causeɛ
despite Mohammedan apathy, a considerable stir in th
neighbourhood. During many days deputations used t
arrive from the neighbouring villages, headed by th
Ayam, or mayor, with salutations of respectful greetin;
and offers of service. Needless to say, they were receivеɛ
with the strictest conformity possible to their own usageɛ

whose genuine, if somewhat ceremonious, hospitality was
thoroughly congenial to their host.   One can easily picture
Lamartine seated on the divan of Jacoub Pasha, at once
awing and fascinating the guests, whom he, on his part,
describes in very pleasant colours: They were of all classes
and conditions, ranging from the humble villager to the
many-camelled sheikh.   There was but little difference in
their dress.   The poorest had richly chased mountings to
their pistols ; a courteous self-possession, common to them
all, testified to the antiquity of their civilization, which had,
in process of time, penetrated even to the lowest social
stratum.   The intercourse between man and man in the
old subject land of Syria is governed by unwritten laws,
at least as old as the Seleucidæ.   The meanest peasant
addresses his superior with perfect freedom and polish,
but without a tinge of self-assertion.   And what is more
surprising is that education was diffused with the same
impartial quality.   Every village had its school, in which
reading and writing were taught by the Imaum, who, having
scarcely any other duty to perform, fulfilled that of teacher
most scrupulously.   Grave and taciturn by nature, these
Asiatics spoke little, and never for the sake of talking ;
their words were well weighed and well chosen.   The dark
side of the picture is that their severer labour was done by
women and slaves ; but, as Lamartine assures us, such was
the universal gentleness and kindliness, that the position
of the slaves, trusted as members of the household, differed
little from that of hired servants in Europe.

Social relations having been established on a satisfactory footing, the next task was that of surveying the
limits and estimating the capabilities of the grant with

which view the party started before daybreak on a lovel:
August morning. Lamartine was accompanied by MM. d
Chamborand and Barraud—the latter a young Frenchma
who studied at the Agricultural College of Grignan, an(
had since been employed for some years in developing th
resources of several large Syrian estates, M. de Champeaux
whose health had suffered a good deal from the fatigue
of the voyage, remaining with Madame de Lamartin(
The leaders of the expedition were mounted on six Aral
horses purchased at Constantinople; Lamartine on ;
chestnut mare, "ardent and high spirited, but witha
sagacious and reflective, careful to husband her strengtl
so as to be fresh at the end of the longest day's marcl
contrasting agreeably in colour with the flea-bitten grey
barb which carried M. de Chamborand." For the rest o
the party and the baggage, some of the small wiry ponies
which wandered in large herds over the surroundin;
steppes, had been provided.

Very soon after leaving Achmet-Sched all trace o
cultivation ceased. On the vast plain before them, th(
sparsely scattered trees were low and stunted, the groun(
producing little but grass or heather. Yet here and ther(
brilliant patches of wild flowers clothed the desert witl
beauty, the soil showed traces of moisture, and was pro
nounced to be good mould to the depth of eight or ter
feet. To turn the wilderness into a garden nothing wa:
needed but man's skill and labour.

The road they followed was a bridle-path, which, skirt
ing the mountain range that separates the valley o:
Burghaz-eva from those of Magnesia, led to the caravar
route of Bainder and Tireh. After reaching it, a few more

ours of easy march brought them to the Khan of Gourgour, or "the bubbling water ;" so the host (if an Eastern khan which provides nothing but bare walls and an undying flame of charcoal to light the narghilé can be said to have a host), on being informed that he was in the presence of his landlord, the friend of Abdul-Medjid, was profuse in salaams and civilities.

The party were conducted over the buildings and adjoining grounds, all in a state of dilapidation, which told of the evils of absenteeism ; and, as a substantial proof of the advent of better times, M. Barraud was directed to note down the necessary expenditure for improvements to the amount of a year's rent. After a well-earned break-fast, laid, not in the caravansera, but under the shade of a group of willow-trees, they went a little way up the stream to a mill of primitive arrangement, for the renewing of which a second advance of six hundred piastres was promised. The stream, which even in the hottest seasons fulfilled the promise of its name, would, in the opinion of MM. Barraud and de Chamborand, have sufficed to irrigate eight thousand acres.

Before resuming the march, Lamartine, charmed by the beauty of the spot, fixed on the site of a new mansion which was to supersede the castle of Achmet-Sched, while his companions traced the outline of a scheme of irrigation by which the waters of Gourgour were to work a factory and turn into a garden at least four hundred hectares of barren waste—a plan which, probably very fortunately, never went beyond paper. But it is pleasant to know that all the promises made to the proprietor of the khan were scrupulously fulfilled.

A march of nine hours brought them to Teni-chifflic
the largest and most flourishing village on the estate,
time for the evening meal. As their coming had not bee
notified, they proceeded quietly to encamp under the larg
sycamore-trees which shaded the village green. But hard
were the carpets spread, than the villagers, among who
the news had spread like wildfire, came to welcome the
new master, offering cordial and respectful hospitalit
This, however, was declined. They then brought little gif
of milk, butter, fruit, sherbets, and all they could think o
the Ayam insisting on being allowed to provide coffe
which his slaves brought in a vase of antique bronz
"which might have been in the treasury of Crœsus, Kir
of Lydia."

The collation, followed by a few hours of sleep, refresh
them completely, and they then spent some hours in admirin
the fertility of the gardens and fields surrounding Ter
chifflick, and in pleasant converse with the people. Mai
favours were asked, which Lamartine, who thorough
enjoyed the *rôle de bon prince*, graciously accorded; 1
even promised to obtain from the Pasha of Smyrna tl
freedom of a young man said to be cruelly punished for
very trifling offence. On asking the use of a large an
lofty building standing a little way from the town, 1
received the agreeable intelligence that it was the store
which his share of the harvest would be placed until
pleased him to dispose of it.

Towards evening they started again, and, passing ov
some parallel lines of wooded hills, came to a clump
giant oaks, called the "Forty Thieves," which serve as
landmark for miles. They saw below them the beautif

alley of Syra and the town, where they decided to stay
or the night. Sending a horseman forward to give notice
f their arrival, they remained for some time in delighted
contemplation of a landscape which combined something
of the sublimity of Switzerland with the rich luxuriance of
Italy, while below them gleamed the marble walls of Syra,
with her thirty minarets, which, illuminated in honour of
some Mohammedan festival, glittered like fountains of fire.

As they approached the city, a fresh surprise awaited
them. A long line of horsemen, mounted on richly
caparisoned steeds, came out to meet them. These were
the Governor and principal inhabitants of Syra, who,
having heard of their arrival, would not suffer them to lodge
at the khan, and came to offer hospitality, which was
gratefully accepted. After many courteous and flowery
speeches had been exchanged, they entered Syra amid a
salvo of fire-arms and the acclamations of the inhabitants.

The next day brought them to Touloum, the most
picturesque spot on the estate. So delighted was Lamartine
by its beauty, that he sent a messenger, who, riding through
the night, reached Achmet-Sched before dawn, with an
invitation to Madame de Lamartine to join them, which,
accompanied by M. de Champeaux, she accordingly did.
A delightful day was spent in receiving the homage of the
inhabitants and in sketching the beautiful architectural
remains, gems worthy of their setting, ending by a moon-
light ride home. The excursion was the prelude to others
equally pleasant; besides which there was enough interest
and occupation at Achmet-Sched to make time pass quickly
and confirm the intention they then seem really to have
entertained, of making it a permanent residence. Lamar-

tine, always somewhat vague in his narratives, does n
make it plain what was the nature of his proprietorship
the tract of country, larger than the Duchy of Lucca, whi(
had been conceded to him.   In one place he mentioi
that a third of the produce of the soil belongs to the lan
lord ; over the countless herd of wild cattle and hors
ranging the plains, he also had seigniorial rights.   But su(
was, he tells us, the admirable fertility of the soil, tha
colonized by sturdy Burgundian peasants, it would speedi
surpass in productiveness the finest districts of Europ
and his project was to start a company to undertake i
cultivation.

The time fixed for their return to France came on
too quickly.   After a fortnight spent with the lively ar
hospitable foreign colony at Smyrna, they embarked in
French steamer which lay out in the offing. . By Kha
Pasha's orders a Turkish sloop was at their dispos;
Many friends, both old and new, accompanied them (
board, and, with promises of a speedy return, they start(
amid auspices on their homeward journey.

"But to no one," writes Goethe, "is it given to wand
with impunity under palm-trees ; " and for the second tin
in the East an unexpected sorrow overtook the Lamartin(
The season was unhealthy ; the black flag of cholera fo
bade their landing at Athens, and an almost equally fat
epidemic of fever pervaded the air.   Madame de Lamartii
was the first to succumb.   M. de Champeaux, an elder
man, already suffering from heart disease, was still le
able to resist the contagion.   Nothing could exceed tt
kindness of all on board ; the first lieutenant at on(
gave him up his more airy cabin, two French missionar

priests who were on board tended him night and day, and
Dr. Crawford, an English passenger, of whose skill and
kindness Lamartine writes enthusiastically, volunteered his
services to help the rather inexperienced ship's doctor.
M. de Champeaux bore his sufferings with such fortitude
as almost to deceive his friends ; but one evening, with his
usual cheerful composure, he gave Lamartine his last wishes
and messages for his family, and three days before France
was reached he passed quietly away.   Lamartine has done
his best to pay a fitting tribute to his friend's talent and
virtues, in a passage of much eloquence and pathos, which
concludes the otherwise cheerful record of the " Nouveau
voyage en Orient."

Leaving his wife at Monceau, Lamartine started for
London, with the object of organizing a company for the
cultivation of the territory of Burghaz-eva.   The moment
was not well chosen.   " All the world is out of town," he
writes ; "gone to hunt the fox."   But he was received
everywhere with tokens of respect and even of enthusiasm,
deeply gratifying to one who in his own country was no
longer a prophet.   A banquet offered to him by the City
of London he declined, but at a dinner given in his honour
by " fifty friends of peace, moderate politicians and philo-
sophers," Lamartine spoke amid much applause.

Lamartine's tenure of his Eastern possessions proved
very brief.   Unexpected difficulties arose in the management, and ultimately he resigned them, receiving a sum of
money in compensation.

On his return to France he found that in his absence the
march of political events had been rapid.   The hostility of
the Parliamentary party to Louis Napoleon was becoming

daily more undisguised. They rejected a proposal for re placing the nomination of mayors in the hands of th Executive, although all the industries of the country wer being paralyzed by the election of Socialists; and the went so far as to appoint a commission, of men avowedl opposed to the President, to watch over his conduct durin the recess. On this, Louis Napoleon threw himself on th support of the provinces, where his popularity was rapidl increasing. He made a progress through Lyons, Stras bourg, Rheims, and Cherbourg, which was at every stag an increasing triumph. The cries of " Vive le President ! were only drowned by those of " Vive l'Empereur !"

The next move of the Assembly was one which showe at once their irritation and their weakness. On the 2nd of January, 1851, a journal known as the organ of the majorit reported certain instructions to the troops, requiring ther to obey no orders but such as had been issued by the Com mander of the Army of Paris. On the day following, Lou Napoleon went down to the Assembly, and demanded tha they should declare the instruction apocryphal, or suspen General Changarnier, who had issued it. The Assembl hoped to gain time by passing to the order of the day whereupon the President divided the military command i such a way that Changarnier was superseded, without hi name being mentioned. The Assembly were furious, an threatened to raise an army of fifty thousand men, and plac it under Changarnier. Finding this impossible, they wishe to establish a " Commission d'Enquête," with the power of a Star-chamber. Lamartine adjured them not to stultif themselves by an illegal and unconstitutional course, whic could only end in their defeat.

After five days of tumult and uproar, a vote of want of confidence in the Ministry was passed. The President at once dismissed them, but replaced them as quickly by others equally serviceable to him. The proper course for the Assembly would have been to refuse supplies and run the risk of a dissolution. But, aware that the verdict of the country would be against them, they were afraid to do this, and continued an undignified and hopeless struggle, showing their anger against the President by reducing his income, and other paltry measures, and finally took to quarrelling among themselves.

Lamartine, seeing with all the world that it was not in an impotent and discredited Assembly, but in the force of public opinion, that the last hope of maintaining the Republic lay, took no further part in the debates, but devoted his energies to upholding Republican principles in political pamphlets and through the press. About this time he joined M. de Laguerronnière in founding a new journal, *Le Pays*, which nowadays, having changed its politics, is the accredited organ of the Bonapartists. But it was a forlorn hope, for it was evident that the advent of Imperialism was only a question of time; nor to such foreigners as visited him at this period did the President make any secret of his intentions, or of the means he relied on to carry them out. Whether there really was, as he seemed to think, a conspiracy formed with the object of sending him to Vincennes, is open to question, but no one could deny that the situation was untenable. All through the spring and summer of 1851 a catastrophe was almost daily expected, but, as we now know, it was not till an evening in August that the famous meeting of five—Morny, Persigny, Carlier,

Rouher, and the President—was held in an arbour at S
Cloud, with coffee and liqueurs on the table, and the *coi*
d'état planned ; Rouher, who, as the only lawyer presen
was employed to draft an imperial constitution, quietl
lining away in his pocket-book the liberties of Franc
Even then the President was disinclined to immediat
action ; it was only in November, when the Assembly pro
posed, by a flagrant violation of the existing law, to usur
the control of the army, which had been expressly conferre
by the Constitution on him alone, that the anniversary o
Austerlitz was fixed on as the date of his 18 Brumaire.

Lamartine, who resolved not to identify himself eithe
with the undignified and illegal conduct of the Assembl;
or, on the other hand, to have any share in establishing th
form of government which above all others he detestec
had not, since the beginning of May, taken part in an
debate. The autumn found him at St. Point, and i
October he was stricken down by a severe attack o
articular rheumatism, which kept him for more than tw
months confined to bed. An invalid's company is no
generally very cheerful, but M. de Lacretelle, who, wit
Charles Alexandre, was seldom absent from Lamartine
sick couch, tells us that, painful as it was to his friends t
see him suffer, Lamartine's unfailing sweetness of dispositio
and his brilliant talk made his sick room the most delightfi
of *salons*. He bore his sufferings with the patience o
a Mussulman. If extreme pain sometimes drew from hii
"quelques exclamations soldatesques," he quickly made u
for them by increased gentleness and affability. He ofte
asked to be read to, but his friends were never afraid of h
imposing any heavy tax on them in that way, for ever

page suggested a reminiscence, every argument a discussion. As soon as the swelling in his hands had diminished, he took up his pen and wrote off " Le Présent, le Passé, et l'Avenir de la République," of which Lacretelle says : " Le prophète s'y versa tout entier. Les événements y furent prédits presque à leur date. Le livre n'est pas fait de pages mais de rayons." But as it did not appear in print till Republics were out of fashion, the book only had a *succès d'estime.*

One morning, in the first week of December, a flood of visitors rushed in from Mâcon to announce the events of the 2nd—the Assembly dissolved, half the deputies in prison, the electors ordered to the poll by a discharge of musketry. Lamartine's explosion of wrath was, according to Lacretelle, Titanesque. He inveighed against Napoleon as " one of those wild beasts which from time to time come out from their lair with the semblance of men, and are called Tiberius, Nero, Caracalla. They told you there had been no massacre ? and I tell you that men have been walking the Boulevards with blood up to their knees ; that women and children have been slaughtered by thousands. No matter what the appearance of civic virtue may be, there is always somewhere a woman carrying in her arms a child that will one day be called Cæsar. And this Cæsar will reign by corruption. You will see the despotism of beadledom. He will make war in order to hide under flags and trophies the corpse of Liberty. And he will last long ; and he will wear many masks, till at last he will bring on France an invasion ! "

But after having poured out his soul in this torrent of mingled commination and prophecy for a considerable

time, Lamartine kept his head better than any of hi
friends. They wanted to rush out into the streets an
highways and raise the people in defence of their libertie:
"You will do nothing of the sort," was his reply. "You
bounden duty is, on the contrary, to go back each to you
own home.. Everything will be accepted ; as you knov
the peasantry have been fanaticized by the name c
Napoleon. And even if it were otherwise, how could w
deliberately drive them up to the bayonets of an army tha
remembers nothing but Austerlitz ?"

But some letters written about this time show best hi
feelings and his own position with regard to the events c
the day.

To the MARQUIS DE LA GRANGE.

"December 15th.

"What has happened grieves but does not surprise m
I deplore the *coup d'état* of the Bonapartists. With
little patience the Constitution might have been legall
revised and improved. The great misfortune of France :
that she now rests on a single bayonet, and if one man
pulse ceases to beat, hers too will stop. I have been doin
my best, as far as I could from the bed on which I hav
been two months a prisoner, to prevent the people roun
me from taking part in any wild or foolish acts of violenc
A few hundred mountaineers came down from Griseu:
passing within about twelve leagues of us, to attack Mâco
it was said, but nothing came of it. Far from my havin
been abused or threatened, as they say in Paris of me, th
villagers came up to ask if they could be of any service t
us : they are excellent people. I shall publish my reasor

for not voting, couching them in moderate terms ; then I shall take up my pen and keep to literary work. But the generous friendship of your letter will never be forgotten by me. It is by adversity hearts are tested."

To another friend, a few weeks later :—

" Your letter is one of those cries of eloquent indignation which pierce the heart. It is well when one is young to be indignant; as one grows old, one learns to be compassionate. Those who remember 1815 understand 1851. Always Gauls, never men ! Do not let us speak of it. Time is the instrument by which Providence works, and it will bring back, though I know not when, dignity to the people. We must pity them and console them, even in their weakness. They loved Liberty for the sake of her name, and now, for the sake of another name, they have given themselves up to despotism. Still the world goes on, and you, who are young, will yet see many changes come to pass. But I look elsewhere for other and better things."

To M. DE LAPRADE.

"July 4th, 1852.

" Your letter has given me almost more pleasure than your speech, because it is more directly personal to me. It has been a consoling balm after much bitterness. But do not let us be sorrowful beyond measure ; God wills to humble the pride of nations as He does that of individuals. But He will not utterly crush the spirit of man. That such as you are weeping at the sepulchre, is a token that soon the stone will be rolled back. We have sinned by excess of liberty, and of this sin despotism is the unfailing chastisement. But this despotism, which has begun by a great crime, will only last long enough to bring France back to reason, and then we shall have that perfect balance o authority and liberty which is the glory and the morality of government. I am much better in health. In a few days I shall go to Pàris to roll up our tent, and then I return here to live, like you, in solitude,—to think, write, pray hope, and act—if ever Providence brings us back to honest and moderate action."

A few months later, it was reported, in some of the Parisian journals, that Lamartine had accepted a seat in the Senate ; whereupon he wrote as follows to the editor of the *Siècle* :—

"M. LE RÉDACTEUR,

"You quote from the *Indépendance Belge* a list of the political men whom the present Government is about to call to the Senate, in which list my name occurs. In the interests of truth, which should always be respected, will you allow me to contradict a report which has not, and which never could have, any foundation."

Lamartine persevered to the last in his resolution o entire abstention from political life during the Imperial *régime*, and, as it lasted longer than his life, all the remaining records of his biography are literary or personal.

CHAPTER XII.

LAMARTINE'S early years, once the morning mists had lifted, were, as we have seen, illuminated by a considerable share of literary and social success. During his manhood, he played a leading part in the political history of his country; an amount of personal popularity such as falls to the lot of few had come to him, almost without an effort; and, finally, a career of more than ordinary brilliancy had culminated in a moment of the highest, if not of sustained, achievement. But the crowning blessing of a serene old age was not vouchsafed to him. Besides the very bitter trial of seeing his most cherished aspirations for the future of France hopelessly blighted, he was himself all but crushed beneath an overwhelming burden of debts and difficulties. To those who knew the simplicity of Lamartine's habits and tastes, and the utter absence of luxury or ostentation which characterized both him and his wife, the amount of his liabilities was an insoluble enigma. M. de Lacretelle, speaking with thorough knowledge, says that Lamartine's household expenses in Paris never exceeded £2000 a year; in the country, where his hospitality was unceasing, his table was simple, supplied chiefly, he used to

say, by presents from his humbler neighbours,—but omitti
to add that they ultimately received back far more th
they gave.

In the management of his estates he was hard-workir
intelligent, and to outward appearance successful. H
crops were more luxuriant, his labourers better off, th
those of the surrounding estates. But, apparently
account of the difficulty winegrowers on a small scale fou
in disposing of their produce, it was the custom in t
Mâconnais for the large proprietors to buy up their tenan
and those of the smaller owners' crops on foot for rea(
money, reselling them at leisure. This Lamartine, alwa
speculative and sanguine, unfortunately did, on a very lar;
scale, usually giving a price far beyond the value, and r
selling at a loss. That the peasants round Milly, Moncea
and St. Point were becoming capitalists at his expen
rather pleased him ; the idea of his difficulties ever becor
ing serious never occurring to him. " I shall always arrang(
he used to say, " so as to.have a good balance of ou
standing debts. For individuals, as for nations, debt is
stimulus necessary for production."

The rental of his estates was considerable, and for e:
traordinary expenses he knew he could at any time reali
a considerable sum in a few weeks of literary labour. B
though his gross income was large, it was subject to mar
reductions. His uncles and aunts had followed cla
traditions by making the whole of the landed estates of tl
family revert to him, but so encumbered with legacies 1
their five nieces and innumerable great-nieces and nephev
as to be a burden rather than a possession. Already, i
1846, Lamartine's embarrassments were becoming seriou

and it was a matter of consideration whether he should
not resign his seat in the Chamber, which made a winter
residence in Paris obligatory, and, selling a portion of his
estate, live modestly on the remainder.   However, an
opportune legacy from his last surviving aunt, together
with the large sum he received for "Les Girondins," averted
this necessity, and in 1847 he was able to look forward
confidently to the speedy payment of all his debts.   But in
February, 1848, came the Revolution, of which the most
abiding result was Lamartine's ruin.   Besides suffering,
in common with the rest of the world, from the depreciation
of every kind of property, he was driven, by his intense
patriotism and almost morbid horror of bloodshed, to
spend every shilling he could command in averting fresh
disturbances.   What he actually disbursed was never
known, but it was said that, to postpone a single rising
till.troops sufficient to overawe the insurgents could be
brought into the field, had cost him seventy-five thousand
francs.   Most of the men who have since occupied similar
positions found means of at least recouping themselves, but
Lamartine, at the end of his three months of power, owed
more than three millions of francs.   Still he could not
realize his situation, and when some leading financiers,
MM. Mirés, Pereira, and others offered, with rare but real
disinterestedness, through Lamartine's friends, MM. Roland
and Chamborre, to advance money sufficient to meet his
most pressing liabilities, and secure him an income till all
was paid off, provided he agreed to the immediate sale
of a portion of his estates, and undertook to refrain for
the future from buying up his tenants' wine, Lamartine
dismissed the offer with a smile.   He who spoke so diffi-

dently of himself as a statesman and as a poet, had, bʒ not uncommon infatuation, implicit faith in his talents a financier. Blinded, by the enormous sums that had be realized from his works by publishers, to the real difficult of his situation, he was firmly convinced that, if only 1 health and strength lasted, he could save by degrees a sι sufficient to liberate all his estates, and thus be enabled bequeath to his representatives an undiminished inheritan

Hence came the enormous productiveness of Lama tine's last years, which at one time reached the almc appalling amount of fifteen volumes in a single yea besides which he undertook, singlehanded, three volumino periodicals, " Le Conseiller du People," " Le Civilisateuι and " Cours familier de Littérature," the last of which w continued for several months after his death, from man scripts he had left. And if it be true, as is sometimes sai that original literary composition is the hardest and mc exhausting of all work—what days and nights of cru unintermitting labour does not this catalogue represen The pen, once a toy in his hand, was changed into a wor man's tool, nay, into the oar of the galley-slave. Jul Janin, himself no idler, tells how, one summer day, whι he was in *villeggiatura* near Mâcon, he went over to pɛ his respects to the owner of Monceau. " A winding paː leads up to a great and illustrious house. There, in h study, stretched on a simple camp bed, lay M. de Lama tine. He was ill, but he was writing, whether prose ι poetry I know not ; but piles of manuscript scattered aboι betrayed the secret of many sleepless nights. Not a daː nay, not an hour of rest does he allow himself. Yet it wɛ a time of overpowering heat ; the birds were singing in th

shes, dogs were barking cheerfully in the courtyard ; in
e cool, dark stall an Arab mare was neighing for her
ster ; feathered fowl were taking their food without
bour ; in the valley the vine-dressers were resting in the
easant shade, for their work was light, and they knew
ey could trust to their master's indulgence. In that
ppy secluded spot all but he were singing, resting, or
joicing. Yet you were worth labouring for, valleys,
ountains, St. Point, Monceau! You were worth being
nsomed, even at the price of a poet's genius! But no
her man living could with impunity have imperilled his
putation by undertaking such a task."

During many long years the odds were terribly against
amartine. All that was of value—books, heirlooms,
rniture—he gradually parted with, and at last a day came
hen Monceau, Milly, and St. Point were put up to auction.
amartine's friends then exerted themselves to the utmost.
n appeal was made to the public in the form of a com-
ete edition of his works for the author's benefit. But
ost readers had them already in detail, and the result
as hardly what had been hoped. The Emperor, with
aracteristic generosity, offered more than once to pay
amartine's debts out of his private purse, at first under
e condition that he would accept a seat in the Senate,
en without any condition. The offer was renewed re-
atedly with the greatest possible delicacy, M. de Laguer-
nnière being the negotiator. But even in his darkest
ys, sick in body, worn out by the strife with his
editors, Lamartine's only answer was a courteous refusal.*

---

* In 1868, Lamartine's relatives accepted for him an annuity of 25,000.
ncs, voted by the Legislative Chamber.

At last, however, the long struggle, which recalls Hugo's terrible picture of the duel between the man and the octopus, ended like it in victory, chiefly through the success of the "Cours d'Entretiens littéraires," which kept up the number of thirty thousand subscribers ; and before Lamartine's lofty intellect became darkened by the shadows of approaching death, an arrangement was made by which all just claims against him were satisfied.

As the last volume of Lamartine's published correspondence closes with a letter dated March, 1853, and his life from that time forward was devoted to literary work there is not much record of his closing years, save an occasional notice, in memoirs of the time, of evenings spent in the little *salon* of the Rue Ville l'Evêque, when Madame de Lamartine nightly received her friends. Mr. Senior's volume of "Recollections of the Second Empire" records some interesting conversations. In the earlier ones, politics and history past and passing are discussed, especially during the Crimean war. The alliance between France and England pleased Lamartine, though he blames the irresolution and dilatoriness of the Imperial Government, "qui pirouette sur l'Autriche," and predicts the disastrous consequences.

Another evening Lamartine had been speaking at a hall lately opened for the delivery of lectures on social science. M. Pelletan, another of the guests, related how when Lamartine had left the hall, the audience, composed chiefly of working-men, stood talking eagerly of him and of 1848, and of the scenes before the Hôtel de Ville. " We came," they said, "determined to overthrow the Provisional Government, and Lamartine as its head. But we were children in his hands. We were cowed when he reproved

s, proud when he praised us, and obedient when he
ommanded us."

On this, Lamartine turned the conversation on public
peaking generally, saying—" I have addressed different
udiences, but the only one worth speaking to *c'est la foule.*
n an assembly your friends, or rather your party, treat the
debate as a game, yourself as a piece or as a pawn, your
peech as a move ; your adversaries think of you only as
n enemy, and of your speech only as a thing to be refuted.
The rest, the impartial part of the audience, go to a debate
as they go to an opera, consider your speech as a work of
art offered them to criticize, and praise or blame you
accordingly as they have been bored or amused. No one
changes his opinion ; no one is convinced ; no one is even
moved. The best speech does not alter a vote. It merely
renders the vote, which every hearer had premeditated to
give, more or less pleasant to him. No one cares whether
the speaker is or is not sincere. Indeed, it is well known
that he must often be insincere, since he speaks not his
own opinions, but those of his party, or rather those which
it suits his party to profess for the time being. No one
cares for their truth. What is wanted is that they be
plausible, and offer a good excuse for the vote. *La foule* is
sincere. It comes to you for information and for counsel.
The first, almost the only quality it demands from you is
sincerity. You may reproach it, you may laugh at it, you
may run counter to its prejudices,—it will bear anything
from you while it believes you to be honestly anxious to
give it good advice. But beware how you are found out in
flattering it ! Beware how you are found out in saying
anything which it believes to be insincere ! That instant

your influence is gone. Inferior men may be powerful mob-orators, if they have the same prejudices and feelings as their hearers. They reveal to every man that he is sympathized with by them, and sympathized with by his neighbours. They render every folly contagious. They strengthen every opinion, and excite passions already too violent. The real triumph and the real usefulness is not to stimulate, but to moderate, to control, to alter, often to reverse. So far as I effected these things, or any of these things, at the Hôtel de Ville, I was useful."

Other conversations turned on literature, which, as time passed on, grew more and more the one engrossing and all-absorbing interest of Lamartine's life, till all that remained to him of the years of troubled strife in the forum and the market-place was a rapidity of thought and phrase which could never have been acquired in study. His mind was not suited for analytic or scientific methods. In his historic and biographical sketches he does not attempt to go below the surface of things ; nor does he in his classic studies often go further afield or nearer home than Plutarch and Rollin,—writing of the Tarquins and the Brutuses as if Niebuhr and Mommsen had never existed, but fulfilling admirably the object he had in view—to stimulate the thoughts and recreate the jaded minds of the limitless audiences he addressed. And, despite the overwhelming stress of work to which he subjected himself, the traces of weariness in his style are wonderfully few ; he is often diffuse, repeats himself frequently, but keeps to the last the "luminous and sustained phrase" of his earlier manner. His judgments are wonderfully clear and discerning ; it is remarkable how many passages of Lamartine's least-known

books have become current coin of thought and expression.
And though he did not often in latter days exercise his
poetic power, it remained undiminished to the end, as is
shown by the lines headed " La Vigne et la Maison," which,
in almost his seventieth year, he improvised to supply
some copy which had gone astray of his 15th " Entretien "
—lines which, despite some obvious negligences, show the
touch of the master's hand, " the power of sweet and
constraining suasion, the tender elegiac grace," of the
Lamartine of old. The poet is gazing once more on the
home of his childhood, as it lies faintly illumined by
the feeble rays of a November sun.

> " La nuit tombe, ô mon âme ! un peu de veille encore !
> Le coucher d'un soleil est d'un autre l'aurore.
> Vois comme avec tes sens s'écroule ta prison !
> Vois comme aux premiers vents de la précoce automne
> S'envole brin à brin le duvet du chardon.
> *   *   *   *   *   *
> Le soir qui tombe a des langueurs sereines
> Que la fin donne à tout, aux bonheurs comme aux peines,
> Le linceul même est tiède au cœur enseveli,
> Cette heure a pour nos cœurs des impressions douces
> Comme les pas muets qui marchent sur les mousses. . . .
> Je ne sais quel lointain y baigne toute chose,
> Ainsi que le regard l'oreille s'y repose ;
> On entend dans l'éther glisser le moindre vol.
> *   *   *   *   *   *
> Viens, reconnais la place où ta vie était neuve.
> N'as-tu point de douceur, dis-moi, pauve âme veuve,
> À remuer ici la cendre des jours morts ?
>
>> " N'y trouves-tu pas le délice
>> Du brasier tiède et réchauffant
>> Qu'allume une vieille nourrice
>> Au foyer qui nous vit enfant ?
>>
>> " Où l'impression qui console
>> L'agneau tondu hors de saison
>> Quand il sent sur sa laine folle
>> Repousser sa chaude toison ? "

But how all has changed! How silent and deserted is
now the house which, in bygone days, used to be from
earliest dawn full of life and joy!

> " Tous les bruits du foyer que l'aube fait renaître
> Les pas des serviteurs sur les degrés de bois.
> Les aboiments du chien qui voit sortir son maître
> Le mendiant plaintif qui fait pleurer sa voix,

> " Montaient avec le jour ; et dans les intervalles,
> Sous des doigts de quinze ans répétant leur leçon
> Les claviers résonnaient ainsi que des cigales
> Qui font tinter l'oreille au temps de la moisson."

And now only pale ghosts of the past flit through the
deserted rooms, in which spiders weave their nets ; nettles
choke up the pavement once echoing such joyous footsteps—

> " De la solitaire demeure
> Une ombre lourde d'heure en heure
> Se détache sur le gazon :   ,
> Et cette ombre, couchée et morte,
> Est la seule chose qui sorte
> Tout le jour de cette maison ! "

Then, with one of the swift lyric changes in which
Lamartine excelled, another chord is struck—what has
been so loved, so cherished, cannot perish wholly.

> " N'as tu pas, dans un des pans de tes globes sans nombre,
> Une pente au soleil, une vallée à l'ombre
> Pour y rebâtir ce doux seuil ?
> Non plus grand, non plus beau, mais pareil, mais le même."

Reading these lines, one can understand what M. E. de
Montégut, who, when a very young man, frequented the
salon of the Rue Ville l'Évêque, tells of the unfailing charm
of a mind which never wholly lost its youth, clothed in the
dignity of gracious, serene old age. " Mais ce qui dominait

sur tout était une expression ineffaçable de mansuétude et de douceur."

Madame de Lamartine aged more quickly than her husband, though she was energetic and active, and, as long as her strength lasted, an early riser, giving much time to works of active benevolence. But of late years her one engrossing occupation was assisting her husband in his literary work; at this she laboured night and day. There had been a time when, by wise counsels, and by the sacrifice of the greater part of her own fortune, she had striven hard to avert his impending ruin; but she now, with rare discretion, refrained even from giving advice, wearing her poverty with the same graceful simplicity that had characterized her as the hostess of one of the most brilliant *salons* of Paris. Still she retained to the last a certain degree of elegance in her own person. It used to be remarked that, even at the Rue Ville l'Évêque, and in the days when the Republican element most predominated, she retained her English habit of dressing for the evening, though she no longer exacted it of her guests. At last a day came when, feeling herself beaten in the long struggle against increasing years and failing health, she devolved her duties as hostess on her nieces, and reclined quietly on her sofa, always sympathetic, but conversing little. What strength she had she reserved for writing and correspondence; numerous letters show how bright was the now flickering flame of that noble soul.

In the spring of 1867 her sufferings increased, yet was she so calm and cheerful that those around her did not observe how quickly her life was drawing to its close. But in May a sudden and severe attack of erysipelas com-

pletely prostrated her. For many days M. Clavel, the
family physician and friend, with two other doctors, watched
her unceasingly. Most of the time she seemed unconscious,
just able from time to time to inquire anxiously for her
husband, who lay in the adjoining room, stricken with
rheumatic fever, unable to move, listening in mute anguish
to her last painful struggles, which ended on Thursday,
May 21st. Her obsequies were, according to her wishes,
simple in the extreme. It might have been otherwise, for
M. Ulbach says that the Government offered to have her
remains conveyed to St. Point at the public cost, and with
much ceremonial. But the offer was declined, and, after
a short religious service at the church of St. Augustin,
M. Louis de Ronchaud and the Comte d'Esgrigny accompanied the coffin to Mâcon. Here they were met by several
members of the Lamartine family, the principal inhabitants
and functionaries, and a large concourse of people, who
had come unbidden to follow the *cortège* to St. Point, to
do honour to one who, though a stranger to them by birth,
was for her own sake, as well as for the name she bore,
loved, and revered. A recumbent statue in marble, with
the inscription, *Speravit anima mea*, marks her resting-place.

Lamartine's sorrow was shared by his friends. " I
venerated her whom you mourn," wrote Victor Hugo to
him two days later, "and feel the need to tell you so. But
far beyond these horizons you already discern a brighter
future. Not to you need we say, ' Wait and hope.' You
are of those to whom life is already but an expectation.
She whom you loved is invisible, but present to you. Dear
friend, let us live in our dead."

The years during which Lamartine survived his wife

were few and sorrowful, but not altogether without solace ;
his niece and daughter by adoption, Madame Valentine de
Cessia de Lamartine, watching over him with unflagging
devotion. He still continued to labour with his pen. His
last and posthumous work, "Vingt cinq ans de ma vie,"
which he left unfinished, though unequal in style, has many
interesting, charmingly written pages. But, clear and unclouded as was his intellect, the oil was visibly failing. A
few laboriously, slowly written paragraphs were now the
limit of his daily task. In the evenings, always carefully
dressed, seated in his arm-chair, he welcomed his friends
with his accustomed gracious urbanity ; his features, clear
cut and noble to the last, lighting up as he listened to or
took part in the discussions going on around him. But he
could not keep up the strain for long, becoming gradually
silent and abstracted, till his thoughts wandered visibly to
other and brighter scenes.

The last occasion on which he was quite himself was at
a dinner he gave to the elder Dumas, Stendhal, Lacretelle,
and a couple of other guests, one of whom was a country
neighbour. Dumas talked with more than his usual brilliancy, though the presence of Madame Valentine imposed
a restraint on the conversation to which he was not accustomed, but which he scrupulously observed.

"If we had only known," Lamartine afterwards observed, "we might have invited all the clergy of the parish ! "

Dumas' sonorous laugh had the effect of an elixir on
Lamartine ; his spirits rising with the occasion, he over-
flowed with sallies and epigrams recalling the best days of
Gallic wit. The other guests were too amused to do anything but listen and laugh. M. de Lacretelle maliciously

adds, " As they talked French, not Parisian, even the
country neighbour was able to enjoy every point."

A few months later there came a visible change. M.
Vaucorbeil was bringing out his opera of " Mahomet," for
which he had borrowed the *motif* from Lamartine's " Histoire de la Turquie," in which the prophet, whom Voltaire
had accustomed the French people to look on as a fanatical
impostor, stands out a glowing type of ardent humani-
tarianism. M. Vaucorbeil asked leave, before the opera was
produced on the stage, to express his thanks in person for
the permission accorded him of making use of the work,
and to explain his own interpretation of it in the language
of harmony. Lamartine was gratified by the attention,
and touched by the enthusiasm of his visitor, but he who
was once almost unsurpassed in his command of thought
and language, had now considerable difficulty in keeping
up a few minutes' conversation, and an expression of relief
passed over his face when M. Vaucorbeil rose to depart.

After this, conscious of his failing powers, he saw none
but very intimate friends. During the few remaining
months, Madame Valentine redoubled her loving care and
watchfulness. At last, in the latter days of February, on
an anniversary recalling one of his noblest triumphs, the
physician, who in the morning had found nothing amiss,
told Lamartine in the evening that his end was near. He
received the summons with quiet cheerfulness, sent for his
kind and frequent visitor, the Abbé Duguerry, Curé of the
Madeleine (who before another year closed laid down his
life in the cause of faith and justice), and received from him
the last Sacraments. For another day and night Lamartine's nieces, Mesdames de Pierreclos and Belleroche, with

their children and Madame Valentine, watched by his bed-side. MM. Texier, Chamborand, Desplaces, and many others came to receive a parting glance and smile, till gradually, almost imperceptibly, the end came.

Notwithstanding the seclusion of Lamartine's latter years, Paris did not hear of his death without emotion. During the days which followed, hundreds passed up and down the staircase leading to the chamber where death wore an aspect of singular peace and majesty. In M. Wastyns' words—"Le poëte grandissait tout ce que touchait son génie, et la mort même sur ses traits rayonnants se montrait dans une indéfinissable splendeur." Genuine and widespread as were the regrets for his loss, there was nothing in the simple rite of Lamartine's burial resembling the splendid tribute of spectacular grief since lavished on the remains of Victor Hugo. The offer of a public funeral made by the Emperor was respectfully but firmly refused, and the coffin privately conveyed to the Cathedral of Mâcon, where, in the early morning, the requiem was sung; after which the funeral procession, followed by more than two thousand silent and sorrowful mourners, started for St. Point. The distance was more than eight miles. From time to time a halt was made as the inhabitants of the neighbouring villages fell in. Those Parisians among the following who had known Lamartine only as a literary man or as a politician wondered at this spontaneous tribute of grief from a whole country side. Not so they who had seen him living among his own people, respected, honoured, almost adored. The "Académie française" was represented by MM. Emile Augier and Jules Sandeau, who, in accordance with usage, should have

delivered orations over the grave. But this Lamartine's
will strictly forbade. When the last words of prayer were
said and the final blessing given, no sound broke the silence
save a sweet and solemn peal from the village belfry, recalling to many the lines written by Lamartine more than
thirty years before—

> " Moi, quand des laboureurs porteront dans ma bière
> Le peu qui doit rester ici de ma poussière,
> Après tant de soupirs que mon sein lance ailleurs ;
> Quand des pleureurs gagés, froide et banale escorte,
> Déposeront mon corps endormi sous la porte
>   Qui mène à des soleils meilleurs ;
> Si quelque main pieuse en mon honneur te sonne,
> Des sanglots d'airain, oh ! n'attriste personne ;
> Ne vas pas mendier des pleurs à l'horizon !
> Mais prends ta voix de fête et sonne sur ma tombe
> Avec le bruit joyeux d'une chaine qui tombe
>   Au seuil libre d'une prison ! "

THE END.